Catching Air

**Center Point
Large Print**

**This Large Print Book carries the
Seal of Approval of N.A.V.H.**

Catching Air

SARAH PEKKANEN

CENTER POINT LARGE PRINT
THORNDIKE, MAINE

This Center Point Large Print edition is
published in the year 2014 by arrangement with
Atria Books, a division of Simon & Schuster, Inc.

The text of this Large Print edition is unabridged.
In other aspects, this book may vary
from the original edition.
Printed in the United States of America
on permanent paper.
Set in 16-point Times New Roman type.

ISBN: 978-1-62899-119-2

Library of Congress Cataloging-in-Publication Data

Pekkanen, Sarah.
  Catching air / Sarah Pekkanen. — Center Point Large Print edition.
  pages (large print) cm
  Summary: "Two married couples pursue a dream to open a bed-and-breakfast in small-town Vermont:—Provided by publisher.
  ISBN 978-1-62899-119-2 (library binding : alk. paper)
  1. Bed and breakfast accommodations—Vermont—Fiction.
    2. Life change events—Fiction. 3. Sisters-in-law—Fiction.
    4. Large type books. I. Title.
  PS3616.E358C38 2014b
  813'.6—dc23
                                                    2014011300

For Robert, Saadia,
and Sophia Pekkanen

Part One

Part One

Chapter One

Dawn Zukoski was scared of lots of things—spiders, lightning bolts, the way New York cabbies drove—but only once in her life had she known true terror.

She was eight years old back then, and visiting her elderly neighbor. Mrs. Rita's home was cluttered with gold-framed photos of her long-grown children and towers of *Reader's Digest* magazines, and it smelled of dog pee from her two yippy terriers. But Dawn loved going there because the cookie jar was stocked with Nilla wafers, and the television was always tuned to game shows.

Lacy curtains over the windows hid the sight of other kids on the street playing kickball or hide-and-seek on summer mornings, but Dawn could hear their shouts and cheers. She didn't care, though; she and Mrs. Rita were busy competing in their own games of Plinko or One Away.

"You're overbidding by a thousand!" Mrs. Rita would admonish the contestants. "Dawn, we would've walked right off with that camper!"

Dawn would nod and reach for another cookie, savoring the sweet crumbles on her tongue and the feeling of safety she never experienced at school, where her classmates put two straws in their mouths to imitate her buck teeth, or held their noses and giggled when she walked by, no matter how hard she willed herself to become invisible.

It happened when a young guy spun the big wheel at the end of the first half of *The Price Is Right*. Dawn was sitting cross-legged on the maroon wall-to-wall carpeting that itched her bare legs. A plate of cookies rested on her lap, and the dogs—who enjoyed Nilla wafers as much as she did—were watching her from a few feet away. Staring, really.

Dawn stared back. It was funny at first. The dogs, who were usually hyper, had become as still as statues. Dawn locked eyes with one of them. It was just like the no-blinking contests the boys in her class loved to hold. How long could she last? Five seconds . . . ten . . . Then Mrs. Rita let out a whoop and clapped her hands sharply—"He landed smack-dab on the one dollar! Did you see that, Dawn?"—and at the sudden noise, the spell was broken and the dogs charged.

Dawn fell backward, cookies spilling all around her. "No!" she could hear Mrs. Rita yelling from what seemed like a great distance away. Dawn thrashed and screamed, but every time she pushed one dog away, the other found its way forward, raking her face with its teeth. The attack seemed to go on forever.

Mrs. Rita finally managed to get up and whack at the dogs with her cane, and then Dawn was flying out the door, past the cluster of kids in the street. The kids stopped playing and turned to stare at her, too.

Her vision grew blurred, but she managed to run up three flights of stairs and get inside her apartment and slam the door before collapsing into her mother's arms. Her mother was a nurse's aide, the one neighbors called when their children spiked a high fever or their elderly parents tripped on the stairs.

Her mother didn't scream or hesitate. She lifted Dawn up and carried her to the sink and cleaned her face—luckily the dogs had small mouths and their bite marks weren't deep, and it was blood running into her eyes, not trauma to them, that had impaired her vision—and then she took Dawn to the hospital to get a half dozen stitches.

Even though her father explained that the dogs had thought Dawn was issuing a challenge by staring into their eyes and that they were only trying to protect their home, Mrs. Rita's living room never felt safe for her again. But that wasn't the worst part. The worst part was being trapped under the snarling, biting mass, terror weakening her body as her heart threatened to explode. The inability to escape; that was the sensation that still haunted her.

So much had changed for her since that long-ago day, though. She was twenty-seven now, and gone was the girl who sat at the last table in the lunchroom, at the end closest to the bathrooms, so she had a ready place to hide. Braces had pulled her teeth straight, and even though the rest of her hadn't transformed—her thighs were still a little pudgy, her dark blond hair remained lank despite the fact that she'd put misguided faith into every shampoo in CVS that had the word *volumizing* in its description, and she had two slim, silvery scars forming parentheses on her right cheek—she felt beautiful for the first time in her life.

All set for tonight? her boyfriend, Tucker—her boyfriend!—had texted her that morning as she'd waited for the bus to take her uptown to her job at the investment firm on Sixth Avenue.

All set, she'd texted back, giddiness welling up inside of her. It was a rainy, dreary morning, yet she felt as if she were standing beneath a sunbeam. Tucker was the reason why she felt beautiful; he told her she was, every single day, while she drank up his words like a parched plant taking in water.

A guy holding a cup with the Starbucks logo was waiting beside her, and Dawn smiled, remembering how Tucker had taken her to the coffee shop after he'd dropped a huge pile of papers on the floor directly outside her cubicle on his third day of work.

"I'm such a klutz!" he'd said when she rushed to help him.

"So am I!" she'd said, feeling her cheeks heat up. Maybe that wasn't her most flattering confession, but looking into his navy-blue eyes made her dizzy. She'd noticed him the moment he'd walked through the etched-glass doors of the investment firm. What female wouldn't? His hair was sun-streaked and slightly rumpled, his nose was long and thin, and when he smiled, twin dimples flashed. He looked like a J. Crew model, or a Kennedy, like the type of guy who was born knowing how to sail and play croquet, who drove a zippy red convertible, who was always throwing barbecues on the beach. He wasn't just a man—he also carried the promise of a golden life.

Dawn had been working at the firm as an assistant to a vice president ever since she graduated from Queens College. She lived in a studio apartment next to a couple who drank, fought, and made up with equal enthusiasm— then kicked off the cycle all over again. She bought her suits at Macy's and her pink lipsticks at Duane Reade, and she ordered tuna-salad sandwiches or chicken Caesar salads at the corner deli for lunch. A lot of people came to New York for excitement—nightclub hopping and Broadway shows and shopping sprees—but Dawn followed the city's quieter rhythms: week-end walks in Central Park, trips to the grocery store, girls' nights out with the other adminis-trative assistants. Before Tucker Newman blasted into her life, twirling it upside down, her biggest excitement was debating whether she should join Match.com.

Tucker was, without a doubt, the sweetest and most considerate man she'd ever met. The last guy Dawn had gone on a date with had watched the Knicks game on a television above her head at the bar the whole time, but Tucker wanted to know all about her. He asked lots of questions about her job and her boss, and leaned in to hear the answers. *What do you see in me?* Dawn wondered as she watched his long, elegant fingers encircle his coffee cup. She stopped herself from asking the question because she could practically hear the women's magazines she subscribed to chastising her: *Don't sell yourself short! He's lucky to have you! Now sit up straight and project confidence!*

Maybe those magazines were onto something, because after they'd had coffee, he'd invited her to dinner that very same night.

"I'm sorry, you probably already have plans—" he'd started to say, just as she'd blurted, "I'd love to!"

They'd both laughed and had quickly become inseparable, at least in the evenings and on weekends. At work they still kept up a façade of barely knowing each other, because Tucker's father was a founder of the firm and Tucker didn't want him to know. "He's too controlling. And your boss might not like it either," Tucker had said.

"Controlling?" Dawn had repeated, hungry to know more.

Tucker had sighed, then he'd told her everything: the harsh spankings his father had administered when Tucker was a little boy; his dad's insistence that Tucker learn lacrosse, because that had been *his* sport, even though Tucker yearned to play the piano instead; the hefty donation to Yale during Tucker's junior year of high school to ensure the college's acceptance letter. Tucker's life had never truly been his own.

"He wanted a son who was exactly like him. That's why I changed my name to Tucker Newman when I turned twenty-one," Tucker had confided as Dawn stroked his hair and made sympathetic noises. "I couldn't bear being John Parks Junior."

Then he'd kissed her, and swooped her up to carry her into the bedroom—she prayed his back wouldn't give out from her weight—and later, as they gobbled cold cereal for dinner, he'd answered the question that had been buzzing around in her mind: Why had he decided to come work for his father?

"I want his respect," Tucker had said. "I'm going to show him I'm not the screwup that he thinks I am."

"Of course you're not!" Dawn had said, her

voice loud. "And he's an idiot if he thinks that."

Tucker had started to laugh—it was such a beautiful sound—and he'd pulled her close, giving her a kiss that tasted sweetly of Cap'n Crunch. "Do you know you're the first person to ever take my side against him?"

Dawn hadn't told Tucker that she'd once been walking behind him in a hallway, and she'd seen his dad pass and give him the briefest of nods. How painful that must have felt, as if Tucker was somehow beneath him. Tucker's father seemed to be much harder on his son than on his other employees—despite the fact that Tucker had a degree from Yale, he'd insisted that Tucker begin work as a mail clerk.

Tucker had asked about her family then, and when she'd told him that her parents had died in a car crash several years earlier, she could've sworn she saw tears fill his eyes.

"So you don't have anyone?"

"Just a few aunts and uncles and cousins, but we're not close," she'd said. "Most of my parents' families are back in Poland. They got married really young and immigrated here when they were both nineteen."

Tucker had brushed her hair away from her face and looked at her as if she was a movie star. "Let's be each other's families from now on," he'd whispered. Happiness had buoyed her like helium.

They'd been dating only four weeks. How could someone like him fall for someone like her? It was a miracle. *Her secret lover,* Dawn thought, a smile playing on her lips. It was a title snatched from the romance novels she adored but never had the chance to read anymore because she was actually living the story. Tucker brought her red roses every single week, even though she protested that they were too expensive, and he kissed the insides of her wrists. He winked whenever he passed her cubicle at work, then showed up at her apartment hours later, pressing her against the wall and kissing her hungrily.

Her iPhone was buzzing again: *Nine hours and thirty-eight minutes to go until I see you . . . and then in four days, we make it official.*

Tucker loved to divide time into segments like an orange; he was a whiz with numbers. She could see him taking over the entire company someday. Dawn knew his father would regret doubting Tucker.

Where was the bus? Dawn ducked out of the shelter and peered up the street, but she could see only a snarl of yellow taxis. The rain was picking up, soaking through the bottoms of the blue Keds sneakers she wore for commuting. Dawn was tempted to take a cab, but she always rode the bus to work and it was important that she go about her usual routine, that she act as if this was a normal day.

She'd pick up a triple espresso for the vice

president on her way in, filter his calls, send his faxes, manage the stream of visitors to his office, and order a tuna-salad sandwich for lunch, though she doubted she'd be able to eat a single bite. Then, at precisely 2:00 P.M., she'd take a stack of clients' checks to the bank. Simple.

She heard something that made her blood freeze: a bark. A German shepherd was straining against his leash, bearing down on Dawn. She froze and averted her eyes while the dog sniffed at her.

The owner finally seemed to notice Dawn's fear. "Hey, he's friendly," she said.

Get him away from me! Dawn wanted to scream. She always kept an eye out for approaching dogs and managed to evade them; how had this one slipped through her vigilance? Her heartbeat thudded in her ears. The giant, hairy beast was still there, sniffing all around her, when the bus finally pulled up, its brakes squealing. Dawn almost slipped on the steps in her haste to board. She took a deep, shuddering breath when she was safely in a seat. It was as if that dog had sensed her anxiety, had been drawn to it. Hadn't she heard somewhere that dogs could smell fear?

Four days, she repeated. She only needed to get through the rest of the week, and then it would all be over. No one would be harmed, no one would be upset with her. And her golden life with Tucker could officially begin.

She leaned her cheek against the cool glass of

the window and watched the heavy raindrops slide past, turning the city into a blur.

Heavy raindrops pelted down on Kira Danner as she grabbed her purse, her briefcase, and two bags of groceries out of the trunk of her Honda Accord. She felt one of the brown paper bags begin to slip out of her grasp as she hurried toward her apartment building and climbed the steps to her second-floor walk-up.

She twisted her key in the lock and pushed the door with her shoulder just as she lost her grip. *It had to be the one with the eggs,* she thought as she watched the contents tumble to the floor.

"You know how to make an entrance," her husband, Peter, joked as he walked into the living room.

Kira rolled her eyes at him and wrestled her phone out of her purse as it began to buzz. She checked the caller ID: It was Peter's older brother, Rand. Rand didn't phone often, but he had a sixth sense when it came to picking the worst possible moments. The last time he'd called, he'd interrupted the first nap she'd managed to take in three years, and the time before that, she and Peter had been in the middle of repainting the living room.

She pushed her wet hair out of her face before answering. "Hi, Rand," she said, keeping her irritation out of her voice.

"Hey, K, is Peter around? He didn't answer his cell."

"Sure, he's right here." Kira handed Peter the phone and scooped up the carton of eggs— miraculously, none had broken. That was probably the best thing that had happened to her since she'd left for the law firm fourteen hours earlier, she reflected as she set down her heavy briefcase.

"Hey, man, long time," Peter was saying. Then: "Vermont? Whoa."

Kira left the rest of the groceries for Peter to collect while she went into their galley kitchen. She loved cooking, but she was too exhausted to find anything inspiring in the vegetable drawer or on the condiment shelf tonight, so she reached for a Tupperware bowl of puttanesca sauce in the freezer.

"Looks like pasta and pellets tonight, Fred," she told the goldfish circling the glass bowl by their tiny window. "Don't get too excited, though. You're the one getting the fish food."

She salted a pot of water and put it on to boil, then shook a bit of food into the fish tank. Fred ate quickly, then kept circling, moving quickly but going nowhere. She watched him for a moment: How had it come to this, that she felt such a deep kinship with a thumb-size vertebrate?

She was julienning a carrot for a salad when she heard Peter's footsteps approach.

"So what's in Vermont?" she asked.

When he didn't answer, she turned around to see him leaning against the doorframe, his tall, lanky body nearly filling the opening. His sandy blond eyebrows were tightly knit above his clear blue eyes.

"Is everything okay with Rand?" she asked quickly. Rand had a magnetic attraction to risk—he rode motorcycles too fast, quit jobs before he had new ones lined up, and, until he'd met his wife, Alyssa, had chatted up pretty girls without checking to see if they had jealous boyfriends nearby. Somehow he always landed, catlike, on his feet.

"He's fine," Peter said. He cleared his throat. "He and Alyssa are moving to Killington."

"Sounds nice," Kira said. "Actually, it sounds a little menacing. What's in Killington?" All she knew about the area was that it was a big draw for skiers.

"Remember that lawsuit from when the moving truck rear-ended him?" Peter was saying. "Rand finally got a settlement."

Kira nodded. *Rand's luck,* she thought. He'd been stopped at a red light when the brakes on the truck behind him had failed—brakes worn so thin that they should have been replaced months earlier. Rand's Jeep was totaled, but when a fireman wielding the Jaws of Life cut him out of the crumpled metal, Rand had emerged with only a broken arm, two cracked ribs, and a bump on his forehead. He'd walked out of the hospital four hours later with a fiberglass cast and the card of a personal injury lawyer.

"He wants to use the settlement to open a bed-and-breakfast near a ski slope," Peter said.

Of course he does, Kira thought, stifling a laugh.

"Does he know anything about running a B-and-B?" she asked. "You have to keep books and do marketing and build a website and cook fancy breakfasts every day . . . I can't see Rand and Alyssa doing all that stuff."

She glanced at Peter, whose eyebrows seemed to have inched even lower, which meant he was contemplating something. Peter, her tech-savvy husband, whose start-up company aimed at providing mobile technology services was faltering. She glanced down at the container of homemade puttanesca sauce she'd cooked the previous Sunday.

"Oh, no," she said involuntarily.

"Hear me out," he said. "Don't say no yet."

I think I just did, Kira thought, but she nodded.

"You hate your job—" he began.

"I wouldn't say I hate it," she interjected. "It just . . . Well, it isn't what I thought it would be. Whoever invented the concept of billable hours was a sadist. I work all the time, Peter, and it isn't ever enough . . . They want me to pad my time, to—to *lie* to clients to make the firm even more money, and it's disgusting—"

Peter reached over and began massaging her neck with one hand. For such a thin guy, he had fingertips of steel. "Oh," she sighed, feeling the tight cords along the sides of her neck yield. A headache she hadn't even noticed began to ebb away.

"My business hasn't taken off the way we'd hoped," Peter continued.

"It hasn't been that long . . . ," she began loyally before her voice trailed off. Peter was a whiz with computers. The problem was, so were a million other people who were willing to work more cheaply, like college students.

"We'd live in a beautiful home," Peter said, his voice deep and soothing. His fingers kept digging into new spots of tension, and it was hard for Kira to remember why she'd been arguing. "No more crappy apartments. Rand is offering us a one-third share if we help get the B-and-B off the ground. And if things go well, we could hand it over to a professional inn-keeper in a year and keep making money."

Kira tried to think of what to say next. "I've never even been to Vermont" was what she finally came up with.

Peter let go of her neck and wrapped his arms around her waist. She could feel the heat coming off his body, and the steam rising up from the boiling water, and the humid Florida air filtering in through the window. It seemed, suddenly, as if she'd been hot for her entire life, her thighs always sticking to the vinyl seats in her car, her hair forever matting against the back of her neck.

Vermont, she thought, testing out the word, envisioning snowflakes drifting onto her cheeks and pine trees spreading open under an enormous blue sky.

Peter was right; she hated her job. She worked so hard, arriving at her windowless office by seven every morning, writing long, excruciatingly detailed reports, gobbling a Cobb salad at her desk, poring over documents until her eyes felt gritty and her entire body ached. She lived in the Sunshine State, yet she sometimes went days without ever glimpsing the sun.

And instead of being grateful, the firm had punished her. She'd been put on a kind of probation—her partnership delayed for a year— because she didn't beef up her hours like the other associates, and had spoken the truth to a client and embarrassed the partner who'd overbilled him. She was still reeling from the injustice. Wasn't the law supposed to be an honorable profession? When she entered law school, she'd envisioned taking on pro bono cases for persecuted immigrants and abused women. She'd thought she'd change lives—stand up in a courtroom, her voice ringing with passion as she fought for truth and justice. Instead, she was the one who'd been changed. At thirty years old, she felt as brittle and worn-out as an old cornhusk. And she had yet to help a single pro bono client.

"You could hand in your notice and we could leave in a couple weeks. I'll teach you to ski. We could spend some time together for a change," Peter was saying. "If we don't like it, we can always move back."

Her left-brained, sensible husband—so different from his spontaneous, irresponsible brother—had already made up his mind. How had that happened so quickly?

"I don't know," she said. For some reason, tears filled her eyes. Peter was offering her the escape she'd been yearning for, and now that she was standing on its brink, it felt terrifying.

"It's such a big decision," Kira said. And they saw Rand and Alyssa only once a year or so. Wouldn't it feel strange to suddenly be with them constantly?

"Sleep on it," Peter said as he carried their plates to the little wooden table in their dining nook. "We can talk more tomorrow."

But as he came back into the kitchen and slid past her to get the salad, he whispered words that spilled into her mind like blue ink into clear water, clouding her thoughts. She knew their echo would keep her awake for the rest of the night.

"We'd both be home all the time," he'd

whispered as she instinctively stiffened, some-how knowing what he'd say next. "Maybe we should have a baby."

The rain had finally tapered off, and gauzy clouds hung low in the sky. Alyssa stepped out of the Jeep, stretched her back, and took her first look at the B-and-B. The A-frame house sat perched atop acres of sprawling land like a pioneer surveying uncharted territory and deciding that yes, this would be the perfect place to settle. Alyssa was a firm believer that houses had personalities, and she liked this one's style; it looked strong and welcoming. She lifted the Nikon hanging on her neck, framed the shot, and snapped.

In a few months, the panoramic vistas would be transformed when a white coating erased the vibrant summer colors. But the view would still be every bit as spectacular. Just imagining it made Alyssa's lungs expand and her heart feel lighter. Back in D.C., where Rand had worked as a carpenter and part-time guitar teacher at a kids' music school and she'd photographed weddings and babies and family reunions, she'd often felt as if everyone were trying to rush her along—brushing past her with an impatient exhalation on the sidewalk or honking when she didn't step on the gas the second the light turned green.

Out here in the minty air, under a sweeping

sky, she probably wouldn't hear a car horn for weeks at a time.

Rand slung an arm around her shoulders. "Tonight we're gonna uncork a bottle of wine, grab a blanket, and hit the hot tub. This"—he used his hands to draw an invisible square around them—"is an unpacking-free zone until tomorrow."

Alyssa turned in to him, feeling the rasp of his chin stubble against her forehead. "Perfect," she whispered, thinking again of how lucky she was to have found this man. Chance had been their Cupid: She wasn't supposed to be waitressing at the diner that morning six years ago, but someone had asked her to trade shifts. Five minutes after she arrived at work, Rand had walked in.

Yummy, she'd thought, taking in his thick, dark hair and a face that belonged to a hero on an action-movie poster. He was dressed in a T-shirt and old jeans, which she vastly preferred to an Armani suit.

"Coffee?" she'd offered. Granted, not her most seductive opening line ever.

"Yeah," he'd said, then he'd looked up and their eyes had met. She'd instinctively reached to smooth down her hair, not because it was messy but because she felt certain it was standing straight up from the sudden jolt of electricity running through her body.

She'd been saving up her tips, planning to leave

the next week for Portugal, the latest in her string of traveling adventures. Instead, she and Rand had gotten married within three months and her life's real adventure had begun.

"Admit it," Rand was saying now. "You thought there was a Wal-Mart next door."

Alyssa laughed. "Was it wrong not to tell Peter and Kira we didn't see the place before we bought it? Technically they didn't ask. And the real estate agent sent us lots of photos."

But Kira had e-mailed them a dozen times, asking questions that had never occurred to Alyssa. *Do you have a business plan?* she'd written. *Could the B-and-B be considered an investment property when filing taxes? What's the square footage of the structure?*

That was far from the only difference between her and Kira. Kira was barely five foot two and slender, with the cornsilk-blond hair of a child and dainty features. *A pixie,* Alyssa had thought the first time she'd seen her. Alyssa was seven inches taller and curvy, with a one-size-too-big hook of a nose that had been the bane of her adolescence, until the rest of her face filled out to blunt its impact. Their family's bloodline, her mother used to laughingly say, could rival any mutt's at the pound: Latin American mixed with Italian ancestry, topped off with a dash of Native American blood, which revealed itself in Alyssa's olive skin and high cheekbones.

While Kira was plowing through college, Alyssa was dropping out, reasoning that she'd get a better education by slinging a camera around her neck, shrugging into a backpack, and hopping aboard trains to cross Europe and Asia. She rode elephants in Chiang Mai, slept on a sidewalk in Budapest when she couldn't find a room, ate a boiled frog in Shanghai, and sunbathed nude in Corfu. Whenever she ran out of money, she returned to the States and worked as a nanny or waitress until she could afford another airplane ticket. Her life was glorious in its simplicity, her focus always on the next train, the next country, the next adventure. There were men along the way—plenty of men—but none who captivated her the way traveling did, until she met Rand.

Now her husband reached into his pocket and pulled out the big brass key the previous owners had mailed to them. "Could be dead bodies inside," he whispered. "No one has lived here for what, three years?"

"The guests who never checked out," Alyssa intoned.

Rand swung open the door to the house and they stepped inside. The entrance hallway took a sharp right turn and spilled into a large living room with a giant stone fireplace. Aside from dust and spiderwebs, the room was perfect, with its wide-planked, honey-wood floors, a nook that would work well as a dining area, and built-in bookcases.

"Tell me the rest of the place looks this good," Alyssa said, walking past the dining nook and pushing through a swinging door to the kitchen. Rand followed, and they were silent for a moment.

"Tell me the rest of the place doesn't look this bad," Rand said. He ran a shoe over the peeling linoleum floor.

"It's not that awful," Alyssa lied.

She squinted, envisioning a fresh coat of paint on the scarred wooden cabinets and a new floor. "Guests probably didn't come in here, so they didn't keep the kitchen up as well as the rest of the place."

"Let's check out the rooms," Rand said. They retraced their steps through the living area and climbed the steps to the four guest bedrooms. The smallest one had twin beds, a big picture window, and its own bathroom. Two others held queen beds and private bathrooms, and the largest boasted a king-size bed and Jacuzzi tub. The ivory paint on the walls had dulled with time, but there were bureaus, beds, and curtains that the previous owners had left as part of the settlement agreement.

"We just need sheets and comforters . . . maybe a few throw rugs," Alyssa said as she wandered around. "And Pledge. A truckload of Pledge."

"Your photos on the walls, too," Rand added. He gave her ponytail a tug and led the way back downstairs, to a door off the living room. Rand leaned against it and pretended to push against something heavy.

"The bodies must be stacked behind here," he said, and she swatted his butt. He swung open the door and it creaked—"Gotta oil that," he said—and they ventured down a narrow hallway to where the final two bedrooms awaited.

"Oh." Alyssa gasped when they stepped into the first doorway.

One entire wall was composed of windows, and a love seat faced a gas fireplace. She looked in the bathroom, which was tiled in sea green and featured a huge, glass-walled shower with five spray nozzles. "You know how I'm not really into material things?" she said. "This shower just changed my mind."

"Room for two," he said with a leer. He began opening windows, letting fresh air chase out the musty smell as Alyssa walked over to the corner across from the fireplace.

She and Rand had lived in six different apartments and homes since they wed, and in every single one, Alyssa had known where a rocking chair would go.

She stood in the empty space, thinking of a long-ago scene: the doctor in his white office, wearing a white coat, staring out at them from underneath heavy white eyebrows. By then, Rand's sperm had been scrutinized and deemed perfectly shaped, mobile, and robust in number. They were practically supersperm. The problem, it was clear, lay somewhere deep within her.

Yes, they told the doctor, they'd been trying for more than a year. No, she'd never been pregnant. Although she had irregular periods, she'd never had an abortion or miscarriage. No sexually transmitted diseases either, other than a brief bout with chlamydia that was a parting gift from a guy she'd met in Spain. And she'd never had any major surgeries.

"Well, other than a ruptured appendix," she'd added.

The doctor had been scribbling something on his pad, but his hand had suddenly stilled.

"I was only fifteen," she'd said.

"Abdominal diseases can cause scarring in fallopian tubes," the doctor had said. He'd cleared his throat and reached for a cartoonish-looking plastic replica of the female reproductive system. "Eggs travel down the tubes from the ovaries to the uterus, but if they're blocked—"

Alyssa had held up a hand. "I know how it works," she'd said. "Or doesn't work, as the case may be." She'd made a noise that was meant to be a laugh but had turned into a kind of bark. The doctor had mentioned dye tests, an ultrasound, and laparoscopic surgery.

"Would that fix it?" Alyssa had asked.

"It can, in some cases," the doctor had said.

"If indeed a blockage is preventing you from getting pregnant. It could also be stress—"

"We're probably the least stressed people you've ever had in your office," Rand had interrupted.

Well, not anymore, Alyssa had refrained from saying. Appendicitis. And to think her biggest worry after waking up in the operating room all those years ago was that her scar would show when she wore a bikini.

The doctor had cleared his throat. "Successful surgery depends on the location of the blockage, and the severity of scarring . . . IVF may be an option, too."

They'd left his office half an hour later and had walked silently to Rand's Jeep. Rand had slid inside and started the engine. But he didn't pull out of the parking spot.

Does he blame me? The thought had seemed to rip apart all the muscles in her chest, and she'd nearly gasped. She might be able to live without having children, but she couldn't live without Rand's love. She'd twisted her hammered silver wedding band around and around on her finger while she waited for whatever would happen next.

"All those tests," Rand had finally said. "And then what? I have to go jerk off in a cup, and we've gotta come up with the money, and maybe that doesn't work either . . ."

"I know," she'd whispered. *I'm sorry,* she'd thought.

"Fuck it," he'd said and finally turned to look at her. When she saw his smile—a real one that made the corners of his dark eyes crinkle—she'd felt weak with relief. "Who needs kids anyway? Diapers stink, and I don't want to spend every Saturday coaching soccer. If the kid got any of my genes, he'd drink all my liquor. Why does anyone reproduce?"

She'd never loved him more than at that moment, she'd thought. True, she was the one with a much stronger longing to have children. Rand had been a little resistant at first—more scared than anything else, Alyssa had thought—but he knew how much it meant to her, and so he'd come around.

"Maybe this is one of those signs you're always talking about," he'd said.

"Or maybe it's another kind of sign," she'd replied. "Would you . . ." Her voice had failed and she'd begun again. "What would you think about adopting?"

He'd stared at her for a moment, then shrugged. "I dunno."

"I thought I could look into it . . . Okay?"

"Okay," he'd said, and she'd let out her breath.

So she'd found an agency that connected prospective parents with little girls from China and had put together a packet of information, including photographs of her and Rand together. They'd met with a social worker who was young and anxious and had spilled the glass of water they'd given her all over the couch. They'd filled out forms—actually, Alyssa had filled them out, because Rand had a moderate case of dyslexia and paperwork was torture for him—and had accepted a generous check from Alyssa's father to cover the cost of the adoption, which they never could've afforded on their own.

Rand had accepted the change in their course so easily that Alyssa was ashamed to tell him she still harbored a small, secret hope that she'd become pregnant. That maybe the blockage in her tubes had a sliver of an opening.

But as the months and then years passed and her period continued to show up despite the fact that she'd taken up meditation, swallowed daily doses of the herb chasteberry, and switched to a vegetarian diet, her hopes had withered. She was thirty-five now, and her age was yet another enemy of fertility. Rand never seemed to mourn the child they wouldn't have together, but she couldn't shake the image of a son. Sometimes she even dreamed about him, a little boy with Rand's eyes and plump cheeks. He was always in her arms, always laughing as she spun him around in circles.

She walked away from the empty corner. She didn't think about their phantom son quite as much these days; the passage of time was dimming his image, like the reverse of a Polaroid photo forming. Maybe someday, he'd fade away for good.

She headed into the bedroom next door. It was much smaller, and darker, but sliding glass doors led to a little patio framed by hedges for privacy.

"It's . . . cozy," Alyssa said as Rand followed her in. She opened the curtains on the single window. "Do you think Peter and Kira will like it, if they decide to move here? I feel kind of bad that our room is so much nicer."

Rand shrugged. "They're getting a sweet deal. We're covering the down payment and two-thirds of the mortgage."

"True," Alyssa said. "So do you think they're going to do it?" Peter and Kira were supposed to give their decision that day.

"Let's find out," Rand said. He reached for his phone and dialed.

Alyssa suddenly felt nervous. She knew Rand wished he was closer to his brother—they'd fought a lot growing up, and there had been a deep rift around their mother's death nearly a decade earlier that had never been fully repaired. Alyssa still didn't know the full story, but she knew Rand regretted whatever had happened. When Rand had suggested inviting Peter and Kira along, she'd said yes quickly. Embracing new experiences was a reflex for her. But now it hit her: She'd spent so

36

little time with her in-laws. Was this a mistake?

Alyssa liked Rand's younger brother. When she and Rand had driven to Florida for Thanksgiving a few months after their wedding, Alyssa had watched Peter chase a spider across the kitchen, capturing it in a paper towel before shooing it out the door, and when he'd noticed her, he'd shrugged and said, "I figured the little guy probably has a wife and kids at home who were getting worried about him."

Kira was trickier. She was friendly enough, but she seemed stuck in high gear. She'd fluttered around, making sure they had extra pillows and their preferred kind of juice for breakfast. Alyssa had noticed Kira kept a grocery list on her refrigerator with items divided into sections labeled "Produce" and "Dairy," and during dinner—which rivaled some of the best meals Alyssa had ever eaten in restaurants—Peter had mentioned that Kira was one of the smartest associates at her law firm.

"She'll be running the place in another ten years," Peter had said, as Kira blushed and passed around a bowl of her roasted root vegetables spiked with fresh herbs *grown in little pots on her fire escape.* Kira had skipped the second grade, she'd broken a local track record in junior high school, and she'd worked part-time in college to pay for her expenses while pulling in straight A's.

It was a little intimidating, frankly.

Alyssa watched Rand's face as he listened to Peter talk. Then Rand smiled.

"Awesome," he said.

Chapter Two

"How are you today, Ms. Zukoski?" the bank teller asked.

"Great!" Dawn said, and the teller gave her an odd look.

Tone it down, Dawn warned herself, softening her overly broad smile. She thought again of the German shepherd at the bus stop and imagined scent cones of fear spreading out around her body.

She slid the checks forward, under the Plexiglas divider, and the teller looked through them one at a time. Her red fingernails clicked against her computer's keyboard as she began to slowly enter the amounts.

Dawn glanced around. The bank was wood-paneled and opulent, with a trio of dark leather sofas clustered over an Oriental rug. A few people stood behind her in line, and an armed security guard, a muscular young man, kept watch by the door. He met her gaze, and Dawn quickly looked away.

Why was it so quiet in here? Dawn could hear

her own shallow breathing. She opened her mouth to comment on the relentless rain, then closed it. She needed to get out as quickly as possible.

"Three hundred and forty thousand dollars," the teller finally said. She pushed the deposit slip toward Dawn. "Thank you, Ms. Zukoski."

This was how their routine always ended. But today Dawn was working from a new script.

"I need to wire some money into a client's account," she said. She'd rehearsed that line a hundred times, saying it aloud as she paced her apartment at night to get just the right inflection, but now the words felt sharp and coppery in her mouth. She realized she was clutching her handbag so tightly that her fingers were turning white, and she loosened her grip.

"Of course," the teller said, her face betraying no surprise. "Could you step over there"—she gestured to the couch closest to the security guard—"and wait for our manager?"

"The manager?" Dawn asked. She felt faint. "Is that . . . the standard practice?"

"Yes," the teller said.

Was she lying? Dawn wondered. Maybe the firm had learned of her plans. An errant e-mail, a conversation overheard—she'd thought she'd been so careful, but what if she'd made one tiny, crucial mistake? This could all be a setup. Maybe the other customers were undercover cops. Maybe the teller had been wired by the FBI.

"Lady, let's get a move on," called an older man with a gruff voice from the back of the line.

As Dawn walked over to the couch, one of her pumps skidded on the polished floor. She regained her balance just before she fell.

The manager approached, his hand extended. "Ms. Zukoski?"

How did he know her name? Dawn almost bolted, then she realized the teller might have told him.

"I need to wire some money into a client's account," Dawn repeated, hoping her hand didn't feel clammy in his. Her rehearsed line kept running through her mind, like one of those continual advertising loops in Times Square. Dawn wished she were there now, losing herself in the crowds of tourists, blending into the masses.

No one will get hurt, she reminded herself. She was just shifting funds around for a few days—something banks did all the time, ironically.

"Certainly," the manager said. "Will you accompany me to my desk?"

She followed him, and he pulled a form and pen from a drawer. "Please fill out the necessary information," he said. "And I'll need your identification. Do you have the account numbers for the transfers?"

Dawn nodded. She tried to swallow, but her mouth was too dry. She'd been entrusted with some of the firm's banking duties her first month at work. It had surprised her, until she'd realized that the firm had copies of her passport, driver's license, address, and social security number as well as bookkeepers who regularly scrutinized every transaction.

She pulled her license and a slip of paper out of her purse. She'd printed a fake document on the firm's letterhead, so it would look official, but she'd used her home computer to do so. She copied down the account numbers carefully, pressing hard with the pen so her numbers wouldn't reveal that her hand was shaking.

"One hundred thousand dollars?" the bank manager asked as he reviewed the form.

Dawn nodded again.

"Just a moment," the manager said.

This was it. If she was going to be arrested, it would happen now. She couldn't help it; she looked toward the security guard, but he was gone. Where was he? Could he be behind her? She glanced around wildly before she spotted him opening the door for an elderly woman with a walker.

She exhaled slowly. The manager was coming back now, and he was smiling.

"Excellent," he said. "The transfer will go through by the end of the day. Is there anything else we can do for you?"

"No," Dawn said. She got to her feet quickly. "Thank you."

In twenty steps she'd be out the door. Maybe she wouldn't go back to work today; she could pretend she'd come down with the stomach flu. But no, she had to go back—she had to act normally! Fifteen steps . . .

"Ms. Zukoski?"

She froze. The bank manager was calling her name, and the security guard stood between her and the door, his gaze fixed on her. She knew when she turned around she'd see her boss flanked by a dozen police officers.

I'm sorry, Tucker, she thought. She felt the bank manager's hand touch her arm.

"Lollipop?" he offered, holding out a bright orange one.

"There's got to be a gas station nearby," Kira said, peering into the darkness.

It was close to midnight. They were somewhere near the border of North Carolina at the end of their first day of traveling, and all Kira wanted was a hot shower and a soft bed. At this point, she'd happily settle for a cold shower and a lumpy sleeping bag. She yawned and rubbed her eyes, then resumed searching the road ahead for a sign indicating the way to a gas station, a motel, a McDonald's . . . anything resembling civilization.

"Check your iPhone again," Peter said.

She glanced down and shook her head. "Still not getting a signal." All they had to guide them was a map Peter had purchased when they'd set off, and that crinkly rectangle of paper seemed hopelessly antiquated now. It could show them a few different routes to the highway, but not which ones featured gas stations.

Instead of taking I-95, which cut a straight, industrial path along the East Coast, they'd decided to travel along smaller back roads and stop to visit fruit stands and wineries and antique shops on their way to Vermont. "It'll be fun," Kira had said to Peter in what now seemed like one of the more foolhardy statements of her life.

But it *had* been fun, at least for a while: They'd sung along to a Miranda Lambert CD, affecting a country twang, while Kira had dangled her bare feet out the window as the stress of the past six years seemed to peel away in the wind. They'd followed the signs to a state park and had spread out a blanket and taken an afternoon nap by a pretty lake.

The nap had left them feeling so refreshed that they'd decided to drive late into the night, and now they seemed to be the only ones on the two-lane road. Their easy chatter had tapered off into silence as the line on their gas gauge had dipped into the red zone.

"There!" Kira shouted, pointing at a flash of color in the distance. "A gas station."

"Thank God," Peter said.

They pulled in next to the single pump, and

Peter looked at the small structure with a wooden sign advertising cold drinks and cigarettes in uneven lettering.

"It isn't open," he said.

"Are you sure? Maybe if you knock on the door, someone will answer it. They could be in the back or something."

"Kira, there is no back. And the lights are off." Peter started the engine again and drove around to park behind the gas station.

"What are you doing?" Kira asked as he killed the headlights.

"We need to stop for the night," Peter said, his voice as low and calm as ever. She'd seen her husband lose it exactly twice—once when he'd dropped a can of juice on his bare toe and once when they'd lost power during an electrical storm and he'd fried an expensive computer belonging to a client.

"We're about to run out of gas," Peter said.

"Don't you think we should keep going?" Kira asked. "There could be another one up ahead."

"If there is, it's probably closed, too," Peter said. "At least this way we can choose where we get stuck. We'll gas up as soon as they open."

Kira exhaled loudly, but she knew he was right. Peter's logical mind and his steadiness were among the traits she'd always prized most in him. She reached into the glove compartment and grabbed a napkin.

"I have to pee," she said. "Yell if anyone's coming, okay?"

"Trust me, no one's coming," he said.

She squatted down a few yards away from their Honda, trying to avoid splattering her flip-flops. A young couple running out of gas on a shadowy, deserted road . . . wasn't this how most horror movies started? She finished up quickly and hurried back to the car, then reclined her seat as far as it would go as Peter took his turn using nature's facilities.

"I hate not brushing my teeth before bed," she said when he returned. "It feels disgusting."

"We'll find someplace that has a bathroom first thing tomorrow," he said. He popped the trunk and walked around to the back of the car. "Need anything?" he asked.

"Did we pack a Marriott?" she said.

"Hang on, let me see. No . . . we've got a Holiday Inn here, but that's about it." He got back into the car and handed her a sweatshirt to use as a pillow.

"Thanks," she said, shifting around to find a comfortable position. The night air was thick and moist, and their windows were unrolled, so the sounds of crickets chirping drifted toward her. Of course, the open windows would also make it easier for a psychopath in a hockey mask to get into the car, but it was too hot to roll them up, so she'd have to risk being hacked to death.

If only it wasn't so *dark* out here. She tried to focus on the crickets' melody and not on the fact that something smelled—she had a sneaking suspicion it was her armpits—and that her back was already sore from so many hours of sitting in the car.

"Yuck," she whispered. This wasn't how she'd envisioned starting a new chapter of their life together. A carefree road trip had sounded romantic and spontaneous, and those were two elements sorely missing from her life these days. She was always so tired after work that some-times a week or two—sometimes longer—passed before she and Peter had sex. That wasn't normal for a healthy young couple, was it?

She doubted Rand and Alyssa ever let a week pass without having sex.

Whoa! Where had that thought come from? She glanced over at Peter, feeling guilty, but he seemed to be asleep. His pale profile was barely discernible in the moonlight. His arms were folded across his chest, and he'd taken off his glasses and placed them on the dashboard. He always looked a decade younger without them.

She closed her eyes and reclined again. As they'd packed for the move, she'd wondered if she would miss Florida. But today, as they'd driven past her old elementary school and the spot that once held the frozen yogurt shop where she'd worked during high school, and so many other physical locations that were emotional landmarks for her, she'd realized she was relieved to leave the state behind.

Kira had lived in Florida for her entire life, save the years when she attended college and law school at Duke, and at least in the beginning, she'd loved it. Back then, though, her father was still around.

As a child, Kira had always felt a deeper connection with him. Her mother was harried and snappish, but her dad flung open the front door after work, filling the quiet rooms with his loud voice. He read bedtime stories and gave princesses funny, growling voices. He pulled quarters out of her ears and flipped her over his shoulders and sang to her in his low, sweet voice, changing the lyrics to lullabies: "Hush, little baby, don't say a word, Papa's going to buy you an elephant . . . and if that elephant won't dance, Papa's going to put him in underpants . . ." She'd giggle hysterically until her mother appeared in the doorway, telling them to settle down, that Kira needed to go to sleep. Her father would turn on a flashlight and make shadow bunnies on her wall before he left, giving her the flashlight with a wink. He was larger than life; he was coated in glittering magic dust, like a character in her storybook.

If his gait wasn't perfectly steady as he entered the house, if he forgot to ask about her track meets, if she sometimes thought she caught a whiff of perfume that smelled as sweet as Juicy Fruit gum clinging to his clothes—well, it didn't matter. Not back then, anyway. But as she matured, Kira's eyes grew clearer, and her sympathies tilted toward her mother, who was always bent over the sink or laundry basket, mending and cooking and sweeping. Creating the illusion of a nice home, as if that could help tamp down the turmoil swirling within it.

"Why do you and Daddy sleep in different rooms?" Kira had asked her mother once.

"Because he snores," her mother had responded, and then she'd turned on the vacuum cleaner, which was her favorite way to end conversations.

Sometimes Kira wondered: Had her parents ever been happy? And if so, who had taken the first steps toward destroying their marriage? Or maybe it wasn't anyone's fault. They could just have been a mismatch, another young couple who'd mistaken passion for love, and whispered promises for lifelong commitments.

By the time Kira was near the end of her elementary school years, her mother's face had seemed creased in a permanent frown, her features sunken inward like a prune. Her dad often came in at dawn, pretending he'd had to work through the night. It was almost comical, given that he was so often between jobs. At least it would have been comical, if it didn't hurt so

48

much. Because he wasn't just abandoning Kira's mother, he was leaving her behind, too.

His bag of tricks no longer enthralled her, and she was old enough to read her own books. Her father didn't seem to know what to do with her once she was no longer a little girl and had questions and accusations of her own, so he stopped trying and began to avoid her. His sparkle dust had worn off, revealing the flawed, ordinary man beneath it.

"Let me guess: You slept at the office, right?" she'd said once when he came in as she was leaving for school, his clothes rumpled, his expression guilty. At that point he was selling men's suits at a retail store. "It must be so *busy,* fitting in your nocturnal clients."

Nocturnal was a word she'd studied for the school spelling bee she'd won—the one he hadn't attended.

One night he and her mother had had an explosive fight—Kira could hear them yelling even after she'd pulled her comforter over her head and plugged her fingers in her ears—and the next day, her father had moved out.

"I'll see you soon, K," he'd said as he carried armloads of trash bags stuffed with his belongings out to his car. He'd tossed her a wink, but she'd just walked past him, down the front steps and onto the sidewalk and into town, where she'd gone to the library and had hidden for hours in the reference section, flipping the pages of a heavy book and watching the words blur. He'd called her that weekend, and the next one, but she'd refused to talk to him, which she knew secretly pleased her mother.

No matter how tight things became—and they became almost suffocatingly so, after her father left and sent only sporadic checks and they moved from the house to an apartment—her mother wouldn't accept help. She wouldn't *take* anything.

It wasn't as if they ever didn't have enough to eat. It was just that sometimes they ate rice and beans, or peanut butter sandwiches, for a few days running. Kira's clothes and shoes came from the thrift shop. She didn't mind wearing other people's old clothes, but used shoes were the worst. No matter how clean they looked, they always smelled sour. Plenty of people had it worse, though, Kira's mother always reminded her.

Kira understood that her mother was proud, but there was a time when Kira's most fervent wish was for a little charity. She was about eleven years old, and she'd spotted a rack of Hostess cupcakes by the checkout line in the supermarket. Those cupcakes were symphonies of sugar and starch, the most delectable things imaginable.

Her mother had seen her staring and, miraculously, had plucked a cellophane package from the rack, putting it into their cart alongside a carton of milk, a box of cornflakes, iceberg lettuce, eggs, chicken breasts, and bananas. The treat stood out like an emerald glittering atop a pile of dirt. Kira could almost taste the smooth chocolate icing on her tongue, and savor the sensation of licking the creamy filling.

But then the cashier with the seen-it-all-before gaze had handed back the credit card and said, "It was denied." It had happened to them dozens of times before. This time, though, a woman had stepped forward. She had long gray hair, although her face was young, and she wore clogs and a flowery dress. Even all these years later, Kira still remembered the pattern of those soft blue flowers.

"May I?" the woman had asked, holding out her own charge card. "I've had the same thing happen myself. Sometimes those silly machines just don't work."

Kira had looked at the woman's kind face, then at the cupcakes, so close she could touch them. She wouldn't even wait until she got home to eat them with a glass of milk. She'd rip apart the cellophane and devour them in the car and lick every sticky crumb off her fingertips.

"You're too kind, but my husband must have just forgotten to pay the bill," Kira's mother had said, forcing out a small laugh. Kira could still remember how her mother's lipstick had seeped into the vertical lines above her mouth, and how she couldn't tell if her mother was angry or just embarrassed.

"We can send her the money," Kira had said, looking at the woman with gray hair, who was nodding encouragingly.

"Don't be silly," Kira's mother had responded, grabbing Kira's upper arm and squeezing hard.

They'd left the cupcakes behind and driven home silently, and Kira had eaten another peanut butter sandwich for dinner, choking down bite after miserable bite. She was furious; she had enough money in her piggy bank to repay the woman! Why hadn't her mother let her? Later that night, her mother had come into her room and rested a hand on Kira's shoulder. Kira had pretended to be asleep, but her mother had spoken anyway.

"Two cupcakes aren't worth our pride, honey," she'd said. "We'll buy some next time with our own money."

Her mother had remembered, too: A few weeks later, there was a cellophane package on Kira's pillow when she came home from school. Kira had sat on the edge of her bed, remembering the knowing eyes of the cashier and the sympathetic ones of the gray-haired lady, feeling the hard pinch of her mother's fingers against her upper arm. The frosting and creamy filling and cake had turned into a paste in her mouth and she'd had trouble swallowing it.

Maybe, in an odd, circular sort of way, her father was the reason why she'd been put on probation at the law firm, since the idea of taking anything rankled her, too. Or maybe there was more of her mother in her than she cared to admit: After all, in the first grade she'd seen a classmate with a rainbow-colored eraser that she knew belonged to another girl, and she'd raised her hand and announced it to the teacher in front of everyone, ignoring the whispers of "Tattletale!" Brutal honesty was probably woven into her DNA, a genetic gift from her mother, along with a faster than normal resting pulse and the inability to relax.

"Are you still awake?" Peter was leaning up on one elbow, staring at her.

She started. "It's just so hot."

"It'll be cooler in Vermont," he said.

"Maybe we should get onto I-95 at the next chance," she said. "We could be there in two days if we don't take a lot of breaks. This was a dumb idea."

Peter studied her for a minute, then reached for his door and opened it.

"What are you doing?" she asked. Instead of answering he walked around to her side of the car, opened her door, and reached for her hand.

She followed him to a patch of grass, where he lay down.

"It's better out here," he said.

"But the bugs," she began.

"Shh," he said. "Come on."

So she lay in the crook of his arm and looked up at the stars. The air was soft and velvety, and though Peter smelled as bad as she did and the grass was itchy under her legs—at least she hoped it was grass and not the angry occupants of an anthill—a slight breeze cooled her skin.

"Was this a mistake?" she whispered. "I thought we needed a change, but maybe Vermont isn't the answer."

Peter sighed. "I don't know."

We're stuck, she thought, feeling fear grip her chest. They'd quit their jobs, sublet their apartment, and bequeathed their goldfish to a neighbor's little girl. Maybe instead of leaping into something new, they should've analyzed their life to see where it had gone off track. How could Peter be thinking about having a baby, creating a new life, when they didn't even know which direction their own would take?

But she hadn't felt like analyzing, endlessly discussing, and carefully weighing the pros and cons. She'd lived her entire life that way. Just once, she'd wanted to be spontaneous and impractical—to leap headfirst into a thrilling new experience. Like Rand and Alyssa were always doing.

Fine, so she was a little jealous. It was hard to escape her envy when she'd schlep home, her feet aching and her mind feeling simultaneously jittery and dull from too much caffeine and too little sleep, to discover Peter turning over a postcard with a palm tree or Mayan temple pictured on the front. "Rand and Alyssa are taking up cliff diving," Peter would say, reading off the back of the postcard. Or "They decided to go to Guadalajara for a month after they finish building a Habitat for Humanity house in Honduras."

Sometimes Rand would e-mail a photo instead, and Kira couldn't help but notice that Alyssa had the kind of long, sleek hair nature had denied Kira, and the toned body of a yoga devotee. Alyssa always seemed to be tanned, smiling, and free from the worries that jarred Kira awake at three on the nights when she was the most exhausted.

That was why she'd spent days deep-cleaning the carpets and washing down the baseboards before she'd labored over the Thanksgiving dinner she'd served them. She wanted them to admire the lovely home she'd created, even if it was just a rental apartment, and be awed by the juicy, brined turkey and rhubarb-apple pie she'd concocted. She wanted to show off a snapshot of her life with Peter at its best, too.

"It's only a year," Peter was saying now. He yawned and stretched his back.

Kira nodded. They still had their savings, and a small 401(k), and she'd put most of her paychecks toward paying off her school loans, so she now owed only about ten thousand dollars.

"One year," she repeated, the words carried out on a sigh.

The next twelve months would be a kind of life pause for them, breathing room to figure out what they really wanted. Kira knew, for Peter, that meant a family. He'd often talked about having three or even four kids, while Kira thought two seemed like plenty. She needed to figure out a way to tell Peter she wanted to get through this year before they shook up their lives again. It wasn't that she disliked kids. But something she couldn't identify was holding her back; she didn't feel ready yet for a child of her own. She dreaded having that conversation.

She sighed and stared up at the full, bright moon overhead.

The bright overhead fluorescent lights pierced Alyssa's eyes. She stood in the aisle of the sprawling megastore and stifled a scream. She was starving. She felt dizzy. She desperately wanted to be anywhere but here.

She steered her cart down another aisle—naturally she'd gotten a cart with a faulty wheel that required her to hurl herself against it every few steps to keep it moving—and looked around as a headache clamped down on her temples. She was in the wrong place again; she needed sheets, and this aisle was filled with coffee-makers and Crock-Pots.

Did they need any of this stuff? Maybe she should pick up a coffeemaker; guests would definitely want coffee.

But . . . which one? Her morning caffeine ritual involved dunking a tea bag into a pot of hot water, but here were devices that let you put a little circular pod into the top of a machine, and then a latte or caramel cappuccino or hot chocolate would magically spurt out. Alyssa loaded the coffeemaker and a few boxes of pods into her cart, then reconsidered.

If they filled all the rooms in the house, they'd have eight guests. Some people drank two or three cups of coffee in the morning. Alyssa wasn't a math whiz, but she could easily see that if they made one cup at a time, they'd be constantly running back and forth from the kitchen.

So, none of those cute little pods. She unloaded the boxes and put them back on the shelves and stared at the other coffeemakers until the features advertised on their glossy boxes danced and grew blurry before her eyes: *Programmable settings! Built-in grinder! Auto-shutoff!*

Maybe she should get something to eat, even if the only offerings at the little snack bar were junk—huge, gooey slices of pizza, candy bars, and sodas in plastic buckets. No, all that sugar and starch would make her feel even worse. She'd kill for a banana. But if she tried to locate them, she'd get lost forever, finding her way out the exit door only when she was a gray-haired old lady with a cane—which they probably sold here, too.

She snuck glances at the people around her. None of them seemed to be having trouble. They were trotting briskly through the aisles, their carts filled, their wheels behaving. They looked happy, even! One woman passed, snatched a package of coffee pods from the shelf by Alyssa, and sailed on by, barely breaking her stride. Alyssa was definitely the outsider here. She'd never gotten the hang of shopping, never seen its appeal. She lived in cargo pants and T-shirts for work, slept in one of Rand's old T-shirts, and had a few dresses for evenings out. What else did she need? She owned a lot of jewelry, but it was all hand-crafted pieces she'd picked up on her travels, inexpensive trinkets that held memories and meaning.

When she and Rand were getting ready to move to Vermont, it had taken her only a couple of hours to pack her personal belongings: her photography equipment, her journals, a few sentimental items like the pressed wildflowers from a bouquet Rand had picked for her. She'd never felt the desire to accumulate stuff; it made her feel weighed down, tethered in place.

Cooking was Kira's domain; she should let her sister-in-law pick the coffeemaker, Alyssa finally decided, knowing it was a cop-out.

She'd been in this store for almost an hour and her cart was empty, save for a trio of black picture frames that she'd tossed in on a whim. She'd driven an hour to get here. No way could she go home empty-handed. Rand was wielding a sander to refinish the big dining room table they'd bought secondhand, and Kira and Peter were driving up from Florida. Everyone else was managing this transition just fine—she needed to do her part. She turned her cart down a new aisle, then felt her iPhone buzzing in her pocket. The number was unfamiliar, but she answered it anyway.

"Alyssa? This is Donna Marin with Children from China."

"Oh!" Alyssa said. She stopped moving, her cart squeaking to a halt. She'd never met the adoption liaison, but they'd spoken a few times during the past couple of years.

"Things are moving along, so I was calling to check in. I tried you at home," Donna was saying, "but that number has been disconnected."

"Actually, we just moved," Alyssa said.

Donna Marin's voice chilled by a few degrees. "Did you notify our agency? I don't see any notation in your file . . ."

"No, not yet," Alyssa said, feeling the smile drop off her face. "I mean, I was going to . . ."

There was a pause. "This is the third time you've moved in four years, correct?"

Why did she make it sound like that was a

terrible thing? Alyssa pictured a frowning woman in severe glasses, making a big red X over the file Alyssa had so carefully constructed, the one with a photo of her and Rand holding hands on the cover and their "letter of intent" in which they promised to love and cherish an adoptive child.

Alyssa clutched the phone closer to her ear. "But one of our moves was just from D.C. to Virginia. A dozen miles, and only because the owner of the house we were renting decided to sell."

"I see."

"Did we do something wrong?" Alyssa asked. "We had this great business opportunity in Vermont, and we'll be up here at least a year—"

"A year?" Donna asked.

Alyssa squeezed her eyes shut. "Probably longer," she said quickly.

"It's just that you understand the Chinese government has some rigid requirements for adoptive parents," Donna said.

"I know," Alyssa said. She and Rand had needed to show proof that they'd graduated from high school, and they'd been fingerprinted, and demonstrated that they had a stable income . . .

The salary requirements. Would they be in violation if the B-and-B didn't earn a good income this year?

"When we did the home study, you were living

in Virginia," Donna said. "Obviously we'll have to do another one now."

"Of course," Alyssa said. "That would be fine!"

"So, a B-and-B . . . Will you have any long-term guests?" Donna asked.

"Um . . . no, I don't think so. Most people will just stay for a few days," Alyssa said. "Can I ask why?"

"If they stay a certain amount of time, we'd need to consider them as living with you. Which would mean they'd also have to undergo background checks, as you did."

"A week. Tops," Alyssa said. "No one will stay longer. I'm certain of it."

She cringed as she thought of something. "Except my brother-in-law and sister-in-law. They're moving here to help us run the B-and-B. But she's a lawyer! And he's a really nice guy."

"We'll still need to do checks on them," Donna said. "And we'll be back in touch about the home visit."

"Wait!" Alyssa said, sensing Donna was about to hang up. "Um, is there anything we can do? I'm so sorry we didn't tell you about the move . . . I wasn't trying to hide anything, it just never occurred to me . . . ."

Donna's voice finally softened. "Look, this process is difficult and time-consuming, as you're well aware. It's best to avoid major changes while the adoption is ongoing . . . After you have your daughter, you'll be free to do whatever you'd like."

Your daughter. No one had ever said those simple, beautiful words to Alyssa before. Her breath caught in her throat as the twelve letters seemed to float around her, soft and downy as tufts of cotton.

"We won't move anytime soon," Alyssa said. "Nothing will change."

"Good," Donna said.

"When you said we were getting closer . . . how close, exactly?" Alyssa asked. "Another year, or two?"

"It's probably more like a matter of months," Donna said. "I'll be in touch."

Alyssa kept holding on to her phone long after Donna had hung up. All the preparations they'd made for the adoption had been so sterile and academic that it was hard to equate them with a warm, living child. Maybe, too, she hadn't let herself believe the adoption would ever go through, because she'd been so badly disappointed once before. She'd closed off her heart until this very moment.

Grace. The name blossomed in her mind like it had been waiting for permission to surface all along—a prayer, a blessing, a promise.

She was going to be the mother of a little girl! Her daughter already existed. She was probably asleep now, since it was nighttime on the opposite side of the world. Maybe Grace was curled up in a crib with her little hands tucked under her cheek.

Something miraculous happened: The new aisle Alyssa had turned down was filled with things for babies. There were impossibly tiny sleep sacks in pink and blue and yellow, teddy bears, soft-looking blankets, and little rubber bathtubs. There were even miniature bathrobes with pockets made to look like ducks. They had to be the sweetest things she'd ever seen.

"Oh," Alyssa breathed, reaching out to touch one.

"They're adorable, aren't they?" An obviously pregnant woman picked up a bathrobe, too.

"I can't stop buying stuff," the woman confessed. Her ankles looked painfully swollen, and after she put the robe into her cart, she began rubbing her knuckles into her lower back. "I'm due next week, and suddenly I had this urge to run to the store and get more things for the baby! I don't even know why; we have everything we need. Nesting, I guess."

"Next week?" Alyssa said. "Congratulations."

"Thanks," the woman said, and as she smiled, Alyssa realized the cliché was true: Despite her apparent discomfort, the woman really was glowing, as if she'd been lit from within.

The woman's eyes flitted down to Alyssa's flat stomach, then back to the baby items. *It's okay,*

63

Alyssa wanted to say. *I'm part of the club now, too!*

"We're expecting a little girl," Alyssa blurted. "Do you know what you're having?"

"We're having a girl, too!" the woman said. "Wow, you look amazing. I started showing at eight weeks."

"Oh, I'm not pregnant," Alyssa said. "We're adopting."

"Oh," the woman said. "Well, congratulations!"

"Thanks. We've been waiting a long time," Alyssa said. She felt a lump form in her throat, and she swallowed hard. She wouldn't have this —the swollen ankles and pink cheeks and the feel of that glorious, curving belly under the palm of her hand—but she could still be a mother. That was the important thing.

"Maybe you should get one of these, too," the woman said, gesturing to the bathrobes. She smiled and briefly touched Alyssa's hand: "For good luck."

As the woman headed off, Alyssa sorted through the robes until she found one labeled *12–18 months*. Grace would fit inside of this, Alyssa marveled, smoothing the robe and tying its sash into a floppy bow.

Grace. She whispered the name to hear it aloud for the very first time, and her heart swelled. She'd fashion a sling from printed fabric and tie her daughter close to her chest when she went out for walks, like she'd seen women do in Africa. She'd teach her little girl to go sledding, and run behind her holding the seat of her bike until she was steady enough to pedal off on her own. They'd practice tying shoes, and bake banana bread together, making the kitchen steamy and warm and wonderful-smelling on winter afternoons. Suddenly, the emptiness of the preceding years crashed over Alyssa, stealing her breath away. She felt the ache of missing her daughter so sharply she could hardly bear it.

Oh, my sweet baby Grace, she thought as she cradled the robe in her arms. *I cannot wait to hold you.*

Chapter Three

Dawn cradled her oversize purse in her arms, holding it as she would an infant. The cash it contained felt as heavy as a cement brick, and she was worried the shoulder strap would break, spilling the money out onto the street. She hurried down Sixty-second Street, knowing guilt was as visible on her face as a sunburn.

She'd been unable to sleep the previous night. Every creak in the hallway was the police coming to break down her door, and the shrill cut of her phone ringing had nearly caused her heart to stop. She'd been so grateful to hear the voice of a telemarketer that she'd stayed on the line for ten minutes, then agreed to send in two hundred dollars to a charity she'd never heard of. It was her penance.

Then this afternoon, when she'd left early for a "doctor's appointment" and had gone to the bank to withdraw the money . . . Well, the only way she'd managed to get through it was by taking an old, crumbly Xanax from a prescription she'd gotten years ago after her parents had died. She'd felt so woozy that she'd needed to lean on the counter to keep her balance.

But now Phase One of the plan was complete. She needed to get the money to Tucker quickly, so he could invest it in the initial public offering of his college classmate's company. The funds would triple, quadruple, or more . . . and then Tucker would stride into his father's office to show him the profits he'd made for their clients. To prove that he had what it took to succeed.

"What if the IPO doesn't work?" Dawn had asked, her voice hesitant, when Tucker had first mentioned the idea, one week earlier. The pain washing across his face felt like a knife twisting in her stomach.

"So you don't have any faith in me either," he'd said and turned away from her.

"No!" she'd cried. She'd wrapped her arms

around him, but he hadn't yielded. "I just don't want you to get in trouble!"

"It was a stupid idea," he'd said. He'd wiped his eyes with a quick, rough movement. "You're right."

She'd felt him slipping away, and she'd panicked. She'd ruined their relationship by doubting him; it was the single cruelest thing she could've done to a man who desperately needed to be believed in. No one else understood that beneath Tucker's golden looks lived a wounded little boy.

Besides, she knew the IPO *would* work. He'd showed her his old roommate's e-mails listing the investors already lining up to pour money into the electronics company. Even she recognized a few of the names. He'd printed out an article from an industry trade publication raving about the company's potential. His college friend was doing Tucker a huge favor by letting him in on the deal.

Then there was the safety net that Tucker didn't know about.

If something catastrophic happened and the money was lost, Dawn could just barely cover it. She was the beneficiary of a small life insurance policy from her father, his final gift to her. She'd held on to it all these years, letting the interest accumulate, thinking that she'd use it for her wedding someday. And she would: her wedding to Tucker. He was planning to propose. She'd seen the ring box on his bureau one night, just before he'd observed her noticing it and had quickly pulled a shirt over the box.

Three more segments of time to endure, she thought. Today Tucker would give the money to his roommate. Tomorrow, the company would go public. And the day after that, they'd cash in the profits and bring his father a six-figure check. Maybe even seven figures!

Dawn turned in at the entrance of Tucker's apartment building. It was a plain, run-down building, with a dirty floor and rusty metal mailboxes lining the wall. Tucker lived in a tiny studio because he refused to accept any money from his father, which only made her admire him more.

As she climbed the stairs to his fifth-floor walk-up, she heard men's voices. One of them was Tucker's, but there were at least two others— loud, angry voices. She hesitated on the landing.

"Tucker?" she called out, her voice sounding unnaturally high.

She heard a quick murmuring, then he appeared. "Hey, baby," he said, and she almost fell into his arms before she noticed his eye.

"What happened?" she cried, reaching out to touch the puffy skin. It was so swollen it looked like a baby bird's eye.

"This?" he said. "I walked into the edge of a bookcase. It's nothing."

"We need to get some ice on it!" she said. She started to move toward his apartment, but he grabbed her arm.

"The money," he said. "Where is it?"

He was squeezing her arm too tightly, and her head was still a little fuzzy from the Xanax. Was that why Tucker seemed so different all of a sudden?

"The money?" she repeated.

Two men came into view. One was big and rough-looking, but it was the smaller, well-dressed one who made Dawn's heart pound. Something in his expression . . . Were they robbers?

"Jesus, Dawn." Tucker exhaled. "You've got it, right? The hundred grand?"

Out of the corner of her eye, she saw the smaller man take a step closer to her.

"I'm about to go to the bank," instinct made her say. Her mouth was bone-dry, and she tried to swallow but couldn't. Something was off. The air around her felt thick and oppressive.

"You didn't bring the money? The bank's about to close!" Tucker had turned into a stranger. He always looked so put together, but now his shirt was untucked and his face was sweaty. The smaller man's gaze drifted down to the purse she was cradling in her left arm. Her bulging, heavy purse. Then the man looked at her and smiled.

"Is this your old roommate?" Dawn asked.

"Yeah," Tucker said. "My roommate."

The men were too still. They were staring at her without blinking. Just like the dogs in Mrs. Rita's living room all those years ago right before they attacked.

This time Dawn ran first.

She twisted out of Tucker's grasp and tore down the stairs, hearing a shouted curse behind her as the men came clattering after her. She cast a look behind her as she spun around the fourth-floor landing. Tucker was leading the way in pursuit. He was with *them*, not her.

She knew they would hurt her; she'd seen it in their faces. Her panty hose shredded and she heard a rip in the fabric of her skirt, but she kept her right hand on the railing, using it to swing herself around like a gymnast. Terror had given her the coordination and strength she'd been denied most of her life, but it had also robbed her of her voice. She wanted to scream— they were in New York, surrounded by people— but her voice had dried up.

She burst through the outer door and ran straight into a miracle. A yellow cab was letting a woman off at the building next door.

"Wait!" Dawn called, her voice finally returning. She imagined she could smell the hot breath of the men behind her, feel their fingers clawing at her. The woman by the cab turned to look at her, one hand still on the open door, her mouth forming a perfect O of surprise. Dawn leapt into the back of the cab and slammed the door and locked it just as Tucker grabbed the handle.

"Drive!" she screamed, and the cabbie obeyed, tearing away down the street. Dawn glanced behind her. The two men were getting into a black car parked on the street, but Tucker was still coming, his face grim as he sprinted behind the cab. Who was he, this man who'd whispered he'd loved her, who'd held her in his arms and kissed her so sweetly?

The cab turned a corner, and the driver slammed on the brakes as they encountered a traffic jam.

"Your boyfriend?" the cabbie was asking. "He hurts you?"

"Yes," Dawn said, because how else could she explain?

"I have three daughters," the cabbie said. He got out of the car and locked his door, then put the keys in his pocket. He was an older man, with white hair and a big stomach. He stood there with his hand out like a stop sign as Tucker approached, and Dawn prayed that Tucker would listen, that the cabbie would somehow talk her sweet boyfriend into coming back. But Tucker just reached out his fist and punched the driver in the face.

"No!" Dawn screamed. Bright red blood streamed from the cabbie's nose.

Dawn opened the door—she wouldn't be

trapped, not again, not ever again—and began to run. She looked back and saw Tucker pulling away from the cabdriver to resume the chase.

She tore down the street, her lungs growing tight, weaving through taxis and delivery trucks. She turned down another, busier avenue lined with cafés and stores, and she stepped on something sharp and almost screamed at the burst of pain; she'd lost one of her Keds. She limped a few steps, then ducked inside a restaurant, hurrying toward the back. She found the bathroom and locked herself inside and waited, her breath loud and ragged in the small space. Someone knocked on the door, and she flinched. She curled up into a ball and hid behind the toilet, thinking it might protect her in case the men had guns and tried to shoot their way inside.

She heard an odd noise, and it took a moment to realize it was coming from inside her purse. Why hadn't she thrown it off when she'd been racing down the stairs? They might've left her alone then. But terror had stolen her ability to think clearly.

She pulled out her phone and stared at it. *Mr. Wonderful,* read the display. She hit the Talk button but didn't say a word.

"Hey, baby," Tucker said, like nothing had happened.

"Tell me where you are." He was panting and

she imagined him pacing the street outside the restaurant, peering into windows.

She saw the ruby-red blood running down the kind cabbie's face. She shook her head.

"I need the money," Tucker was saying. His voice had been soft and cajoling, but now it grew rougher. "You've got to get it for me, understand?"

"He wasn't your roommate, was he?" she whispered.

"What? Dawn, come on. You can't hide from me forever."

She wrapped her arms around herself and rocked back and forth. "I thought you loved me."

"I do love you, baby," Tucker said.

"No," she whispered. "I won't do it."

She could feel the darkening in Tucker, like a blind snapping shut over a sunny window.

"Your fingerprints are on everything," he said. "Understand, Dawn? I know you're not too bright, but think about it. You wired the money. You *stole* it."

"I did it for you!" she burst out, but he continued, speaking in a low, calm voice that scared her more than a shout.

"I barely even know your name," he said. "Ask anyone at the office."

"But . . ." Her head swirled. *Her secret lover.*

Someone knocked on the bathroom door

again, then rattled the handle. "Is anyone in there?" a woman called out.

She had to think. She had to find a way out of this.

"I'll tell your father!" Dawn cried.

"Sure, you do that," Tucker said. "My father lives in Michigan, Dawn. He's a plumber."

Everything had been a lie. She dropped her head onto her knees as nausea roiled in her gut. Tucker had tricked her, used her for money. He'd never cared about her. Was there even a ring in that jewelry box? She'd seen enough *Lifetime* movies to know this sort of thing happened to women like her—silly, trusting women. They dated charming serial killers, they fell for con artists, they swallowed lie after lie because they were so desperate for love . . .

"I use disposable phones," Tucker was saying. "So it's going to be hard to prove I ever called you. But you can tell all that to the police when they arrest you."

Her head snapped up at a sudden thought: Could Tucker be tracing her location through this call? Maybe the men with him had the means. She lifted the lid of the toilet tank and dropped her phone inside, then did the scariest thing possible: She stood up and opened the bathroom door.

At the sharp clatter of a dish smashing against the floor, her knees buckled; then she realized it came from the kitchen, just a few feet away. She rushed through the swinging doors, running past the chefs in white aprons, nearly crashing into a waiter holding a tray full of plates, and then she found the back exit and spilled out onto the street. She waited to feel hands pull her into the black car as she walked briskly, favoring her injured foot, keeping her head low and trying to blend into the crowds. Someone bumped into her and she stifled a cry, but it was just a woman pushing a baby stroller.

She came to a corner drugstore and went inside and gave the clerk five dollars and begged him to call her a cab. She hurried through the aisles, grabbing a pair of flip-flops, a plastic blue rain slicker that came in a small rectangular packet, and a box of Band-Aids. She began to pull out her credit card to pay, then she realized: It would be another way to track her. She had seven dollars in her wallet, not enough for her flimsy disguise and the cost of the cab she'd just called. She slid a hundred-dollar bill off the top of the cash brick in her purse.

It's starting, she thought. If she hadn't been a criminal before, she was turning into one now.

She pulled on the slicker and covered her hair with its hood and stayed in the doorway until she saw the bright yellow taxi pull up outside. She ran for it and kept her head low, beneath the window, once she was safely inside.

"Where to?" the cabbie asked.

She had no idea how to answer. Tucker was

probably waiting at her apartment. Maybe if she found her boss's home address and went to him, begging him to understand . . . But he was a brusque, busy man. She didn't think he'd help her; he'd just call the police. When she didn't show up for work tomorrow, her absence would cause questions. How long would it take for the firm to notice the missing money and report her?

"Lady?" the cabbie asked.

She'd never missed her parents so desperately. She thought of her father in his red apron at his cashier's job at the neighborhood grocery store, slipping her a piece of gum or a soda when she went in to say hello, and her mother coming home from a long day as a nurse's aide, where she'd tried to dispense comfort by singing to her youngest patients as she tended to them. They were such good, dear people, and all they'd ever wanted was for her to be happy. She remembered the way they'd always reached out their arms for a hug, even when they'd seen her only the day before, and she choked back a sob.

She wanted to go home, but her home had disappeared when her parents died. "Penn Station, please," she finally said. She curled up on the seat and buried her face in her hands and cried as quietly as she could.

Kira cut a small piece of a banana-pecan pancake, chewed slowly, then sprinkled more cinna-

76

mon into the bowl of batter on the counter. It needed something else, but what? Vanilla? No, the pancakes were verging on too sweet already, she decided. Maybe a bit of bran, to add heft and texture. She scribbled a note in her new cookbook.

"Breakfast in ten minutes," she called out to the others. She and Peter had arrived at the B-and-B three days ago, and this would be her first test meal.

"You're killing me," Rand called back. "It smells insane."

"Hand soap!" Alyssa said, coming into the kitchen. Her wavy hair was tied back in a red bandanna, and her skin was nut brown from so many hours in the sun. "I knew I forgot something. The guests will need it for their bathrooms. And we're low on milk. Do you want me to pick up anything else while I'm out?"

"I think I'm good," Kira said as she used a small measuring cup to pour more batter onto the sizzling griddle.

"A measuring cup?" Alyssa asked.

Kira shrugged. "It makes all the pancakes come out a uniform size."

"Right!" Alyssa said, nodding, and Kira smiled. She'd been pleasantly surprised by how much she found herself liking Alyssa. When Alyssa and Rand had come to Florida a few years back, Alyssa had remained in the guest room meditating one morning while everyone else had coffee, which Kira had found a little rude. And Alyssa and Rand had stayed up late the first night, giggling and whispering, then Kira had heard the rhythmic creaking of their bed, which made her intensely uncomfortable. She couldn't imagine having sex with Peter with their relatives just a thin wall away.

But the moment they'd arrived at the B-and-B, Alyssa had come running out to the car to meet them. She'd given them a tour while Rand carried in Kira and Peter's bags, and when Kira had commented on the fresh blue paint on the kitchen cabinets, and the pretty yellow-and-orange countertop tiles, Alyssa had said she'd picked out the color palette.

"Do you like it?" she'd asked, looking so hopeful that Kira had smiled.

"It's perfect!" she'd answered.

Now Alyssa picked up a pancake with her fingertips and began nibbling on it. "Oh," she moaned. "These are incredible. Do you know what I usually eat for breakfast?"

"What?" Kira asked, opening the oven door to check on the bacon.

"A granola bar," Alyssa said. "And lunch is sprouts and hummus in a pita with canned soup or something boring like that." She shrugged. "I've never gotten the hang of cooking."

"It's not as hard as you think," Kira said. "You could do it."

Alyssa hoisted herself up onto the counter. "Maybe sometime you could show me," she said.

"Sure," Kira said. "I've got a bunch of gourmet dinner recipes you can make in under half an hour."

Alyssa hesitated. "Well, I was thinking we could start with mac 'n' cheese, or spaghetti and meatballs. Just something basic."

"Okay," Kira said. Spaghetti and mac 'n' cheese? Those were entrées from the kiddie menu. Why in the world would Alyssa—

Kira looked at her sister-in-law more carefully. Could she possibly be pregnant? Alyssa sure didn't seem to be suffering from morning sickness, given the way she was gobbling down that pancake. Kira had once asked Peter if he thought Rand and Alyssa would have kids. "I dunno," he'd said, shrugging. "Rand's never mentioned it."

Peter, on the other hand, had mentioned it twice on the drive up alone. Kira's stomach clenched remembering it. They'd just upended their lives; the timing was all wrong, no matter what Peter said. Kids needed stability, and right now, the ground felt very wobbly under her feet—

"Are those pancakes okay?" Alyssa asked.

Kira jerked back to the present and stared down at the smoking mess on the griddle. She lifted up two blackened pancakes and flung them into the sink.

She could feel her cheeks turning pink. "I can't believe I did that."

Rand's voice came from the living room: "Is something on fire in there?"

Kira turned off the burner and waved around a potholder to dissipate the smoke. What if this had happened when the dining room was filled with hungry guests? She'd secretly envisioned visitors raving about her cooking, posting glowing reviews on Yelp and the B-and-B's website: *Kira's eggs Benedict are the best I ever had! Go taste Kira's homemade raspberry scones—they're worth the trip!* Now she saw a different kind of review: *Keep 911 on speed dial during breakfast—this place is run by amateurs.*

The stress she'd been pushing away since she quit her job came snapping back at her like a rubber band. She and Peter had made a mistake; she was certain of it. She should've swallowed her pride and accepted her punishment and stayed at the law firm. She and Peter weren't anything like Alyssa and Rand—why had she pretended they could be?

"These ones are perfect." Alyssa's voice broke into her thoughts, and Kira turned to see her lifting up the platter. "And I can't believe you warmed up the maple syrup to go with them! Should I carry this into the dining room?"

"Sure," Kira said, feeling her spirits lift a fraction. She pointed to a blue-and-white china pitcher on the counter. "I squeezed some orange juice this morning, too."

"Fresh-squeezed orange juice is my favorite thing in the world, but I'm too lazy to ever make it," Alyssa said.

Kira reached into the refrigerator for the bowl of hulled strawberries she'd spiked with fresh mint, welcoming the rush of cool air on her warm face. She walked back out to the dining room, noticing the acrid smell hadn't completely dissipated, and sat down at the table.

"Did you seriously cook all this for just us?" Rand asked.

"You should've seen her in the kitchen," Alyssa said. "It was like watching a . . . a musician or something. It was art!"

Everyone was being so kind to her; it was amazing how grateful people became when they were served good, hearty food.

"So what's the plan for today?" Kira asked.

"I'm going to take more photos for our website," Alyssa said. "And run into town for supplies."

"I'm going to shower," Peter said.

"Thank God for that," Rand cracked, and Peter threw a piece of bacon at him. Rand picked it up off the floor and ate it.

"I was thinking," Kira began. Peter's cell

phone rang, and he got up to take the call.

"Alyssa, would you want to offer photography services to our guests?" Kira continued. "I bet a lot of them will come here for special occasions . . . anniversaries or whatever. Maybe you could snap pictures and people could buy them if they wanted?"

Alyssa looked at her. "What a great idea!"

"And I could offer an après-ski package for folks," Kira said. "Spiked rum drinks and nibbles, things like baked Brie with apricots . . . just something that would taste good after a day out in the cold. We could charge extra for it."

"Do you have any more ideas?" Rand asked. "Because you're batting a thousand."

"Maybe I've been a frustrated innkeeper all my life," Kira joked as Peter came back to the table.

"I've got a little announcement," he said, holding up his cell phone. "We just booked our first guests."

"What?" Alyssa squealed. "How did they even know we were open?"

"Peter's been doing some marketing," Kira said. "He got us listed on the chamber of commerce's website."

"You're amazing!" Alyssa said. "So when are they arriving?"

"Today," Peter said. "They'd booked some other place, but there was a reservations mix-up, so we got them. They asked how much we charged and I had no idea what to say, so I made something up—one twenty-five a night for the big room, and a hundred for one with a queen bed. Sound about right?"

"Actually, that's too low," Rand said. "No way will we make a profit with those rates."

Alyssa saw Peter stiffen. The pride on his face slipped away.

"Call them back if you want," Peter said, his voice tight. "I didn't want to lose customers by revealing we didn't have our act together."

Rand folded his arms in front of his chest. "Hey, little bro, I've been busting my ass for three weeks to make sure it's together."

Whoa, Kira thought. *They're fighting already?*

Alyssa placed a hand on Rand's arm. "Honey?" Her voice broke the tension arcing between the men.

"You probably made the right call," Rand finally said, and Kira let out the breath she didn't realize she'd been holding. "They're our trial run. They should get a discount."

"Cool," Peter said. And just like that, their spat was over.

Maybe her concern about getting along with Alyssa was misplaced; it was their husbands she should've worried about, Kira thought. But Rand was probably just tired from working so hard these past few weeks; she'd noticed dark circles under his eyes and the thumbnail that was turning black from where he'd banged it with a hammer. Peter must still be exhausted from the long drive, too. That was the cause of the momentary tension between them.

Surely the brothers wouldn't be bickering all the time. *No!* Kira thought. This was going to be a wonderful year—for all of them.

The B-and-B had never looked better. Alyssa sat in a rocking chair on the front porch, feeling the late-summer breeze tickle the fine hair on her arms. Dusk was beginning to settle, and solar-powered torches illuminated the sweet gale and chokecherry bushes hugging the edges of the house. The windows were thrown open, and James Taylor was singing about going to Carolina in his mind.

A Toyota 4x4 began to climb the long drive-way, and Alyssa poked her head inside the front door, calling, "They're here!"

The bedrooms looked warm and welcoming. Pitchers of water with floating lemon slices were on the bureaus, and bouquets of violets brightened the bathrooms. In the living room, Kira was setting out a tray of goat-cheese-and-walnut-stuffed figs and a crusty loaf of French bread with a warm artichoke dip. There was also a pitcher of pomegranate martinis—a complimentary spread for their first guests.

Alyssa opened the door to the two young

couples, and Peter and Rand hurried out to help them with their bags.

"Oooh! Are those snacks for us?" squealed one of the women. She appeared to be in her mid-twenties, like the other three, and was petite and blond enough to be Kira's little sister. "We munched all afternoon when we were wine tasting at the vineyards, so we never ate a proper dinner and suddenly I'm hungry again!"

"Of course," Kira said. "Help yourselves. And we've got plenty of pomegranate martinis."

Alyssa grabbed two of the suitcases and carried them upstairs. She took a moment to turn back the covers on the beds and to switch on the nightstand lamps. When she came back down, she ducked into her room to find her camera before heading into the living room, where the couples were settled on the sectional couch and Rand had pulled up a chair to join them.

Rand looked like he'd been an innkeeper for decades. He had one foot up on the coffee table and was enthralling their guests with the story of the time he'd bumped into a member of Coldplay in a men's room at a little dive bar in New York.

"Kind of weird that he was singing one of his competitor's hits in the stall— Oh, hey, babe," Rand said, patting the chair next to him. "Come say hi."

Alyssa extended her hand to the blond woman, who was the closest to her. "I'm Jessica," said the woman. She had a slightly squeaky voice, skin so pale it appeared almost translucent, and a pink tinge to the tip of her pert little nose. If she were an animal, she'd be a hamster.

"This is Scott, my fiancé." Jessica put a little emphasis on her last word as she nudged the knee of the beefy, ruddy-cheeked guy sitting next to her.

"Jessica and Scott just got engaged last weekend," said Rand. Jessica held out her hand so Alyssa could see her ring, which looked huge against her tiny finger.

"Congratulations!" Alyssa said as she sat down next to Rand.

"And meet Maria and David," continued Rand, master of ceremonies, as he gestured to the other couple. "They've all been best friends since college."

"This is our celebratory trip," Jessica explained. "Maria and David are going to be our maid of honor and best man."

"Wow," Alyssa exclaimed, because she couldn't think of anything else to say. She'd never understood the fuss some people made over weddings, or why they focused more on the celebration than the meaning behind it. She and Rand had gotten married in a friend's living room, with her mother, who'd been ordained for the occasion, serving as minister. Everyone had eaten pasta off paper plates and sipped glasses of wine. Alyssa had woven white flowers into her hair, and Rand had been barefoot and in jeans. It had been absolutely perfect.

"Mmm . . . try one of these," Jessica said as she grabbed a fig and popped it into Scott's mouth. Alyssa raised her camera and captured the moment.

"Did you just take a picture of us?" Jessica asked.

Alyssa called up the digital photo on the screen and handed the camera to Jessica. "Take a look," she said.

"I love this!" Jessica squealed. "This may be the best photo we've ever had taken. See, Scott . . . the candles behind us and the expression on our faces . . ."

"I'll print it out and give it to you before you leave," Alyssa said. "As an engagement gift."

"Alyssa's a professional photographer," Rand said.

The sound of a guitar being strummed made everyone look at David, who'd found Rand's guitar leaning against the side of the sofa.

"Do you play?" Peter asked.

"Not since seventh grade," David said. "I thought about taking it up again, but I don't have the time. Maybe after I'm done with my medical residency."

Rand reached for the guitar and began accompanying James Taylor. "I needed the shelter of someone's arms, and there you were," Rand sang, his low voice caressing the words. "I needed someone to understand my ups and downs, and there you were . . ."

"Maybe that should be our wedding song," Jessica said to Scott. "For our first dance."

"You know what?" Maria blurted. "You guys should get married here!"

"Here?" Jessica repeated.

"I mean, the food's great," Maria said, gesturing to the tray of appetizers. "And it's so intimate and pretty. You'd have everything you needed in one place—even a photographer. It could be spectacular!"

Jessica was staring at Maria, her mouth slightly open. Maria shrugged. "It's just an idea."

"Actually," Jessica said, drawing out the word, "that could be brilliant."

"Brilliant?" Kira echoed faintly. She was standing in the doorway coming from the kitchen, holding a tray containing a bowl of warm spiced nuts and a fresh round of pomegranate martinis.

"My mom keeps pressuring us to have the wedding in my hometown, in Connecticut," Jessica said, leaning forward and speaking even more rapidly. "But most of our friends are out here now. Plus I don't want to be traveling back and forth to Connecticut all the time to do wedding stuff; I just started a new job a few months ago."

"And my grandparents think we're going to do it at their club, which is like retirement central," said Scott, who hadn't even spoken until now but suddenly seemed as animated as Jessica. "They'll probably want to serve dinner at four-thirty and kick us out by six."

Jessica jumped to her feet and looked around the room. "This could really work," she said. "We could have the wedding party stay here. Everyone else could drive in for the day or stay at a hotel. Are there any close by?"

"Um, yeah," Peter said.

"When were you thinking of getting married?" Rand asked.

"We hadn't really nailed that down," Jessica said.

"A winter wedding would be cool," Scott said. "People could go skiing the day before."

"I've always wanted to be a bride in the wintertime! So December? Or maybe January would be better, after the holidays." Jessica drained her martini. "These are yummy. Should we serve them at the wedding?"

"Nah," Rand said, and Alyssa turned to look at him in surprise. She'd thought he'd be more diplomatic about turning down their guests for a venture they weren't remotely qualified to pull off. "We should create a special drink just for your day," he continued. "A Jessica-tini. Scott scorpions."

"Ha ha," Kira said, looking a little pale. She put down the tray on a sideboard instead of bringing it to the guests. "I— Do you think we should talk about it a little more before we decide? I mean, were you thinking about a sit-down dinner?"

"A sit-down dinner sounds great," Jessica said. "With passed appetizers first, though, right, Scott?"

Scott ate another fig as he nodded. "Can we serve these?" he asked.

Kira cleared her throat. "Um, are you sure you want to have it here?" she began. "There isn't a ton of space, so you might have to limit your guest list . . . How many people were you thinking of inviting?"

"Our families, so that's ten. Friends, our parents' friends . . . Let's say that brings us to sixty. Oh, and grandparents and aunts and uncles . . . maybe seventy-five?" Jessica said.

Seventy-five wasn't so bad, Alyssa thought. They could handle seventy-five. She glanced at Kira, who shook her head violently.

"We've gotta invite my cousins, too," Scott said. "That's another eight right there. No, nine. I always forget about the quiet one. He smoked too much weed in high school." Scott tapped a finger against his temple. "Never been the same."

Jessica was counting on her fingers. "Gosh, I guess if you count all our relatives, it might be over a hundred."

"Over a hundred," Kira repeated. Alyssa swore she could read Kira's mind: *Including feuding relatives who'll resent the location, and a stoner cousin who'll eat all my appetizers in the first ten minutes!*

"I'll help," Alyssa whispered.

"You can't even make mac 'n' cheese!" Kira hissed. "And you're the photographer!"

"A heated tent for dancing and eating, a blanket of freshly fallen snow, nothing around you but pine trees and starlight—it'll be gorgeous," said Rand as Kira glared at him from across the room. "And if you want to have your bachelorette party here, too, it's on the house. Our wedding gift to you. You and your girls could have drinks in the hot tub, then go barhopping while Scottie and his crew head to Vegas . . ."

"What a great idea!" Jessica cried. "I'll talk to my bridesmaids!"

"A toast!" Maria cried, raising her glass. "To the wedding!"

"Wait!" Kira cried. "I'm sorry, but I've never cooked for that many people before . . . ," she began.

Jessica turned her big blue eyes up at Kira. The tip of Jessica's nose grew even pinker, and she sniffled. "But this is the first time I'm feeling truly happy about my wedding," she said in her squeaky little voice. "Please?"

Rand moved his right hand down low, so the

guests couldn't see what he was doing, and he rubbed his right thumb across the pads of the index and middle fingers on the same hand. Alyssa saw Kira notice the gesture that meant "money."

Kira's shoulders slumped. "Okay," she said. "We'll do it."

"To a winter wedding," Rand said. "To Jessica and Scott!"

Jessica and Scott clinked glasses with everyone as Kira reached for one of the martinis on her tray and took a big gulp. Alyssa wondered if she was the only one who noticed that Kira hadn't joined in the toast.

Chapter Four

A hairbrush. A packet of tissues. Her wallet, which held two credit cards—useless now, of course—as well as a library card, a photograph of her parents on their wedding day, her New York driver's license, coupons, her bus pass, and the seven crumpled dollar bills.

Dawn continued to remove the contents of her purse, placing each item on the empty seat beside her. The box of Band-Aids. A small cosmetics bag. Hand sanitizer gel. A roll of peppermint breath mints, which she'd taken to carrying so she could pop one in her mouth before kissing . . .

No. She couldn't think about him now.

The only thing left in her purse was the brick of cash, but no way was she going to pull *that* out. The grungy-looking guy across the aisle had turned sideways in his seat, and Dawn could sense his stare; it made her feel unclean and even more jittery. She rubbed her hands up and down her arms, wishing the driver would turn off the air-conditioning. She was freezing in her silk shirt and torn skirt and thin layer of plastic— or maybe shock was settling into her body.

She looked down at everything she had in the world, then packed it all back into her purse and stood up and limped to the bathroom at the back of the bus. She locked the door, then closed the lid on the toilet and sat down. She twisted her left leg around so she could see the bottom of her foot. It was covered in a layer of black grime, and though the bleeding had stopped, a gash bisected her heel. She dampened a paper towel and cleaned it as best she could, wincing, then she squirted on hand sanitizer and bandaged it before slipping on her flip-flop again. Her toes were growing numb, and she had to clamp her teeth together to keep them from chattering.

What next? She tamped down her panic by summoning a comforting image of her father: his eyes, soft and brown and a little watery behind his thick glasses, his salt-and-pepper hair, the gentle swell of his belly beneath the suspenders he always wore.

He'd taught her to play chess. She hadn't been very good at it, but she remembered his advice now: "Always tink more den one step ahead," he'd say, his voice holding on to the influences of his native Polish. "Dat's key."

Maybe her credit cards weren't useless, after all.

Dawn walked back to her seat and looked out the window. The sky had darkened, but city lights glittered all around them.

"I'm stopping in Baltimore for ten minutes," the driver announced as he pulled into the Greyhound station and cut the engine. "If you're not on the bus when I'm ready to leave, we're going to D.C. without you."

The grungy guy had fallen asleep, his mouth hanging open as he snored. Dawn stood up and let her Visa card slip out of her fingers and land on the floor next to him. Maybe he'd use it and create a false trail.

Think more than one step ahead, Dawn reminded herself. She had to keep moving, but how? A rental car would require an ID, and so would train or airplane tickets. Hitchhiking wasn't safe. She didn't want to stick with Greyhound; mixing up her modes of transportation would better muddy her trail.

There were other buses linking cities along the

East Coast, though—Dawn had seen people lining up on street corners in New York, clutching cups of coffee and overnight bags while they waited to board. The buses all had company names emblazoned on their sides . . . She just needed to remember them.

She pulled up the hood on her rain slicker and walked toward the line of cabs waiting outside the bus station. Cabs were good. The drivers never looked at you, and if you paid with cash, there wasn't any way to trace you. She slid into the back of one. "Do you know where the closest Megabus station is?" she asked.

The cabbie stopped talking on his cell phone for a moment. "The one at White Marsh Mall?" he asked, and she nodded. A mall? She couldn't believe the stroke of luck.

Her first stop was Macy's. She whipped through the sale racks, grabbing black track pants, an inexpensive T-shirt, and a soft, zip-up athletic jacket. She added cheap sneakers and socks and paid with two of the stolen hundred-dollar bills. She found a bathroom and tore off the tags with her teeth, then crammed her ripped skirt and white blouse into the trash can. The new clothes helped a bit, but she felt like she'd never truly be warm again.

What else? She caught sight of her reflection in the mirror, studying her round, brown eyes and thin lips. It was the first time she'd ever been grateful that her looks were so forgettable. She used the elastic wound around the bottom of her brush to secure her hair in a ponytail, thinking that she needed to get hold of dark hair dye and scissors as soon as possible.

She walked toward the mall exit and glanced at her wristwatch: 7:45 P.M. It seemed like days had passed since she'd gone to Tucker's apartment. What she'd give now to never have met him—to be sliding a Lean Cuisine into her tiny oven and turning on a movie. Even the sounds of the couple fighting next door would be a symphony.

Dawn blinked back tears as she thought about her little studio with the bright yellow curtains she'd taken from her parents' house because her mother had sewn them, her sunflower plant, her well-loved novels lining her bookcase. She wondered if she'd ever see the place again.

Again she yanked her thoughts forward. She needed to concentrate on getting to a safe place. Then she could try to figure out a way to fix things before the police—or Tucker—caught up with her. *Which would be worse?* she wondered briefly.

The yeasty smell of fresh-baked dough drifted past her like a cloud. She looked to her left and saw an Auntie Anne's pretzel stand. She watched the server scoop ice into a cup and top it with soda, and she was gripped by a thirst so intense it was dizzying. She'd had nothing but a few sips of tea and bites of toast for the past two days. She bought a Coke and guzzled it, then purchased a bottle of water and a plain pretzel and tucked them into her purse. She wasn't hungry now, but she had no idea where the next Megabus was heading, and it might be a long ride.

She was going to take the first one out, leave her destination to chance. And if there were no more buses traveling tonight, she'd find a cheap hotel and go in the morning.

She found the bus stop across from the Red Lobster. The next Megabus was an overnight one to Boston, leaving at 8:10 P.M.

Her instinct had been to head south—to warmth and sunshine, where she could move about more easily. So maybe the opposite move was the smarter one because it would be unexpected. Tucker had accused her of being dumb, but she wasn't. She'd only been too trusting. She wouldn't ever make that mistake again.

Boston, she decided as she settled onto the bench. She'd never been to the city, and knew no one who lived there.

It would be a good start.

Soup would be a good start, Kira decided as she reached for her stack of cookbooks and began flipping through the pages of the first one. Everyone liked soup on cold winter days, right?

Plus it could be made a day in advance, in big batches. That would simplify the first course—assuming Jessica approved. Which was far from assured, given that their bride was proving to be a lot more picky when she wasn't chugging Jessica-tinis. When they'd chatted on the phone last night to discuss possible menus, Jessica had shot down three of Kira's suggested entrées before deeming chocolate dessert fountains "tacky." Kira had swallowed hard and refrained from mentioning she'd had one at her own wedding.

Alyssa came into the kitchen as Kira began jotting down a grocery list.

"Butternut squash, vegetables for stock, garlic, and nutmeg," she read over Kira's shoulder. "So you're making cheeseburgers?"

Kira laughed as Alyssa switched on the heat beneath her teakettle—she was forever sipping from a chunky pottery mug that smelled of peppermint or chamomile—and hoisted herself up to sit on the counter.

"I hope we get a lot of snow this winter," she said. "I've been dying to hit the slopes and get in some boarding."

Kira frowned. "Maybe I should check into the snowplow service," she said. "Just to make sure people can get through for the wedding."

Alyssa smiled. "Are you really worried about too much snow? It would be great for business."

"No," Kira said, opening the refrigerator to

check the supply of butter, realizing they had only two sticks left and adding a notation to her grocery list. "Well, maybe just a little. I don't have any experience driving in heavy snow. And it just hit me: It's going to get really cold. I kept picturing Vermont in the fall when we planned to move here. Orange leaves and apple cider and roaring fires. I didn't think about the depths of winter."

"It won't be that bad," Alyssa said. "We'll eat a lot and sleep a lot, like bears. Then spring will be here."

Kira turned to look at her sister-in-law. "You don't worry much, do you?" she asked.

"Me?" Alyssa thought about it. "No, I guess I don't. I've always believed the universe has some kind of a grand plan, and that things unfold as they were meant to, even if we don't understand why at the time."

"See, I think the opposite sometimes," Kira said. "Take tragedies. How can anyone say an accidental death is meant to be? I knew this girl in college who died—I mean, I didn't know her well, but she was in a few of my classes—and she was hit by a car as she was crossing a street. At her funeral one of her friends got up and talked about how this girl had walked a dog for a neighbor who was out of town that morning, because she was that kind of person. Someone who did favors for others. And I couldn't help obsessing for a while. What if this girl had forgotten the key to the neighbor's house and had to double back to get it? What if the dog had stopped to smell one more patch of grass? So many little things had the potential to save her, and she only needed one of them."

"Mmmm," Alyssa said. "I didn't mean that every single thing that happens to us is positive in some way. It's more like we're all on journeys, and there's something to be taken away from all of our experiences. Good and bad."

"I worry that I worry too much sometimes," Kira said, trying for a joking tone.

"About anything in particular?" Alyssa asked. The teakettle began to shriek, and she reached over to turn off the burner.

"Money, where we're going to live next, what jobs we're going to get, whether quitting the law firm and moving here was a smart thing to do . . ." Kira's voice trailed off. *Whether to have a baby,* she thought.

"Is that all?" Alyssa asked lightly.

"But see, you're in the exact same spot as us," Kira said. "And you don't stress about it, do you?"

Alyssa didn't answer immediately. She poured steaming water into a mug and added a tea bag and some honey; then she asked, "Have you ever been snowboarding?"

"What?" Kira shook her head. "No. I've never been skiing either."

"Then maybe this metaphor won't make sense," Alyssa said, "but for me, the best part of snowboarding is going over jumps. You feel like you're flying. It's completely exhilarating. The first time I did it, though, I immediately tensed up for the landing, and of course I fell. It's like the mountain *knows* when you're nervous. But gradually I learned to just be in that glorious moment of catching air. Once I began trusting that I'd land safely, I always did."

She shrugged and took a sip of tea. "I try to live life that way, I guess."

"Huh," Kira said. It sounded lovely, but completely impractical. What if you fell on your head, or soared right off the edge of the mountain?

Alyssa had probably grown up with money, she thought. People who did never seemed to worry about it much. "What do your parents do for a living?" Kira asked.

"My mother teaches pottery classes. And my father's a corporate lawyer," Alyssa said. "He's worked at the same company his entire life. He just keeps moving into nicer offices."

"Ah, so you'll probably get a big inheritance someday," Kira said. Then she clapped a hand over her mouth. "Oh, God, I didn't mean that the way it sounded. It's just—"

"It's fine," Alyssa said, but she looked a little taken aback.

"I should probably just take up meditation, like you," Kira said, her smile an apology.

"Hey, you're teaching me to cook," Alyssa said. "We could do a trade. I could lead you through a few meditation sessions."

"Thanks," Kira said. "I'll think about it."

Alyssa slid off the counter and stretched her arms over her head, arching her back as she released a big yawn. She looked ridiculously fit and flexible, Kira thought. Maybe there was something to this yoga and meditation business, but Kira doubted she'd be patient enough to sit through a single session, even if the reward was washboard abs.

"So what's the plan for today?" Alyssa asked.

"Brace yourself for the excitement: wedding menus," Kira said. "Jessica wants something called 'amusements' during cocktail hour."

"Seriously?" Alyssa said. "If you drink a lot of cocktails, doesn't that make it amusing enough?"

Kira pretended to scribble something on her pad: " 'Get Jessica and Scott plastered.' Actually, that's not a bad idea. Then maybe they won't notice when something goes wrong."

"Nothing's going to go wrong," Alyssa said.

"But something always does at weddings," Kira said.

"It didn't at mine," Alyssa said.

"Are you sure?" Kira asked. "Because I've tested this theory before, and I'm always right. It doesn't have to be a huge thing, but it's usually dramatic."

"Nope. Oh, wait—someone opened a bottle of champagne and the cork flew out and hit a little kid in the face. He cried for a minute, and everyone freaked out, thinking it had gotten him in the eye, but he was fine. The noise just scared him. Does that count?"

"Absolutely," Kira said. "It isn't as good as the groom fainting and landing in the wedding cake, but I'll take it."

"So what went wrong at yours?" Alyssa asked.

Kira looked at Alyssa, wondering if she was joking again. Her sister-in-law honestly didn't know?

"Um," Kira said. "There was this . . . incident."

"That sounds bigger than a champagne cork misfiring," Alyssa said.

"Yeah." Kira gave a little laugh and rechecked the butter supply.

"So," Alyssa prompted.

"So, Peter and Rand kind of got into a . . . dispute."

"An argument?" Alyssa asked.

Kira shook her head. "A fistfight."

"Are you kidding me?" Alyssa gasped. "What happened?"

Rand should have been the one to tell her—so why hadn't he? Kira wondered. She felt uncomfortable revealing the story, especially after she'd just put her foot in her mouth, but she'd never believed in keeping secrets.

"You know they didn't speak for a while after their mother died, right?" Kira asked.

Alyssa just nodded, so she continued. "Peter took a semester off from college to care for her while she had chemo and radiation," Kira continued.

Alyssa blinked. "Really? How wonderful of him."

"She and their dad were separated by then, and he completely checked out. And when Rand didn't come around much, and then their father got married again six months after their mom died . . . well, Peter felt abandoned. By everyone in the family. Even their mom, for dying."

Alyssa nodded. "I can understand that."

"At the funeral he and Rand sat separately," Kira continued. "They didn't talk for a while after that, but then we invited him to our wedding."

She looked at Alyssa. "You know what? I'm not sure I should be the one to tell you all this, after all . . ."

"Go on," Alyssa said. "Please."

Kira sighed. "At the reception someone opened a bathroom door and gave a little shriek, so of course everyone looked. And there was Rand . . . with one of my bridesmaids. Anyway, Peter flipped out because he was friends with the bridesmaid's boyfriend, who was home sick. So

Peter started shoving Rand and he knocked him into a wall and Rand began pushing him back. Everyone turned and stared. Finally a few guys got between them and held them apart."

"Oh my God," Alyssa said. "That's horrible!"

"I know," Kira said. "But then they snapped out of it. Rand apologized to Peter . . . he said something about knowing he'd screwed up. But the way he said it, it seemed like he was really apologizing for leaving Peter to deal with all the stuff with their parents. Anyway, Rand stuck out his hand and Peter shook it and the DJ put on the song 'Wipeout'—that part was pretty funny, actually—and it was like nothing ever happened."

She looked at Alyssa, wondering how much of Rand's past his wife knew, and if the story about the bridesmaid would come as a surprise. But Alyssa didn't seem like the jealous type, and Kira suspected her sister-in-law had a pretty spicy past of her own.

"I'm glad you told me," Alyssa said. She sipped her tea and seemed lost in thought for a moment. "Did you know their mother well?" she finally asked.

Kira shook her head. "I remember her being around. Bringing cupcakes into the classroom one year for Peter's birthday—you know he and I went to school together, right? Seeing her pick him up, and cheering at the football games when Rand played, that sort of thing. But she died before Peter and I got together."

"I always sensed she was the glue of the family," Alyssa said. "Rand doesn't talk about her much, though. I think it's too hard."

"Peter still has one of her crossword puzzles. She never finished it. That always kind of broke my heart," Kira said.

"I think that's part of the reason Rand wanted you guys to come live here," Alyssa said. "To get closer to his brother."

"Oh," Kira said, surprised. She looked out the window as she thought about it. She'd figured Rand wanted them for more practical help. But maybe what Alyssa said was true. Rand could still be trying to make amends; it could be the reason for the generous financial deal he'd offered them.

Kira had always assumed the reason Rand and Peter had fought so much growing up and weren't close now was that their differences formed a wedge between them. Rand had been athletic, popular, and a terrible student, which Kira had attributed to his being lazy, since he was certainly bright enough to rebuild a carburetor or rewire a lamp. But there were always girls eager to do his homework, or classmates who tilted test papers so Rand, the star athlete, could see their answers. Peter was smaller, shy, and uncommonly bright, with little interest in sports. Even their coloring was different, but if you looked closely, you could see a faint echo in their almond-shaped eyes and strong jawlines.

If they'd had something—anything—in common, or if their mother had lived, things might have been different. On a superficial level, the brothers got along well enough—they exchanged wisecracks and shared occasional meals. But neither man seemed to want to deepen their relationship. Rand was always working outside, while Peter stayed glued to his computer.

A flash of color outside the window caught Kira's eye—the leaves on the big sugar maple tree in the backyard were beginning to turn, with gold and red patches weaving through the green. Already a few nights had been cold enough for the ski resort to make snow. Soon it would be time for roaring fires and bulky sweaters and toasted marshmallows. And, of course, the wedding.

She sighed and looked back down at her grocery list.

"How about I make dinner for us all tonight?" Kira suggested. "Kind of a taste test for the wedding meal."

"Only if I can help," Alyssa said. "You need to start training me!"

"Okay," Kira said. "You're in charge of the side dishes."

Steak filets, she wrote on her list. *Broccoli rabe. Wild rice with cranberries and slivered almonds.*

No. Wasn't one of Scott's cousins allergic to almonds? And Jessica would probably object to broccoli since it wasn't fancy.

She sighed, crossed out, and started over again.

Chapter Five

Rand turned up the music, singing along with the Killers, as Alyssa watched the scenery rushing past. She never tired of Vermont's vistas: the white-capped mountains, the dreamy, low-hanging wisps of clouds, the picturesque restaurants they drove past on their way through town. Finally they turned onto the street that led to their secluded B-and-B, climbing the long hill toward their pretty home.

There was a minivan parked outside the B-and-B's garage, with stick-figure stickers depicting a family on the back window. There was a father, a mother, a little girl, a smaller boy, and two dogs.

"Who've we got today?" Rand asked.

"A family," Alyssa said. "They're just in for a night."

"Tell me they didn't bring the dogs, too." Rand pulled into his spot and cut the engine.

Before they saw their guests, Alyssa and Rand heard them. As they opened the front door, sounds poured out: A baby was crying—no, *yowling*—and someone was screeching, "Watch the juice! The juice! Oh no! Honey, can you—"

Alyssa closed the door, stepped into the living room, and surveyed the scene. A young mother was walking across the room, patting the back of a plump, red-faced baby draped over her shoulder. On the sofa was a young girl, maybe three, who was clutching her stomach and looking miserable. The father—who appeared far less cheery than his waving stick-figure representative on the back of the minivan—was bending over to pick up a glass that had fallen onto the carpet, sloshing out its contents.

"Shit," Rand breathed.

Alyssa elbowed her husband in the ribs. "Hi," she said loudly. "We're the co-owners . . . What can we do to help?"

The mother turned to look at Alyssa with grateful eyes. "We had a little spill," she said over the noise of the baby, who was hitting an impressive new octave. "I'm so sorry. And my daughter's sick . . . I think it was the food we got on the drive up here. She said her hot dog tasted bad . . ."

"Hot dog," the little girl said with a frown. Then she promptly threw up all over herself as well as the couch.

"Sweet Jesus," the father moaned.

"Paper towels!" the mother yelled, but before

anyone could move, Peter came in from the kitchen holding a small plastic trash can containing a plastic liner.

"Oh, hey, Alyssa and Rand." He looked down at the couch. "Guess I'm a few crucial seconds too late."

He put the trash can down next to the little girl, then walked over to the mother. "Here, why don't you give me Freddie," he said, reaching out his arms for the baby, who sounded like a furious cat. "You can take your daughter to your room and give her a bath, and we'll clean up in here."

"Are you sure?" the mother cried. "I'm so sorry! We didn't know she'd get sick . . ."

"Of course you didn't." Peter settled Freddie into the crook of his elbow. By the sound of things, Freddie wasn't any happier in his new position. "Could he be hungry?" Peter asked.

"Probably," the mother said. She sighed and pushed her hair off her face. "Yes, I'm sure that's exactly what it is. I was about to feed him, and then I got distracted when . . . Anyway, I think I've got a banana in the diaper bag." She rummaged through it, pulling out a juice box, a bag of crushed Goldfish crackers, and a single tiny blue sock before locating the banana, which looked like it had seen better days.

"I found some saltines!" Kira said as she swung through the kitchen door. And then, "Oh. Oh dear."

"This is why we Scotchgarded the sofa," Peter said. "Look, everything's going to be fine. A little throw-up never hurt anyone. Let's get your daughter taken care of first, then we'll fix up the couch."

He sat down on a chair opposite the sofa, balancing the baby while peeling the banana. "K? Can you get me a spoon? Maybe one of the tiny ones you use for measuring will work."

Alyssa felt a slow smile spread across her face. *Look at you!* she wanted to say to Peter. She'd never seen this side of him before.

The father picked up his daughter and headed upstairs, with the mother trailing close behind, as Peter began talking to the baby: "Now, you're not going to puke on me, are you? Because we're getting along so well. Let's make a deal: You don't throw up on me, and I won't throw up on you. Okay?"

Miraculously, the baby's yells were decreasing in volume. And when Kira came back with a plastic teaspoon and Peter scooped out a bit of banana and popped it into Freddie's mouth, a surprised look came over the little guy's face and he stopped crying completely.

"You liked that, didn't you?" Peter said. "More where it came from if you remember our deal."

"Come on," Alyssa said to Rand. "Let's get the couch." Kira had brought out paper towels and fabric spray cleaner along with the teaspoon, and Alyssa began to mop up the mess and toss the soiled towels into the trash can.

"Eww," Rand said, scrubbing at a spot on the carpet. "This stinks. What did that kid eat, turpentine?"

They got up the worst of the mess, and Rand went to bring the trash can back into the kitchen while Alyssa sprayed cleaner onto the couch and left it to soak in.

"You, my friend, would probably like a new diaper," Peter was saying to Freddie. He talked like he was chatting with a peer instead of using the high voice most adults put on when faced with a baby. "I'm going to let your parents handle that one, though."

Alyssa leaned back on her heels, considering Peter. He scooped out a little more banana, fed it to Freddie, and used the edge of the spoon to wipe away the excess from the baby's chin. He was a natural. No—it was more than that.

He'd done this before.

Of course, she thought. His mother had been ill, and he'd cared for her while she was dying. Alyssa watched the easy movement of the spoon Peter held as it carried nourishment to the little boy, and the scene blurred and was replaced by one in which she saw him feeding soup to his mother, wiping her chin, and settling blankets around her more securely. What a comfort he must have been to her.

Peter looked up and caught her eye. "He's cute, but he's a little porker," he said of the baby.

"Can I try?" Alyssa asked.

"Sure," Peter said.

Alyssa straightened up and walked over to the chair, and Peter started to hand her the baby boy. "You know what?" he said. "You might want to wash your hands first, so he doesn't get his sister's germs."

"You're so right!" Alyssa said. Something else Peter had probably learned during that painful time, she thought. She ducked into the kitchen, where Kira was busy at the stove, and scrubbed her hands with antibacterial soap.

"Can you bring a dish towel?" Peter called. "We've got a little spit-up."

She grabbed a clean one and walked back into the living room.

"Why don't you take my seat?" Peter offered.

"Okay," Alyssa said as he started to hand her the baby. Suddenly she felt nervous. She'd held babies before, but not recently. "Do I have to support his neck or something?"

"Nah, he's holding it up well himself," Peter said. He handed her the baby, then stood and took Alyssa's elbow to help guide her down into the chair.

"Hello there," Alyssa said, staring into the little boy's impossibly wise blue eyes. "Oh, aren't you gorgeous."

Freddie broke into a gummy smile, and Alyssa squealed. "He smiled! I think he likes me!"

"Oh, sure, forget all about who fed you the banana," Peter joked. "I feel so used."

Alyssa adjusted the baby into a more comfortable position in her left arm, then reached out with her right hand to smooth his downy, dark hair.

She began to sing: "Twinkle, twinkle, little star, how I wonder what you are . . ."

"You're a natural, babe," Rand said from behind her. He bent down and kissed her forehead, then picked up his guitar from its spot next to the couch and began to accompany her.

Freddie's eyes were growing heavy, and he felt deliciously warm in her arms. Alyssa segued into "Rock-a-bye, baby," despite Peter's whispered protest that it was a sadistic song involving innocent babies tumbling down from treetops, and Rand was still strumming his guitar.

By the time Freddie's mother came downstairs, he was sound asleep, his rosebud lips parted, his long lashes resting against his plump cheeks.

"You are miracle workers," the mother said. She approached the chair and looked down at her son.

"He's the miracle," Alyssa said.

The mother put a hand on Alyssa's shoulder. "Thank you," she said and gave a little laugh. "I must look as tired as I feel. I think that's why my in-laws gave us a night here as an anniversary present. They thought it would be a break for us. Some break, huh?"

"You don't look any more tired than any other mother with young kids," Alyssa assured her, even though the woman had bluish gray smudges under her eyes and her face was drawn. "I'm Alyssa, by the way."

"Susan."

"Is your daughter okay?" Alyssa asked. "I'm sorry, I didn't catch her name either."

"It's Katie." Susan sighed and sat down on the edge of the sectional couch, close to Alyssa. "She's watching a video right now. We brought along an iPad for that." She rolled her eyes. "Before I had kids I vowed they wouldn't get exposed to television too soon. But not three weeks after I had Freddie, I was begging Katie to watch *Barney*. She's got the theme song memorized by now."

Rand strummed a few more chords and set down his guitar. "I'm going to head out to the garage," he said. "See you in a few." He exited the room, and a moment later came the sound of the front door closing.

"Was that your husband?" Susan asked, and Alyssa nodded.

"I hope we didn't scare him away," Susan joked. "We're probably not your favorite guests."

"Hey, real men don't mind a little puke," Peter said.

Alyssa was staring at Freddie, marveling over the sweet creases at his wrists, but she lifted her head at Peter's tone. Was there an edge in his voice?

She must've imagined it, she decided. Peter was smiling at Susan now, and Kira was coming into the room with a bottle of wine, and the baby was warm and deliciously heavy in her arms.

Everything was fine here now, she thought. Everything was good.

Chapter Six

Dawn tucked her newly darkened hair behind her ears as she walked through the doors of the Apple Store. The wind had picked up in the last hour or so and the air held a bite; she needed to find a thrift store so she could buy a coat. It would push the total amount she'd spent to close to eight hundred dollars, including the twenty-nine bucks she'd been paying nightly for a bunk in a youth hostel, but she was keeping track so she could repay it someday.

"Can I help you?" A young guy greeted her, his index finger poised over an iPad.

"Just looking," she said, slipping past him. The store was busy, but she found an empty computer with a stool positioned in front of it. She sat down and pulled up a fresh Google search. Typing her name felt a little risky, but it was a chance she had to take.

She waited, her heart thrumming, but the search turned up only two hits: the brief newspaper obituary for her parents she'd paid for years earlier, and the investment banking firm's employee list. Maybe her crime wasn't big enough for the papers to pick up, given all the murders and robberies out there—or maybe the firm hadn't reported it to the police. Perhaps it was being kept quiet in order to prevent clients from panicking.

She erased her search history. Now it was time for her big gamble. She was going to write an e-mail to John Parks, the man Tucker had pretended was his father. She'd tell him everything, including the fact that she still had almost all of the money. She'd offer him her entire inheritance as penance. She'd be fired, of course, but maybe they'd let her walk away.

They could probably find a way to trace her e-mail if the police were involved, but it seemed safer than sending an actual letter with a postmark, especially since there would be no way for her to get a reply to a physical piece of mail without giving away her location.

Her fingers shook as she called up her personal e-mail account, and she had to retype her password twice.

Someone slid into the seat beside her, and she reflexively hunched over, trying to hide the screen. It was just a guy in a pair of dark hipster glasses almost identical to the ones Dawn now wore. His were probably cosmetic, too. The guy was too busy staring at his own screen to notice hers.

Dawn reached into her pocket and pulled out the folded piece of paper containing her confession. She started to type the first line—*Please read this all the way through to the end*—into a new message, then hesitated.

A flurry of new e-mails were waiting in her in-box. Most were junk or from concerned friends with subject lines like *Are you okay?* There was one from her landlord—her rent was overdue—and another, similar message from Visa.

And one was from Tucker.

She recoiled as violently as if snakes were striking out of the computer screen.

"You okay?" the guy next to her asked.

She nodded. "Just . . . thought I saw a bug."

"You mean a mouse?" the guy said, laughing as he pointed to the one attached to her computer.

She swallowed against the nausea rising in her throat and opened the e-mail, which was dated and sent the night that she'd fled from New York.

Dear Ms. Zukoski,

I'm writing this to ask that you please stop sending letters and cards to my home. I was alarmed and disturbed to find you on my doorstep this afternoon. It's obvious you've developed a fixation on me for some reason, but let me assure you, it's not reciprocal.

I don't want to have to go to Human Resources to report your harassment or the fact that you must have accessed company records to get my home address, but if this continues, I will.

You obviously need help. It's clear you are on a dangerous path. I expect your assurance that you will comply with my request, and if I don't hear back from you with your explicit agreement, I will be forced to take action.

Sincerely,

Tucker Newman

It was a code. He was threatening her.

There was one unread message just beneath it, with the subject line *Mr. Wonderful.* Her nickname for Tucker. He was the only one who knew about it.

With shaking fingers, she clicked on it. It was from an unfamiliar address. It contained a single line: *I will find you.*

She logged off the computer and burst out of the store, looking wildly up and down the street, half-expecting Tucker to leap out at her at any moment. He must have saved the dozen or so notes and cards she'd mailed to him. Of course they'd never corresponded through their office e-mail accounts, because of Tucker's "father."

She'd written flirty, sweet things, like "Your eyes light me up inside" and—oh, God—"I can't wait to watch your cute butt when you walk down the hall at work tomorrow."

He was using her love letters to craft an alibi. Maybe he'd already told John Parks that Dawn was obsessed with him, about his concern that she seemed to be becoming unhinged.

She couldn't contain her nausea any longer. She found a trash can by the street corner and leaned over it and threw up. She straightened and fumbled in her purse for a tissue, her mouth tasting foul and her body shaking.

"You okay, lady?" A Boston cop was approaching her. He looked at her closely. Did he recognize her from some APB? The police could have already traced her here.

The cop was frowning. Maybe he thought she was on drugs. Oh, God, if he searched her purse and found the brick of cash . . .

She nodded. "I'm fine. I'm just . . . pregnant."

It scared her, how quickly the lie formed on her lips. Who was she becoming?

"Ah," he said, a smile slicing across his beefy face. "I don't know why they bother calling it morning sickness. My wife had all-day sickness, too. She carried around these ginger chew things she got at a health-food store. Maybe you should get some."

"Good idea," Dawn said.

He continued on and she felt her legs nearly give out, but she forced herself to begin the nearly three-mile walk back to the hostel, hoping the cold air would clear her mind.

Tucker was sealing off the few avenues she had left. She visualized him sidling up to other assistants—her former work friends—as he delivered mail around the building, speaking her name and asking if they'd heard the news: *She's nuts . . . Oh, you haven't heard? Yeah, she had this crush on me . . . really creeped me out . . .*

The firm would never be safe for her again. And neither would anywhere else, if Tucker was still chasing her.

A car blared its horn, and she leapt backward. She'd almost walked into traffic.

For a wretched, fleeting moment, she contemplated doing it: closing her eyes and stepping off the curb and into oblivion. But she thought of her parents, and knew she couldn't. How heartbroken they'd be to know her life had turned out this way.

She thought about Tucker's swollen eye, and the small man with the cold smile. Maybe he owed money to drug dealers, or gambling bookies. He'd invested so much time and energy into duping her; he was probably growing more desperate with every passing day.

Dawn wrapped her arms around herself as she walked, ducking her head into the wind as it picked up. It was dark now, and she was heading through a seedy section of town. She passed by a liquor store, and a few men sitting on the stoop hooted at her, but she ignored them.

She finally reached the hostel and went to the women's dorm room and crawled into her bunk. Two girls from England were giggling and chatting as they got ready to head out on the town. They wanted to meet American men, and dance, and flirt the night away.

Be careful, Dawn yearned to tell them. But they were vibrant and happy; they expected the future to hold only good things. They hadn't even looked at her when she came in.

Maybe that was why she'd fallen for Tucker's lies so easily—because he'd seemed to really see her, rather than skimming his eyes past her the way others did. For as long as she could remember, she'd been the girl standing against the wall at school dances, the one chosen last for kickball. Once in elementary school—it must have been third or fourth grade—a substitute teacher had taken over the class. After circle time on the rug at the front of the room, the sub had called the names of the students from the roster one by one, dismissing the kids so they could go back to their desks to read.

The students were listed alphabetically, which meant Dawn was last. She was always last, with a name like Zukoski.

Because she was sitting to one side of the sub—or, let's face it, because she was Dawn—the sub didn't notice she hadn't called Dawn's name. She simply stood up and went to her desk and began marking papers while Dawn sat there, unsure of what to do, hearing the titters of her classmates as she drew in her arms and legs, trying to make herself smaller.

Now she turned her head into the pillow to muffle her sob. The worst part, the most pathetic, awful part, was that she missed Tucker. She hated him and felt shamed by him, but she couldn't erase the memory of how he'd held her, his breath warm against her ear as he'd whispered that he loved her. She hadn't felt so safe or special since her parents died.

It had been so wonderful, even for a brief stretch of time, to feel her loneliness lift and believe she was loved again.

Kira stirred nutmeg into a pot of simmering mulled cider and wondered how the day had slipped away.

She'd spent more than an hour talking with Jessica this morning—or, technically, listening—before Jessica settled on dinner entrées: salmon filets with an option of pasta primavera for the vegetarians.

"I won't change my mind again!" Jessica had said, giggling, and Kira was trying to forget the fact that Jessica had made the same promise, using those precise words, during their last conversation, when she'd settled on filet mignon with vegetable risotto.

Kira hoped the others liked fish and pasta, because she'd be making variations of them all week, searching for recipes that would marry the elegant with the easy.

She'd also gone to the Union Street grocery store in town, because Peter had updated their online reservations to include a line for guests to check if they'd like late-afternoon snacks and a hot beverage for an extra fifteen dollars per person, and two couples who were staying tonight had opted for the snacks. It was only sixty dollars, but every bit helped: She and Peter needed to start earning money, fast. Their health insurance was exorbitant, and she didn't want to scrimp on coverage, since they'd need good care when she became pregnant.

She sighed. Last night she'd reached for her birth control pills in the medicine cabinet as they'd gotten ready for bed, and Peter had stilled her hand with his own.

"Leave them there," he'd whispered as he kissed her neck, his usual prelude to sex. She'd felt herself freeze.

"What's wrong?" he'd asked.

"Nothing," she'd said, trying to unclench her body. She could always take a pill later. She kissed him back, but this time he pulled away.

"You don't seem as happy as I thought you'd be," he'd said. "Don't you like living here?"

For a moment she'd wished she'd married the type of guy who'd be happy to have sex under any conditions. Why did she have to get the sensitive one who wanted to talk first?

"No, I do," she'd said. "It's just that I'm not sure it's the right time for us to get pregnant. Shouldn't we wait a little while?"

"We've *been* waiting," Peter had said. "You wanted to put it off until you made partner. That was our deal."

"Well, I'm not a partner yet," she'd said, trying to make a joke even though speaking those words made her flinch. But Peter hadn't laughed.

"I just feel like we should get the B-and-B off the ground before we get pregnant," she'd said. "What about waiting until we've been here a year?"

He'd been silent then, and she'd thought he was considering it, perhaps seeing the wisdom in her careful planning. But when he'd finally spoken, his voice was tight.

"Do you really want to have kids, Kira?" he'd asked. "Because I'm beginning to wonder if there will ever be a good time."

He'd gone to bed then, yanking the covers up around his neck, and even his breathing had sounded angry.

She'd stared at his rigid back, knowing Peter yearned to create a family of his own, perhaps to make up for the one he'd lost. He'd probably been ready to become a father since shortly after his mother died. But he didn't appear to understand that something seemed to be physically holding her back—something even stronger than fear.

The lean times after her father left had been bad enough. But once things got so bad that Kira actually went to her father's house to ask him for money. She was in high school by then, and she and her dad were back in touch, mostly through phone calls on her birthday and at Christmas-time, or quick visits. She'd never accepted an invitation to his home, though. Stepping over the threshold of the place he shared with a new family represented a line she didn't feel able to cross.

He sent child support, but Kira's mother had been hospitalized for nearly a week after catching pneumonia, and they didn't have good insurance. Kira had seen her mom staring at bills stamped with a threatening-looking red ink, and she'd made a quick decision: If ever there was a time to ask for help, this was it.

She found her dad's address on an old envelope and drove there in her mother's beat-up Hyundai after cheer practice. It was early evening, and unusually warm out. Daffodils bloomed in his yard. She still remembered those bright pops of yellow.

He didn't live far away, only about thirty minutes, but it may as well have been another country, because the difference between their homes was so dramatic. He lived in a cheap row house, but she could smell chicken roasting as she walked up the front steps. The front door was open, with just the screen separating her from the family inside, and light was pouring out. The steps were swept clean, and there was a welcome mat by the door. She could hear a child laughing.

As she lifted her hand to ring the bell, she overheard her father, just a dozen or so feet away, reading a storybook to his new stepdaughter— by now he was on his third marriage—and making a growling voice for the princess. Kira sank down onto the steps, listening. She could hear a woman's low, melodic voice calling the family to dinner, and the little girl squealing. Kira imagined her father was flipping her over his shoulder.

She was suddenly so hungry and tired. Her belly felt hollow, and her joints ached. She folded her arms over her knees and dropped her head. She didn't want to go home and cook spaghetti again. She wanted to walk into the light, and taste the chicken, and listen to the end of her father's story.

"Honey?" she heard her father's new wife say. "Do you want a beer?"

Kira got up and slipped away without having knocked on the door. She was the one who'd told her father to leave her alone all those years ago, she reminded herself. She'd refused to attend his subsequent weddings, even though he'd invited her . . . She just wished it hadn't been so easy for him to let her go.

She'd ended up taking an added shift at the frozen yogurt shop—Sundays from noon to seven—and the extra money had pulled them through. Her mother had gotten better. They'd moved on.

Kira had grown up in a house of uncertainty, where financial worries had helped rip apart her parents' fragile union, and she'd always imagined things would be different when she was married. But she and Peter each had a failed career now, and their bank balance was dependent upon the whims of vacationers. She tried to push away the unsettling thought, but it kept gnawing at her: If the B-and-B was a bust, they'd have to start over again.

The timing was all wrong. She only wished Peter could see that.

Chapter Seven

It had been a happy day, a golden day, but nothing could prepare Alyssa for the miracle blossoming within it.

As they cleaned up the breakfast dishes from

their only guests—a quiet family with two teenage sons who'd come for a weekend of hiking and bike riding—Peter announced that the long-range forecast called for the snowiest winter in Vermont in a decade.

"Awesome," Rand said. "That'll bring in the skiers and boarders like crazy."

Peter kept their bookings listed on an oversize calendar posted in the kitchen, and the stretches of empty white squares had them all worried. The B-and-B needed to be busy through the winter months or they'd never make a profit, even with the wedding.

Alyssa finished loading the dishwasher and scrubbing the omelet pan, then she took a cup of tea out to the porch and sat on a rocking chair. There was a nip in the air, but the sun felt warm on her face. She leaned back her head and closed her eyes, letting her mind drift back to her conversation with Kira and the story of Peter and Rand's tangled history, as it had so many times in the past few weeks.

Families were so complicated, she mused. Take hers—her parents had split up before she was out of diapers, but the most surprising thing was that they'd gotten married in the first place. Her mother was a hippie who'd brought cloth bags to the supermarket decades before it was fashionable; her father's favorite way to cap a day was with a marbled steak and a martini.

Once, Alyssa had asked her mother, Bee, why she'd gotten married to a man so different from herself. "Maybe we hoped we could change each other," Bee had said, smoothing Alyssa's hair back from her face and kissing her forehead as Alyssa caught the scent of patchouli her mother always wore. "Or maybe you were the whole point."

And Alyssa's stepsisters, who came from her father's first marriage, felt more like acquaintances than relatives. They'd been teenagers by the time Alyssa was born, and now they led lives that looked nothing like hers. One was an executive at a Fortune 500 company and the other had started a make-your-own jewelry business that had grown to franchises in five states. They lived in gorgeous homes, had well-dressed kids attending expensive colleges, and seemed stretched so thin that they could snap at any moment.

Alyssa adored both of her parents, but she was closer to her mother. Still, her father was always there for her. She thought about Kira's pronouncement that she'd never have to worry about money. And it was true: Her father sent her an exceedingly generous check every year on her birthday. Other checks along with professionally wrapped gifts arrived at Christmastime, and he'd been the one to cover their adoption fees. Maybe those slim paper rectangles had provided an invisible safety net that allowed her to soar, to erase the kind of fear that could freeze someone in place in a safer kind of life.

The sun, the soothing motion of the chair, the omelet and toast she'd eaten for breakfast lying heavily in her belly . . . Alyssa adjusted the pillow behind her back and yawned.

When her cell phone rang, she was completely disoriented. Had two hours passed, or two minutes? She rubbed her eyes and looked down. This time she recognized the number, and she jumped out of her chair, suddenly wide awake.

She snatched it up on the second ring, knowing even before Donna with Children from China spoke a word that this was a seismic moment in her life, a dividing line that would forever separate everything into a before and an after.

"Congratulations!" Donna said, and Alyssa burst into tears.

"The Chinese government has approved your application and we have a match for you. A little girl, estimated age of eleven months," Donna said.

"Thank you," Alyssa whispered, suddenly loving Donna, who was a conduit to such miracles every day. "Thank you so much."

Did Donna sound a little choked up, too? "I'm sending you an e-mail right now with a photo and brief history. Once you and your husband have a chance to read through everything, we can go through the formalization of your acceptance. There are a lot of papers involved!"

"When can we—" Alyssa began, but her throat tightened and she couldn't finish.

"Go to China?" Donna said. "You'll have to get travel permission from the Chinese government, and a consulate appointment. Things are really backlogged now, so it'll take months."

"Thank you so much," Alyssa said again, and then she hung up and ran across the yard, her feet barely skimming the prickly grass, to where Rand was cutting dead limbs off trees. She grabbed him by the hand and pulled him through the house, into their bedroom. She collapsed onto the bed next to the laptop she'd left there.

Rand misread the look on her face. "Lyss? What is it?"

"Our daughter," she managed to say, turning the computer screen toward him so they could both see the photograph filling it. A little girl in a simple white shirt, sitting in a straight-backed chair, her feet dangling above the floor. Her hair was so glossy it almost looked wet, her eyes were narrow and exquisitely shaped, and her smile looked shy yet brave. This inexpensive, staged picture was the most precious thing Alyssa owned, the one item she would run into a burning building to save.

She heard Rand's quick, fierce inhalation of breath, and she felt her tears coming hard now, streaming down her cheeks. She wanted to laugh and cry and dance and shout. They'd been waiting so long, and their daughter was arriving at the best possible moment, almost as if she'd known they were finally ready to be parents. As if she were the teacher and they were the students.

She can sit up, the accompanying note reported. *She eats all her meals. She sleeps eleven hours a night, and naps three hours every afternoon. She is a happy and healthy child.*

Alyssa wiped her cheeks with the backs of her hands, but the tears kept coming. She was so glad Grace was happy; she couldn't bear to think of her daughter in a crib in a crowded orphanage, holding out her arms and sobbing, yearning for someone to pick her up. For someone to tell her she was beautiful, and loved, and good. Alyssa would tell her those things every single day, and whisper them into her ear at night as she drifted off to sleep, to make up for all the times Grace hadn't heard them.

Alyssa thought of the little bathrobe tucked away like a talisman in her bottom drawer. She could finally take it out and hang it alongside her own robe. She'd buy a rubber ducky, too, and some of those soft sleepers. Diapers! She'd need diapers, of course, and maybe a rattle . . .

Rand looked stunned, and younger, somehow. His hair was wild, and he had a smudge of dirt on his cheek. "Is it, like . . . official?"

"Don't move," Alyssa said and grabbed her camera off the dresser. She'd frame this picture of Rand at the moment he learned he was a father and pair it with their first one of Grace. Rand was a father now; they had a child, she just happened to be thousands of miles away. And that meant Alyssa was finally a mother.

"It's official," Alyssa said when she lowered her camera with trembling fingers. "They wouldn't have sent her photo if it wasn't."

"We're going to have a kid," Rand said and blinked a few times. He gave a little laugh. "Holy shit."

Alyssa leaned close to him and gave him a long, hard kiss. "She's coming, Rand." A great, joyous sob welled up in her throat, and when she closed her eyes, it was her daughter's face she saw. "Grace is coming home to us."

"I . . . What should we do?" Rand asked. He stood up and started to pace.

"We can tell a few people," Alyssa said. "My mom. And we should call our dads, too. And then we need to tell Peter and Kira. They're going to have to run this place while we go to China for a couple weeks."

Rand was still pacing, still looking stunned. "Okay," he said. "Do we need anything? A crib?"

"I was thinking she could sleep with us," Alyssa said. "Babies do, in most cultures."

"With us?" Rand repeated. "What if I roll over and mush her?"

"We'll figure it out." Alyssa closed her eyes.

"I want to send out a little light to Grace right now, okay?"

Rand didn't believe, as she did, that energy could travel between human beings, but he stayed next to her as Alyssa closed her eyes and willed a message across the miles. She sent it over the tips of treetops and past the Atlantic Ocean, through the misty, thin clouds, and beyond the border of another continent, where she visualized it traveling like a ray of golden light straight down into Grace's soul.

We're waiting for you. We love you already. We've always loved you.

Kira put down her long-handled wooden spoon and retrieved a wheel of Brie out of the refrigerator. She was pulling off the plastic wrap when Alyssa swung open the kitchen door.

"In the mood for a walk?" Alyssa asked. "Rand and I are going and thought you and Peter might want to come."

"A walk?" Kira repeated.

"It's this thing where you put one foot in front of the other," Alyssa teased. "Come on, it's gorgeous out!"

Kira hesitated. "Did you ask Peter?" Things between them had felt strained since their argument a few nights earlier.

Alyssa nodded. "He's waiting outside."

Kira left the Brie to soften on the counter and

set the burner for the cider to low. She found her coat and wound a blue-and-white scarf around her neck, then walked out onto the porch, where Alyssa was snapping photos.

Kira inhaled a breath that chilled her lungs as she took in the explosion of colors at the tops of trees—russets and golds and crimsons that mirrored the sunset just above. It was probably close to eighty degrees in Florida now. If she were still there, she'd be stuck in her windowless office, reading a dry report, her eyes burning.

"Deer," Alyssa whispered, pointing. There were five of them—two bucks and three does— munching on bushes that edged the lawn.

Rand clapped his hands, trying to scare the animals away. "Hey, it'll save us from clipping the hedges," Peter said, putting out a hand to stop his brother. "Besides, they're pretty thin."

"One of those dudes must be getting lucky," Rand said. "I'm thinking he's got a sister-wife thing going on."

Their reactions to the deer pretty much summed up the differences between the two brothers, Kira thought. She walked over to Peter, slipped her hand in his, and felt a knot in her chest loosen when his fingers squeezed hers back.

"Let's go this way," Alyssa said, steering them away from the deer. They walked in silence for a moment, leaves crunching beneath their feet.

"So," Alyssa finally said. She stopped walking.

"We, ah, wanted to tell you something." She took a deep breath, and her eyes filled up.

"Everything okay?" Peter asked as Kira squeezed his hand more tightly, suddenly worried.

Alyssa nodded. "It's good news. Rand, you say it. I don't think I can get through it without crying!"

"We're adopting a little girl from China," Rand said.

"Whoa!" Peter said. "That's fantastic!"

"We've been waiting for years . . . I still can't believe it," Alyssa said.

Kira hugged Alyssa as Peter offered Rand his hand and the men shook.

"We're so happy for you, too!" Kira said. "And for us! We're going to be an aunt and uncle!" She was surprised to discover her eyes were also wet. "Do you have a name picked out?"

It was the first time Kira had ever seen Rand look ill at ease. He toyed with the zipper on his coat before answering. "It's Grace," he said. He glanced at Alyssa. "I was thinking her middle name could be Elizabeth."

For their mother, Kira thought.

Peter stared at Rand as Kira caught her breath. Rand was looking back at Peter steadily, waiting for him to react.

But Peter didn't, at least not immediately. He seemed frozen in place. Later, Kira would wonder if Rand had started to reach his arms out toward his brother, or if the faint ripple of movement had existed only in her imagination.

A red Jeep came up the road, and the driver tooted the horn as the vehicle passed by, breaking apart the moment.

"Must be our guests," Kira said. "They're early."

"Let's celebrate when they leave, okay?" Peter said. "We'll take you guys out to dinner in town."

"Cool," Rand said.

"So we're going to have to go to China at one point for a few weeks to get Grace," Alyssa said as they began to walk back to the B-and-B. "We can hire someone to help out while we're gone . . . I just hope we don't have to be there during the wedding."

"This is a little more important than the wedding," Kira said.

"You should say that to Jessica," Rand said. "I'm sure she'd agree."

Kira punched him lightly on the arm. "Tell us more about Grace," she said.

"She's about eleven months old," Alyssa said. "She can sit up! I keep picturing her . . . I wonder what she's doing all the time. If she's sleeping, if her diaper is wet, what foods she'll like . . ."

"Like mac and cheese, or spaghetti and meatballs?" Kira asked, and Alyssa laughed.

"My arms actually feel empty now, without her," Alyssa said.

"I can't wait to see her picture," Peter said. "I can't wait to see *her!*"

Kira glanced at him. She couldn't help wondering if Peter would feel even more strongly that they should get pregnant now, and fear tightened her chest. She was truly happy about Grace's impending arrival; she couldn't wait to meet her niece, and rock her, and give her a bath. Oh—and steam some sweet peas so she could watch Grace pick them up in that adorably focused way babies had when they were learning to control their hands.

How could she be feeling more excitement about the prospect of someone else's child than her own? Peter deserved better; maybe there *was* something wrong with her.

Rand was grabbing Alyssa from behind, picking her up and swinging her around, and she was laughing. They were both wearing jeans and brightly colored fleece jackets, and they looked as perfect and happy as a couple in a television advertisement. Meanwhile Kira and Peter were walking side by side, not touching, and Kira knew what Alyssa meant about her arms feeling empty—because her hand felt the same way without Peter's in it.

Kira couldn't think of anything to say to her husband, except, once again, *I'm sorry.*

But she held the words inside. If she spoke them, she knew she'd burst into tears, and she couldn't do that. This was Grace's day.

Chapter Eight

The only people Alyssa had confided in about her infertility were her parents. Her father had been sweetly supportive, offering to send her to the Canyon Ranch spa, and Bee had been positive and reflective, as she was about so many things in life, telling Alyssa that everyone took a different path to motherhood.

"The children who are meant to be ours find us one way or another," Bee had said, her gentle voice a balm to Alyssa's pain. "You'll know when you meet him or her."

"Did you feel that way about me?" Alyssa had asked, flopping back onto her bed and letting her mother's voice soothe her as it had countless times during her childhood. She envisioned her mother's round face with the deep smile lines radiating out from the corners of her eyes like beams from the sun, and imagined her curling up on a sofa under a patchwork quilt, a mug of tea close at hand.

Her high-achieving half sisters took after their dad, but Alyssa was indisputably her mother's daughter.

Alyssa knew the story of her own birth well: Bee had panted her way through labor at home, attended by a midwife who lit incense and Alyssa's father, who rushed home from work and ducked into the room, grew pale and loosened his tie, and ducked back out. Nine glorious, agonizing hours later, Bee had reached down and pulled Alyssa out herself. The story had half-thrilled, half-horrified Alyssa as a child; as an adult, she yearned for a similar experience.

"When I first looked into your eyes, I recognized you," Bee had said. "As if we'd been connected across time."

As she looked into Grace's eyes in the photograph sent by the adoption agency, Alyssa finally understood what her mother meant.

Alyssa cupped her chin in her hand as she considered the photo now. She'd printed out a copy on her best paper and had mounted it on a frameless canvas. Every detail of Grace's face was carved into her heart; she could pick her daughter out of a crowd of hundreds of children in China. The tiny scar just above her lip—how had that happened? Alyssa's heart contracted; she hadn't been there to comfort her little girl, to draw Grace into her arms and kiss her boo-boo, and now she'd never learn the real story behind the scar. Grace's chin jutted out the tiniest bit, and in that feature Alyssa could almost feel the strength of her daughter, who'd traveled so long and far to find her mother, as Alyssa was searching for her from the other side of the world.

"Aren't you going to hang that on the wall?" Rand passed by, his skin gleaming wet from the shower, a towel twisted around his waist. She'd thought of buying him a bathrobe for Christmas the first year they were married, then decided against it. She loved the way his tight stomach muscles looked when they were damp, and the trail of dark hair disappearing under the towel.

Alyssa shrugged. "I like holding it," she said.

"You'll get to hold her soon enough," Rand said.

"Not soon enough," Alyssa corrected.

Every time her cell phone sounded, her heart leapt in her chest. She knew it would be a long time before they were told to get on a plane, but her bag was already packed and sitting in the closet. It held three changes of clothes for Alyssa and a few toiletries, but most of the space was reserved for things Grace would need: packages of diapers and wipes, shampoo and lotion and rash cream, a half dozen soft cotton shirts with matching pants, a sweet little coat, a fuzzy orange blanket, and a few chunky board books. The last item Alyssa had tucked in the bag was the ducky bathrobe. Her good-luck talisman.

"Don't you want to get your bag ready, too?" Alyssa asked Rand. He was standing in the closet, swapping his towel for a pair of jeans.

"We've got plenty of time," he said. He slid on a black Henley shirt and used the towel to dry his hair.

"I know, but . . . ," she said.

He turned to look at her. "But what?"

She shrugged. "It's part of the fun."

He leaned forward and dropped a kiss on her lips.

"Your hair's getting long around the ears," she said, reaching out to touch it. "Want me to trim it?"

"Nah." Rand jerked away from her and walked into the bathroom. She could see him through the open door; he was fiddling with his hair, brushing it forward onto his forehead as he examined it from different angles in the mirror.

A ten-second combing was the most attention he usually paid to it, so he must've noticed what she already had: his hairline was beginning to recede and the top was thinning. Genetics were working against Rand; his father was almost completely bald, and Rand had inherited his dark hair and blunt features. Peter, on the other hand, took after their mother, who'd been tall and slim, with thick blond hair.

She thought of making a joke—she didn't care if he lost his hair—but something told her Rand wouldn't laugh. He had a streak of vanity, probably honed while he was growing up, when his dyslexia prevented him from performing well in school so he earned admiration in other ways, like through his athletic prowess and his good looks. Rand still did fifty push-ups every morning and kept his free weights in the garage for daily workouts; he was proud that he could fit into the same size jeans he'd worn when he was twenty. Maybe it was scary for him to lose control over this aspect of his appearance, Alyssa thought as he frowned into the mirror.

"Want to go snowboarding?" she called out. "I checked the website for the slopes, and it was cold enough last night to make snow."

"Sure," Rand said. He came out of the bathroom. "Is anyone coming today?"

"Nope," Alyssa said. "We've got Jessica's bachelorette party tomorrow—or her 'pre-bachelorette-party party,' as she's calling it, and then a full house at the end of the week."

"Pre-party party?" Rand asked.

"Apparently she and the girls are going to Vegas, too, closer to the wedding," Alyssa said. "But I don't think they wanted to turn down a free trip here."

"Pain-in-the-ass bride." Rand rolled his eyes. "Let's hit it," he said, putting a baseball cap on his head. "I'll grab my board."

"Okay," Alyssa said. "In twenty minutes."

She grabbed his hand and yanked him down onto the bed next to her. "You're gorgeous," she whispered, slipping her hand under his shirt and stroking his broad chest.

She couldn't tell him that his hair loss didn't matter, that he was still as attractive as ever. But maybe she could show him.

• • •

Routines meant danger. The folks who ran the hostel in Boston had begun to take an interest in Dawn, asking where she was from and how long she planned to stay. Most travelers came through for just a night or two, so she'd started to stand out.

That, combined with Tucker's chilling e-mail, meant it was time to move on.

She was sitting in a diner near the Boston University campus, stretching her early-morning breakfast of tea and an English muffin and thinking of where to go, when she overheard a few students in the next booth chatting about a ski trip.

She'd been skiing once, long ago, with her dad. He'd saved up for the day trip because he wanted his daughter to experience all that his glorious adopted country had to offer. They'd driven in his old Pinto from New York to a small resort town—she couldn't remember its name—and he'd rented her what had to be the world's shortest skis and half-carried her to the bunny slope, since she kept slipping. She'd been terrible at it, but her father's patience had never wavered. He'd stayed right next to her, steadying her with his arms, reminding her to fall backward, onto her butt, if she needed to. At the end of the day, when her nose was running and her cheeks ached from the cold, he'd taken her into the resort's

145

lodge and bought her a hot chocolate. It had arrived smothered in a pile of whipped cream with chocolate shavings on top. She'd drunk every rich, delicious drop, her fingertips tingling as the feeling returned to them, then she'd fallen asleep on the ride home. She'd awoken briefly to feel her father carrying her up the stairs of their apartment building. There wasn't any better feeling than having your dad carry you to bed when you were a child.

She sensed that her father was somehow by her side again, guiding her just as he had on that long-ago day when she'd navigated the scary slopes. He was such a smart man. He'd immigrated to the United States with Dawn's mother when they were both nineteen. He'd only been able to find work as a grocery store cashier, but he'd taught himself how to repair their car and handle plumbing problems, and he'd learned English by watching sitcoms at night and repeating the actors' lines. What would he tell her to do now?

Stay unpredictable. She could almost hear his voice.

"I see the bus," one of the students said, and they all stood up and grabbed their skis and boots and headed outside. A sign, Dawn thought, and she paid her bill and followed them. The driver was stowing the equipment under the bus when she approached him.

"Excuse me," she said. "Is there room for one more?"

He shrugged. "Twenty bucks."

She handed him the fare and found an empty seat in the last row. She pulled the backpack containing the change of clothes she'd bought at a thrift store onto her lap and took a black wool cap out of the pocket of her secondhand down coat as her eyes scanned the pedestrians outside the window. She was looking for Tucker again, just as she'd done every time she'd walked down the hallways at work, but now whenever she saw a tall blond man, her heart stuttered for a very different reason. When the bus began to move, she eavesdropped on the conversations around her, trying to glean details about where they were going so she could formulate a plan. She was equal parts watchman and private detective lately, she thought. The thought made her flinch: Could the investment banking firm—or Tucker —have hired a private detective to find her?

She was still retracing her path in her mind, probing for missteps, when they arrived in Killington, Vermont, three hours later.

Dawn stepped off the bus into the ski resort's parking lot and looked up to see a tall wooden lodge, not dissimilar from the one she'd visited with her dad so many years ago. She went inside and found a table by a big window overlooking the slopes. The cavernous room was mostly empty, and it felt toasty warm. She'd chosen a seat that faced the entrance, so she could see whoever came into the restaurant, but everyone seemed to be out on the slopes.

A deep weariness settled in her core. She'd been on high alert for so long, sleeping in snatches, tensing every time she turned a new street corner or heard a loud sound. There were fewer people here, and it was blessedly quiet. Getting out of the city had been a good idea, she thought.

What was she going to do next, though? She tried to come up with a mental list of options. She could consult a lawyer, but would the lawyer have an ethical obligation to turn her in? She didn't know enough about the law to determine if it was safe. Maybe she should just turn *herself* in. But if the police didn't believe her story, she'd go to jail. She'd be trapped there—unable to escape. Her worst fear. She didn't realize she'd reached up to touch the scar on her cheek until her fingernail scratched her skin.

She slouched lower in her seat as her eyelids began to grow heavy. She'd gotten up at 4:30 to leave the hostel so no one would see her depart. Now the exhaustion she'd built up over the preceding weeks overtook her. She rested her head on the long wooden table and closed her eyes. She'd allow herself the luxury of drifting off for a few minutes. When she woke up, she'd plan her next step.

• • •

What sadist had invented the concept of skiing? Kira wondered. Who was the first person to decide it would be fun to rocket shakily down an icy mountain on two pieces of metal with wind attacking your face and snow spraying into your eyes and people whipping all around, waving spiky poles like gladiators closing in for a kill? She was shocked lawyers hadn't shut down the sport yet; the potential for catastrophe was rampant.

"Come on," Rand said. "You'll love it."

"I bet you'll catch on really quick," Alyssa said encouragingly. She and Rand were carrying their personal snowboards and wearing goggles and boots and helmets they hadn't had to rent. They looked like they'd been born atop a mountain and had soared down it in lieu of learning how to walk.

"It looks like fun," Kira lied. She'd lived in the South for her entire life. She wasn't cut out for this crap.

She slid a foot forward and promptly fell over. She tried to get up and fell again, like a slapstick character in a cartoon.

She glared up at Peter, who was helpfully holding out the pointed tip of his pole, like he expected her to clutch on to it. He was the one who'd suggested they join Alyssa and Rand on the slopes. Peter had gone skiing a few times before, naturally, so he looked perfectly at ease on his flippers of death.

"Here." Rand handed his snowboard to Alyssa, walked over behind Kira, and bent down to grab her around the waist. He lifted her to a standing position, then kept his hands on her as she took another, tentative shuffle forward. She would've wiped out again if it weren't for Rand. As it was, she fell backward against his chest and nearly took them both down.

"This might not be a good idea," Kira said. "I should probably go straight to the après-ski part."

"Let's try the bunny slope," Rand suggested. "I'll stay with you until you get your legs. It's like riding a bike—it'll click after a little bit."

"I broke my wrist when I was learning how to ride a bike," Kira muttered, but Rand kept helping her slide along, a few inches at a time. His closeness was distracting, as was his firm grip on her waist and his deep voice in her ear. She glanced over at Peter, keeping pace alongside them on his own skis. Her husband didn't look overjoyed.

"I think I've got it now," Kira said. "Let me try it on my own."

Rand let go of her, and she tumbled forward, landing spread-eagle.

"Yeah, I can see that," Rand said. "Come on, Lindsey Vonn."

Kira raised her head and spit out some snow,

then Rand lifted her up into a standing position again.

She nearly wiped out a dozen more times on the way to the bunny slope, but by the time they arrived, her legs were adjusting to the unfamiliar sensation and her body's excellent sense of balance—due to her years of gymnastics and cheerleading—was kicking in.

"I think I can do it now," Kira said when she reached the chairlift. It looked like a subway escalator for underage commuters; a dozen little kids were riding it, but no adults, which felt more than a bit humiliating. Why did people like this sport again? Hadn't a comedian once likened it to standing in a freezing cold shower while tearing up hundred-dollar bills?

"Are you sure?" Rand asked. "I could stay with you on your first run."

"She said she's fine!" Peter said, his words clipped.

No, her husband definitely wasn't happy.

"Hey!" Rand released Kira so quickly she almost fell again. "Just trying to help."

Peter muttered something under his breath, his voice too low for Kira to make out the words.

"What?" Rand asked.

Peter held his eyes for a moment. "Nothing," he finally said.

"Whatever," Rand said. "Lyss, let's hit the diamonds. We'll catch you later."

"Thanks," Kira called as he turned away. She grabbed the handrail and rode the escalator up, managing to exit without incident with the help of a member of the ski patrol. She positioned herself sideways to the mountain so she wouldn't go zipping off and waited for Peter to come up next to her.

"Are you okay?" she asked. Peter wasn't the jealous type, but his brother seemed to push all kinds of buttons in him.

"Yep," he said. He looked a little less tense now that Rand was gone, but Kira couldn't help wishing her brother-in-law had stayed to help her on her inaugural run. She looked down at the bottom of the mountain, which seemed ridiculously far away.

"I have no idea what to do next," she confessed.

"Follow my tracks," Peter said. "I'm going to make gentle, wide turns. If you feel yourself falling, just sit down."

"Okay," she said, wondering if this would somehow end up on YouTube.

Miraculously, her balance held and she was able to trace Peter's path all the way down the mountain without a single fall. "I did it!" she cried. Sure, a few dozen four-year-olds had done it a lot faster, but she still felt triumphant.

Peter reached over and clinked poles with her. "You were great," he said. "Let's do it again."

"You don't think we should quit while I'm

ahead?" she joked, but already her competitive spirit was kicking in. One more run on the bunny slope, she decided, then she was hitting the real ones.

She banished the ridiculous thought almost as soon as it entered her mind, but for a fleeting moment, she imagined Rand watching her sail past him, her knees bent and her hair flying in the wind, his handsome, rugged face filled with admiration as he cheered her on.

Chapter Nine

Alyssa stood on top of the mountain and inhaled deeply, tasting the sharp tang of frost. The sun was ablaze in a brilliant blue sky, and the slopes were shining ribbons of white.

The first run was always her favorite. She grinned and adjusted her goggles.

"Ready?" Rand asked, and she nodded and set down her snowboard.

She waited until a group of skiers had moved out of her way, then stepped onto her board, squatted low, and took off. Adrenaline coursed through her veins, and she laughed aloud. She picked up speed and went into a turn, feeling her core muscles contract as she counterbalanced to avoid falling.

"Woo-hoo!" she yelled, pumping her fist in the air.

Out of the corner of her eye she saw Rand approaching fast, carving up the slope as he cut back and forth and sent up sprays of powder.

She crouched lower, feeling her thighs burn, and aimed her board toward a little jump. Another twenty feet . . . she tucked in her elbows and kept her knees loose. This was it, the moment when she always felt the most alive.

The jump swam before her eyes. She blinked away a feeling of disorientation. Ten feet . . . five . . . Her legs abruptly turned weak and shaky, and she knew she couldn't hold her squat. She straightened and tried to steer to the side of the jump so she could stop.

Too late, she thought as she hit the edge of the jump at an angle. Dizziness overpowered her, and the ground tilted and turned blurry. She landed hard on her left side and lay there, trying to catch her breath.

"Lyss?" Rand was bent over her, touching her cheek. She took stock of her body. Her shoulder throbbed, and there was a chunk of ice trickling down the inside of her jacket, but she'd escaped serious injury.

She could hear someone call out, "Is she okay?" and she slowly sat up and waved.

"Did you catch an edge?" Rand asked.

"I don't know," she said. "I just got dizzy."

Her head was clearing now, but she still felt shaky. "I skipped breakfast. I think that's it."

She got to her feet, holding on to his arm for balance. "I can make it to the bottom," she said. "Then I'll go grab some oatmeal."

"I'm right behind you," he said. "Take it slow."

She made it to the entrance of the lodge and unstrapped her board and set it in the snow. "You go ahead," she told Rand. She knew how much he loved to board, and he'd already lost time by helping Kira, which had been sweet of him, even though it had seemed to irritate Peter. "I'll catch up with you."

"You sure?" he asked.

She leaned forward and kissed him. "I already delayed you by twenty minutes this morning, remember?"

He grinned. "Call me when you're ready," he said.

She went into the lodge's restaurant and bought a banana and oatmeal and some orange juice; then she took it all to a table. The eating area was mostly deserted, except for one woman slumped over napping at a nearby table.

Alyssa sipped the juice and forced herself to taste the oatmeal. She felt a little nauseated, which happened sometimes when she forgot to eat. She reached around to the base of her neck to try to rub away the headache that was forming.

Maybe she'd wrenched something when she fell.

An odd squeaking sound made her turn to look at the sleeping woman. The woman must be in the throes of a vivid dream—now she was muttering, "No . . . please . . ."

Alyssa turned back around and took another tiny bite of oatmeal. It tasted a little off. Could she be coming down with the flu? She managed to eat most of the banana, then pushed her tray aside. She was going to stay in the lodge and rest, she decided. There would be plenty of other days to snowboard. She was just pulling out her cell phone to tell Rand when the sleeping woman gave a half moan, half scream. It was an awful sound, hollow and wretched.

Alyssa leapt out of her chair and rushed over.

"Hey," she said as the woman jerked up her head and looked around, her eyes wild. "You're okay. I think you just had a bad dream."

The woman blinked rapidly, then glanced up at Alyssa, her lips trembling. "He's not here?" she asked.

"Who?" Alyssa asked.

The woman shook her head instead of answering, then wiped the tears from her eyes with her fingertips.

Alyssa reached for a napkin from the dispenser on the table. "Here," she said.

"Thanks." The woman had a round face and ink-black hair, and oddly, she wore an exercise outfit instead of ski clothes. "I'm sorry if I disturbed you," she said.

"No worries," Alyssa said. She was about to go back to her table when the woman's face crumpled and she bent over, her body erupting in wrenching sobs.

Alyssa didn't hesitate. She'd never shied away from engaging with strangers—years of traveling solo had erased those sorts of social barriers for her. She sat down next to the woman and rubbed her back and made soothing sounds as the woman wept.

"I'm sorry," the woman said again, rubbing the napkin over her eyes.

"Please don't apologize," Alyssa said. "There's nothing wrong with having a good cry when you need one. Tell you what, I was just going to get a cup of tea. Can I bring you one?"

"Tea?" the woman asked, like it was a foreign word.

"Or coffee, or hot chocolate," Alyssa said.

The woman stared at her for a moment. "I would really love some hot chocolate," she said. She began to reach into the purse in her lap, but Alyssa waved away her offer of money.

When Alyssa came back to the table, the woman had composed herself and was sitting up straight, her purse still clutched in her lap like she was worried someone would steal it. She was younger than Alyssa had first thought—

maybe in her mid-twenties—and she looked exhausted, with her slightly matted hair and dark circles ringing her eyes.

"They asked if I wanted whipped cream," Alyssa said. "I wasn't sure, but I figured yes would be the safer answer."

The woman smiled. "What's the point of hot chocolate without whipped cream?" she asked. She took a sip and closed her eyes. "I can't tell you how good this tastes," she said. "Thank you."

Alyssa squeezed a lemon wedge into her tea and added the contents of a packet of honey before speaking again.

"So, who is he?" she asked.

The woman tensed. "What do you mean?"

"You asked if he was here when you were waking up from your dream." Alyssa shrugged. "I figured it must have been a bad breakup. I'm Alyssa, by the way."

"My name is . . . Dawn," the woman said.

"You don't have to tell me if you don't want to," Alyssa said. "But I've found it can be really therapeutic to talk to a stranger, someone who doesn't have an opinion about your history."

Dawn took another sip of hot chocolate. "It's complicated," she said. She gave a little half laugh. "Supercomplicated."

Alyssa nodded. She could imagine what had happened: Dawn had walked in on her boyfriend with another woman, or maybe he'd wanted only a bit of fun but she'd fallen in love. She had that look about her—innocent and vulnerable and unsophisticated. Maybe it was the first time she'd had her heart broken. But what was she doing at a ski resort, sitting in the lodge's restaurant in those black track pants and hoodie, carrying a big leather purse?

She was completely unprepared for what Dawn said next, in a voice so small and wispy that Alyssa had to strain to make out the words: "He . . . hurt me."

Dawn hadn't meant to lie. But she'd been feeling so achingly alone and then, miraculously, she wasn't any longer. The beautiful woman with the kind smile had patted her back, and given her a napkin, and bought her a hot chocolate—a bitter-sweet echo of her father's gift from long ago. She couldn't bear to tell Alyssa the truth and see the smile slip off her face while she pushed back her chair and got up and walked away.

Her dream was so vivid it was hard to believe it hadn't happened: Tucker had come into the ski lodge, his eye still raw and swollen, wearing the same blue oxford shirt he'd had on the day he chased her, and she'd suddenly realized her mistake. The table she'd chosen in the back of the restaurant—the one that let her see everyone coming in—also provided a good view of *her*.

Tucker had spotted her instantly. She'd been

unable to move or scream; she just sat there, fear flooding her body, while he came closer, his face twisting in rage and hatred. She'd awoken as his hands tightened around her neck.

When Alyssa had asked, "So, who is he?" Dawn remembered how the cabdriver had tried to protect her because he thought Tucker had hit her, and she wondered if the fib might make Alyssa stay beside her a little longer. Technically Tucker *had* hurt her, just not in the way she'd implied, though she'd sensed simmering violence in him during their last encounter that might've exploded if he'd caught her. He'd gutted her emotionally, upended her sense of safety, destroyed her life.

"My God," Alyssa said. She reached forward to grasp Dawn's hand. "Can I call someone for you? A friend?"

Dawn shook her head. "No. There isn't . . . anyone."

"You're safe now, okay? I'm here and I'm going to help you," Alyssa said.

Dawn closed her eyes and heard those beautiful words again. *I'm going to help you.*

She couldn't do this alone, not any longer. Someday soon Tucker would catch up with her, or the police, or some scary guy would follow her and mug her and take all of her money . . .

"I'm scared he's going to find me," Dawn whispered. She needed to stick to the truth as much as possible.

"Is he here? In Killington?" Alyssa asked.

Dawn shook her head. "I don't think so. I came from—from a big city. I've been taking buses, staying in different places. I just got here today."

"You did good," Alyssa said. "Do you have a place to stay tonight?"

Dawn shook her head again. "Not yet. I was going to see if I could find a cheap motel . . ." *Honesty,* she reminded herself. "Or maybe find an empty condo and try to sneak in there to stay until I got things sorted out . . ."

"I think you should come stay with us for the night," Alyssa said. "We run a B-and-B, and all the rooms are empty at the moment. You can have a good meal and a hot bath and figure out what to do next."

Dawn's breath caught in her throat. She felt her tears rise to the surface again. "But you don't even know me," she said. *You don't know what I've done,* she thought, but Alyssa was already talking over her protests.

"I used to travel a lot, and there was one time when I took a train to Germany late at night. There was a girl sitting across from me, and we started talking. She spoke English really well, which was good, because my German is terrible. Anyway, we talked about everything: the job she had, which was babysitting, and the job she wanted, which was to be an actress. She wanted to know about my life, growing up in the U.S., and she said she dreamed of visiting Hollywood someday. At the end of the ride we both got off the train and then it hit me: I'd forgotten to exchange any money into German currency before leaving Poland—this was before the euro —and I hadn't booked a place to stay. Normally that wouldn't be a big deal, but it was dark out, and there weren't any other trains. Everyone else was walking away, and the booth for the train attendant was empty, so I just stood there with my heavy backpack, looking around in the darkness. And then, naturally, it started to rain."

"What did you do?" Dawn asked.

Alyssa smiled. "The girl came back. She said she'd been about to get into her boyfriend's car when she'd seen me standing there. I spent the night on the floor of her apartment, and the next day they dropped me off at a bank where I could exchange money."

Dawn looked out the window, watching as skiers and snowboarders worked their way down the mountain. "I think my problems are going to be harder to solve," she said.

"Yes," Alyssa agreed. "But at least I can help with one of them. I can give you a place to stay tonight."

Dawn looked down at her cup of hot chocolate, wondering if she dared trust a stranger. She'd grown so suspicious and careful lately that Alyssa's offer seemed fraught with danger. What if Alyssa called the police to report the "abusive" boyfriend? Or what if Dawn slipped up and revealed the truth?

But in the end, the draw of kindness, a meal, and a hot bath overpowered Dawn's fear. She had to stop and rest or she'd collapse, and she sensed Alyssa wouldn't press her to reveal her full story. All she was offering was the reprieve Dawn desperately needed.

"Okay," Dawn said. "Thank you. Thank you so much."

Alyssa smiled. She wasn't wearing any makeup, and her natural beauty shone through —big eyes the color of licorice, wavy hair that tumbled halfway down her back, and a strong jawline with a hint of a cleft in her chin.

"We'll have to hang out here for a while first," Alyssa said. "My husband's snowboarding, and my brother and sister-in-law are skiing. We all own the B-and-B together, so you'll meet them soon."

So many new people. But maybe Alyssa would run interference for her so the others wouldn't ask questions.

"You're not a skier?" Dawn asked, trying to turn the conversation to focus on Alyssa, so she didn't slip up by revealing too much.

"Oh, I am," Alyssa said. "More of a snow-boarder these days. But I started to feel sick out there, and then I took a fall. I just got dizzy all of a sudden; it was weird. So I came in to get something to eat. Anyway, I'm feeling a lot better now."

"Dizzy?" Dawn repeated.

"Yeah, and nauseous. I could barely stand to eat anything," Alyssa said. "This tea is the only thing I want." She gave a little laugh. "Usually you can't keep me away from hot chocolate, but the thought of it made me feel a little ill. Maybe I've got a touch of food poisoning."

Dawn studied her for a moment, thinking of the times women in the neighborhood had knocked on her mother's door, seeking relief for the exact same symptoms Alyssa had just described. Instead of handing out samples of flu medication, her mother had always ruled out another possibility first.

Dawn wasn't sure if she should say anything to the woman she'd just met, and before she could decide, the moment passed. Alyssa was pulling out her cell phone to call her husband, and Dawn turned away but still overheard Alyssa's end of the conversation: "Hey, I'm going to sit it out today . . . No, just still feeling kind of yucky . . . You go ahead and get in some runs for me . . . Sure, I'll meet you here for lunch. Love you."

Alyssa hung up the phone and put it back in her pocket.

She wrinkled her nose. "Yuck," she said. "Lunch."

Chapter Ten

Kira ladled butternut squash soup into a big serving tureen and filled a basket with thick slices of her homemade honey-wheat bread. She hesitated, then went to the freezer and pulled out a dozen of the tomato-and-cheese tarts she'd made as a test for wedding appetizers. Dawn hadn't eaten any lunch at the lodge. She must be hungry.

Alyssa had filled her in on Dawn's story while their surprise guest took a bath, but Kira's mind still buzzed with questions.

"Where did she come from?" Kira asked as she slid a tray of the tarts into the oven.

"I didn't ask," Alyssa said.

"There's got to be some organization that can help her," Kira said. "Can't the police do anything?"

Alyssa shook her head. "Even with a restraining order, she isn't safe."

Kira nodded, remembering the news stories she'd heard about abused women and the law's inability to protect them. "So she just ran? With nothing but a change of clothes?"

"She said she didn't have anyone to turn to," Alyssa said. "Maybe she was worried if she went to her family or a friend's house, the guy would track her down."

"How awful," Kira said. "What is she going to do next?"

"Keep running, I guess," Alyssa said.

Kira found some butter for the bread and uncorked a bottle of red wine. The wine was intended to relax Dawn, who'd nearly jumped out of her seat when Peter walked up to the table at the lodge, wearing dark sunglasses and brushing snow out of his thick blond hair. But Kira was craving a glass, too; her muscles were sore and shaky after just a few hours on the slopes.

Kira hadn't spent much time with Dawn, but she'd always had a good sense about people, and she knew Dawn wasn't crazy, or on drugs. Her story had the ring of truth.

"Let's get some food into her," Kira said. "Then we can think about the next step."

Alyssa looked up at the sudden sound of water rushing through the pipes overhead. "I think she just pulled the plug on her bath. I was worried she'd fallen asleep in there."

"She did look exhausted," Kira said.

Peter came into the kitchen and grabbed a piece of bread out of the basket, devouring it in three huge bites. "Skiing always makes me hungry," he said.

"Is that why I can't stop eating?" Kira asked. "I've already had two pieces."

"Clearly my stomach bug isn't catching," Alyssa said. "Though come to think of it, I feel a lot better now."

She reached for a slice of bread, too. "I'm sorry I didn't ask you guys before offering her a room," Alyssa said. "I should've checked, but I just kind of blurted it out."

"Hey, I would've done the same thing," Peter said. "She's obviously at the end of her rope."

"As long as she's cleared out when Jessica and her bridesmaids arrive tomorrow, it's fine," Kira said. "They booked all the rooms, so we don't have any to spare." She frowned. "But I hate the thought of just sending Dawn off without doing anything to help her."

"Me, too," Alyssa said. "Maybe we can think on it tonight."

Peter went to set the table, and Alyssa made a salad while Rand built a fire. By the time Dawn came downstairs, everything was ready. Their unexpected guest stood on the threshold of the dining room, staring at the food heaped on the table. Her hair was still damp, and she wore another pair of black stretchy pants and a gray waffle-knit shirt. Dark colors, Kira noted. Maybe she'd chosen them in an effort to blend into crowds. Oddly, Dawn's purse still hung from her shoulder.

"This looks wonderful," Dawn said. She blinked hard and looked down, appearing on the verge of tears until Peter stepped forward and handed her a glass of wine. "Unless you'd like water?" he offered. "Or juice?"

Dawn took a sip and sighed. "This is perfect," she said. "Thanks."

"Come and eat!" Kira urged. "I'm the house chef, and I get offended if people don't gobble down food. If you don't feel like soup, I can throw together a sandwich. And I think we've got some chicken in the fridge . . ."

"Soup sounds really good," Dawn said. She took a seat at the end of the table and carefully set her purse beneath her chair. Alyssa filled her bowl, and Dawn dipped in her spoon and closed her eyes as she savored her first taste. She ate reverently, Kira thought, wondering how long it had been since the young woman had had a proper meal.

The only sounds in the room were the clinking of spoons against bowls and requests to pass the butter or bread. Kira found herself at a loss for words for perhaps the first time in her life. Or maybe so many words were bubbling up inside of her that she had to cork them for fear she'd ask the wrong question. Then Rand reached for a second helping of soup. "I wouldn't want to offend Kira," he said, tossing Dawn a wink. Her only response was a brief smile.

She was being very careful, Kira thought. With her purse, with the way she slowly ate her soup, with the few words she parceled out . . .

Suddenly Alyssa exclaimed, "It's snowing!" She pointed to the fat flakes drifting down outside the window.

"You brought us good luck," Peter told Dawn. "The more snow we get, the busier we'll be."

"I can't imagine anyone not wanting to stay here," Dawn said. "It's the prettiest place I've ever seen."

"Just for that you get the last piece of bread," Kira said, putting it on Dawn's plate. She added another splash of Merlot to Dawn's glass. Dawn protested, but Kira noticed she ate and drank everything.

When dinner was over, Kira stood to clear her plate, but Dawn jumped up quickly. "Can I clean up?" she offered.

"It's usually a group effort around here," Kira said. "And you're our guest!"

"Please?" Dawn asked. "I'm not a real guest, and it's the least I can do. You made me this wonderful dinner, and you're letting me spend the night . . . I would really like to contribute something."

Kira hesitated. "Okay," she said. "Thanks."

She sat back down and caught Peter's eye as Dawn collected her purse from under the table and put the strap on her shoulder before she began clearing the table. Peter raised his brows, and she shrugged. It was clear Dawn didn't want the purse out of her sight for even a second. It made Kira intensely curious: What could it possibly hold?

Alyssa awoke early the next morning to the smell of coffee. She climbed out of bed, slipped on her robe, and went into the kitchen. It was spotless; Dawn had spent a long time last night wiping down cupboards and mopping the floor, and according to Kira, she'd even scrubbed the inside of the refrigerator. They'd decided not to protest, since everyone sensed Dawn craved the activity, and not just as a way of providing compensation for the night's lodging. Sometimes physical work gave one's mind a rest, and Alyssa suspected cleaning had provided Dawn with a temporary peace.

She was relieved to see Dawn sitting at the counter, her ever-present purse beside her. She'd been secretly worried the young woman would slip away during the night.

"I hope I didn't wake you," Dawn said. "I made coffee for everyone."

"Thanks," Alyssa said. She noticed Dawn hadn't poured herself a cup, so she took down two mugs from the cabinet above the stove. She filled one and set it on the table before the young woman, then grabbed a carton of cream from the refrigerator and slid the sugar bowl in front of their guest.

"You're not having any?" Dawn asked.

"I'm a tea drinker," Alyssa said as she switched on the burner beneath the kettle. She breathed in the sharp, earthy aroma of coffee and felt her stomach twist. She clenched the edge of the counter to steady herself.

"Are you okay?" Dawn asked. "You just got a little pale."

"Yeah," Alyssa said. She eased herself onto the stool next to Dawn, grimacing. "Weird. I thought I'd kicked this stomach bug, but it seems to be back." She took in a few slow, deep breaths.

Dawn took a sip of coffee. "You're nauseous again?" she finally asked.

"Mmm-hmm," Alyssa said. "A bit dizzy, too." She gave a laugh. "No snowboarding for me today. Maybe I'll go sit in the hot tub and get out the toxins."

"I don't know if I should say anything," Dawn began. "But maybe the hot tub isn't a great idea."

"Why not?" Alyssa asked.

Dawn hesitated. "Is it possible . . . Do you think you might be pregnant?" she finally asked.

Alyssa's mind went blank as she stared at Dawn. She'd heard the word, but her mind was incapable of processing it.

"I only asked because my mother was a, ah, in the medical field, and sometimes female patients came to her thinking they had the flu, only they were actually pregnant," Dawn said. "Are you okay? I'm sorry, I wouldn't have said anything

. . . I was just worried because hot tubs aren't good for fetuses . . ."

Alyssa braced herself against the counter again as she stood up. "It's okay. I'll be right back."

As if in a trance, she walked into the bedroom and sat down on the edge of the bed where Rand still slept, her mind spiraling back over the previous weeks. She couldn't remember when she'd last had her period. It had always been irregular, and she'd stopped tracking it a long time ago, as part of her acceptance of her infertility.

Six weeks, maybe?

There had been something odd about her last period, whenever it had been, she suddenly recalled. It was much lighter than usual, and had lasted only two or three days. Alyssa hadn't thought much of it at the time, other than feeling vaguely grateful.

Pregnant, she thought. *Could it actually be possible?* An image of one of Rand's sperm wearing a bright red cape and pumping its fist triumphantly in the air popped into her mind, and she suppressed a hysterical giggle.

A couple of years ago, the possibility would've sent exhilaration shooting through her body. But now Grace was coming, and Alyssa had made peace with her infertility. She'd not only accepted the change in her life's course but truly believed it was her destiny.

She started to lean over and shake Rand awake, then paused. She could be going through early menopause, or her nausea really could be the onset of the flu. Her symptoms could be rooted in a dozen causes, even though the one Dawn had suggested seemed the most likely.

Alyssa closed her eyes and sat cross-legged on the floor, trying to quiet her racing mind. She needed to absorb this possibility before she did anything else. Later she could decide whether to pick up a pregnancy test in town, or maybe phone a doctor. But she wouldn't say anything to Rand just yet. Jessica and her bridesmaids were coming today, and their giddy energy would be overpowering. She'd talk to Rand in the morning, after she'd centered herself.

After a few minutes she felt calmer. She opened her eyes, uncrossed her legs, and stood up. She'd take a little time today to do yoga, or meditate, she decided. Or perhaps she'd take a long walk outside in the clear, crisp air.

But as she reached for the water glass she kept on the nightstand, she noticed something: Her hand was shaking.

Chapter Eleven

Dawn methodically removed every trace of her existence. She scrubbed the toilet and sink, washed out the tub, and mopped the bathroom floor, then moved on to the bedroom. She stripped the sheets, dusted the furniture, and straightened a glorious photograph of a tide pool reflecting the sunset.

Last night's sleep, after the good soup and rich wine and cheesy tarts, had been the best one in her recent memory. When she'd awoken this morning, the view from her window had revealed strong-looking trees spreading their branches under a lightening sky, as if they were saluting the day ahead. She'd felt a glimmer of something that it took her a moment to recognize as happiness.

But now she had to go. She'd washed out her change of clothes in the sink using a few squirts of hand soap last night, and even though they were still a little damp, she folded them carefully and tucked them into her backpack. She took a last turn around the room to make sure she hadn't missed anything, then put on her coat, slung her purse and backpack over one arm, and picked up the bundle of dirty laundry with the other hand.

She was still unsure if she should have said

anything to Alyssa about her hunch, but she'd thought the news would be welcome. It was clear Alyssa and Rand's marriage was a happy one: His hand had rested on his wife's thigh during dinner, and she'd leaned into him and given him a kiss when he refilled her wineglass.

As Dawn was bumping her sack of laundry down the stairs, she ran into Peter.

"Where are you off to, you Santa Claus impostor?" he asked, and she smiled despite herself.

"I figured I should head out," she said. "I can walk to town and see about getting a bus somewhere."

Peter studied her face for a moment. "Tell you what," he said. "It's gorgeous out and I was about to go for a short hike. Come with me, and then if you still want to go, I'll drive you to a bus station."

Dawn didn't know how to say no, or maybe the truth was she didn't want to. She wasn't ready to head off into the unknown again. Peter went into the kitchen, saying he wanted to grab some granola bars and water, and she put the bundle of sheets into the washing machine and turned it on. She left her backpack in the closet by the front door but kept her purse strap firmly in place on her shoulder. She saw Peter notice, but he didn't comment on it. Another reason to like him.

They walked in silence for a while, with Peter

leading them to a trail a short distance away from the B-and-B. A few determined leaves still clung to the trees despite the frost in the air, and Dawn pushed her hands deeper into her coat pockets, making a mental note to pick up mittens the next time she came across a secondhand store. At first the woods seemed too quiet, but after a few moments, Dawn realized it was full of noises: Squirrels rustled, birds twittered and called, twigs snapped underfoot . . .

"The anniversary of my mother's death is coming up soon," Peter said without preamble.

"Oh," Dawn said after a surprised moment. "I'm really sorry."

She almost blurted out that her mother had died too young as well, but she held back. The fewer details Peter and the others knew about her, the better.

"What was she like?" Dawn asked instead.

"Amazing," Peter said. The trail was just wide enough for them to walk side by side, so she couldn't see Peter's expression, but she heard a catch in his voice. "She stayed home with my brother and me when we were growing up, but as we got older, she began to volunteer. She worked at an animal shelter for a while, and she delivered Meals on Wheels. Things like that."

Dawn wasn't sure what to say. "She sounds . . . like she was really nice."

"And she worked at a shelter for abused

women," Peter continued. "It was the last big thing she took on before we found out about the cancer. She told me it was the most important thing she'd done with her life, besides getting married and having children."

The rush of guilt Dawn felt was so powerful she nearly gasped. Peter thought she was like one of the women his mother had helped—maybe he wanted to help her as a kind of tribute to his mom, a way of honoring her good deeds. If only he knew.

"It isn't—like that with me," she blurted.

He gestured to a large gray rock by the side of the path, and they sat down. He passed her a granola bar and bottle of water, and she was glad to have something to occupy her hands even if holding the chilled water made them feel even colder.

"I don't know exactly what happened to you," he said. "I don't need to know. But you need help and we all want to give it."

Dawn finally found the courage to look him in the eye. How had she mistaken him for Tucker when he'd first walked up to the table at the ski lodge? Aside from being tall with blond hair, the men were opposites. Peter had a gentle voice and an unassuming manner, and he was being better to her than she deserved.

"Here," he said, taking off his gloves and giving them to her. "Your hands must be cold."

That did it; guilt ripped through her again, and she knew she couldn't trick him any longer. She'd tell Peter her story, then grab her backpack and go.

"I fell in love with the wrong guy," she began. "He was really handsome and charming and—and I thought he loved me, too."

A blue jay swooped down to land near them, and Peter tossed it a bit of his granola bar.

"He was involved in this . . . scheme . . . at the place where we both worked," Dawn went on. She couldn't bear to see Peter's expression flip from sympathy to disgust, so she looked down at her sneakers, which had been white at the beginning of her journey but were stained and dirty now. "I didn't realize he was trying to steal money. I thought . . . Anyway, it doesn't matter what I thought. I got involved in the theft. It was wrong, and I shouldn't have done it. But I loved him so much."

She watched the jay eat his breakfast, feeling her own rise up in her stomach.

"And then when I realized he'd tricked me, I ran away. I didn't give him the money he was trying to steal. But he chased me. This cabdriver tried to make him stop, but he hurt the cabdriver. I got away, though. I'm still running. Sometimes I think I always will be."

She waited a moment to see if Peter had any questions, but he didn't say a word. She slid off the rock and removed the gloves and placed them next to Peter. She'd taken only a step or two in the direction of the house when he spoke.

"So he hurt you," Peter said. "Just like you said."

Dawn was stunned. "But . . . not that way," she protested. "He didn't hit me—it wasn't—"

"There are a lot of ways to hurt a person," Peter said. "Is he still after you?"

Dawn nodded. "He wrote me an e-mail implying that he was."

Peter was turning his bottle of water around in his hands, and she could almost see him turning her dilemma around in his mind, too.

"I really appreciate you not being angry with me," she said. "But I don't think there's anything anyone can do."

"You can't go to the police?" Peter asked.

She sat back down. "I was involved in taking the money," she said. "Actually, I was the one who took it."

"Ah," Peter said.

"I was supposed to give it to Tucker, and then he was going to double it and give it all right back, but . . ."

It sounded so foolish now. "Please don't tell the others," Dawn begged. "They were so nice to me. I don't want them to hate me."

"I promise they won't hate you," Peter said. "I won't tell them, though. Not until you're ready."

He took a long drink of water. "Look, this is too complicated for us to figure out today. Stay a little longer."

"But you have guests coming," Dawn protested. "Kira said something about a bachelorette party . . ."

"There's a little space up over the garage," Peter said. "I think the previous owners used it for storage. It isn't fancy, but we all talked about it last night and agreed it's yours for a while if you want it. I've got a sleeping bag you can borrow, and there's a space heater somewhere in the house."

For a moment, the tantalizing possibility floated before her: another good meal, a warm bath, sliding into a soft sleeping bag and feeling enveloped by a sense of safety rather than dozing upright on a hard bus seat and jerking awake in a panic every time someone coughed . . .

The blue jay took off, and she watched it soar away. At first she'd admired its beauty, but now she thought about its typical day: It was constantly in search of its next meal, always trying to evade predators . . . Such an exhausting existence.

"I would really love to stay for just a little longer," she finally told Peter, and she bowed her head so he wouldn't see her tears of relief.

It was one of the few times Kira had ever been alone in the B-and-B. Alyssa and Rand had gone into town, and Peter had invited Dawn on a hike, hoping to draw out a little more information. They were all worried her life could be in danger, and no one was comfortable sending her off yet, so Kira hoped Dawn would take them up on the offer of staying in the little storage space for another few days. Kira glanced over at the backpack Dawn had left by the front door. She'd never violate Dawn's privacy by peeking inside, even if she was curious about their too-quiet guest.

The house was very clean—Dawn must've gotten up early and straightened the living room, too—so Kira curled up on the sofa with a new cookbook she'd picked up at the Book King in nearby Rutland. Jessica and her friends were arriving in a little while, but they planned to go out to dinner and then barhopping, so all Kira needed to do was serve cocktails and appetizers tonight and breakfast tomorrow morning, and she had plenty of supplies for that. Rand and Alyssa were making a run into town to pick up champagne and white wine, and the fridge was stocked with cheese and crudités and other nibbles.

Tomorrow, though, every bedroom would be filled again with a family of four and two couples. All eight guests wanted the après-ski package, which meant Kira needed to hit the store. Maybe she'd make three-bean chili in mini–sourdough bread bowls, or baby potato skins smothered with cheddar cheese and chives, she mused as she turned the glossy pages of her cookbook.

She could, of course, rotate the same few appetizers since the guests would never know, but this was pure fun: reading recipe books like novels and fantasizing about how she'd tweak the ingredients. Her days were scheduled around the creation of meals now, ruled by the length of time it took to bake a squash, or allow a loaf of tarragon-and-olive-oil-infused bread to rise. It was such a sharp contrast to her years at the law firm, where she'd always worn a watch and had a clock on her desk, as well as a larger one hanging on the wall in her office.

True, here in Vermont she was aware of the pressures of time in a different sense. She and Peter still hadn't come to an agreement about when to have children, and she knew his considerable patience was running out. Unspoken words simmered between them, thick and oppressive as the air just before a summer thunderstorm.

Kira sighed and glanced out the window, seeking solace in the view: a swath of blue sky and pristine snow capping the evergreen trees. Her life had changed so dramatically in the past few months. Some mornings she woke up and automatically stumbled toward the shower before realizing that she didn't have to rush to make it into the office by 7:00, and that her days were no longer a series of competitions to see who could stay at the firm longer and make the partners more money.

She'd been very good at her job, excelling at research and billing a minimum of sixty hours a week—sometimes much more. But it never seemed to be enough. In the office next door, a guy named Rich, who was a sixth-year associate like her, always came in later than she did and regularly left earlier. He went to happy hours and took weekend trips and even boasted a golf handicap of seventeen.

Yet Rich had billed two hundred more hours than she had during her final year at the firm, a fact that the firm's managing partner had pointed out on more than one occasion. Obviously Rich padded his hours, even if some of those hours on the golf course were spent with clients. Everyone at the firm stretched out numbers like taffy on their time sheets; it was as routine a practice as the firm's weekly softball games for summer associates. Yet Kira couldn't bring herself to join in; she was like a vegetarian at a pig roast, watching everyone happily gorge themselves while she worried about whether the animal had been humanely treated. The eraser she'd made a classmate return back in elementary school, her inability to ask her father to contribute a little more when she and her mother needed it most, her refusal to peek at the calculus final exam the rest of the senior class passed around after a student broke into the teacher's desk and made a copy—it hadn't started with the law firm culture; she'd been this way her entire life.

Even so, she still might've made partner, if it hadn't been for the firm's twentieth anniversary party. She'd been wedged in a corner of a fancy country club's ballroom, sipping a gin and tonic and watching a few tipsy lawyers attempt the macarena, which was disturbing on too many levels to count. The firm's managing partner—a red-cheeked, florid-looking guy named Thomas Bigalow—had walked past her, his arm slung around the shoulders of one of their clients.

"Here she is!" Thomas had bellowed upon spotting Kira. "One of our rising stars!"

She wasn't flattered; he doled out praise and criticism with an equally heavy hand, which meant his words canceled each other out.

"I'm Kira Danner," she'd said, extending her hand to the client and wondering if Thomas had forgotten her name. It was possible, depending on whether the empty glass in his hand contained his first martini or his fifth.

"Chris Woods," the client had said. He was completely unremarkable: gray hair, gray suit, bland face. How could she know her brief encounter with him would torpedo her career? He should've looked more menacing.

"Skyrim Holdings," Thomas added meaning-fully. One of the firm's biggest clients.

"Of course!" Kira said. "I worked a bit on the government lawsuit." She'd been one of the folks in the trenches, digging through thousands of pages of research, while Thomas handled the client interaction—he was like the elegant hostess who met diners at the door of a fancy restaurant while the cooks sweated and scrambled in the kitchen.

"Kira's the one who found the precedent we needed to get the antitrust suit dismissed," Thomas had added. He might've struggled to remember her name, but Thomas had a near-photographic memory of all the major details of every case he'd overseen for the past decade. There was a reason he was the managing partner. Besides, he was the one who'd cut Kira a thousand-dollar bonus check when she'd burst into the office, clutching a printout of her discovery.

It had been Kira's biggest triumph in her six years at the firm; her research had been directly responsible for saving a client hundreds of thousands of dollars—maybe even millions. She'd used the bonus check to pay off her school loans a bit faster, but only after deducting fifty bucks to buy a bottle of champagne.

"So she's the hero?" Chris had asked, and Kira had blushed.

"Well, her along with the brilliant name

partner who argued on your behalf in court," Thomas had said. "Brilliant and dashing, I should say."

They'd laughed—backslapping, hearty, rich-men laughs—while Kira took another sip of her drink and tried to think of something to say.

"It was just luck that I found the precedent so quickly," she'd blurted. "Usually it takes me a few weeks of research instead of an hour!"

Chris Woods had cocked his head at her, then turned to stare at Thomas, and Kira had instantly realized her mistake: Associates weren't the only ones who overbilled.

"An hour," Chris Woods had repeated. He wasn't laughing any longer.

Kira had frozen, knowing whatever she said would only make things worse. Thomas could've billed for a few dozen associates working overtime for a solid week—he probably *had*—and Chris Woods never would have questioned the enormous check he'd had to cut.

"Let's remember this when you submit your next bill," Chris Woods had said. "Or perhaps we should renegotiate your last one."

"Touché!" Thomas had shouted, pretending they were still joking around. He'd steered the client away from her quickly, and she'd known her punishment was coming. It was administered the next morning: a one-year "deferral" before she would be considered for partner. Terms like *team player* and *maturity* were kicked around while Kira's nails dug into her palms and she fought back tears of anger and humiliation.

Gossip spread through the firm quickly, and everyone had acted like she was contagious—at least for the next few weeks, until another scandal had erupted when a married partner slept with a paralegal. Even her administrative assistant had given Kira's arm a squeeze and brought her a latte after Thomas finished dressing her down. Which only made Kira feel worse: She was an object of pity, a cautionary tale. The firm's screwup. The injustice of it still made her breath come faster and her face grow hot. Weren't lawyers supposed to be agents of truth?

After the Incident, she'd begun to dread going into the firm—or, more accurately, dread it more than usual. She'd tried to quiet the persistent voice that kept asking if this was what she wanted, and instead she drove herself harder and put in even longer hours, determined to earn a second chance. Then Rand had called with his strange, spectacular offer, and for once, his timing was exactly right.

And so, Vermont. Her chance at a new life.

The front door opened, letting in a blast of cold air, and Dawn and Peter appeared on the threshold of the living room.

"How was your walk?" Kira asked, shaking off her dark memories.

"It was good," Dawn said. "It's so beautiful here!" She pulled off her gloves and handed them to Peter. "Thanks for these."

Dawn looked better than she had the previous day, Kira thought. Some color brightened her cheeks, and the circles under her eyes weren't as prominent.

"Dawn's going to stay with us again tonight," Peter was saying. "I'll rustle up my sleeping bag, and then let's go check out the space above the garage, okay?"

"Sure," Kira said, closing her cookbook. "We've got an electric lantern in the closet. I'll bring that, too."

She got up off the couch and passed by Dawn. "I'm really glad you're staying," she said.

She was rewarded with a smile—the first one she'd seen from the young woman.

In the end Alyssa had done both yoga and meditation, then she and Rand had walked through town together, stopping at Outback Pizza for a cheese-and-pepper pie.

When they'd arrived home, Kira reported that Jessica had just called to announce she and her girlfriends were on their way in. Kira was busy in the kitchen, putting the finishing touches on appetizers with Dawn's help. Tomorrow, she'd find a quiet place to talk to Rand, Alyssa thought. And then she'd take the pregnancy test she'd picked up at a drugstore in town, and they'd view the results together.

She unloaded the dishwasher and closed the door of the machine. "What else can I do?" she asked Kira.

"I think it's under control," Kira said. "Maybe just take drink orders when the girls arrive? Would you mind?"

"I think my years of waitressing prepared me well for that," Alyssa joked just as the doorbell rang. She hurried to open it, and a half dozen young women piled into the house.

"Brrrr!" Jessica said, surprising Alyssa with a hug. "It's freezing out!" She wore what looked like a handmade bridal veil, and she smelled like alcohol—which probably explained the hug.

"Welcome!" Alyssa said. "Come on in, everyone!"

"I swear my nipples just froze and fell off and clinked against the pavement," drawled one of the women, who had an accent. Maybe South Carolina, Alyssa thought. The girl could've been *Miss* South Carolina, she was so pretty, with her wavy, honey-colored hair and toothpaste-ad smile. Her friends shrieked with laughter.

Kira collected the women's coats to hang in the hall closet. "Get near the fire," she urged. "It's warmer there."

There was a flurry of introductions—Alyssa knew she'd never remember the names—and

Jessica's five friends showed off their matching long-sleeved white shirts with the words *The Bachelorettes!* written in a dark cursive. Jessica's shirt was identical except for the wording: *He Put a Ring on It!*

"Love the shirts!" Alyssa said. The women all seemed so young—a tangle of slim limbs and glossy hair and giggles. Had she ever been that young? she wondered.

"Hey, ladies," Rand said as he came downstairs and entered the living room. Jessica flung herself at him and gave him a much longer hug than she'd bestowed on Alyssa.

"Rand!" she squealed. "He's the guy I told you about—the guitar player," she explained to her friends.

"Are you going to serenade us?" one of the woman asked.

"Maybe," Rand said, his expression turning grave. "But first there's a problem."

"And what is that?" asked Miss South Carolina, arching a perfectly shaped eyebrow.

"None of you are holding drinks!" Rand said, and the girls erupted in laughter again. "We've got wine, we've got hot buttered rum, and I can put together just about any other kind of cocktail you want."

"You can?" said Miss South Carolina, putting a hand on her slim hip. She was the leader of the group, the outspoken one who made things happen, Alyssa thought. "How about a Nutty Irishman to warm us up?"

"We've got plenty of Baileys and Frangelico," Rand said. "I'm on it. A round of six, with tequila shots to start?"

A whoop went up from the girls, and he disappeared into the kitchen.

"He's hot," someone whispered, and another woman made a low, appreciative noise in her throat.

"You know what I want to do?" Jessica asked. "Get in that hot tub!"

"Oooh!" one of her friends squealed. "But isn't it too cold?"

"It's called a *hot* tub for a reason."

"Drinks first," Miss South Carolina said. "Priorities, ladies. Then we can get in the hot tub or go into town and hit a bar or do whatever our bride's little heart desires."

"Are there any bags in the car? I can get them and put them upstairs for you," Peter said, and one of the girls handed over her keys.

Rand was coming back into the room with the tray of tequila shots and a shaker of salt and cut-up lemons, and Jessica was asking if anyone could put on some music, and Alyssa could see the long night stretching out ahead of them: drinks, a late dinner, barhopping, the hot tub, more drinks . . .

Just the thought of it was exhausting. She hid

her yawn with her hand as she walked over to the couch and collapsed onto it. Her body ached for her soft sheets and fluffy comforter . . . The fire was crackling and glasses were clinking and the room was very warm . . . Her eyelids felt so heavy . . .

"May your wedding night be like a kitchen table: four legs and no drawers!" Miss South Carolina was shouting.

Alyssa's eyes popped open and she looked around. Had she really nodded off, right here in the living room? Exhaustion weighed down her limbs like stones, and she could barely force herself to stand up.

She picked up the empty shot glasses and carried them into the kitchen so she'd have an excuse to leave. She slipped back out and walked down the hallway toward her bedroom, chased by another gale of laughter. She was so exhausted she fell into bed without even changing her clothes or turning out the light. She managed to pull the comforter up over herself, and within moments, she fell into a deep, dreamless sleep.

When she awoke, she felt disoriented. She blinked in the semidarkness until her eyes adjusted and she saw Rand fumbling for something on the dresser.

"Sorry," he said when he saw that she was awake. "Jessica and the girls want to hit up some bars in town and they're too drunk to drive, especially with the roads so slippery. So I'm going to take them."

"Oh." Alyssa rubbed her eyes and looked at the digital clock on the nightstand. It was only nine-thirty, but it felt so much later. "Are Peter and Kira going, too?"

"No, they're staying here," Rand said. "They're hanging out with Dawn."

"We could call the girls a cab," Alyssa began.

"It's no big deal," Rand said. "There's a band at the Pickle Barrel I want to check out."

Maybe she should go, too, Alyssa thought. But her bed was so comfy . . . and she wouldn't even be able to have a single drink since she might be pregnant, she suddenly remembered. The thought of the cold outside and blaring music and crowds held no appeal.

"Do you want me to come?" she asked Rand. "I'm really tired, but . . ."

"Nah, you get some rest," he said. He came over and kissed her on the lips, and she thought she tasted tequila. Had he done a shot with the women?

He's hot, one of them whispered in her mind.

"Just . . . be careful, okay?" Alyssa said. "Don't drink much if you're the designated driver."

"Sure," Rand said.

She didn't have any reason to feel insecure, Alyssa reminded herself. Rand was a very social guy. And yes, the women were young and beautiful, but they were also drunk, and he could be saving them all from an accident or lawsuit or worse . . . Really, it was a good thing he was going along.

She saw him slip out the door, his shoulders broad in his maroon sweater, a baseball cap atop his dark hair, and for a moment she was seized with regret. She really should get up, and splash water on her face, and follow him out to the car . . .

She sighed and rolled over, and within a minute, she'd succumbed to a deep, hard sleep again. She never even heard Rand come back in.

Dawn lay in her borrowed sleeping bag in the small room above the garage, lost in the memory of the time a few years earlier when she'd been in another empty space, not much bigger than this one.

She was twenty-two years old and she was moving out of her parents' Brooklyn apartment into a studio in Manhattan. By the end of the day, her single bed and IKEA dresser and standing lamp were in place, and her mother had filled Dawn's miniature refrigerator with neat stacks of glass containers of food: sour zurek soup and pierogi dumplings stuffed with mushrooms and cabbage rolls smothered in tomato sauce. And Dawn's favorite: paczki, the Polish donuts with sweet cheese and strawberry filling.

That weekend, Dawn had invited her parents

to dinner. She'd wanted to cook a special meal, something representing their adopted country, so she'd baked a meat loaf and set a card table with a lacy cloth that had belonged to her grandmother. She'd lit a candle, and poured a California red, and they'd toasted to her first apartment.

"Your own place," her father had said, looking around with pride. He'd grown up in a family with five brothers, and they'd all shared one bedroom. "Stinking feet and snoring," he'd joked. "Dat was the worst part."

Dawn was the embodiment of their dreams: a physical vindication of their decision to come to America. They'd given up so much—leaving behind family and friends and the security of the known—and though their lives hadn't been easy, they'd been determined to pave a better path for future generations, to give Dawn and their grandchildren opportunities that weren't available in their poor, small country. They'd made no secret of the fact that they wanted Dawn to get married and have lots of children.

"Maybe five?" her mother had suggested. "Or six." She'd had an emergency hysterectomy after Dawn's birth, which stole away her own dreams of a large family. Dawn was her last hope.

"Maybe," Dawn had told her mother, laughing. "But only if their grandma and grandpa babysit all the time!"

She'd brought out the strawberry shortcake

she'd bought from a bakery—it was the most American-seeming dessert she could think of— and cut them each a generous slice, and then they'd all had another glass of wine.

Dawn loved being around her parents and had never understood why other kids seemed to view theirs as annoyances. Only once, in elementary school, had Dawn felt ashamed when her father came to pick her up at school. A horrible boy had mocked his accent before Dawn and her father were out of earshot. Dawn's father didn't react—maybe he was used to it—but Dawn had flushed a deep red, wishing her father hadn't come, that he'd just stayed in the car and tooted his horn. Even in that moment, she'd despised herself for her thoughts.

Sometimes she'd watched her mother or father struggle for a word or phrase, and when salespeople or customer service representatives were impatient, she'd bristled internally. "How well would *you* get by in Poland?" she'd wanted to snap, but she always held her tongue. Her parents were unfailingly polite—too deferential to others, she thought—and she didn't want to embarrass them.

A year after she'd baked that meat loaf, her parents had died while driving home from visiting a distant cousin who'd recently emigrated from Poland to New Jersey. A moonless night, a sharp curve, maybe a deer in the road, or maybe her father had been exhausted from another long week on his feet at work and had nodded off . . . Sometimes when she woke up in the morning, she didn't think about them for a few minutes. But never for longer than that.

Dawn reached across to turn off the lantern and pulled Peter's sleeping bag up over her shoulders. She lay in darkness that was so quiet she could hear her own whispery breaths, and hoped for sleep to come quickly.

Chapter Twelve

Kira had to concede that Rand was the reason why the bachelorette party had gone off without a hitch. He'd entertained the women and kept their drink glasses topped off and had even chauffeured them around. But most important, he'd kept Jessica happy. Kira had secretly worried that with every visit, Jessica would come up with a new list of Miranda Priestly–like demands, dictating that the B-and-B needed to be repainted in her wedding colors or something equally ludicrous.

Sometimes Rand shirked his work duties a bit —or not exactly shirked, but cherry-picked the best chores, like raking leaves on a glorious fall day instead of being stuck inside scrubbing bathrooms. And when the family with the sick little girl and the baby had arrived, he'd essentially disappeared into the garage until they left. But right now Kira felt grateful for her brother-in-law. Last night Dawn and Peter had finished cleaning up while Rand drove the girls into town and Kira indulged in a long, steaming-hot shower before changing into her flannel pajamas and watching a little TV. Later that night, she'd woken up briefly to hear the girls shrieking in the hot tub. She'd thought about braving the cold to check on them—a drowning wasn't the kind of publicity the B-and-B needed—but then she'd heard Rand's deep voice blending with their higher ones, and she'd rolled over with a grateful sigh and fallen back asleep.

Kira had been in such a good mood this morning that she'd made her special banana-pecan pancakes and granola-yogurt parfaits for the queasy-looking bridesmaids, who were, she was grateful to notice, a good bit quieter than they'd been the previous evening.

"Keep the coffee coming," she'd instructed Dawn. "I think it was a late night for them."

The girls had left around ten to go to a spa for massages and manicures, and Dawn had insisted on cleaning two of the guest rooms while Kira straightened the kitchen. Alyssa and Peter had tackled the other rooms, and everyone had agreed Rand was off the hook.

A fresh houseful of guests was due this afternoon but things were under control now. Kira was just topping off her coffee mug when Alyssa came into the kitchen.

"Would you mind if Dawn did the grocery shopping today?" Alyssa asked. "I'm still not feeling that hot."

Her sister-in-law did look pale, Kira noticed, and she'd been quiet this morning, turning down Kira's offer of an omelet and only nibbling on a slice of toast.

"Of course," Kira said. "Do you want to go back to bed?"

Alyssa shook her head. "Rand's taking me to the doctor in case I need antibiotics or something."

"Good idea," Kira said.

She took a closer look at Alyssa. Were those tears shimmering in her dark eyes, or just the reflection of the light? "Sure you're okay?" she asked.

"Yeah," Alyssa said. "It's probably just a bug."

Something told Kira not to press it. Alyssa was usually serene and steady as a cool, clear lake, but she seemed emotionally fragile right now.

Kira thought again of the giggling girls in the hot tub. She'd assumed Rand had just been hanging out nearby, but now she wondered: Had he joined them? The Jacuzzi was large, but with seven bodies, it would've been a tight fit. Maybe Alyssa was upset about that, even though she didn't seem like the jealous type. But a hot tub full of pretty, tipsy girls could make even the most secure wife uneasy.

"We'll be back before the guests arrive," Alyssa was saying.

"Take your time," Kira urged. "Everything's under control here."

Kira leisurely finished her coffee, then puttered around the B-and-B for a while, flipping the last load of sheets from the washing machine to the dryer and kneading some dough so she could make mini–bread bowls to go with the chili. Her cell phone interrupted her just as she was replenishing the stock of toilet paper in the guest rooms. She was surprised to hear her mother on the other end. They'd talked less than a week earlier, and they rarely chatted more than twice a month. Their phone calls always covered the same basic ground—the weather, the B-and-B, her mother's book group and receptionist job. Their relationship was pleasant enough, but it wasn't what Kira would call close. They always talked about events, not emotions, and as soon as they'd covered the facts—a fresh snowfall, this month's literary bestseller, the raise her mother was hoping to get—their conversation ran dry.

"Your father phoned me this morning," Kira's mother began.

Kira felt a little electric shock. She didn't think her parents ever spoke. Their divorce had been like a blazing wildfire that left nothing but charred wreckage behind.

"He did?" Kira finally managed to say.

"He wanted your new address," Kira's mother said. "Apparently his stepdaughter is getting married, and you're invited to the wedding. She's only twenty-two, if you can believe it. I have no idea why people get married that young nowadays."

Kira held on to the phone for a long moment, feeling her breath stick in her lungs. Why hadn't her father wanted to phone her directly? she wondered.

"Of course you don't have to go," Kira's mother said, a comment that could probably be translated to mean that Kira's mother didn't *want* her to go.

"Did you give him the address?" Kira asked.

"I did," her mother confirmed. "I probably should've asked you first, but he caught me off guard. As you can imagine. He walks out almost twenty years ago and now, all of a sudden, he wants to be back in touch? The arrogance of this . . . this *person* is breathtaking."

"Mom," Kira broke in when her mother paused to take a breath. "It's fine." She knew from experience her mother could continue on in this vein for a while.

"Well." Her mother seemed to gather herself. "I just thought you should know, so you wouldn't be surprised when the invitation arrived. I wonder where he's throwing the wedding. He'll probably spend more than he can afford, trying to impress everyone, and—"

"Oops, the doorbell just rang. Our guests are here. I'll call you later!" Kira managed to keep her voice cheery as she ended the call.

She held on to the phone for a long moment after hanging up, the cold receiver pressing against her cheek.

A wedding, she thought. She wondered if her father would walk his stepdaughter down the aisle, and raise his glass in a toast while everyone watched and wiped away tears. Probably, she thought. That was what dads did at weddings.

She had met her stepsister twice, both brief encounters, but she knew what her laughter sounded like from that long-ago night when Kira had sat on the front steps of her father's home, unable to knock on the door.

Her own relationship with her father was more stable now. He'd taken her to a baseball game once when she'd come home from college for spring break—she knew nothing about the sport and had suffered through nine sweaty innings, praying something would finally happen on the field—and they'd had lunch a handful of times, including shortly before she'd left for Vermont. His life seemed quieter now that he'd found what appeared to be real happiness with his third wife.

She'd invited her father to her wedding. She'd fretted about it, not knowing how her mother would respond, but Peter had urged her to do so. "They're adults," Peter had said. "And it's not fair of them to put you in the middle." So she'd sent off the invitation, still with a knot in her stomach.

But her father hadn't come. He'd injured his leg in a fall the day before the ceremony, he'd said, which smacked of an excuse to Kira. He probably just hadn't wanted to face her mother, or to answer questions from all the people who might wonder why he was largely absent from Kira's life. Her father wasn't good when it came to dealing with difficult emotions—he was the party guy. He'd sent her a check for a thousand dollars, which she'd briefly thought about tearing up (after also briefly wondering if it would bounce), but in the end her practical side had won out and she'd deposited it.

He was throwing a wedding for his step-daughter, but he hadn't even bothered to show up for Kira's. She sank down on the edge of the bed in the guest room and wrapped her arms around herself.

She barely ever thought about her father nowadays. Why did it sting so much?

Chapter Thirteen

Alyssa leaned back on the exam table, trying to appear nonchalant as a doctor—one far more handsome than an ob-gyn had any right to be—reached for a pair of gloves and prepared to take a look.

"So this was a surprise?" the doctor asked. His white coat was crisp, his shoes polished, and his eyes slate blue under dark, well-shaped brows. Alyssa half-expected him to turn toward an unseen camera to give viewers a meaningful soap-opera-star stare. The only thing that didn't fit his image was his name: Ernest Natterson.

"Definitely a surprise," Alyssa said. "I thought I couldn't get pregnant. We're on the verge of adopting a little girl from China. Her name is Grace. So I guess we're going to have two kids this year."

"Double congratulations, then," Dr. Natterson said.

Everything had happened in a rush that day: After Jessica's gang had left and they'd finished cleaning up, she'd pulled Rand aside and he'd waited outside the bathroom door while she took the pregnancy test. He'd been remarkably calm upon seeing the double blue lines, but maybe shock was overpowering his emotions, as it was hers.

She'd found an ob-gyn through an Internet search and had scheduled an appointment for the following week. Then she'd thought to mention to the receptionist that she'd had a bad fall on the ski slopes, and she wasn't quite sure how far along in her pregnancy she was, but that she hadn't had her period in a long time, and suddenly, an appointment had opened up for that very afternoon.

Two children, after so many years without any! *Pregnant.* The word had become steeped in hope and pain and then resignation for her through the years. After all this time—at the strangest possible time—she was with child. Thirteen or fourteen weeks along, according to the doctor.

While she'd been waiting to see Dr. Natterson, Alyssa had asked the nurse why her morning sickness was beginning now instead of during the first trimester. The woman had shrugged. "Pregnancy doesn't follow any specific rules," she'd said. "Some women have it for nine months, and for others, it comes and goes."

Dr. Natterson finished making a notation in Alyssa's chart and gave her another dazzling smile. "Any questions for me before we get started?"

"Not really," Alyssa said. She looked at Rand, who shook his head.

"I mean, I've been having wine almost every night," she said. "Is that okay?"

"How many glasses?" Dr. Natterson asked.

"One or two. Well, sometimes more."

Rand cleared his throat. "Remember that time at the Wobbly Barn a few weeks ago?"

Alyssa squeezed her eyes shut. "Once I smoked a little weed, too."

"Do you plan on continuing to drink and smoke marijuana?" Dr. Natterson asked.

"God, no," she blurted. "I never would have, if I'd known . . ."

"I wouldn't worry," Dr. Natterson said. "That doesn't mean I'd recommend you continue, though."

Alyssa laughed, relieved. She'd phoned her mother before they left for the doctor's because Rand's nonreaction had left her wanting to talk to someone. She knew Rand probably just needed time to absorb the possibility, as she had, but she'd been gripped with the urge to share the worries that had sprung up in her mind despite her best efforts. Bee had assured her that she'd sipped gin and tonics throughout her pregnancy. "Oh, how I craved the lime!" Bee had said, adding that she even knew women who smoked cigarettes as a method of weight control back then, before the dangers of smoking and drinking during pregnancy were understood. Still, getting an official pass was the only thing that completely eased Alyssa's fears.

Alyssa sat back up and tugged the gown over her knees, suddenly feeling cold in the sterile white room.

"Maybe just one more question," she said. "I'd always planned to breast-feed, back when I used to think about getting pregnant. I know that's healthiest. But . . . is it—" She struggled for the right word, finally coming up with "fair?"

The doctor used his heels to gain traction on the floor and wheeled his stool closer to her. "Fair to Grace?" he asked.

She nodded, feeling grateful that he understood. That he remembered her daughter's name, even if she wasn't the focus of this visit.

"Because you think it will take time away from her?" the doctor asked. "Or because you don't think she was breast-fed?"

Alyssa bit her lip. "Both, I guess. I could read to her while I nurse the baby, but what if she's learning to walk and I have to chase after her or something? I mean, I know it's all going to work out. Plenty of women have more than two children and they manage . . ."

"It's going to be a major life adjustment, so don't minimize it," Dr. Natterson said. His gaze took in Rand, who was standing in the corner, looking as shell-shocked as Alyssa felt. "For all of you. No matter how badly you want children, no matter how long you've waited for them, your life is going to change in the next few months. Dramatically. You're going to deal with sleep deprivation, and hormonal changes that can affect your mood. Do you work outside the home?"

"Actually, our home is our work," Alyssa said. "We run a B-and-B."

Dr. Natterson nodded. "One word of advice? Schedules," he said. "It'll be easier on all of you if you can get your children to nap at the same time."

"We're not really schedule people," Alyssa said. "I guess we could try, though . . ."

"Tell you what," he said. "Let me check things out, and then I can give you a list of some good information sources: books, websites . . . You've still got plenty of time to prepare."

Alyssa took a deep breath and tried to relax as Dr. Natterson bent down between her legs. Her regular gynecologist always chatted during her Pap smears, but this doctor was silent.

After what seemed like an unusually long time, Rand began to hum the theme song to *Jeopardy!* and Alyssa laughed, glad to have the tension broken. But Dr. Natterson didn't join in. He straightened up and took off his gloves.

"Everything looks good with the baby," he said. "He or she seems to be growing fine, based on how you're measuring."

His voice was somber, out of sync with his words, and in the pause that preceded his next sentence, Alyssa felt an electric twinge work its way down her spine.

"Have you heard of an incompetent cervix?" the doctor asked.

"Incompetent?" Alyssa echoed.

"It's a terrible term. It sounds pejorative, when in fact it's just a quirk of anatomy," Dr. Natterson said. "Basically as a baby grows and puts weight on the cervix, the cervix can weaken."

"Is that normal?" Alyssa asked.

"It's not all that uncommon," he said. "But it's not desirable. We want to keep your cervix closed up tight until the baby's big and healthy and ready to come out."

"Is it starting to open?" Alyssa asked. Tears sprang into her eyes, and she blinked them away. She wished Rand were closer. Why was he standing so far away?

"It's thinning a bit," Dr. Natterson said. "So we're going to keep it closed."

"Okay," Alyssa said. They had a solution. "Let's keep it closed. What do I need to do?"

"You'll go to the hospital for a transvaginal ultrasound, and then they'll put in a stitch around your cervix. It's called a cerclage. We'll keep the cerclage there until you're ready to deliver."

"Do I have to stay overnight or anything?" she asked. "Is it a big procedure?"

"You'll probably need to stay just one night," he said. "So you and the baby can be monitored before and after the procedure. It's not terribly complicated, but you will need anesthesia. An epidural, probably."

Alyssa inhaled and exhaled slowly, trying to calm her racing heart. "When do we need to go?"

"I'm going to try to schedule it for tomorrow morning," he said.

"That soon?" Rand asked.

"It'll be better to get it done quickly." The doctor stood up and put a hand on Alyssa's shoulder. "I'll give the hospital a call. I'd like to see you back here after the cerclage."

Don't go! Alyssa wanted to wail. Was it unreasonable to ask Dr. Natterson if he'd consider moving in with them for the next year or two, perhaps sleeping on the floor by the foot of their bed, so he could answer all of their questions in his reassuring doctor voice?

By the time Alyssa had gotten dressed, the nurse had come back into the room with a prescription for prenatal vitamins and the information on the cerclage, which Dr. Natterson had scheduled for 9:00 the next morning. They'd have time to go home and pack a few things, but then Dr. Natterson wanted them to go straight to the hospital. Alyssa and Rand rode the elevator down to the lobby and went out to the parking lot and found their Jeep. Alyssa shivered, even in her puffy down coat. She rubbed her hands up and down her upper arms while she waited for the heat to kick in.

She was pregnant. Grace was coming. There was an abused woman hiding out at their B-and-B. Her cervix wasn't competent. They had a houseful of guests arriving today. She needed a "procedure." So many thoughts swirling through her head—she grabbed on to the one that seemed most manageable.

"Do you think the Jeep's safe?" she blurted. She double-checked her seat belt to make sure it was latched and found herself scanning the side of the road for any deer that might leap into their path and crash through the windshield.

"Huh?" Rand turned to look at her. He had the wheel in a death grip, but that wasn't the way he usually drove. He typically leaned back in his seat, one hand low on the wheel and the other thumping out a bass line on his thigh, the picture of relaxation. She'd loved his driving style back when they lived in D.C., where everyone else seemed to be jockeying for position, measuring triumph in an extra inch or two gained, or a fellow motorist cut off. But now it seemed a little . . . irresponsible.

The day of his accident rushed back to her, vivid and sharp: the phone call from the hospital; her frantic, burry race to get there; the plastic bag containing Rand's wedding ring and wallet, which she'd clutched while he was in surgery.

She remembered kissing his bruises and scratches as gently as possible, and throwing his bloody clothes into a trash bin, knowing that even if the stains came out, she'd never want to see them again.

"Okay, don't laugh, but what would you think about trading in the Jeep for a minivan?" she suggested.

He raised an eyebrow.

"Or a station wagon," she said. "A Volvo!"

"That's even worse," Rand said.

"I know you love your Jeep," she said. "But it was totaled. What if Grace and the baby had been in the back?"

"That was a fluke," Rand said. "One in a million. It's not gonna happen again."

You don't know that for sure, Alyssa thought.

"Let's focus on one thing at a time, okay?" Rand said.

"Okay," Alyssa said, and she put her hand on his leg. They never squabbled, and this was a ridiculous time to start. There was a person inside of her, the size of an orange, with fingernails and a heartbeat and a spinal cord. It was unfathomable. Grace was going to be a big sister. They'd need more diapers! Would life ever feel calm again?

Then she looked down and realized that somehow, during the last mile or so, her other hand had moved to gently rest on her belly.

· · ·

Dawn steered her shopping cart down the aisle of the grocery store, searching for the black beans Kira needed to make her chili. It felt good to help, to step in and take over the task for Alyssa—especially since Dawn had enjoyed eight glorious hours of sleep. After a hot shower and a veggie omelet for breakfast, she felt some of her strength returning. The only awkward moment came when she realized she'd have to ask Peter for a ride to the store. Kira had raised her eyebrows at that.

"You don't drive?" Kira had asked.

"I . . . used to, but my license expired," Dawn lied. Outside, it was flurrying again and the roads were slick; she couldn't risk losing control of an unfamiliar car and crashing. Or what if the police pulled her over for a faulty taillight and she had to reach for the New York driver's license in her wallet, then wait while they ran her name through a database?

"No problem," Peter said. "I need to hit the bank anyway."

Kira didn't ask any more questions, but Dawn could see them lingering in her eyes.

Another lie. They seemed to be tightening around Dawn, ensnarling her like a thick vine.

She found the beans and continued checking items off Kira's list, filling her cart with a packet of fresh chives and cheeses—*a block of good aged cheddar and a Gruyère, or if they don't have that, smoked Gouda,* Kira had written in her precise script. Dawn passed by a display of wine and hesitated. She yearned to add a nice bottle as a gift for Kira and the others. But spending the stolen money when it wasn't essential for her survival felt like she was tempting bad karma.

She finished her shopping and checked out, making sure to keep the change from the cash Kira had given her in a separate envelope in her purse; then she went outside to wait for Peter, who was running errands of his own. Killington was such a pretty town, with its well-kept shops and unique restaurants lining the streets like jewels tucked into a necklace. A recent snowfall had dusted the treetops, and overhead, the sky was a dazzling blue.

She began to wander down the street, a bag of groceries in each arm, gazing into the windows of a snowboarding shop and a bookstore. Dawn passed by a family of five—one of the little kids was on the verge of a tantrum and the parents were cajoling her out of it with promises of pizza—and then a couple strolling hand in hand. The sight made her pull up short, her throat aching. Tucker had been the first man she'd loved, but everything about him was an illusion. She wondered if their kisses and lovemaking, which felt almost sacred to her, had been repulsive to him.

She caught a glimpse of her reflection in the next store window she passed. Even with her new glasses and dark bob, anyone who looked closely would recognize her. She couldn't change her body shape, or the curves of her features, or those tiny but distinctive scars on her cheek.

She was about to move on when something inside the store caught her eye: a display of electronics, including disposable phones.

She stared at them, thinking hard. Weren't disposable phones impossible to trace? She thought so but couldn't remember for sure. She'd seen enough thrillers to know that either way, she should stay on the line for only a short time.

She went into the store and juggled the groceries while she dug into her purse for some cash. Then she stepped back outside to look for Peter. He hadn't pulled up in front of the grocery store yet, so she wrestled with the plastic clamshell packaging on the phone, using her teeth and nails to wrest the device free. She had five hundred minutes of connection time, but she was planning to use fewer than two of them.

She dialed the phone number of the investment banking firm and in a low voice asked for Kay, one of the administrative assistants who'd been part of the weekly group happy hours. Kay was forever rescuing animals in need. Every month or so, a notice would go out on the firm's Listserv:

Kay had found a one-eyed tabby cat that needed a home, or a pregnant mutt at the pound was about to give birth to puppies who'd be up for adoption as soon as they were weaned. Kay had a good heart, and she wasn't Dawn's closest friend at the office—two reasons why Dawn had chosen her. If someone were monitoring incoming calls in an effort to track Dawn, they might overlook one to Kay.

"Kay Dunning, may I help you?"

The gravelly voice almost undid Dawn. She hadn't spoken to anyone from her old life since fleeing New York. She imagined Kay sitting in her cubicle, sucking on the electronic cigarette she used in a seemingly endless battle to quit, surrounded by photographs of the unloved animals she was driven to help.

"Hel-loooo?" Kay sounded impatient now.

"Kay?" Her voice was a croak.

"Yes, who is this?"

"It's Dawn."

She could hear Kay's gasp of breath. "Dawn! Where are you, girlfriend?"

"I'm . . . not in New York anymore," Dawn said. "I had to leave."

"Well, we've got a dozen rumors going around here. Someone said you stole some money and took off for Mexico, and then there's the theory that you quit to work for a competitor and took all the company files with you. Personally I was hoping George Clooney kidnapped you and took you to that villa of his in Italy."

Seconds were ticking by too fast.

"Can you tell me anything else?" Dawn whispered urgently. "Is anyone looking for me?"

"Yeah," Kay said. She lowered her voice. "Two cops were in here last week. They took some stuff from your office."

She had maybe half a minute left. "Anyone else?" Dawn asked. "What about that guy Tucker from the mailroom?"

"Oh, Dawn," Kay said, her voice too kind. "You know he has a serious girlfriend, right? She came by the office for lunch last week."

Kay's tone told Dawn everything she needed to know: Tucker had gone public with his story about her crazy infatuation with him.

Dawn almost dropped the phone when someone jostled her from behind. She was momentarily swallowed up by a group of snowboarders who were walking down the sidewalk.

"What's it called again?" one of them shouted to a friend.

"The Pickle Barrel," shouted the guy right as he passed by Dawn. "I think it's in the next block."

Dawn raised the phone back to her ear with a shaking hand, wondering how much Kay had heard. The guy's voice had been so loud.

"Kay?" she said. "I'm in trouble. Please don't tell anyone I called. I'm begging you."

She was counting on her old co-worker's big heart, hoping it would trump her sense of duty.

"I didn't do any of the things they said I did," Dawn cried. "I promise. Tucker—he tricked me—"

She'd been on the line too long. She didn't have time to explain what had happened, or to try to get Kay on her side.

"I won't bring it up to anyone," Kay finally said. "But if they ask me, I have to tell the police you called. I need this job, Dawn."

"Okay," Dawn whispered, then she hung up.

Even if Kay had caught the snowboarder's words, there had to be other places in the world called the Pickle Barrel, Dawn thought as she gripped the phone tightly in her hand.

Why wasn't Tucker content to annihilate her heart? Why did he have to destroy the rest of her life, too? If he appeared before her right now, she wouldn't run. She'd launch herself at him, clawing his face and shouting obscenities. Her rage felt like a beast living inside of her.

The phone had the capability to send texts, and she'd memorized Tucker's number. He'd probably gotten rid of that phone now, but she had to do it anyway: *FUCK YOU,* she typed, then she hit Send.

She threw the phone on the ground and crushed it with her shoe, grinding her heel into the plastic and relishing the loud crack as it broke apart.

Then she walked back to the grocery store and saw Peter was now waiting outside.

"I'm sorry it took so long," she said. He popped the trunk so she could stash the groceries, then she slid into the passenger's seat.

"Did you get everything you needed?" he asked.

She nodded, clenching her teeth, thinking, *No, not by a long shot.*

Kira was kneeling on the floor, scrubbing every last trace of soot from the fireplace hearth when Rand and Alyssa came home. She understood Dawn's compulsion to clean—after the phone call from her mother, she'd needed to do something requiring no thought but lots of activity.

"Everything okay?" Kira asked, pulling off her rubber gloves.

When Alyssa didn't respond immediately, Kira looked at her more carefully. Something in her sister-in-law's face had changed.

"Yeah," Alyssa said. "Kind of." She glanced at Rand. "We, ah, just got some news. Crazy news!"

"Good news?" Kira asked.

"Of course," Alyssa said, but she didn't sound completely convincing. "We're, um, pregnant."

Kira was perfectly still for a beat. "But—you were adopting—you said—Grace," she sputtered.

"We still are, of course," Alyssa said. "This was a . . . a little surprise."

"One of those little surprises you need a

defibrillator to recover from," Rand added wryly.

"Somehow I got through the first trimester without even noticing—"

"Wait," Kira blurted. "You're in your *second* trimester?" She looked at Alyssa's midsection, but it was impossible to tell if she was showing because of her coat.

"Barely," Alyssa said. She ran a hand over her forehead. "It's all so crazy. Anyway, we can't stay long. We have to go to the hospital . . . Apparently my cervix is trying to open and they need to keep it shut so I have to get this stitch . . ."

"A cerclage?" Kira asked. At Alyssa's surprised look, Kira added, "One of my old college roommates had one a few years ago, and she shared every detail on Facebook." Including photos that belonged only in a medical textbook.

"Yeah," Alyssa said. "It's supposed to be really simple. I know we've got a bunch of guests coming, but maybe Rand can come back for a few hours tonight to help—"

"Hey." Kira stood up and walked over to envelop Alyssa in a hug. Her sister-in-law was shaking slightly, and she seemed to be a thin layer away from tears. Although Alyssa was the taller and stronger of the two women, Kira felt as if she were holding her sister-in-law up.

"Rand is going to stay with you and take care of you," Kira said in a gentle voice. "Don't worry for one second about the guests. We're pros at this by now. Peter and I can handle it."

"Will you tell Peter?" Rand asked. "Don't think we should wait around."

"Of course," Kira said. She gave him a hug, too, but he felt stiff and unyielding. Shock, she thought, and worry for Alyssa and the baby.

"Thank you," Alyssa whispered.

Kira smiled. "You are never boring, did you know that?" She felt good when that coaxed a little laugh.

"I need to pack a bag," Alyssa said. "Can you come help me figure out what to bring? You're so good at that stuff, and I'm not thinking clearly. We're supposed to check in tonight so they can monitor the—our baby . . . It sounds so strange, doesn't it? I think that's the first time I've said those words aloud. I can't get used to them. Anyway, I don't know what time we'll be back tomorrow . . . Rand will call you—"

"Just relax," Kira interrupted again. Usually she was the chattier one, but Alyssa was clearly releasing stress by babbling. "All you have to do is take care of yourself and my other niece or nephew."

She walked with Alyssa into the bedroom, keeping her arm around her sister-in-law's waist. "You'll need a nightgown and toothbrush and toothpaste and clean underwear. Maybe a book?" She pulled one off the nightstand. "Hmm . . . this looks soothing: *Guided Meditations*?"

Alyssa shook her head. "I won't be able to concentrate."

"I highly recommend *People* magazine, then," Kira said. "Tell Rand to get you one at the hospital gift shop. Don't forget cozy socks . . . Do you need face cream? Good. And how about a charger for your phone?"

Alyssa zipped up her bag and gave it to Rand to carry to the car, and Kira stood in the doorway, smiling reassuringly and waving while they drove off.

The moment they were out of view, she marched into the kitchen and poured herself a large glass of wine.

Chapter Fourteen

Kira blurted out the news the moment Peter and Dawn returned from the store, and a wide smile instantly broke out over Peter's face.

"That's wonderful!" he said as he bent down to untie the laces on his snow boots.

"I know, but don't you think it'll be a little . . . overwhelming?" Kira asked. She wished she could recall the words when she saw Peter's smile drop away.

"I just meant it might complicate things for guests staying here. What if the baby cries all night, or Grace gets into something because the place isn't childproofed . . ."

"The guests will be sleeping on another floor, remember? A little soundproofing, a white-noise machine . . . it'll be fine." Peter shook his head. "They're having a baby. Most people consider that happy news."

There was a moment of silence, then Dawn spoke up: "So, should I put the grocery bags in the kitchen?"

It wasn't the most subtle attempt to change the subject, but Kira was grateful to her nonetheless.

"Sure," she said, avoiding Peter's eyes. "I'll start the chili."

An hour later, Kira was just stirring the last spoonful of cinnamon into the big pot on the stove when she heard a vehicle roar into the B-and-B's parking lot. She peered out the window and saw a Jeep pull to a stop, skis attached to the roof rack.

"Peter!" she called out. "We've got visitors!"

His voice floated down from somewhere upstairs, but she couldn't make out his words. Maybe he was checking on the guest rooms.

It was barely one o'clock, hours before check-in. Their guests were very early, but what could Kira say? If she pretended the rooms weren't ready, they'd probably just plop down on the couch. B-and-Bs inspired informal etiquette, Kira was learning. Most people walked right in instead of knocking, and once, at midnight, a guy had rapped on Alyssa and Rand's bedroom door because he had heartburn and wanted Tums. Alyssa had staggered to the bathroom to get a bottle out of the medicine cabinet. When she'd relayed the story to everyone the next day, she said it wasn't until she'd gone back to bed that she'd realized she was wearing a short T-shirt with nothing at all underneath.

"We should charge extra for that," Rand had cracked.

Kira went to open the front door, her smile evaporating as she took in the scene: An injured skier was being supported by another man as he navigated the steps, dripping blood everywhere. His pants were ripped at the knee, and his face was pale.

"What happened?" Kira gasped.

"He fell in the parking lot. Everyone thought he was okay, because he got right back up," one of the women reported.

"I had a little alcohol cushioning," the injured man explained. He was as tall and beefy as a defensive tackle, with thinning blond hair. He looked to be in his mid-forties, as did his three companions.

"Yeah, like five Heinekens of cushioning." The woman snorted.

"Shouldn't you see a doctor?" Kira asked, thinking, *Five beers before one o'clock?*

"It's a scratch," the guy said and let out a burp.

"Okay," Kira said, her mind whirling. No way was she going to let this guy bleed all over their floors and new couch, especially since the wholesome-sounding family of four was en route. She pushed one of the rocking chairs closer to him. "Why don't you sit down and I'll go get you a bandage or something?"

The woman who'd come to the door first followed Kira inside.

"I told him to stop drinking," the woman said, like she and Kira were in the middle of an argument. "I told him!"

And how much did you *have to drink?* Kira wondered as she went into the kitchen, grabbed a bowl, and splashed in some warm water.

"Why don't we take this outside?" she said, unspooling a wad of paper towels and leading the way back through the swinging door. She really hated it when guests invaded the sacred space of her kitchen. "I'm Kira, by the way."

"Gina," the woman said as they returned to the porch. Gina had a slight accent—New York or New Jersey, maybe. "That idiot is Terry, and the other couple is Chuck and Bridget."

"Terry's your husband?" Kira guessed.

"Unfortunately," Gina said. "Let's fix him up so I can kill him later."

Once they'd washed Terry's leg, the injury didn't look too bad. He'd sheared off a good bit of skin, but he could move his leg freely and insisted it wasn't too painful.

"He carves up black diamonds all morning, then he trips on a pebble," recapped Chuck. He swatted Terry on the back of the head.

"Let me find you some Neosporin and bandages," Kira said. "Keep applying pressure until the bleeding stops. Don't move!" The last two words came out with a little more force than she'd intended.

She collected the bowl of disgusting blood-tinged water and used paper towels and hurried to the bottom of the stairs. "Peter!" she hissed.

He appeared a moment later, holding a wrench.

"What are you doing?" she asked.

"There's a leak in one of the bathrooms," he said.

"You're kidding." She looked at his face. "You're not kidding."

"Dawn turned on the sink, and water started dripping inside the vanity," he said.

"Do you know anything about plumbing?" she asked. Home repairs were Rand's domain.

"I'm looking it up online," Peter said.

"Hurry!" she said. "We've got guests! Drunk guests!"

She raced into the kitchen, dumped Terry's mess into the sink with a shudder, and scrubbed her hands with hot water and soap. She pulled antibiotic gel and a roll of gauze out of the first-aid kit and put them on a tray, then filled a pitcher with water and added a few slices of lemon to four tall glasses. She hesitated, then grabbed a few beers and a wedge of cheddar from the refrigerator as well as some crackers and a jar of mustard, and arranged everything on a platter. Maybe if she served them snacks, they'd stay outside until the bathroom was fixed.

"Hey, um . . . Katie?"

Kira's shoulders tensed. The woman was back in her kitchen.

She rearranged her expression before turning around.

"This guy wants to see you." Gina gestured to a man who looked like a college student; he was clean-cut and skinny, with horn-rimmed glasses and a sprinkling of acne on his chin. Kira started to take a step toward him, assuming he was part of the family that was also due to arrive today. Then she saw the clipboard in his hands.

"I'm Hugh Jepsen from the health department," the guy said. "I'm here for an inspection."

No, Kira thought, closing her eyes. When she opened them again, skinny Hugh Jepsen and his clipboard were still there, and *his* eyes were tracking toward the mess in the sink.

"We had an injured guest," Kira said quickly, moving to block his view. Why hadn't she taken ten seconds to dump the soiled paper towels in the trash can? Chili ingredients littered the countertops, along with a cutting board that held the remnants of an onion; a tray of mini–bread loaves was cooling atop the stove; and a bulging bag of trash was hanging from the knob of the back door. Kira knew they'd be having unannounced inspections a few times a year; it went along with getting a license to serve food. But today of all days? Hugh Jepsen could win an Olympic gold medal in a bad timing competition.

"So I heard," Hugh said. Kira could only imagine how Terry and Chuck had welcomed the young inspector when he'd stepped onto the front porch.

"I need to take a look around," Hugh continued.

"A look around?" Kira echoed, stepping backward toward the sink. They couldn't be closed down if they violated some health-code standards, could they?

She heard a loud clank overhead, and a vision of Peter attacking a pipe with the wrench, water spewing everywhere, swam before her eyes.

"Hi."

Kira's head whipped around as Dawn entered the kitchen. The younger woman seemed to take in the scene with a single glance, and she quickly extended her hand toward Hugh. Because of her position, he had to shift to shake it. Which meant he was no longer looking directly at the sink. Kira grabbed the mess, bowl and all, and dumped everything into the trash can.

"The guys outside said the health inspector was here. Are you from Vermont?" Dawn asked, still vigorously shaking Hugh's hand, which prevented him from turning back around.

"Yes," he said. "Born and raised."

"Oh, I just love it here," Dawn said as Kira reached for a sponge and frantically wiped down the countertop and sink. "The snow is gorgeous! I bet you had a lot of fun sledding as a kid. Did you learn to ski at a young age?"

"Uh, yeah, I did," Hugh said as Kira slid the cutting board into the sink.

"How wonderful," Dawn said, finally releasing Hugh's hand.

Thank you, Kira mouthed behind his back.

"Shall I take this tray out to our guests?" Dawn offered, reaching for the tray.

"That would be wonderful," Kira said.

"I just need to check a few things," Hugh said, taking a thermometer out of his pocket. He looked back at Kira and the newly clean counters behind her and blinked. She met his eyes and smiled in a way that she hoped conveyed pure innocence.

Hugh put his thermometer inside the refrigerator, bent to look under the sink, opened and closed cabinet doors, and made more notes.

"We've never had an injury before," Kira said. "It was a little scary. I thought it was best to keep him outside to prevent contamination. The scrape isn't that bad, though, it just looked awful at first."

Stop talking, she ordered herself. She waited while Hugh bent down to scrutinize the edges of the floor and peered inside the microwave and oven. He retrieved his thermometer from the refrigerator and checked it.

"Okay," he finally said. "I'm all set."

Kira breathed a sigh of relief. She swept the floors every day, and the shelves in the refrigerator were sparkling clean thanks to Dawn, so maybe he'd overlook the drips of blood on the front porch.

"Is there anything else we need to do?" she asked.

"Nope, that should cover it," he said.

She couldn't read his expression and still wasn't sure if he'd glimpsed the disaster in the sink.

"It sure is a snowy day for you to be out," she blurted. "Of course, I guess this weather isn't anything out of the ordinary if you live in Vermont. I just moved here from Florida. My in-laws are the co-owners. They're adopting a baby from China and they're also pregnant, so they're at the hospital right now getting checked out . . ."

Take pity on us, she thought. *We're nice people!*

Hugh began edging toward the door, and she followed him, trying to glimpse the notes on the pad tucked under his arm. "Can you . . . would you mind . . . I mean, did everything go okay with the inspection?"

"I'm really not supposed to discuss the results," he began, opening the storm door and stepping onto the porch. Which, Kira noticed with a rush of relief, Dawn had miraculously cleared of any traces of blood.

"The libations were a hit!" hollered Terry. "Time for another round, señorita!"

Kira slumped against the doorframe. She'd budgeted the après-ski package carefully, allotting one or two drinks per person, but she had the feeling that Terry and his friends were just getting started. At this rate she'd lose money tonight.

She noticed Hugh looking at her. He seemed a little older than she'd first thought, and he wore a slim gold wedding ring. She couldn't read the expression in his eyes.

"Good luck with your guests," he said. "I'm sure everything will be fine." Then he winked, and she exhaled. They were safe.

"Another round coming up," Kira said, heading back into the kitchen.

Dawn carried in the tray and began to scrub the dirty platter. "Is there anything I can do to help?" she asked.

"Are you kidding?" Kira said. "You just *saved* me."

"I'm so sorry about the sink," Dawn said. "I turned on the faucet because I was cleaning in there, and I noticed water coming out through the bottom of the vanity . . ."

"Hey, it's not your fault," Kira said. "I'm glad it was you who discovered the leak instead of a guest."

She took stock of the kitchen. "Tell you what," she said. "Can you hollow out the mini–bread bowls and I'll finish the chili?" She demonstrated how to pull out the bread innards, leaving the crusty shells intact. "We can use the leftover bread to make croutons or something later."

"Sure," Dawn said. She picked up a knife and got to work.

With any luck, Kira thought, they'd get the food ready quickly and then she could call a plumber about the sink—not that she didn't have faith in Peter, but the biggest home improvement project he'd ever tackled was hanging pictures that always ended up crooked.

The kitchen door swung open again, and Kira fought back the urge to pick up the nearest frying pan and bop the intruder over the head. Luckily, it was just Peter.

"Any luck with the sink?" she asked.

"Um . . . it's leaking faster," he confessed.

"We need to call a plumber," Kira said. "Oh, crap!" She caught sight of the hot buttered rum on the stove beginning to boil over and raced to turn down the burner.

Too many crises were colliding. The fear she'd tried to push out of her mind came rushing back full force: Alyssa and Rand's baby was at risk.

What Kira hadn't mentioned about her Facebook friend was that her baby had ended up coming seven weeks early and had spent the first few weeks of its life in the ICU. But Kira had to tamp down her worry and keep smiling, because their new guests would be arriving soon, and Gina would probably come through the door at any moment to demand more drinks. Plus, she'd planned to stay up late tonight making soup for Jessica's first-course tasting, then she had to prepare passed appetizer samples, and the salmon and pasta with side dishes, and it all had to be perfect, or Jessica would demand more changes. And then there were all the rooms and bathrooms that would need to be cleaned tomorrow and the next day . . .

She felt a hand on her arm, and she looked up at Dawn, with her light hair growing in at the part of her dyed dark bob and her big, blocky glasses. Dawn, their strange, sweet guest who'd saved her only moments ago.

"I can help," Dawn said.

Beep, beep, beep went the hospital's machines, relentless and methodical as a dripping faucet.

It was 2:00 A.M. and Alyssa couldn't sleep. The woman in the next bed kept moaning and thrashing. Nurses and aides seemed to come in every few minutes to dispense medicine or take readings or write something on charts. Why did people ever go to hospitals to get well?

She tried to quiet her mind because she and the baby both needed rest, but she felt intensely alone and very scared. She wished Rand were there, even though she'd been the one to tell him to go home.

"One of us might as well get some rest," she'd said, knowing the only other options were the hard chair in the corner of the room or the couch in the waiting area. His discomfort was obvious; while she was checking in and getting settled, he kept jingling the change in his pocket, then he made an excuse to go to the cafeteria to bring her a cup of tea she didn't want. Being at the hospital seemed to conjure a kind of panic in him that was probably rooted in his mother's death. Still, it hurt that he'd left so quickly, without even putting up a feeble protest.

She felt guilty for thinking it, but it was the truth: If their places had been reversed, she would've slept on the hard chair.

Luckily, her mother had been the perfect combination of laid-back and supportive when Alyssa had phoned right after Rand went home.

"I just don't know how I'm going to do it," Alyssa had confessed, keeping her voice low so the woman a thin curtain away didn't overhear. She thought about Kira, with her lists and schedules and endless energy. Kira had even created a three-ring binder for Jessica's wedding, with tabs for sections like "photography" and "flowers" and "food." Meanwhile, Alyssa had failed to notice that she was three months pregnant. How could she possibly take care of a human being she hadn't even realized was growing inside of her?

But her mother had said the perfect thing: "You will *thrive* doing it." The absolute certainty in her voice had made Alyssa shudder with relief.

"Is it a bad sign that I didn't notice?" she'd asked, wrapping and unwrapping one of her long, loose curls around her index finger. "I thought I had a really light period about six weeks ago, but the doctor said it was just spotting. Apparently it's not uncommon."

Bee had answered Alyssa's more important, unspoken question instead: "Your love for the baby will grow right along with the baby itself, you know. They'll both get stronger every day."

A nurse swung through the door and checked a readout on a machine next to Alyssa.

"Still awake?" she asked.

"I guess I'm nervous," Alyssa said. The nurse touched her shoulder briefly. "You're in the best possible place," she said before moving past the green curtain to check on the woman in the next bed.

Alyssa adjusted the pillow under her head, trying to find a more comfortable position. They should probably call Donna Marin at the agency to let her know, she realized. Alyssa frowned, imagining Donna's reaction. *"Another* change?" she could almost hear the adoption liaison saying, her lips pursing in disapproval.

A thought made Alyssa's mouth grow dry: Her pregnancy wouldn't delay their trip to get Grace, would it? She didn't think she'd be able to bear that.

Maybe no one at the agency had to know. Aside from a slight thickening of her waist that she'd attributed to Kira's good cooking, she wasn't showing. And the weather was her partner in camouflage—it was the season for bulky sweaters and scarves. It was wintertime in China now, too.

It was better not to tell, she decided. Why risk it?

She couldn't remember falling asleep, but the next thing she knew, the room was brighter, and soon Rand arrived, holding a bag containing warm blueberry muffins Kira had baked, and then they were wheeled into another room for the surgery.

"First we're going to check things out," said the doctor—a woman who barely looked old enough to be babysitting. She held up a probe attached to the ultrasound machine. "You shouldn't feel anything but a little pressure between your legs."

"Should I be jealous?" Rand joked, and Alyssa grimaced. Maybe he was nervous, but was this really the time? She and the doctor both ignored him.

The doctor adjusted the ultrasound screen so Alyssa could see it clearly. "There's the heartbeat," she said.

Alyssa stared at the small, bean-shaped figure on the screen and watched the steady light throbbing near its center.

"Isn't that too fast?" she asked.

"No, fetuses have much faster heartbeats than we do," the doctor said. "This one is about a hundred and thirty beats per minute. Everything looks good."

Alyssa ran her eyes over her baby's head, and its gently curving body. The tiny being seemed impossibly fragile. She could cup her child in a single hand.

"Oh my God," she whispered.

She knew, suddenly, that she could do this. She'd find a sling that let her carry two children at once. She'd buy a bigger bed so they could all pile in, like puppies. From this moment on, she would never feel overwhelmed or complain or worry about having two kids so close together, because she was the most blessed woman alive.

Spark, spark, spark went the baby's heartbeat, like a firefly igniting the darkness.

Well, hello there, Alyssa thought, and she reached out to touch the light on the screen.

Chapter Fifteen

"Excuse me!" Alyssa called to a passing nurse. "Do you know how much longer it'll be before I can leave?"

"Just a few more minutes," said the nurse without looking at them or slowing her pace. Somehow Alyssa wasn't reassured.

Dr. Natterson had been delivering a baby in the same hospital at the time of her procedure, and apparently he wanted to come by to give her recovery instructions. Which made no sense to Alyssa. The cerclage had been ridiculously simple, and she was going to see Dr. Natterson for a follow-up in a few days. Couldn't the doctor who'd performed the cerclage tell her to drink fluids and avoid lifting anything heavy for forty-eight hours and send her on her way?

"Maybe I should go get the Jeep and pull it out front," Rand said. Alyssa was sitting in the hard chair, and he was leaning against the wall next to her, still jingling the change in his pocket.

"But we don't know how long it's going to take," Alyssa protested.

"Right," he said. Jingle, jingle.

"I wish they'd hurry," Alyssa said.

"Yeah," Rand agreed.

They waited for a few more minutes.

"Can you please stop making that noise?" Alyssa finally asked.

"Huh?" Rand followed her gaze to his pocket. "Sorry," he said, withdrawing his hand.

They were silent until Dr. Natterson finally appeared, still in blue scrubs.

"Hi," he said, giving Alyssa a smile that instantly made her forgive him for any past, current, and future transgressions.

"How are you feeling?" he asked.

"Pretty good, just a little tired," she said.

"That's to be expected," he said. "I don't know anyone who sleeps well in the hospital. Make sure you go to sleep early tonight and stay hydrated."

"Okay," she said, glancing at Rand out of the corner of her eye. Was that all they'd been waiting for?

"I talked with the doctor who performed the cerclage," he said. He sat down on the edge of the bed Alyssa had recently vacated and rested his elbows on his knees. "Your cervix is measuring at about three point five centimeters."

"What's the normal number?" Alyssa asked.

"Five centimeters," Dr. Natterson said. "It thinned more than I'd previously thought. So we're going to have to take some precautions for the rest of your pregnancy. You'll need to be on bed rest."

"Bed rest," Alyssa repeated.

"You can take a shower every other day, and walk to the bathroom, but other than that I want you lying down on a bed or couch," he said. "No unnecessary movement for the next five or six months."

It took a second for the realization to sink in— the kind of dazed, fuzzy moment that separates a terrible fall from the resulting crush of pain.

"Grace," she whispered.

She looked at Rand, who was staring back at her, his eyes wide.

"No!" Alyssa yelled. "I need to get her! She's waiting for us, in China! My daughter needs me to bring her home!"

"I'm sorry," Dr. Natterson said. He exhaled and ran his hand over his face. "I don't . . . I've never dealt with this particular situation before . . . I just know two long flights would be the worst possible thing for you and the baby."

"So I have to choose?" she cried.

She looked at Dr. Natterson, then at Rand. Neither man challenged her statement.

"I can't choose! I won't! I will not pick one of my children over the other!"

Why wasn't Rand stopping this from happening?

She was hyperventilating. The room was spinning. She could see Grace's little chin trembling as her daughter stood up in her crib, stretching out her arms and wailing. Crying for her mother to come pick her up, to comfort her in the way that only a mother could. But no one was there, and Grace was crying harder, and now Alyssa was sobbing, too . . .

Someone's hands were on her shoulders. She thought they belonged to Rand, but the voice near her ear was Dr. Natterson's. "You need to calm down," he told her. "Please."

"Why is this happening?" she cried.

And why wasn't Rand yelling and fighting, too? *Do something!* she wanted to scream at him.

But it was Dr. Natterson who spoke again. "You're working with an adoption agency, right? Maybe there's something they can do to help. Delay it, perhaps. Ask their advice."

They don't even know I'm pregnant! Alyssa wanted to cry.

"I am getting on that plane," she said. Grace was crying in her crib! Alyssa's head snapped up, and she looked at Dr. Natterson. "You can't stop me!"

"Listen to me," the doctor said, his voice low and intense. "If your baby is born months early, he or she may not survive. There can also be severe developmental issues. Vision and hearing loss. Intellectual disabilities. You're at a serious risk even without getting on a plane."

Alyssa felt bile rise in her throat, and she gripped the armrests of her chair.

"I don't mean to scare you," Dr. Natterson said. "If you're careful, we have every reason to believe the baby will make it to full term."

His pager erupted at that moment, and he checked the message.

"I'm sorry," he said, sighing as he stood up. "Emergency C-section. I'm going to call you tomorrow to check on you, okay? Just take it easy tonight, drink plenty of fluids, and stay off your feet."

Alyssa nodded. She would do it tonight. Beyond that, she wasn't making any promises.

After a last squeeze of her shoulder, Dr. Natterson shut the door behind him as he left.

"He could be wrong," Alyssa told Rand. "I'm just going to be sitting on the plane. I'll be resting! I'll call my dad. He'll buy us first-class tickets. I can lie down the whole flight!"

He put an arm around her and kissed her forehead. "It's going to be fine."

But his voice was wooden, and she could tell he didn't believe it.

"Don't you dare give up on our daughter," she told him. She felt as if steel was running through her body, pulling her up straight and strong, infusing her with an electric power. "Don't you *dare!*"

"Lyss." He said her name on a long exhale of air. "Grace's life isn't on the line here."

It was as if her ankle was broken, and she'd

gone to lean on him for support, and he'd stepped away, letting her crash to the floor.

"So that's it?" she said. "We just take down Grace's picture and act like she never existed?" She'd never spoken to Rand this way before, in a voice so chilly it resembled a slap.

"Of course not," he said. "I'm just trying to be . . . reasonable."

But there had been too many empty spaces in the preceding minutes that should have been filled with Rand's protests and fears, and in those silences, she'd become aware of something.

He'd already chosen. He'd chosen the baby.

Kira and Dawn were elbow deep in wedding tasting preparations when Peter came into the kitchen.

"Hon, can you hand me that colander?" Kira asked, gesturing with her chin.

But Peter sat down on a stool instead, seemingly unaware of her request, even though he was looking straight at her. "Rand called a minute ago," he said. "They're about to leave the hospital."

Kira walked over and scooped up the colander herself. "How's Alyssa?"

Peter shook his head. "Not good," he said. "I mean, physically she's okay, I guess. But she has to be on bed rest until the baby comes or she could deliver prematurely."

Kira gasped. "But she's barely three months pregnant . . . So she can't do anything for the next six months?" *The wedding,* she thought, then instantly felt ashamed.

"It's more than that," Peter said. Dawn was slicing a melon into small rectangular chunks and silently watching him. "She can't go get Grace."

Kira sank onto the stool next to him, shaken. "They must be so upset," she said. "My God!"

She thought for a moment, her practical mind clicking into gear. "Can Rand go alone? What are the laws in China about that?"

"I hadn't thought of that," Peter said. "I'm not sure what the rules are, and I don't know if they do, either. They're on their way back now. Rand said Alyssa needs a little time alone. She's going straight to their room when she gets here. Actually, I guess that's where she's going to be for a long time."

"Trapped," Dawn blurted, and she blushed when Peter and Kira turned to look at her. "She must feel trapped."

Peter nodded slowly. "Yeah," he said. "I bet she does."

"What can we do to help her?" Kira asked. "I can bring her meals on a tray . . . she'll need a pitcher of water for her bedside, of course. Maybe a DVD player and a stack of movies? We should sign up for Netflix."

"That sounds good," Peter said.

"Okay," Kira said. "Let me think a little more." She stood up and paced the kitchen, passing by her wedding binder on the counter, then she spun around to look at Dawn. "Can you stay a little longer?" she asked.

"Oh!" Dawn said, blinking in apparent surprise. "I mean, sure. I guess so. Whatever you need."

"It won't be forever, obviously," Kira said. "But you need a place to stay and we need help. At least through the wedding. And truthfully, we can't afford to hire someone. You'd be doing us a favor, too."

"I'll only stay as long as you need me," Dawn promised.

"So we need to get your room ready," Kira said. She reached for a pad of paper and pen in a drawer next to the dishwasher. "You can't keep using a sleeping bag. How does a futon sound? That way you can have it as a couch during the daytime."

"Sure," Dawn said. "A futon's fine . . . but really, I'm okay with the sleeping bag."

"Futon," Kira said, scribbling in her notepad. "We've got plenty of sheets and blankets. Maybe another space heater, a lamp . . . oh, and we should get a rug. That'll help a lot. We can pick up a soft, fluffy remnant that covers the whole floor. And you can use the guest showers when they're unoccupied . . ."

Peter walked over and put his hands on Kira's shoulders. "Deep breath," he said.

Kira nodded. "I always get hyper when I'm stressed," she told Dawn.

"The only thing we really need to worry about is the baby and Grace," Peter said. "And keeping Dawn safe."

Dawn looked down and blushed.

"You're right," Kira said, but her mind was clicking as rapidly as ever. "I'm going to check Alyssa's room to see what she needs so I can set it up before she gets home. Peter, could you find some extra pillows? And Dawn, could you get a pitcher of water for her nightstand? I hope Terry and those jerks are quiet tonight. Maybe we should offer them a free dinner in town or something to get them out of here . . ."

Kira stepped out of the kitchen, then popped back in.

"I just thought of something," she said. "The background check."

Dawn's head shot up at her words.

"It's nothing personal—we all had to have them," Kira said. "The adoption agency requires them for anyone staying at the B-and-B longer than a few weeks. It's no big deal, but if you're going to live here for a bit, you'll need one."

"Of course," Dawn said.

"I know you've been worried about telling us your last name," Kira said, putting a hand on

Dawn's arm. "But you're safe now. And we won't breathe a word to anyone. It's just for the security check. I'll get your social security number and birth date later."

"Sure," Dawn said.

Kira seemed to be waiting for something. "So what is your last name?" she finally asked.

"It's . . . Anderson. Dawn Anderson."

Chapter Sixteen

She'd been relegated to the very end of the alphabet for so long that it seemed time for her to claim a spot at the beginning now. Of course, her name wouldn't hold up under scrutiny. The background check would crack apart her story, and then everyone would know she was a fraud. Peter had kept her secret, but Dawn sensed the others wouldn't be as sympathetic.

Kira would be able to find someone else to help out with the wedding—someone who brought fewer complications, Dawn thought as she unrolled her sleeping bag on top of the mattress pad Kira had somehow scrounged up. She'd leave in a couple of days, before the others discovered the truth about her.

The room was cold—the garage wasn't heated—but her sleeping bag felt warm and cozy.

It smelled faintly woodsy and very male. Being enveloped by it, and knowing Peter had been wrapped inside it, too, stirred up odd emotions in Dawn.

Peter was the first man she'd met, other than her father, who seemed to want to take care of her without expecting anything in return. He'd cleared the spiders from this room, brought in an extension cord and electric heating pad to warm her while she slept, and had left a book that she assumed was from his own collection: *Life of Pi*. It was a story of a castaway who'd survived against all odds. She wondered if he'd meant to convey a message of hope to her.

His brother, Rand, so tall and muscular and ruggedly handsome, was the one who'd draw the eyes of women if they were at a bar together. But Peter's quieter charms were the kind that took hold almost imperceptibly.

It wasn't that she had a crush on him, not exactly. And even if she did, it was clear he adored Kira. Dawn had watched them work together to defuse a potentially disastrous situation when their second set of guests had arrived. The parents and their two preteens had retired to their rooms with the Scrabble board and mugs of hot chocolate while she and Kira began prepping for the wedding tasting and Terry and his friends loudly held court in the living room. At ten o'clock, the father had come downstairs.

"My kids need to go to sleep," he'd said, his voice carrying into the kitchen.

Kira had hurried into the living room and Dawn had followed in case she could help, but one look at the scene told her she was in over her head: The father with his sloped shoulders and wire-rimmed glasses was glaring at Terry and his equally beefy friend. *This is not going to end well,* Dawn had thought.

But then Peter had stepped in with an easy smile that belied the tension rising in the room.

"I didn't realize how late it was," he said. "We've got a quiet policy after ten P.M."

Kira had looked surprised, but she'd recovered quickly. "That's right. And with all that fresh powder we got today, you all are going to want to be hitting the slopes early tomorrow," she'd said. Just like that, everyone had headed obediently off to bed and Peter had given Kira a wink.

How could she imagine Peter would even look at someone like her, when Kira was so pretty and capable? She kept four pots going at once on the stove, she wore jeans and winter-white turtlenecks that skimmed her delicate curves, and she calculated the prices of the items she needed at the grocery store in her head and then gave Dawn the right amount of cash. Even Kira's toenails were pretty—perfectly formed and polished a hot pink. Dawn's own toenails were a mess; she'd splurged on mani-pedis and bikini waxes when she and Tucker had been dating, but now her pedicure was growing out and just the tips of her toes were still red. Her hair had the same two-tone look; she had to get hold of another box of dye soon.

She'd stay as long as she could, but as soon as Kira asked for her social security number, she'd slip off without anyone noticing. She'd leave behind a note for the family who had been so kind to her. She began to compose it in her mind. *I'm sorry*, she'd begin. *I'm not who you think I am. I wish I could stay here. I wish it more than anything. I will always remember your kindness . . .*

Alyssa awoke with a scream trapped in her throat.

It was a dream, she told herself as she looked wildly around the bedroom. There was her dresser, and the photograph of Grace on the wall. The house was still, and she was tucked underneath her heavy, wheat-colored comforter.

The dream had seemed so real, though. In it, she'd delivered her baby four months early. It was a boy! Miraculously, he'd been huge and perfectly healthy and they'd gotten on a plane together to go to China. As the plane's wheels had lifted off the ground, though, she'd realized she'd forgotten her bag containing Grace's little ducky bathrobe. Her good-luck talisman.

She'd rung for the flight attendant and begged her to ask the pilot to turn the plane around, sobbing as she tried to explain that Grace needed the robe. But it was too late. And then suddenly they were in Jiangxi, walking off the plane, and a long line of smiling Chinese women were waiting, right there on the tarmac, each holding a little girl wrapped in a red blanket—the color of good luck. Every other person on the plane was an adoptive parent, Alyssa realized. They were racing toward their babies, their arms outstretched, scooping up their daughters and showering them with kisses. Cries of joy rang through the air. Alyssa pushed through the crowds and saw one woman was left, at the end of the line.

Alyssa ran to her, and the woman placed the blanket in Alyssa's arms. Alyssa dug through its folds, searching for a glimpse of Grace's dark curving eyes, that tiny scar. But the blanket was empty and it fluttered to the ground. Then Alyssa realized something: The blanket wasn't red like all the others. It was white, a symbol of death in China.

"Grace!" she screamed as she collapsed to her knees, the rough pavement biting into her flesh. The other parents were getting back on the plane with their daughters now, and the Chinese women were walking away. Alyssa was all alone. She looked down, and her sling was empty; her baby had disappeared, too.

She awoke with her face drenched with tears. The clock on her nightstand said it was just after

3:00 A.M., a time she'd always thought of as the loneliest hour. She'd asked Rand to sleep some-where—anywhere—else, and the space next to her was empty. The house seemed unnaturally quiet.

"It wasn't real," she whispered again, needing to hear the words aloud so they'd feel more solid.

She slowly pushed herself into a sitting posi-tion, then swung her legs over the side of the bed. She stood up and walked to the bathroom. She used the toilet and washed her hands, then slid back under the covers again. It was only then that she realized she was starving. She hadn't been able to eat before the surgery, and her appetite had vanished after it.

Her stomach rumbled, and she wished she'd thought to get a snack when she'd been up. The doctor had said she needed to minimize her movements. Would it harm the baby if she went into the kitchen now?

The enormity of her situation hit her full force: She was completely helpless, yet Grace and the baby were depending on her. Maybe the baby needed nourishment, too. Should she risk getting something to eat? She had no idea which decision was the right one.

Then she saw: There, on the nightstand right next to her cell phone, was a tray containing a full glass of water and a plate covered with Saran Wrap. Alyssa turned on the nightstand lamp, then reached for the tray and settled it on her legs. There were two thick slices of whole-grain bread, a dish of homemade blackberry jam, an orange, a blueberry yogurt, and one of those little milk boxes that didn't need to be refrigerated to stay fresh. And a note, written in Kira's precise script: *For midnight snacking. If you need anything else, use your cell phone to call mine and I'll come running. P.S. I froze the yogurt so it wouldn't spoil. It should be thawed and ready to eat by the time you read this.*

Alyssa uncovered the plate and reached for a slice of bread. She covered it thickly with jam and bit into it, savoring the sweetness. She sipped the milk and nibbled on juicy sections of orange, then began on the yogurt. Kira was right; it was cool and creamy now. She used the crust of the second piece of bread to swipe the inside of the jam pot so she could get out every last bit, then she drank deeply from the water glass. She put the tray back and turned out the light and lay down on her side.

She wasn't scared, not anymore.

She wrapped her hand around her belly and gave it a few strokes. The doctor had advised her to lie on her side, which meant that she was also facing her daughter's picture.

She'd said the words aloud before, but they'd been rooted in terror. Now she spoke them with conviction: "I can't choose."

Her eyelids grew heavy, and she knew she'd fall asleep quickly and easily, and that she wouldn't dream again that night.

"I choose you both," she whispered into the darkness.

Part Two

Chapter Seventeen

Winter held Vermont in a tight embrace. The landscape had been completely transformed during the preceding weeks, and now everything was hushed and still. Little drifts leaned against the B-and-B, and icicles hung from the eaves, reminding Kira of the frosting on gingerbread houses.

Kira had just finished doing a final check of the kitchen when the doorbell rang. Soup simmered on the stove, releasing savory notes of roasted garlic and tarragon, and the two place settings in front of the counter stools were worthy of a Martha Stewart magazine cover—real silver and china from Kira's own wedding set, and freshly ironed linen napkins tied together with delicate sprigs of white freesia and a bit of twine.

Kira wiped her hands on her apron and hurried to answer the door while Peter turned on the "Wedding" playlist she'd created on her iPod.

"Come in!" she said to Jessica and Scott. "Welcome!"

"It's so nice to be back," Jessica said, enveloping Kira in a hug. "Wow, this place looks wonderful!"

At least things were off to a good start, Kira

thought, feeling her cheeks relax into a more natural smile.

"Just one thing. Can you move those big wooden chairs off the porch? I mean, they're fine but nothing special, and it would look so much better if the space was clear. Maybe with a lot of little lights in votives on the railings and some silk ribbons wound around the banisters . . ."

Maybe "good" start was optimistic, Kira thought, but she kept smiling until Jessica finally ran out of breath. For such a petite girl, she had the lung capacity of a Pavarotti.

"We can move the chairs," she told Jessica. "But your florist should be able to handle the ribbons and candles."

"Oh. I just thought, since it was something so simple . . . ," Jessica said, letting her sentences trail off. "I mean, my dad will pay . . ."

Simple? Nothing was simple with Jessica, Kira was learning.

"Let me take your coats," Kira said, deciding distraction was a better course than arguing. "Why don't you and Scott go into the kitchen?"

Kira hung the jackets in the closet by the front door, and by the time she rejoined the couple, Jessica was holding up the china plate, examining it like a pawnbroker might scrutinize a square of cubic zirconium masquerading as a diamond.

"Is this the pattern we're using for the dinner?" Jessica asked, wrinkling her nose. "I'm not sure I like the rim of gold around the edge. Doesn't it kind of scream . . . 'old lady'?"

Kira caught Peter's eye and smiled tightly. She'd spent a long time picking out that pattern, passing dreamy hours in Bloomingdale's as she imagined cooking fancy dinners for Peter, envisioning the two of them ending every day awash in candlelight and happiness. The truth was, though, she'd ended up storing the china in a hard-to-reach cupboard and they'd used cheap plates from Target, ones she didn't mind chipping. This was the first time she'd used it in years, and Jessica's reaction felt cutting. The customer is always right, she told herself, even if the customer is a spoiled, self-centered, greedy Bridezilla. One with bad taste, too—these plates were tasteful and gorgeous.

"Actually, you'll need to rent china and tables and chairs for the dinner along with a tent," Kira said. "Glassware, too. Obviously we don't have all of those things here."

Jessica sighed. "It seems overwhelming all of a sudden. Things are just so stressful, with work and all my relatives nagging me about doing things their way for the wedding . . ."

Her eyes filled with tears and her bottom lip quivered.

No, Kira thought. Unbelievable! How had she ever been foolish enough to fall for Jessica's act? Clearly the girl could access tears like water from a spigot.

She had to take a stand now, before Jessica really began pushing her around. Kira straightened up, gaining a crucial inch over the young woman, and started to say something firm but pleasant to establish reasonable boundaries. But Jessica, perhaps sensing what was to come, beat her to it.

"I thought having the wedding here would be nice, but maybe doing it at a big hotel would make more sense . . . ," Jessica said, looking up at Kira from underneath her damp lashes.

Game, set, and match to the bride, Kira thought, realizing that if they lost this wedding, they'd also lose all the money they were counting on to make up for the slow weeks.

"Okay, we can take care of decorating." Kira sighed. "And Peter, you can find a rental company that will deliver everything, right?"

"Sure," he said. "No problem."

"We'll arrange it and I'll just tack it onto the bill," Kira said.

"That would be so much easier," Jessica said. She smiled the small, private smile of one who has known all along she'd get her own way.

Poor Scott, Kira thought. Did he realize what he was in for? Maybe there was a good reason why he never said much.

"You guys must be getting excited for the wedding," Peter was saying.

"I'm getting excited for the soup," Scott said. "Smells amazing."

"Have a seat," Kira said.

Kira reached for her note card with the words *Roasted butternut squash soup with a garlic-cheese crouton* written on it in her best script, and set it down on the counter in front of the couple.

She pulled the sheet of croutons out of the oven, where they'd been warming, and ladled a bit of the creamy soup into two oversize white spoons. She dotted each with a crusty, fragrant crouton. Vivaldi was coming over the iPod's speakers, filling the room with light, happy notes, and the sun was streaming in through the windows. Outside, the sky was clear and blue, and the snow sparkled as it reflected the sun's light.

"Mmmm," Jessica said, accepting one of the spoons. "Smells delicious."

"It's a house favorite," Peter said, uncorking a bottle of white wine and pouring a bit into their guests' glasses.

"Scottie, what do you think?" Jessica asked after she'd taken a tiny taste.

"It's great," he said.

Jessica took another small sip. "It is," she said, daintily licking her lips. "It's perfect."

One down, seven to go, Kira thought, reaching into the oven and bringing out the tray of latkes.

"Latkes?" Jessica asked.

Kira paused. "Your uncle is Jewish, and you said you wanted to have something representing his faith for the wedding meal . . ."

"Oh, I meant he keeps kosher. So we just need to have a kosher meal for him."

Kira gritted her teeth. She remembered the conversation differently. "It'll be a little tricky to bring in a kosher meal for one person," she said.

"Oh, I'm sure there's a restaurant that can deliver," Jessica responded, waving away the issue with a flick of her hand. "Or mail order or something."

A kosher restaurant willing to make a special delivery all the way up here for one meal? She'd deal with that complication later, put it on her growing list.

"Oh, speaking of, I told you my aunt is allergic to dairy, right?" Jessica said, looking at the tart Kira had put on her plate. "Does this have cheese?"

"Goat cheese, yes," Kira said. She realized she was practically strangling a spatula with her right hand, so she loosened her grip and took a deep breath. "And sun-dried tomatoes. We'll make sure all the foods that contain dairy have cards listing the ingredients. Some will have dairy, but most won't."

"Maybe we should have ingredient cards for all the foods, not just the ones with dairy," Jessica said. "What do you think, Scott?" She didn't wait for an answer. "I mean, that way if people are dieting or something, they can avoid fattening stuff . . . We might want to have a few low-cal appetizers, too—"

"Are you nuts, girl?"

Everyone turned at the sound of Rand's voice. Kira started. She'd barely seen him or Alyssa since they'd returned from the hospital. Alyssa was spending all her time in bed, of course, while Rand disappeared for hours every day, riding his motorcycle or hiking somewhere.

"Seems like he wants to be anywhere but here," Peter had commented yesterday. "Don't you think his wife needs him around a little more?"

"It's probably just his way of relieving stress," Kira had said, but she couldn't help wondering if Alyssa felt lonely.

Kira had been respecting the request for quiet Rand had made on Alyssa's behalf, going into her room only to bring meals or treats or new magazines. But when this tasting was done, she was planning to gently knock on the door and see if Alyssa was ready to talk.

Now here Rand stood, looking like he'd just stepped out of an Eddie Bauer ad, giving no hint of the emotional turmoil that must be consuming him. He wore a gray shirt, jeans, and a baseball cap, and he was holding his guitar.

"Listen, sweetheart, a wedding is the one time people can go crazy and eat whatever they want," Rand said, coming into the kitchen. "Do you really want your guests to be counting calories at your wedding, or do you want them drinking and dancing and celebrating *you?*"

Jessica gave a giggle and tossed her hair over her shoulder. "You're right," she said. "It's my day." She looked at Scott. "Our day," she amended, and Kira muffled a snort.

Rand switched off the iPod. "How about this song for one of your dances?" he asked and began to play his guitar, serenading Jessica with Stevie Wonder's "Isn't She Lovely."

How subtle, Kira thought, but Jessica's smile spread all the way across her face.

"Yummy!" Jessica said, taking a bite of the tart. "Kira, this is so good!"

She watched as Rand put down his guitar and poured himself a glass of wine. He clinked it against Jessica's and Scott's, turning the tasting into a party with that single gesture.

"Have you gotten ugly bridesmaid dresses yet?" he was asking as Jessica giggled again. "Isn't that some kind of girl rule? Make your friends look bad so you look even prettier?"

Kira wondered how Alyssa put up with the fact that every female around seemed to fall prey to the charm Rand spread around like icing on a cake. She thought again of the bachelorettes' giggles coming from the hot tub, mingled with Rand's deep voice. Peter, on the other hand, was so steady and true. Peter, who'd once told her she was the only woman he'd ever loved besides his mom.

She looked over to see her husband clearing away Jessica's and Scott's plates while Rand leaned against the counter, taking another sip of wine. "Get something in fuchsia," he was saying. "And remember: You can't go wrong with ruffles."

Peter was a wonderful husband, Kira thought. He'd be an incredible father, too. He hadn't brought up getting pregnant recently, so maybe he realized the timing was terrible, with Alyssa on bed rest. Or maybe he was waiting for her to start the conversation. She sighed and finished arranging cheeses on a wooden cutting board, dotting the edges with small mounds of raspberries and spoonfuls of apricot and fig chutneys.

"Hoopskirts!" Rand pounded his fist on the table. "No one looks good in a hoopskirt. Come on, you know your friends are going to do it to you when they get married. Lay down the gauntlet early."

Even Scott was joining in now: "Ugly hats?" he suggested. "Maybe parasols?"

"Now you're talking!" Rand said, giving Scott a high-five. Rand had to be upset about the risky pregnancy and Grace, but you'd never know it from the way he was acting. He was putting on a good show.

Kira slid the board in front of Jessica and Scott and reached for the card detailing the items she'd so carefully selected. She waited for a break in conversation so she could announce the next appetizer and talk about how the sweet fig spread should be paired with the creamy Brie on a lightly toasted slice of French bread, and how the raspberries would enhance the goat cheese.

Kira cleared her throat. "Try the Brie," she began. But now Rand was segueing into another story—this one about the time he'd attended a wedding where the best man had slid across the dance floor on his knees and crashed directly into a waiter holding a tray of champagne—and no one was looking at Kira's cheese platter. She waited another moment, then set the note card on the counter and turned off the broiler so the salmon didn't burn. The main course, she supposed, would have to wait.

She had to get rid of the money. It was an albatross, a bad-luck charm, an anchor dragging her down. What if someone looked in her purse and spotted the huge bundle of hundred-dollar bills? Or a thief could snatch it away. And if the police caught up to her, no one would believe her story if she was still in possession of all that cash. They probably wouldn't in any case, but at least it would look better if she returned it. Or most of it, since she'd need a few thousand to keep going. Tucker obviously believed he could still manipulate her from afar, but maybe word would get back to him that she'd relinquished the money, and he'd finally leave her alone.

Dawn was surprised she hadn't realized it sooner, but her mind had been muddy from stress and the lack of sleep or decent food. Until she'd arrived at the B-and-B, basic survival had monopolized most of her brain cells.

The only question now was how to deliver it. Western Union seemed safest, but she didn't know what kind of electronic trail it left. So that left FedEx. She could wrap the cash in a newspaper and address the package to Kay at the office. If she used a two-day delivery method, she could be in a new state by the time the box arrived.

Her plan in place, Dawn unrolled the sleeping bag Peter had left for her and turned down her lantern. It was midnight now, and the house was dark and quiet. The tasting had gone well, and the guests had all packed up and left. It was time for her to go, too. Kira hadn't asked for her birth date and social security number yet—things had been too busy—but she surely would soon.

Dawn slept fitfully, waking every hour or two, fearful of oversleeping and missing her chance to leave unnoticed. Finally she gave up. The sky was still dark, but it was a long walk into town, so she might as well get started. She rolled up the sleeping bag and left Peter's book propped against it, grabbed her backpack and purse, and climbed down the stairs. She entered the kitchen and was reaching for the farewell note in her purse when a sound drew her to the living room.

Someone was sleeping on the big sectional couch, a big guy whose feet were dangling off the end. Tucker! Her heart pounded faster before she could banish that ridiculous thought. She squinted and drew closer.

It was Rand, snores escaping through his open mouth, one arm thrown back behind his head and a few empty beer bottles on the table in front of him. Dawn edged back toward the kitchen. Rand hadn't just fallen asleep out here accidentally; he had a pillow and quilt. What was he doing there?

A fight, Dawn surmised. Alyssa had thrown him out of the bedroom for some reason.

Opening the front door would likely wake Rand, and if she activated the garage door, everyone in the house would startle at the loud, grinding noise. Slipping out the kitchen door into the backyard was equally problematic; there was a dead bolt, but she didn't have the key and had no idea where one was kept.

She stepped lightly back into the kitchen and sank down on a stool. Maybe this was a sign. Maybe she wasn't supposed to leave. She didn't *want* to leave!

Her grandmother had been a big believer in signs. She'd come to live with Dawn's family when Dawn was in junior high school, but she'd never adapted to life in a new country. She spent most days watching reruns of soap operas and baking. On Sundays she joined them for a family walk, which was always truncated by her grandmother's superstitions: A black cat, a ladder leaning against a house, the threat of rain—every direction portended doom. Maybe her grandmother had been right, Dawn thought, since a dark cloud seemed to hang over their family. A year before her parents' death, Dawn's grandmother had suffered a fatal heart attack.

As Dawn sat there, debating what to do, she spotted a folded newspaper on the counter, turned to a page with a mostly finished crossword puzzle showing. She'd seen Peter working on it the previous day. If she stayed, she could ask him for help. He'd understand why she couldn't do the background check. Maybe together they could come up with a new plan; it would be such a relief to have someone to share her burden. Peter liked puzzles. Maybe he could solve hers.

The sun cracked over the horizon, and light spilled into the kitchen. If signs were trying to point her in the right direction, Dawn thought, this could be another one.

She retraced her steps to her makeshift room, unrolled the sleeping bag, and climbed back in, relishing the warmth after the early-morning chill of the house. She picked up Peter's book and lay in Peter's sleeping bag and waited for the house to come alive.

● ● ●

Incredibly, they'd pulled off the tasting. The only difficult moment had come when Jessica and Scott went out to their car and brought in overnight bags, clearly planning to take advantage of another free night at the B-and-B. Kira had started to say something, then she'd swallowed her words. Better to keep Jessica happy, Kira had decided. At least they'd left right after breakfast the next morning.

And Dawn had been amazing, mincing garlic and sautéing vegetables and washing dishes, managing to be exactly where Kira needed help without receiving constant instructions.

"Do you cook a lot?" Kira had asked, but Dawn had shaken her head.

"My mother did, though," Dawn had said, her voice soft. "I used to love helping her in the kitchen."

"She taught you well," Kira had said, noticing the sadness that came into Dawn's eyes. "And that health inspector! I was panicking until you came along and distracted him."

Dawn had smiled. "I used to work for a—um, this guy. He was really busy and a lot of people wanted to see him, so I learned how to get people in and out of his office quickly."

This guy, Kira thought. Dawn seemed determined to avoid giving any hints about her life up to this point. But Kira wasn't complaining:

Dawn had arrived just when they needed help, and she was happy to work for room and board, which was really all they could afford. The match seemed almost too good to be true.

And yet something was nagging at Kira. It was the way Dawn had flinched when Kira mentioned the background check. Maybe she should ask Peter to perform a preliminary one, just to be safe. If Dawn was hiding something, it wouldn't be good for the adoption agency to discover it.

The mail slid through the slot in the door and thumped onto the floor. Kira picked up the envelopes and catalogs and began sorting. Junk, junk, a letter for Alyssa from her mother—those arrived every few weeks, handwritten in a deep purple ink and charmingly old-fashioned—more junk . . . then, at the bottom of the pile, like the cold eyes of a crocodile lurking behind a cluster of lily pads, was a newsletter from her old law firm. The postal service had forwarded it from her address in Florida.

Kira stared at the glossy newsletter incredulously. It had always been a brag sheet for the firm, a mass-produced way to impress present and future clients. On the front page, photographs of the associates who'd made partner were lined up. Rich, the guy with the low golf handicap and even lower work ethic, was grinning toothily in the top row. Then there were color shots of the firm's splashy annual trip—this one to the

Bahamas—as well as highlights from some of the biggest cases won that year.

The case Kira had worked on, the one she'd been at least partly responsible for salvaging, was given top billing.

Kira crumpled up the newsletter and jammed it into the trash can, feeling a hot brew of anger and shame rise within her.

Her photograph should've been there. The years she'd spent grinding away in her office, sacrificing time with Peter and days at the beach and lazy weekend brunches at neighborhood cafés, had been a trade-off for the secure future she craved with an intensity that felt rooted in her very bones. Kira had imagined that once the crunch of her associate years was behind her, she and Peter would become modern models of parenthood. Peter would strap their baby to his chest in a BabyBjörn, and after a Gymboree class or trip to the park, he'd walk to her office—a big, sunny one with lots of windows—so they could all have lunch together. He'd keep his tech-support company alive, of course, but he could work during the evenings or while the baby napped. They'd buy a pretty little house that she could pay off with a fifteen-year mortgage, and she'd max out her 401(k) and they'd start a college fund. Her credit cards would be paid off every single month; their refrigerator would always be full.

A rising star. That's what Thomas, the puffy-faced managing partner, had called her. But he was a man who spewed words like shiny coins spilling from a slot machine; to him they were tools to enrapture clients and entrance juries. The truth meant nothing to Thomas. Winning trumped all.

When she handed in her resignation, she'd thought he'd balk, telling her the firm needed her. She'd hoped he'd leap up from behind his desk and hurry to her side, leading her to one of the love seats by his gas fireplace.

"Let's not be so hasty," she'd imagined him saying as he pulled out the bottle of hundred-year-old scotch he kept on the bar in his sprawling corner office. She'd never tasted a drop of it—only a privileged few had—but she'd visualized him pouring a generous three fingers into a thick-cut crystal glass.

"You know we can't lose you." Then he'd pour himself a glass, too, and take a sip while he surveyed her with the eagle-sharp eyes that contradicted his good-old-boy persona.

"Then you can't postpone my partnership." Kira had practiced that reply—six succinct words. She'd savor the smooth scotch on her tongue and the feel of the creamy leather love seat beneath her legs while she kept her eyes steady on Thomas. She'd make sure she didn't blink first.

"You're tougher than I thought," Thomas would've said. "I like that."

By the end of the day, everyone would have been whispering about her again.

But it hadn't happened that way. She'd delivered her little speech, the one she'd practiced for hours while pacing her small living room. She didn't get emotional or cry, thank God. Her voice had stayed steady and clear as she'd told Thomas she deserved to become partner and if it didn't happen this year, she was going to take another job. She already had an offer on the table.

He'd stared at her for maybe five seconds. Let him think the offer was from a competing firm, rather than a half-baked idea from her irresponsible brother-in-law to run a B-and-B in Vermont.

"All right," he'd said.

Then he'd taken a phone call.

His phone had rung, and he'd actually picked it up. "Johnny boy!" he'd cried, his voice containing such delight that she knew it was a high-paying client.

She'd stood there, feeling her body beginning to tremble. That was it? He hadn't looked at her again. She was obviously being dismissed.

She'd underestimated Thomas. Or maybe she'd just forgotten that winning meant everything to him. She'd packed her things and left the office within the hour.

During her tenure at the firm, she'd managed to

pay off most of her school loans, but she still owed nearly ten thousand dollars for her law school education. She'd given up years of her life, and she'd come out behind.

And now, with reservations trickling into the B-and-B at a slower rate than everyone had hoped, she'd probably be no better off by the end of this year.

She sighed and reached for the wedding binder she kept on the kitchen counter. The wedding was what would pull them through this year and help them at least break even. Her main priority was keeping Jessica happy—and making sure the wedding stress didn't affect Alyssa and Rand, who were burdened by too much already.

At least there was one piece of good news. As it turned out, renting linens, tables, and place settings had been easier than she'd expected. With a few clicks of the keyboard, Peter had found a service that could deliver everything they needed in one batch. Although there were probably cheaper options, Kira was happy to opt for expediency when someone else was footing the bill.

Kira heard the roar of Rand's motorcycle approaching the B-and-B, then the sound of the front door slamming as he came inside. She sat down on a stool to review her proposal before sending it to Jessica. She'd calculated a hundred dollars a head for food and drinks—her cost would be sixty dollars, and the rest would be profit—and she was tacking on the rental items in separate categories for Jessica to review.

"Hey," Rand said as he wandered into the kitchen, his nose and cheeks bright red from the cold. He grabbed a red apple from the fruit bowl and crunched into it. "Where is everyone?"

"Peter's out with Dawn," Kira said. "He found a rug for her room and they went to pick it up."

"Wedding stuff again?" Rand motioned to the binder.

"Yeah." Kira flipped a page. "Can you believe how expensive it is to rent flatware? Thirty-seven cents a fork. At least you don't have to wash it before you return it to the rental company."

"Huh," Rand said. He tossed his apple core into the trash and began rummaging through the refrigerator. "Is this salmon up for grabs?" he asked.

"Yeah," Kira said distractedly. "It's left over from the tasting, but it should still be good."

He pulled out the platter and began attacking a piece.

"Let's see if I've got everything . . . Champagne glasses, wine and water glasses, napkins, bread plates, main course plates—"

"How much are plates?" Rand interrupted, his mouth full.

"Here." Kira started to hand him the papers, but he waved them away. "Just read it off to me."

She started to bristle—she wasn't his secretary!—but then she remembered Alyssa had mentioned a few weeks back, when Kira had asked if she should save the newspaper for Rand or recycle it, that he was dyslexic. Funny how learning something like that could flip your entire perspective. Now Kira wondered: Had she been misjudging Rand all along?

He was tricky, that was for sure. He exuded charm and energy, but she'd never had a deep conversation with him. Even now, when she knew he had to be upset about the risks to the baby and Grace, he acted carefree. Yet she could see shadows under his eyes, as if he hadn't been sleeping well. Rand was the kind of guy who could befriend strangers, but he seemed to let very few people in. Peter, on the other hand, disappeared into a rowdy group, but in a one-on-one situation, he shone.

"Okay." She ran her finger down the first page of the proposal. "Ten-inch dinner plates are thirty-three cents, if we go with plain white," she said. "Hang on, let me find champagne glasses . . ."

"So forty cents a plate," he said. "Sounds about right."

"No, thirty-three . . ." Kira looked up.

"You're not going to tack on a little surcharge?" he asked.

She blinked. "Really?"

"Why not?"

Kira put down the papers and cupped her chin

in her hand. Could she actually get away with it? She was essentially serving as a wedding planner as well as the caterer. And didn't wedding planners traditionally take a percentage of the cost of the event?

She reached for her computer and pulled up its calculator and began tweaking her numbers. She'd been planning to send all the paperwork to Jessica with every cost broken out and itemized. But maybe Jessica wasn't expecting a detailed report. Kira could scale back the proposal and simply lump all the rental fees into one line with the grand total.

She thought about Jessica's 7:00 A.M. texts and her changing menu requirements, her little nose wrinkling as the bride-to-be dismissed Kira's own wedding china.

With a quick motion, Kira's finger hit the Delete key, and her carefully constructed lines disappeared from her screen. When her page was blank, she began again, typing *Jessica & Scott's Wedding* at the top of the page in a pretty font.

She drafted a paragraph detailing the menu, making sure to add elegant-sounding flourishes, like "citrus-infused" and "amuse-bouches," and she highlighted the Jessica-tinis and Scott scorpions the bar would serve. Then she added a second paragraph encompassing all the items that would need to be rented, from bread plates to tablecloths and warming racks.

She pulled up her computer's internal calculator and tacked twenty percent onto the grand total.

"Whoa," she said aloud, leaning back. Was that right? When she added in a surcharge on liquor and a decent hourly rate for Peter's bartending and Rand's music, they'd earn as much from this wedding as they would from a solid month of bookings.

"See?" Rand said, scooping the last bite of salmon into his mouth, still using his fingers. "The surcharge is our friend."

"It may be the best friend I've ever had," Kira said. "Can we really get away with this?"

"Don't act like you're doing something wrong," Rand said. "If she asks, tell her it's standard. And if she doesn't—and trust me, she won't, because there's only room in that cute little head for Jessica-related thoughts—we're golden."

"Okay," Kira breathed. He'd made everything sound so simple. "I'm going to have Peter check over my figures when he gets back, and if you can just make sure Alyssa's okay with it, I'll send the new proposal to Jessica."

The extra money would make all the difference. With their share, she and Peter could pay off some bills, tuck more in their savings account, and maybe they could all pitch in a little to buy some advertising to boost the B-and-B's bookings. One day could turn around their entire year. Rand was right: She wasn't doing anything illegal.

No, no—he hadn't said *illegal!* He'd said *wrong*.

Didn't she deserve to reap the rewards of her hard work for once? She'd found a florist for Jessica, she'd created meal plans, she'd located a mail-order kosher dinner, she'd answered dozens of ludicrous questions, from whether white tulips would be in season in January to the safest placement of candles in a tent (Jessica had an irrational fear of fire, which meant Kira had to add "buy three fire extinguishers" to her growing list). *Haven't you ever heard of Google?* Kira had wanted to scream at Jessica a dozen times. The wedding was consuming so much of her life.

She gathered up the paperwork and her laptop and headed toward her bedroom. It wasn't until she was opening the door that the niggling worry in the back of her brain erupted: All four of them would be in on the plan, but Kira was Jessica's main contact. She'd created the paperwork. If something went wrong, she'd be the one to take the fall.

"I need to ask you something," Alyssa said a few hours later. "It's important."

"Of course," Peter said. "Anything."

Kira sat down at the end of the bed and reached for Alyssa's hand.

"We didn't tell the adoption agency that I was pregnant," Alyssa said. She blinked hard and cleared her throat. "I just— There were reasons. I worried it might affect us getting Grace. I figured the call telling us we were cleared to go to China would be coming soon, and no one would notice."

Alyssa studied their faces, wishing she could view their thoughts as easily. She knew Kira was scrupulously honest; when a store clerk had doled out an extra dime in change a few weeks ago, Kira had handed it right back. And Peter had once told the story of how a few guys in their high school class stole a big calculus exam. Kira refused to look—and she'd gotten the highest score in the class because she'd studied hard, whereas three of the answers calculated by the cheaters had been incorrect.

What did Kira think of the way Alyssa was gambling with her children's futures? Alyssa wondered. But Kira's bright blue eyes stayed fixed on Alyssa, and she nodded for her sister-in-law to continue. For that, Alyssa was grateful. The weight of judgment might've caused her to collapse.

"I don't know what to do now," Alyssa said. Her voice sounded rough even to her own ears, and she took a swallow from the glass of fresh-squeezed orange juice Kira had brought in. It was piercingly sweet and cold and felt like a salve against her throat, which was raw from all the crying she'd done recently. Kira had remembered how much she loved the treat, another reason to be grateful to her sister-in-law.

"If I call, and they say we can't . . ." Alyssa stopped, unable to speak the words and tempt fate. "That cannot happen, okay?"

"Of course not," Kira said. "It *won't* happen."

"You're good at this stuff," Alyssa said. "Can you find out what goes on in cases like this? I keep hearing stories about women who suddenly get pregnant when they decide to adopt. There has to be some . . . some—"

"Precedent," Kira finished the sentence. She thought for a moment, then snapped her fingers. "I'm a newspaper reporter," she said. "Doing a story on adoptions. I'll use my cell phone, which still has a Florida area code so our B-and-B's number doesn't appear on any caller IDs. No one will make the connection."

Peter stepped forward. "I'll do some research, too," he said. "Check around on the Internet. I'll see what I can find."

"Thank you," Alyssa said. "I just . . . I can't lose either one of them."

She wondered if they'd noticed she had said "I," not "we." She'd summoned them now because Rand was outside snowblowing the parking area clear. She hadn't spoken to her husband, other than to answer his questions about whether she needed another pillow or help to the bathroom, since they'd returned from the hospital. But he hadn't brought up anything of substance either. Maybe they were both retreating to their corners, like boxers, and gathering themselves because they knew their next real conversation could be shattering.

"I promise we'll find a way to get both of your children here safely," Peter said.

That did bring on her tears. "Thank you," Alyssa whispered as she wiped her eyes. "Can you do one more thing before you go?" she asked after her breathing was under control. She reached for a small square of paper on her nightstand. "Can you put this ultrasound photo in with the one of Grace? Maybe just stick it in a corner of the frame?"

Peter took the black-and-white image from her hand.

"This is my niece or nephew?" he asked. "God, he's handsome. Or she's beautiful. I mean, you don't see heads shaped like that every day," Peter said. He put the photo in the frame and stood back to study it. "Have you thought about modeling school? It's probably not too early."

Alyssa managed a smile. Kira smoothed the covers over Alyssa's legs, then she and Peter left.

Why had Peter been the one to say it, instead of Rand? Alyssa wondered. That was all she'd wanted from him, to hear that he'd fight to keep their family intact. But instead he'd withdrawn.

She'd fallen desperately in love with Rand on

their very first date, when he'd come to pick her up after her waitressing shift on the same day they met. She'd climbed aboard the back of his motorcycle, and he'd strapped an extra helmet on her, his fingertips making the sensitive skin under her chin tingle as he fastened the buckle, and then they'd taken off down the highway. It had been incredibly sexy, her arms wrapped around his waist, the big machine thrumming between their legs, her breasts pressed against his back. They'd gone to a little dive of a bar to play pool and flirt and drink draft beer. From that night on, they'd been inseparable. They were one of those couples you heard about who basically moved in together on their first date—a vivid example of love at first sight that only deepened with time.

But their relationship had never been truly tested. They'd lived at the behest of their whims, taking jobs that didn't demand much of them and quitting when they got bored, traveling when the mood struck, staying up half the night and sleeping until the sun was high in the sky. Giving all that up didn't seem like a sacrifice to Alyssa, but maybe it would to Rand.

She wondered, suddenly, what had been going through Rand's mind during his mother's illness. She sensed Kira had whitewashed the story of what had happened. Peter had stayed to take care of their mother. But Rand had disappeared when Elizabeth had needed him most. Then there was the time the family with two small children had come to stay for a night at the B-and-B, and Rand had fled to the garage while she and Kira and Peter took care of the baby and brought the little girl crackers and juice. Maybe Rand was the type of guy who ran at the first sign of trouble.

The realization made her curl up into a ball, her tears coming quickly now.

Memories continued to float by, and she grabbed hold of them, trying to piece together the puzzle that was her husband, the man she'd thought she knew better than any other. She and Rand had invited Peter and Kira to their wedding—Alyssa was excited to meet her new in-laws—but a few days before the ceremony, Peter had sent his regrets along with the excuse of a bad stomach flu. By then, it was obvious to Alyssa that a rift lay between the two men.

She'd asked Rand why he talked so infrequently to his brother. "Things got weird around the time my mom died," Rand had said.

"So make things un-weird," she'd suggested, running her fingers through his hair. "Call him and talk it out."

He'd jerked away from her touch. "Please drop it," he'd said. His tone was mild—too mild—and she'd been shocked by the darkness that had come into his eyes.

"Okay," she'd said, lifting up her hands in surrender. "Consider it dropped."

She'd seen Rand explode a few times, usually over stupid things like hitting his thumb with a hammer, but this time his anger had seemed different—sharper, more raw. It had left her feeling chilled, even though she knew it was grounded in the loss of his mother and not directed at her.

That night, though, he'd wrapped his arms around her, then cupped her face in his hands and kissed her sweetly before leading her to the bedroom. *Make-up sex,* she'd thought, even though they hadn't really fought. They hadn't discussed it again either, but then a few weeks later Rand had suggested that trip to Florida to spend Thanksgiving with Peter and Kira. She'd sensed it was his way of extending an olive branch. She'd been proud of him.

She suddenly realized the snowblower had stopped, and she heard heavy footsteps approaching the room.

Okay, Alyssa thought. It was time for them to talk. She filled her lungs with a slow, deep breath. She used her fingertips to wipe away the last of her tears, then looked up and waited for Rand to come into view.

Chapter Eighteen

Dawn rolled down the car window to let in a blast of fresh air. It felt crisp and tangy against her skin, like an early-morning swim. After decades of living in New York, where she'd grown accustomed to inhaling exhaust from belching taxis and the aggressive odors of street vendor carts, she couldn't get over what it felt like to really breathe.

"Is that our exit?" she asked Peter, pointing to a sign.

"Yep." He put on his blinker and began to edge his Honda over to the right.

She stole a glimpse of his pale, blond profile, admiring the way he drove so steadily, keeping the needle at a constant fifty-five miles per hour. She'd been worried about asking him to take her to a FedEx drop box. He'd already helped her so much! But Peter had been the one to approach her this morning as she'd folded a load of laundry.

"Got a minute?" he'd asked.

As if she had anything but time, she'd thought, but she'd only nodded.

He'd tossed out an idea, suggesting that she make an appointment under an assumed name with a lawyer for a consultation. The possibility intrigued and frightened Dawn in equal measures.

"If you want, I can go with you," Peter had said. "And if you don't feel comfortable with the lawyer, you don't have to say anything."

Dawn had considered it while she'd smoothed the wrinkles out of a pillowcase and folded it into a neat rectangle. "What about Kira?" she'd asked hesitantly. "Do you think I should tell her? I mean, she was a lawyer, wasn't she?" Dawn had recently seen a piece of mail from a law firm addressed to Kira Danner, Esq. It had fallen out of the trash can when Dawn pulled out the full bag to replace it with a fresh one.

"She's not practicing anymore, though. And I think it's better to go with someone on the outside," he'd said. "I don't want her to feel any sort of ethical conflict . . . Kira's an incredibly honest person. It might put her in a tough position."

"Oh," Dawn had said. "Of course!" She'd felt her face flush, and she'd reached into the dryer under the pretext of pulling out more clothes to hide her discomfort. She'd known Peter hadn't meant to imply that she, Dawn, was dishonest, but she couldn't help comparing herself to Kira, who never would've let herself get tangled up in something like this. Kira would have seen through Tucker from the moment he dropped those papers on the floor—which, Dawn now realized, was as choreographed a move as everything else in their relationship.

"I've been worried about the background check," Dawn had blurted out.

"I've thought about that, too," Peter had said. He'd sighed and leaned up against the washing machine.

"I didn't give you guys my real last name," Dawn had confessed. Best to get all the ugly stuff out now. "I'm sorry . . . I got scared."

Peter hadn't looked surprised; maybe he'd suspected it already. "Can you tell me what it is? I swear I won't tell anyone. But in fairness to Alyssa and Rand, we need to do the check."

Dawn had nodded. "Okay," she'd said. Her heart had pounded so loudly she worried it would drown out her words. "It's . . . Zukoski. I'm from New York."

"Got it," Peter had said.

Answering Peter truthfully had been a good first step. Now she needed to take another one. "I really want to send back the money," Dawn had said quietly. "I was thinking I could do it if I found a FedEx drop box. It's making me feel ill every time I see it."

"The money?" Peter had asked, then his eyes had landed on the purse by Dawn's feet and realization had dawned on his face. He'd pulled out his iPhone and clicked a few buttons. "There's a FedEx just over the border in New Hampshire," he'd said. "We could be there in an hour."

"You mean go today?" she'd asked.

"Why not?" Peter had said. "We've got guests coming in a couple hours, but we'll be back by then."

"Go where?" Rand had asked, materializing from around the corner.

Please don't tell him, Dawn had thought, instinctively shrinking back.

"Dawn needs to run an errand" was all Peter had said.

"I can drive you," Rand had offered. "I'm a really good chauffeur, if you don't mind me singing along to classic rock." He'd doffed the baseball cap he was wearing and flashed Dawn a smile, his teeth very white against the dark stubble on his chin. Dawn had smiled back, trying to camouflage the fact that something about him made her bristle. Maybe it was because he used his good looks as part of his charm. She was probably reacting to the fact that Tucker had done the same thing, but suddenly, she couldn't wait to get away from Rand.

"I've got it," Peter had said. "I need to fill up my car with gas anyway."

Rand had continued looking at Dawn, waiting for her answer, and she couldn't hide the relief she felt when Peter responded for her. She'd seen something flicker in Rand's eyes. Surprise, maybe. He probably wasn't used to women turning him down.

"Have fun," Rand had said, and he'd walked away.

Now Peter turned off the exit and began following the directions to the FedEx station. The drive had passed quickly—too quickly, since with every passing mile Dawn's heartbeat seemed to quicken—and they'd crossed over into New Hampshire a few minutes earlier.

"Ready?" Peter asked, and Dawn nodded, feeling fear grip her throat. This morning she'd counted up the money—a little over $99,000—then slipped $3,000 out of the bundle to tuck away in her sleeping bag as a safety net, in case she needed to keep running. Along with the money, she was enclosing a one-line note on plain white paper saying she'd return the rest of it soon. After a little deliberation, she had decided against signing her name. She was planning to use a false name on the transit label, too, and pay with cash.

After he pulled up the car in front of the FedEx building, Peter gestured to the newspaper-wrapped bundle in her lap. "Let me send it," he said.

"No." She shook her head. "They probably have cameras everywhere. And if the police are still investigating—"

"Still?" Peter interrupted.

"I called a friend from the office," Dawn admitted. "She told me."

Peter exhaled and thrummed his fingers against the steering wheel. "I don't want you on camera either. Hang on a second."

She felt herself blushing from a combination of pleasure and something else she couldn't quite name. Peter was being so protective of her. It felt lovely.

Peter stepped out of the car and looked up and down the street, then Dawn saw him approach a teenager who was checking his iPhone. The boy listened as Peter spoke, then nodded and went into the FedEx store, coming back a few minutes later with a box and a label. Peter reached into his wallet and handed the kid five bucks.

"What did you tell him?" Dawn asked when Peter returned.

"I just said I was parked down the street illegally, which is true, and I needed to keep an eye on my car so it didn't get towed," Peter said. "I told him he'd get another five if he took the box back in there."

Dawn found a pen in her purse and addressed the box from memory, printing the label in block letters so it wouldn't resemble her usual handwriting.

"Make sure you check the signature-required box," Peter said. "You don't want this left outside a door where anyone can grab it."

She nodded, tucked the newspaper-wrapped bundle inside the package, and sealed it carefully.

She hesitated before giving it to Peter. She'd been desperate to jettison the money. But without it, she felt so vulnerable. Her bank accounts would have alerts on them. Her ability to stay hidden would be threatened.

She felt Peter's hand pat hers twice. "It's okay," he said.

No one had touched her in weeks, not since Tucker had grabbed her upper arm, leaving behind fingertip-shaped bruises. She could feel the warmth of Peter's hand lingering even after he broke contact.

She let go of the package.

"I've got money to pay for the delivery," she said, reaching into her purse, where she'd tucked one of the remaining hundred-dollar bills.

"Is that from the . . ." Peter's voice trailed off as he stared at the cash.

"Yes," Dawn said. She looked down at it like it was a slug in her hand.

"Better not. They might be able to trace it," Peter said.

She hadn't thought of that. Were the police tracking those hundred-dollar bills now? She tried to think of the last place she'd spent one. New Jersey, maybe? No, she'd gotten change at the hostel in Boston after paying for her room—she'd used that change to pay for her disposable cell phone, thank goodness. But her trail still felt too close.

Peter took cash out of his wallet and went back out to talk to the teenager, who hefted the box under his arm and disappeared into the FedEx store.

"It's all done," Peter said. He smiled at Dawn. "The money will be there tomorrow. I told him the box had a couple of books inside in case anyone asks."

She released the breath she hadn't realized she'd been holding, and the tightness in her chest eased. Peter had thought of everything; he'd filled in the gaps she'd missed. "Thank you," she said.

He started up the car again. "Need anything else as long as we're out?" he asked. "I'm going to get a bottle of water."

She smiled ruefully and pointed to her head. "Hair dye," she said. "In case you hadn't noticed. Maybe there's a drugstore nearby?"

Peter laughed. "If we can't find one you can just wear a hat all the time," he said.

"Like Rand?" Dawn asked. She meant it as a kind of joke, even though it was true—Rand never seemed to be without a cap. But Peter looked surprised.

"I guess he does. Only lately, though," Peter said. "He's probably too lazy to wash his hair. Okay, keep an eye out for a drugstore."

Two blocks later, they found one.

"Do you mind grabbing me a water?" Peter asked. "I'm going to get some gas."

"Sure," she said. He gave her forty bucks as she got out of the car. The shipping costs, the gas . . . someday she'd repay Peter, too, she vowed.

She went into the drugstore and found a box of Clairol Midnight Black and a cold bottle of Evian and took both to the cash register. Behind the cashier were racks of disposable phones, which made Dawn wonder if she should call Kay to tell her a shipment was on its way. Kay wouldn't recognize the return address, and suddenly Dawn was gripped with worry that Kay might reject the delivery. It would be better to call here than back in Killington, just in case the signal could be traced.

She decided to buy the cheapest phone, cringing at the added expense for Peter. She paid for everything and tucked the hair dye and water into her purse, which felt so much lighter on her shoulder now. She was once again wrestling with the plastic clamshell when the cashier held up a pair of scissors and cut out the package. Dawn smiled her thanks and stepped outside. She pressed the numbers quickly and felt a surge of unease when Kay answered. She'd hoped to get voice mail.

"It's me," Dawn blurted. "Listen, you're going to get a really important package. I need you to give it to—"

"Hey!" Kay said, her voice sharp. "Slow down a second. Dawn, I don't know what's going on with you, but you need to leave Tucker alone."

Dawn froze. Gone was her friendly colleague; Kay sounded like a different person. "What do you mean?" she asked.

Kay exhaled loudly. "Look, he showed us some of the texts you've sent him—"

"He what?" Dawn blurted. "I haven't texted him!"

"A bunch of us were at happy hour and he happened to be there and he was really upset. Finally he told us why. I looked and those messages came from your cell phone number! I know because I have your number programmed into my own phone, so don't say it wasn't you. Listen, you've got to leave him alone! His arm was in a cast—he said you call him all the time and he can't sleep and he was so exhausted he missed a step and fell down the stairs. His girlfriend broke up with him because it was stressing her out. He even quit work because he can't take it anymore!"

The messages were old, but Kay wouldn't have known that, and Tucker would have deleted his responses. Instead of arguing, Dawn zeroed in on the most critical piece of information. "He's not there anymore?" She gripped the phone tighter. "Do you know where he went? Kay, please tell me. Did you tell him I'd called you a while ago?"

Kay's silence was her answer.

"I let him know you were far enough away

that he didn't have to worry," Kay finally said. Her loyalty had shifted; Tucker had replaced Dawn as her wounded animal now. He would've preyed on her compassion, identifying it as a weak link. Dawn could see him following the administrative assistants to the bar—Dawn had told him about their weekly happy hours—and putting on a mask of surprise when he "bumped into" them. He'd be alone, nursing a beer, trying to anesthetize himself against Dawn's onslaught . . . Of course he felt sorry for her, he'd say as the women drew in more closely around him, but she'd begun to terrify him. Had the others heard the rumor that she'd stolen money from the firm? Who knew what she could do next? Did anyone know if she was still in town? He felt . . . unsafe.

Kay would have taken in his broken arm, his thinness, the haunted look in his eyes. She would've had a drink or two or three—Kay always emptied her glass quickly—and her tongue would have been loose from alcohol. *You don't have to worry,* she would've told Tucker. And he would've fastened those navy-blue eyes on her and motioned the waitress for another round of cocktails. *Are you sure?* Tucker would've said, leaning even closer so their conversation took on a new intimacy. *But how do you know?*

Dawn squeezed her eyes shut. "What else did you tell him, Kay? Did you overhear something during our last call?"

"I don't want to get in the middle of this," Kay said. "Please don't call me again."

She hung up without saying good-bye.

Dawn pulled the phone away from her ear and stared at it. The phone had Internet access, and she typed three words into a search engine: *The Pickle Barrel.* The first hit was the bar in Killington, Vermont.

She couldn't breathe.

She dropped the phone onto the ground and then looked around wildly. Tucker could be on his way to Vermont right now. He could be here!

She heard a car horn toot and spun around to see a blond man waving at her. Her heart galloped faster before she recognized Peter. She took a step toward him, then realized she couldn't put him at risk, or Alyssa and Rand and the baby, or Kira—any of them. A broken arm; it must've been caused by the men who'd been threatening Tucker that day in the hallway. Tucker would be so desperate.

She turned and began running again.

Where was Peter?

Kira had just returned from the grocery store, and while she was carrying four bags in from the car—too many, but didn't everyone overload themselves rather than bothering to make an extra trip?—she slipped on a patch of ice and broke her fall with her hip and elbow. She lay there for a long moment, feeling her joints throb and knowing the pain would only intensify.

This never would've happened in Florida, she thought, struck by an unexpected pang of longing for her home state and its beaches and bright wildflowers that bloomed in highway medians.

A hot bath was what she needed, she thought. A hot bath and some Advil and, in an ideal world, a nap, since she'd woken up at 4:00 A.M. feeling panicky about the proposal she'd sent Jessica. Usually Jessica responded to her e-mails immediately, but not this one. Was she going to question the fees?

Kira pulled herself up, wincing, and dragged her groceries into the kitchen. Unfortunately she had time for only the painkillers. More guests were coming today, and she seemed to be the only one around. Rand and Alyssa were excused, obviously—but where were Peter and Dawn? It would be nice to have some help.

She popped three pills and washed them down with a glass of water, then put away the groceries and checked her cell phone in case a call had slipped through when she'd been driving through a dead zone on the way in from town. Kira had phoned an adoption agency for an "interview," and the receptionist had promised the head of the agency would call back, but she hadn't yet. There was just one message, from Peter: "Hey, sweetie, Dawn and I are running an errand. Back soon."

Kira felt a surge of irritation. True, the upstairs rooms were all clean and ready, but it rankled her that she'd been left alone to greet their guests while Peter and Dawn went out for a latte or whatever they were doing. Her irritation was probably compounded by the fact that she'd skipped lunch and was starving, she realized as her stomach gave a loud growl.

She called Peter back, but it went right to voice mail. "Call me" was all she said.

She started to make herself a sandwich, then put down the knife she was dipping into a jar of peanut butter and walked toward Alyssa's room. She lifted her hand to knock and ask if Alyssa wanted lunch; then something made her pause. She could hear Rand's muffled voice, and she was gripped by an instinct that warned her not to interrupt.

Maybe they were talking about Grace. Peter's initial computer search had shown that adoption agencies had different rules about pregnancy—some didn't have any limitations, but others wouldn't proceed if parents became pregnant during the process. It was unclear where Alyssa and Rand's agency stood. They wouldn't have an answer until Kira talked to the agency directly.

But the most crucial bit of knowledge Peter had gleaned was this: There was no rule or law preventing a father or mother from going to China alone to pick up their child—as long as he or she had been granted power of attorney by the other parent. Now everything depended on the policy of Alyssa and Rand's agency.

Kira went back to the kitchen and fixed her sandwich. There were a few dirty coffee cups in the sink, and Kira started to stack them in the dishwasher along with the sticky knife she'd used; then she realized it was already full of clean dishes. She sighed, her annoyance building. She'd made everyone French toast this morning and had done the shopping, so was it unreasonable to expect someone else could've handled this simple task? Ever since Hugh the inspector's surprise visit, she'd been fanatical about keeping the kitchen clean, and she knew it would gnaw at her if she left dirty dishes in the sink. So she clattered clean silverware into drawers and stacked plates and glasses in the cabinets before carrying her lunch to the coffee table.

She reached for her sandwich, craving the first bite. But before she could take it, she heard her phone buzzing. She ran for it, but instead of a call from the adoption agency or Peter, it showed a new text from Jessica. That wasn't surprising—Jessica texted Kira every day, often as many as three or four times.

But this wasn't one of Jessica's usual lengthy, emoticon-filled missives. The text contained two words: *Call Me*.

Kira stared at it, thinking that it was the identical

message she'd just left for Peter. She'd been short because she was annoyed. Maybe Jessica was, too.

Suddenly Kira's appetite vanished. Even though the room was cool, she felt sweat gathering in her armpits. Was it better to call Jessica back immediately, or wait awhile?

Before she could make a decision, her phone buzzed again. This time, to her relief, it was Peter.

"Hey," she said. "Where are you?"

"Are you okay?" Peter asked. "You sound stressed."

"Jessica just texted," Kira said. "She wants me to call her back. I don't know why she had to text to tell me to call, instead of just calling herself in the amount of time it would take to type a text, but that's Jessica for you. Nothing's ever easy. I don't know what she's going to say. What if she asks for a breakdown of all the costs?"

"Give me her number," Peter said. "I'll call her back."

"What are you going to say to her?" Kira asked.

"I'm just going to breathe heavily and hang up," he said.

"Peter!"

"What do you think I'm going to say? I'm going to ask if she got the proposal and see if she has any questions."

"I don't know," Kira said. "I mean, I'm the one who sent it over, and she might think it's weird if someone else calls about it."

"Just give me her number," Peter said. "Come on."

"No." Kira sighed. "I need to do it. Just come home, okay?"

"Sure," he said. Was Peter upset with her? Something in his tone made her feel as if she'd failed some sort of test.

"Dawn's coming out of the drugstore," Peter said. "See you soon." She could hear the toot of his horn, then he hung up without saying good-bye.

Kira needed to call Jessica and get this over with. She wasn't doing anything wrong, she reminded herself for the dozenth time. Maybe she should tell Jessica about the surcharge, though—casually weave it into the conversation. The simple contract she'd drawn up for the rental of the B-and-B didn't mention the extra fees because they hadn't come up with the idea yet. They'd been focused solely on getting a down payment in case Jessica changed her mind.

Would tacking on a hidden charge be considered theft if both parties didn't expressly agree to it? They *were* doing a lot of extra work for the wedding, but it had taken only about fifteen minutes for Peter to locate the rental company, so she could hardly justify adding twenty percent onto that bill for that.

But they'd have to coordinate with all the vendors, and arrange for the return of the tent and dishes, and tell the florist to bring some damn bows for the front porch, and manage the flow of events all evening . . . They'd earn the extra money!

As she dialed Jessica's number, Kira realized her hand was shaking.

"Hey there!" Jessica said, her voice as high and bright as ever. "So I was thinking about the timing of the toasts. I went to this wedding last year and people were still eating dinner during the toasts, so they weren't really focusing the way they should have been, and it was awful and I don't want that to happen to us. I need you to make sure that doesn't happen, okay?"

"Jessica? Did you get the proposal I e-mailed over?" Kira finally got the chance to ask.

"Hmm?"

Tell her about the surcharge, Kira thought, but the words refused to come out of her mouth. The time to discuss it would've been before she'd put it in the proposal. Then it wouldn't have appeared sneaky. Why hadn't she thought of that before?

"The proposal," Kira repeated. "With the cost of all the stuff for the wedding."

"Oh, sure," Jessica said. "I forwarded it to my dad. He's the one who's paying."

"Okay." Kira breathed. Had Jessica even looked at it?

"Scott's brother is going to give the first one because he's the best man, and you have to watch him, because he cannot hold his liquor. For a big guy he gets drunk faster than anyone I know, and sometimes he spits when he talks, which is a huge problem, but I doubt there's anything we can do about it. I told him he only has three minutes because a lot of people are doing toasts, but I'm still worried he's going to go over it. So just be ready to kind of . . . oh, I don't know, discreetly usher him away from the microphone, okay? You did arrange to have a microphone there, right? And after Scott's brother we'll have the maid of honor, then my dad."

"Microphone," Kira repeated. "Three minutes. Got it."

"My dad can go a little over three minutes, though," Jessica said.

How generous of you, Kira thought.

"But we still have to be careful, because I'm his only daughter, and he might ramble on. You know how daddies are about their little girls."

No, I don't, Kira thought. *I used to, but not anymore.*

"I'm sure your dad will give a wonderful toast," she said. She cleared her throat and tried to make her voice casual. "What does your father do for a living, by the way?"

"He's a prosecutor."

"I can't stop thinking about what the doctor said."

Those were Rand's first words upon walking

into their bedroom. He was standing four or five feet away from Alyssa, but the distance between them felt greater, and she drew up the covers, suddenly chilled.

"The baby could be blind and deaf, maybe intellectually impaired, if it comes too early," he'd continued. "I mean, Jesus . . . that's a hell of a lot to deal with, Lyss."

"It is," she'd agreed. "I'm scared, too."

He'd begun to pace. "I thought we'd give this place a run for a year. Then maybe bike through Italy or something. Travel for a while. Settle down somewhere new. Like we've always done."

A few months ago, she would've been okay with that plan. She would've *embraced* it. So much of their relationship had been cultivated by doing things together, chasing the exhilaration that came from plunging into the unknown. They never read travel guides or even booked hotels beyond their first night of a new trip—they embraced serendipity, courted adrenaline. How many camping trips had they taken over the years, pitching tents in Idaho or New Mexico, watching sunsets, roasting a veggie dog for her and a hot dog for him before zipping their sleeping bags together and making love under the stars? They'd traversed to the bottom of the Grand Canyon, ridden a boat down the Amazon, and eaten fresh-picked pineapple on the beaches of Honduras while sweet juices dripped down their wrists.

That chapter of her life was over now, but Alyssa didn't mourn it. What waited beyond felt much richer.

Alyssa looked at the man she'd loved above any other. He'd always be the handsomest guy she knew, she thought as her eyes grazed over his dark eyebrows, his blunt nose, and that strong chin.

"I'm worried if you stay, you'll resent me," she said. It cost her quite a bit to say those words, to reveal her deep vulnerability at the time when she felt so helpless.

Rand started to protest, but she cut him off. "Maybe not next week, or next month. But you will, eventually. And I'll start to resent you, too. It will poison our relationship. *I'm* the one who wanted children. We never even talked about it much. I just plowed ahead and you went along with it."

He stopped pacing and came closer to her. "Look, Lyss, I know I freaked out . . . I'm still freaking out. But I'm not going to abandon you."

He hadn't mentioned the kids, though. Grace's biological parents had already given her up. Alyssa couldn't—*wouldn't*—risk the chance that Rand would do that to her daughter someday, too.

Rand looked like the bad guy, but she knew she was every bit as complicit, a hidden accomplice in their mutual subterfuge. He'd never packed a suitcase for China, never asked for a copy of Grace's photograph to carry in his wallet. Another detail she'd forgotten until now: Years ago, when the social worker had come for their first home visit, Rand had been late. He'd gone out for a motorcycle ride and had come in fifteen minutes after the appointment began.

The signs had always been there; she'd just refused to see them. She was ashamed of having been so shortsighted when it came to their children.

What should I do? Alyssa wondered. Should she try to work things out with Rand, even though she'd looked into his heart and had seen an absence of something, and she would always love him a little less for it?

But then again, some parents didn't feel an immediate bond with their children. Alyssa's own father, after an extra martini or two one evening, had talked about how he'd been surprised to discover that one of his cronies at a poker game had boasted that he'd never changed a single diaper—things were different for that generation, but still!—and another had said it wasn't until his son began to play Little League that the child became interesting to him.

If they managed to get Grace, could Rand rise to the occasion? She wondered if he'd take Grace for walks in the sling Alyssa had already ordered, and play his guitar to her, and read her story-books. If the baby was born early, would he be by

Alyssa's side in the hospital? She couldn't bear the thought that he'd disappear when she needed him most.

"I just need to ask one thing of you," she said. "If I can still get Grace, you have to be the one to pick her up. Please promise to do that for me."

She saw Rand nod and begin to say something, but his voice seemed to fail him.

She closed her eyes because she couldn't bear to look into his tortured ones, and felt his hand stroking her hair. Suddenly she was transported back to one of the best trips they'd ever taken together. They'd been living in D.C., enduring a gray, slushy winter. Alyssa had come home after a day spent taking photographs of a child's birthday party that had featured a pony, a bouncy castle, a catered lunch, a clown, and a cake by a professional baker. The three-year-old had thrown a temper tantrum—really, a clown?—and the father had spent much of the party on a business call, while the mother kept sneaking into the kitchen to upend a bottle of Chardonnay into her plastic cup.

"Rough day?" Rand had asked. Alyssa had set her heavy camera bags on the floor with a sigh, then massaged her aching shoulder with one hand while she walked over to Rand. She was too tired to answer, so she'd just collapsed in his lap.

"Don't move," he'd said, reaching for something in her hair. "You've got something blue right here . . ."

"Frosting," she'd said. "Don't ask."

"How long will it take you to pack a bag?" he'd asked, stroking her hair.

She'd smiled up at him. "That depends," she'd joked. "Do I need bikinis or a parka?"

"Bikinis," he'd said. "But just the bottoms."

She'd laughed, and had felt a surge of new energy, her second wind kicking in. She could never understand why some people found travel tiring. What could be more exhilarating, more tingling to the senses, than entering a completely new world, tasting unfamiliar food, walking down streets you'd never seen before, and not knowing where you were going to end up? The *sameness* of life was what exhausted her.

"I'll go pack," she'd said.

"Good," he'd said. "Because our flight leaves in six hours."

She and Rand did this sometimes—they surprised each other with trips when they'd scraped together enough money. She'd known one was coming because he'd shown an unusual interest in her work schedule lately, and he'd kept sneaking off to make phone calls.

Once they were on the plane with their backpacks stowed in the overhead compartments, he'd covered her ears so she couldn't hear the flight attendant announce their destination. They'd each drunk a beer, then dozed for a few hours. And then they'd arrived in Portugal.

They'd eaten fish tacos on the beach, made love under the moonlight, and climbed aboard buses without checking the destinations. They'd visited a town entirely dedicated to the Virgin Mary, gone windsurfing, and hitchhiked to the next town. One afternoon Alyssa had admired pottery in a little shop and the smiling owner had come to greet her, his hands stained with gray clay. He'd spoken perfect English, and somehow, he'd ended up giving her a lesson on his wheel in the back of his shop. She'd made a horribly lopsided bowl and given it to Rand, and he'd pretended to be overcome by tears of joy. They'd shared a bottle of red wine with the old man and listened to his stories about the five daughters he was desperate to marry off.

I've never been so happy, Alyssa had thought that night as she'd lain in Rand's arms, watching him sleep and feeling his warm breath against her cheek.

A week after they'd returned to D.C., Rand had been on his way home from giving guitar lessons at the kids' music school, and he'd stopped at a red light and looked down to change the radio station. He'd never seen the moving truck barreling up behind him, the driver pumping the useless brakes. That moment—and the collection of all the moments before it—had led them here, to Vermont.

Alyssa wasn't angry with Rand, not any longer. But she thought she knew what needed to happen next, for all of their sakes.

Chapter Nineteen

Her parents had named her Dawn because it was the most hopeful word they could conjure. Dawn held the promise of the sun rising over the horizon; it ushered in all the glorious possibilities of a new day.

She'd felt as if her mom and dad had been by her side throughout her journey, as close yet ephemeral as shadows, but never had she sensed their presence so powerfully as now, when she sat on a wooden bench in a small, snowy park. Instead of feeling hunger gnaw at her, or the cold seeping in through her cheap coat, she was remembering an evening when her mother had been summoned by an urgent pounding at their door.

A family of six was eating dinner in an apartment one floor below theirs. It took a moment for the parents to realize their youngest boy wasn't joking around, that his frantically wiggling body and scratching at his throat signaled real trouble. He was choking.

"Bring my kit very fast," her mother had shouted to Dawn as she'd fled down the narrow staircase. Dawn had found the kit in the hall closet, where it was always kept, and she'd followed, the heavy metal case banging against her legs with every step. She'd hurried through the open door in time to see her mother standing behind the little boy, jerking him into the air, her fists pressing into his soft belly. Once, twice, three times . . . His arms had fallen limply to his sides as his lips turned blue.

In the background a woman had screeched into the phone, giving a 911 operator their address again and again in heavily accented English, as if the repetition could make an ambulance come faster. But Dawn's mother had been calm, her movements fluid and economical. She'd placed the boy on the floor, reached into the kit Dawn had already opened, and slipped on a pair of surgical gloves. She'd felt around the boy's neck, zeroing in on a precise area and keeping her index finger pressed there while she reached into her kit again, this time for a scalpel.

"I need a straw, like for drinking," she'd said, her voice carrying authority and quieting the murmuring crowd. By now, other neighbors had jammed into the apartment and were straining to see. Someone had raced off and come back clutching a fistful of straws from McDonald's, still in their paper wrappings, which they must have had stockpiled in a kitchen drawer. Dawn had taken one and opened it, then handed the slim plastic tube to her mother. Despite her fear of what might happen next, she'd been fascinated by this side of her mom. She'd watched countless times as neighbors, mostly fellow immigrants who couldn't afford health care, came begging for help: a migraine, a gash that required cleaning, a case of pneumonia . . . Dawn's mother had never turned anyone away, no matter how tired she felt or how late the hour. She'd spent money she could ill afford stocking and restocking her metal kit with bandages and painkillers and sutures.

This was different, though. The boy was very still now, and someone in the crowd was wailing. In the distance Dawn could hear the matching wail of an ambulance siren, but it sounded far away. It was rush hour; it could take long minutes for the vehicle to fight through traffic.

Her mother didn't hesitate. She made a small slice into the boy's neck, her fingers as steady as ever. Dawn watched as her mother slid the straw into the opening she'd created and blew into it until the boy's chest began to rise and fall on its own. Whatever magic her mother had performed had saved his life.

Later that night, Dawn had overheard her parents talking, their words flying fast and fluid in their native language. Her mother had been terrified to risk the procedure she'd only seen a doctor perform once—so much could've gone wrong, she'd said, and she could've been blamed for the boy's death, even though it was already imminent. But that hadn't stopped her from doing the right thing. She'd known there was a blockage in the boy's throat, and she had to create an airway before brain death set in. She'd risked her own safety to try to safeguard his.

The boy had come home from the hospital a few days later with a small scar on his throat, and his family had brought a bouquet of daisies to Dawn's mother. It was all they could afford, but the boy's mother had dropped to her knees and kissed Dawn's mother's hand again and again as she cried.

Dawn's father's life had contained no such splashy events. His heroics had been quieter and steadier—countless, numbing shifts at the grocery store, picking up items off the conveyor belt and packing them neatly into brown paper sacks. He'd smile and politely thank every customer, even the ones who talked on their cell phones and accepted the bags without bothering to make eye contact. Then he'd come home and slide off the brown dress shoes he always wore to work. He'd ease his aching feet in a tub of hot water, the blue veins on his ankles and calves bulging, and he'd released a sigh. Later, Dawn's mom would dress his blisters and cracked toenails with a salve she'd concocted herself, and the next day, he'd get up and do it all over again.

Her parents had never shied away from a challenge. They'd never given in to fear. Dawn now realized that she wouldn't be able to live with herself if she succumbed to it. What kind of life would she have, anyway? Always running, always starting when she saw someone who looked like Tucker, feeling guilty whenever she spotted a police officer . . . She'd tarnish her parents' hard-won legacy.

She stood up and walked back to the drugstore. Miraculously, Peter's Honda was still parked in front.

"Hi," she said, climbing in.

He'd been on the phone, but he put it down quickly when she opened the door. She braced herself for a barrage of questions, maybe some annoyance. But instead, Peter made a joke: "That took a little longer than I expected."

Dawn began to laugh, a deep, rolling sound that started low in her stomach. Peter joined in after a moment, and Dawn giggled harder, feeling her entire body shake. She'd forgotten how good it felt to laugh.

"I'm really sorry," she said. "Can we go home now? I'll explain on the drive."

She'd have nearly an hour to fill him in, to let him know Tucker might be nearby and that she wanted to stop hiding. She'd tell Peter she was going to figure out a way to make this end soon.

The next morning, when Kira padded into the kitchen in her slippers and pajamas to make coffee, she glanced out the window and stopped short. The landscape had been transformed again by another six inches of snowfall. It didn't matter that the B-and-B was cozy and pleasant, that she had a drawer full of new wool socks, that fires always crackled in the hearth. There seemed to be a draft in the kitchen, a tiny gap around the edges of one of the windows, or the back door, or maybe even in the very walls. Rand never could find it, but Kira swore thin, icy fingertips reached in and wrapped around the back of her neck while she worked early in the mornings. Cold snuck deep into her bones and settled there when she stared out at icy mounds that were once trees and shrubs, and when she heard the wind moaning like it was in pain.

While she waited for the coffee to brew, she flipped through the three-ring binder that was her lifeline in planning the wedding. She paused on the printed list of RSVPs that Jessica had forwarded. The majority of guests had picked salmon, with just twelve requests for pasta primavera so far. Jessica had managed to cap the guest list at a little over a hundred, but it looked like most of the guests were actually going to make it.

More snow could be troublesome, Kira thought. What if the plows couldn't climb the hill to the B-and-B? She needed to look into hiring a private plow for the days leading up to the wedding. She made a notation on her ever-growing to-do list at the front of the binder.

She filled a mug with French roast and took it back into her bedroom, shutting the door quietly so it wouldn't wake Peter. He and Dawn had returned from their outing just before dinnertime the previous evening, and she'd been too busy preparing the après-ski package for their six guests to find out what had happened. And, to tell the truth, she'd been too miffed to want to talk to Peter. She'd gone to bed early and had pretended to be asleep when he came in.

Now she eased down next to her husband, being careful not to jostle the bed and wake him up. She would've liked to curl up on the sofa in the living room, where it was brighter and prettier, but she hadn't even brushed her teeth or combed her hair yet, and she didn't want to bump into Rand or Dawn or any of the guests. It was one of the complications of the living situation that she'd anticipated, but it annoyed her more than she'd expected right now. Or maybe she was still irritated by Peter and Dawn's disappearance together yesterday.

Kira took a sip of her dark roast coffee, then glanced over at Peter. She was startled to realize he was already awake, staring up at the ceiling.

"Happy anniversary," he said, his voice early-morning husky.

It wasn't the date of their wedding but the one that marked the beginning of their relationship:

They'd bumped into each other at their old high school, where they'd both gone to sit on the bleachers at sunset for different reasons. Each had been startled and a little embarrassed to discover the other, at least at first.

"Happy anniversary," Kira repeated. *And a sad one, too,* she thought, as her annoyance with her husband melted away.

"Are you thinking about your mom?" she asked, and he nodded.

Peter had gone to their high school to mourn his mother on the one-year anniversary of her death, because he couldn't think of another place that would be deserted on a Sunday night. Kira had arrived moments after him. She'd left college to come home for a long weekend, feeling exhausted, overwhelmed, and worst of all, ordinary. She'd been a standout in high school, but now she was just another pretty face. No one cared about her history as a straight-A student or her old track record. All the achievements she'd held so dear suddenly seemed embarrassingly childish. She'd felt drawn to the place where she'd once mattered.

"Oh!" Kira had exclaimed, startled, when she'd spotted Peter on the top row of the bleachers, his elbow resting on his knee and his chin in his hand.

He'd turned to look at her. "Hi, Kira," he'd said, and she'd fumbled for his name before he'd saved her. "It's Peter. Peter Danner."

"Of course," she'd said. His acne was gone and his voice was deeper, but she would've remembered eventually.

Funny, she'd thought, but the Peter of high school had become the her of today: someone who didn't stand out or command attention; someone not terribly memorable.

She'd wavered for a moment, unsure of whether to sit down. Then she'd noticed him wiping tears off his cheeks.

"Are you okay?" she'd asked.

He'd exhaled. "It's been a rough day," he'd said.

"For me, too," she'd told him, sitting down a few feet away from him. Here was the field where she'd practiced endless cradle catches and spread-eagle jumps, where she'd ridden around the track on the back of a red pickup truck after being named a homecoming princess, waving to the crowd and soaking in the applause. That green field looked so much smaller now.

"What happened to you?" she'd asked.

"It's the anniversary of my mother's death," Peter had said. Kira had heard through the grapevine that Peter and Rand had lost their mother, but she didn't know any details.

"I'm really sorry," she'd said. "Was she ill?"

He'd nodded. "Cancer."

She hadn't known how to respond, so she'd slid closer to him. He'd been really good in math and science, she'd remembered, and had written a funny quote under his photo in the yearbook. What was it again? It had made her laugh when she'd read it over the summer after graduation.

"Your turn," he'd said.

"My reason seems kind of stupid, compared to yours," she'd said.

"Oh, sure, leave me hanging," he'd said.

A thought came to her suddenly: *He's safe.* Peter would keep her confidence, and more important, he wouldn't laugh or make her feel small. The realization had set the words tumbling out of her.

"High school was wonderful," she'd said. "I felt so sure of myself. That's what I miss the most: knowing I belonged. I had a spot at a lunch table with my friends, and there was always cheer practice or a science project and something I needed to do. But now?" She'd shaken her head and looked out at the field again. It was barren and desolate without the bright lights and screaming crowds and loud, excited voice of the football announcer.

"It's like my future opened up—that wonderful, exciting future everyone kept talking about my whole life—and I'm getting lost in it," she'd said.

She'd begun to cry—not quiet, gentle tears like Peter's but big sobs that shook her body. How embarrassing, she'd thought. He was the one dealing with a real tragedy; she was just grappling with some ordinary generational angst. Yet here he was, putting a hand on her shoulder and telling her everything would be okay, like her problems mattered.

"We need ice cream," he'd said after she'd cried herself out. "My mom always used to give me a scoop when I got hurt. She made the homemade kind, and she created flavors. Sliding Superheroes was my favorite."

"Ice cream sounds really good," Kira had said, then she'd laughed. "Sliding Superheroes?"

"It had bananas in it," Peter had said, "and she told me the superheroes would slip on the peels."

He'd laughed, too, but his eyes had still held pain. They'd stood up and walked to his car, leaving hers in the parking lot, and they'd driven to a Ben & Jerry's and found an empty booth. She'd felt completely comfortable with calm, gentle Peter, who held doors open for her, put a dollar in the empty tip jar, and offered her the first taste of his milk shake, then put his mouth on the straw where hers had been just moments before.

She'd savored every bite of her sundae and then dotted her lips with a paper napkin. Peter's mother had been a wise woman: Ice cream did make everything better, especially when hot fudge and whipped cream were involved.

"Can I . . . ah . . . call you sometime?" Peter had asked after he'd driven her back to the high school to retrieve her car. It had been dark out then, and her body had felt loose and heavy from the release of crying. Suddenly, she didn't want the evening to end. By Peter's side, she felt as if she mattered again.

She'd rested her hand atop his, her fingernails just grazing his knuckles, already knowing that later, they'd jokingly argue about who had made the first move. "Sure, you can call me. How about tomorrow?"

He'd stared at her for a moment before smiling back. His eyes were a light shade of blue—almost a violet, in certain lighting—and he had a strong jawline. At that moment, she'd remembered his yearbook quote, the one that had made her wish they'd been friends back in high school: "Sometimes I think the surest sign that intelligent life exists elsewhere in the universe is that none of it has tried to contact us—Calvin and Hobbes."

Of course, if they'd been friends or had dated in high school, their love might have burned out long ago and they wouldn't be here now, living in Vermont. Trying to find their way toward a better life together.

"It snowed again," Kira said, getting out of bed and drawing back the curtains. She wanted to get a little light into the room. "See?"

"That'll be good for business," Peter said, but his voice sounded flat.

Kira knew from experience that her husband would spend much of the day thinking about his mother, remembering how he'd held her hand as his father had paced and Rand had driven to the house, arriving an hour after she'd taken her final breath. Their mother had been cremated and her ashes tossed into the ocean she'd loved, so there was no grave to tend, nowhere to send flowers. Only old memories to revisit.

Kira curled up next to him and put her head on his shoulder and stayed there for a long time, her coffee forgotten. She must have fallen back asleep, because the next thing she knew, the room was much brighter and someone was rapping on the door and calling her name.

"Oh my God!" she blurted, sitting bolt upright. "I forgot to make breakfast!"

She jumped out of bed and ran for the door. Rand was standing there, holding her cell phone, his hand muffling the receiver.

"What time is it?" she asked.

"Nine," he answered.

"The guests!" she moaned.

"It's fine, they all just headed out to the ski slopes," he said. "Dawn made breakfast. But listen, I think it's the adoption agency calling."

Kira instantly went still. She could hear Alyssa shuffling down the hallway; she must've overheard Rand and be desperate to learn the answer to the most important question of her life.

Kira reached for the phone.

Chapter Twenty

Alyssa was reclining on the sectional couch, her legs propped up and two pillows tucked under her head, but she might as well have been turning cartwheels, or leading a brass marching band, or skydiving. Exhilaration coursed through her body, sweeping away her accumulated pain and tension.

Their adoption agency had no pregnancy-related rules. Rand could go alone to get Grace. Her daughter was safe!

She would never ask for anything again; she'd never complain, or take a single moment with either of her children for granted. She ran a hand across her belly, sending light and love to her baby: *You're going to have a sister. You'll have each other for your entire lives.*

"It's incredible!" Kira said. She hadn't stopped moving since she'd heard the news. She fluttered past Alyssa again. "Water! You should have something to drink. Remember the doctor said you needed to stay well-hydrated."

She ran into the kitchen, then popped back out again.

"Or would you rather have juice? Or herbal tea?"

"Juice would be great," Alyssa said. "Thanks."

Kira came out with a glass of pineapple juice. "How about a snack? Some cheese and crackers? Or I could put together a fruit plate with yogurt. The protein might be good for you."

"I'm fine," Alyssa said, laughing. "Really."

She took a long sip of juice and looked across the room, to where Rand sat on a big chair adjacent to the fireplace. She could still see conflict creasing his face, but she wasn't going to worry about that, not right now. This was a day to celebrate her children.

"So you'll go to China alone?" Peter was saying to Rand.

"Yep," Rand said.

"When do you think you'll get the call?" Peter asked.

Rand shrugged. "A few months, I guess?"

"More like a few weeks," Alyssa interjected.

She watched as Peter looked back and forth, staring at her and then Rand as long moments passed. Something in Peter's face changed. He must've read the energy between them, Alyssa thought.

"What's up, man?" Peter asked. "Grace is coming and the baby's doing okay, too."

Rand didn't answer him.

"I mean, I figured you'd be more excited about becoming a father," Peter said, an edge sharpening his voice. "A lot of people would be thrilled, you know."

"Cookies!" Kira jumped up again. "Let's forget calories today. I made some chocolate-chip ones. I'll bring them out."

She hurried back into the kitchen.

"Peter, it's . . . kind of complicated," Alyssa interjected.

Peter leaned back in his chair. Agitation seemed to be vibrating off him in jagged little waves. Where was Kira? The brothers kept glaring at each other, but no one was saying anything.

Alyssa reached for her juice again, just to have something to do, then her hand stilled. She felt as if fizzy, carbonated bubbles were tickling her stomach from within.

"Oh." She gasped softly as she realized what had just happened.

She'd felt her baby kick for the first time.

She cupped her hand around her belly, wondering if he or she could sense her touch. How could life treat her so bountifully? How could one woman be so blessed?

She felt tears begin to trickle down her cheeks, but before she could say a word, she noticed Peter staring at her again, then leaping up out of his chair and stalking across the room toward Rand.

"You're fucking kidding me," he said. "You're bailing."

"What?" Rand asked, looking up and blinking a few times. He appeared dazed.

"That's why she's crying. That's why you're

not excited. Bailing. Someone who fails to appear when you need them. Someone who disappears," Peter said. "Or do you need me to explain it again using smaller words?"

Rand leapt to his feet, towering over his brother. "You have no idea what you're talking about, so back off."

Both men were using their history together as weapons, Alyssa realized. Peter was insulting Rand's intelligence, and Rand was demonstrating his physical dominance over his younger brother.

"He leaves when things get tough, Alyssa," Peter said. He was addressing her, but he kept his gaze locked on Rand. "That's what he does."

"Peter!" Kira was standing on the threshold of the room, holding a platter of cookies, a shocked look spreading across her face.

"You quit the football team in the middle of the season senior year when they started giving your backup quarterback more time. You faked an injury. When Dad got you that job at a construction company, you only did it for a week because you didn't feel like getting up at five A.M., even though he'd called in a favor to help you."

Alyssa was too stunned to say anything. Peter must've been suppressing his emotions for years, judging by the force with which they were gushing out now. Peter's face was turning red, and his fists were clenched at his sides. He looked like a completely different man from the one who'd hugged her earlier, and whispered in her ear that he was going to spoil both of her kids rotten.

"He's got ADD about life; nothing holds his attention. I'm surprised he's lasted here this long, to be honest. I figured he'd go after a few months and we'd stay on alone. I was kind of hoping that would happen, actually," Peter said.

"Peter!" This time Kira's voice was firm instead of shocked.

Alyssa turned to her in relief. Kira would get Peter to stop before he inflicted more pain on Rand. Couldn't he see his older brother was truly hurting?

"Your mom wouldn't want this," Kira was saying. "Especially not today."

"She's right," Alyssa said hastily. "She'd be happy her grandchildren were coming, and she'd want us to be happy, too."

"Kira wasn't talking about that," Peter said. He looked at Rand and waited for a beat.

"Unbelievable," Peter finally said. "You don't remember."

Rand started. "Oh, shit. Is today . . . ?"

"Mom died ten years ago today," Peter said.

The look on Rand's face was so wretched Alyssa nearly gasped.

"I fed her when she was too weak to eat! I washed her! I read to her!" Peter shouted. "Do you know what it was like to hear her cry out in pain and not be able to do anything? No." He narrowed his eyes. "Of course you don't."

Please stop, Alyssa thought, feeling as powerless as if she were a pedestrian watching a terrible car accident unfold.

"She couldn't breathe well at the end," Peter was saying. His loud words seemed to be hitting Rand like physical blows. "She was . . . gasping. It sounded like she was being tortured. Like someone was punching her over and over again."

Rand just stood there, Peter's words raining down on him, his shoulders slumping. He seemed unable to meet his younger brother's eyes.

"I turned up the morphine drip when she needed it," Peter said. His voice broke on his final words: "I held her hand when she died."

The room was absolutely still for a moment, then Rand released a noise that Alyssa could describe only as a kind of anguished roar.

"I didn't get to say good-bye!" Rand yelled.

He launched himself at Peter, knocking his brother against the coffee table before they tumbled to the floor. A vase fell off the mantel and shattered.

"Stop it!" Alyssa cried. She started to sit up, remembered the baby, and forced herself to relax her abdominal muscles. The guys were rolling around on the floor now, grappling, the cords in their necks standing out.

"Peter!" Kira was screaming, but neither man seemed to hear her.

And then Rand stopped fighting. His hands fell to his sides and he allowed his brother to pin him. Peter hit him in the face once, twice, three times. Blood began trickling down Rand's nose, and still he made no move to defend himself or to knock Peter off.

Finally Peter pulled back and rested his hands on his knees. He was breathing hard, and his glasses were crooked.

Rand lay there for a moment, pieces of shattered glass all around him, then he sat up slowly. His baseball cap had fallen off, and his hair was messed up, revealing the bald spot he'd been trying so hard to hide. The small white patch stood out so clearly against the dark of his hair.

"He's right," Rand said, looking at no one. "About everything."

He stood up and walked out the door without his coat.

"Rand!" Alyssa called. She wanted to run after him, but she couldn't move.

Peter began picking up broken pieces of vase and putting them on the coffee table. She could see his hands shaking.

"I'm sorry, Alyssa," he said, not meeting her eyes. "I guess it's better you know now, though."

Chapter Twenty-one

Something bad must have happened in the brief sliver of time between the guests' breakfast and Dawn's return to the kitchen after taking a shower.

Dawn had woken early that morning with a nagging sense of guilt about abandoning Kira. Kira was clearly annoyed; when Dawn and Peter had returned from the FedEx place, the guests had been finishing up an après-ski spread in the living room and Kira had been at the sink, scrubbing a platter with more vigor than necessary.

"Can I help?" Peter had offered.

"I'm almost done," Kira had said, her voice driving home a larger point.

So Dawn had rushed into the kitchen as soon as she'd woken up to start a full pot of coffee and set the table for breakfast. By seven-thirty, Kira hadn't materialized, so Dawn had sliced strawberries and arranged them in ramekins with shards of fresh mint, then she'd fed oranges into the juicer. She'd found a few containers in the freezer labeled *Emergency guest breakfast!* and she'd chosen the one that held batter for blueberry pancakes.

She'd been frying bacon when Rand wandered in—was there any man on earth who wasn't drawn to a kitchen by the smell of bacon cooking? Perfumers should bottle the scent; single women would snap it up.

"Morning, sunshine," Rand had said, stealing a slice.

"Hi," Dawn had responded. "Have you seen Kira?"

Rand had shrugged. "Dunno. Maybe she's sleeping in."

"Good," Dawn had said. "She deserves it. I've got breakfast under control."

"So I see," Rand had said. "I'll just do a little quality control to assist you." He'd taken another piece of bacon and she'd shaken her head but smiled.

A few minutes later they'd heard guests' footsteps clomping down the stairs and Dawn had rushed to finish the pancakes while Rand went to pour coffee.

Dawn had cleaned the kitchen while the guests ate, then, after they'd left to hit the slopes, she'd slipped off to take a shower in the only unoccupied guest room. She'd taken much longer than usual, scrubbing her hair twice and soaping her entire body, then finishing with a long, icy spray. The water had given her a sense of renewal, and she'd reveled in it. She'd been like a frightened little bunny, hiding in the tall grass so the hawk soaring overhead didn't spot her—but yesterday had marked a turning point.

She was going to fight back, starting right now.

Except . . . what had happened while she'd been trying to scour away the last traces of her former self? Alyssa was lying on the couch, red-eyed and staring out the window, while Peter knelt on the floor, picking up pieces of glass. Kira was holding a platter of cookies—which seemed strange, since it wasn't even 10:00 A.M.—and everyone looked a little dazed.

"I can get the vacuum cleaner," Dawn offered, and they all turned to her with startled expressions.

"For the broken glass," she explained when no one responded.

"Thanks," Peter said. "I'm going to . . ." His voice trailed off as he left the room. Kira set the cookies down on the coffee table and hurried after him.

Uh-oh, Dawn thought. Something bad, or strange, had definitely happened. It seemed to be still happening. Alyssa would've rushed to the hospital if it involved the baby, so that couldn't be it. Where was Rand? Dawn wondered. Maybe he and Alyssa were still fighting.

She sensed Alyssa wouldn't welcome questions right now. So Dawn silently vacuumed up the broken glass and brought the cookies back into the kitchen and covered them with a sheet of Saran Wrap. She paused, catching sight of the knives Kira kept in a butcher-block stand.

She listened for a moment to make sure no one was coming, then she eased one out, watching the way it gleamed as it caught the light. Kira would notice if this one was missing from the set, but Dawn knew which kitchen drawer held extra knives. She chose one that was thick and serrated, with a six-inch blade. It came with a plastic protective cover, so she could carry it in her purse, and sleep with it under her pillow.

Kira was perched on the edge of the bed, waiting for Peter to come out of the bathroom. Her mild-mannered husband had erupted like a bomb, and she was still stunned.

She'd always prided herself on being a fixer, but she was flummoxed. Peter and Rand had never been close, but now she wondered if they'd ever speak to each other again. And those things Peter had said, about Rand abandoning Alyssa— could they possibly be true? Alyssa hadn't disputed them, but then, things had unfolded so quickly and violently that maybe she hadn't had the chance.

Kira realized her hands were shaking. She'd known some of what Peter had gone through in caring for his mother, of course. But she hadn't realized how vivid and painful those moments still felt to him. The look on his face, when he'd told of his mother crying out in pain . . . Kira knew it would always haunt her.

She heard the bathroom door unlock, and Peter stepped out. He stopped short when he saw her. His knuckles looked raw, and his face was still flushed.

She didn't hesitate. She stood up and wrapped her arms around his neck and held him. After a moment, his rigid body softened. But then he pulled back. "Is Alyssa okay?"

"I don't know," Kira said.

"The stress probably isn't good for the baby," Peter said. "Maybe I shouldn't have . . . Oh, hell, I just can't believe he forgot. Anything that doesn't fit into Rand's selfish little life gets pushed aside and ignored. What's he think he's going to do when he turns fifty? Play his guitar and pick up girls at bars and ride his motorcycle? Is he still going to be switching jobs and apartments every few months when he's sixty?"

"I don't know," Kira repeated. Peter seemed to be getting agitated again.

"Do you want to go for a walk?" she suggested. "Just get outside and breathe some fresh air for a while?"

He shook his head.

"It'll do you good," she urged. "I know this is such a tough day for you . . ."

"Kira, I said I don't feel like it, okay?" he barked. She took a step back.

"Look," she said. "I know you're furious with Rand. And he was wrong to have disappeared when your mom was sick. It was so unfair that you were left to deal with all that, okay? Your dad should have helped, too, even if they were separated. But I think Rand tried to make up for it by giving us a share in the B-and-B. I think he's sorry—"

"I can't believe you're defending him," Peter interrupted. "Didn't you see Alyssa crying? And Rand acts like he couldn't care less about the baby and Grace. You and I are the ones running around and bringing Alyssa meals and doing everything. You know what he did the day after they got back from the hospital? He took a four-hour hike. And he's always in the garage, doing his own thing, while she has to lie in bed. Tell me he isn't the most selfish person alive."

"I'm not defending him," Kira protested. "But he's dealing with a lot . . . the risk to the baby and everything. Maybe he's just scared."

She fell silent, realizing she was handling this all wrong. Peter seemed to be growing even more upset.

"Why did you want to move here, Kira?" he asked.

The abrupt turn in their conversation startled her. "I . . . I don't know," she finally said. "Mostly for a change, I guess . . . Remember, we didn't even think much about it. We just decided to do it. To be spontaneous."

He nodded slowly. She couldn't see the color

of his eyes, and a shiver ran down her spine. She wanted to turn on a lamp, but she felt locked in place by the intensity of their conversation.

"Why did you want to come?" she asked. Had they really not talked about this before?

There were so many reasons she expected he could give: that he thought it would be a good place to have a baby; that it was a smart financial move; that he wanted to get closer to Alyssa and Rand—although she was pretty sure she could rule out that last reason now. But the words he uttered were so completely unexpected that it took her a second to comprehend their meaning, as if she were underwater, listening to blurry, distorted sounds that were more like echoes of words that came from far away.

"I didn't want to move here," he said.

"But you told me we should!" she cried. "You said so that very first night when Rand called!"

He nodded. "I know," he said, his voice steady, his eyes still opaque. "I liked living in Florida. And God knows I didn't want to be around my brother all the time. But you were constantly stressed-out, Kira. I thought it might . . . help you. Help us."

She ducked her head and took in a deep breath. Peter had done this for *her?*

"We're healthy, but we're not getting any younger," he said. "We have some savings. We own a third of this B-and-B, and yeah, business

isn't exploding but it isn't all that terrible either
. . . So why are you still taking those damn birth
control pills?"

"I just thought we'd give it this year," she
finally said, her voice weaker than she would've
liked. She tried to remember her reasons so she
could form a rational argument, but she felt too
unbalanced. Peter never got mad. What was
happening?

"I know *you* wanted that," he responded. "But
I didn't. I've already been waiting and waiting,
but you keep moving the finish line. When you
make partner, when you pay off all your loans,
when we've been here a year . . . Alyssa's having
two kids this year, and maybe she's going to do
it on her own, and she doesn't seem the slightest
bit worried about it."

Kira felt something ignite within her. "Don't
compare us!"

"I didn't mean it that way," Peter said. "But
why the hell is it so hard? People have babies all
the time. You know how much I want one."

"I've got to get through this wedding!" Kira
said. "It's coming up so fast . . . and Grace will
be here in another month or so, probably . . ."

"There's always going to be an excuse, isn't
there?" Peter said. He looked at her steadily for
a moment. She knew her mouth was gaping
open like a fish's, but she couldn't think of
anything to say. How had Peter gone from

being so furious with Rand to attacking her?

Peter didn't look angry, though, not anymore. He just looked desperately sad again.

"Okay," she blurted. "If you want me to, I'll throw away my pills. It's not that I don't want to have a baby . . . It's just— I don't—"

Peter studied her carefully. "What?" he asked when her voice stuttered to a stop. "What is it?"

"I don't know," she whispered. It was as if there was some kind of blockage, or dam, keeping her from taking the final step. The thought of tossing out her pills caused her heart to hammer in her chest.

"You need to find out," Peter said. His voice still held some metal, and she knew he wouldn't keep waiting for her, not much longer. She couldn't blame him.

Her cell phone buzzed, and she glanced at it instinctively.

"Jessica." She sighed.

"Better get it, then," Peter said.

She'd already picked up the phone and said, "Hello," before she realized that she'd chosen wrong again. She should have finished her conversation with Peter. He was walking out of the room, and Jessica was prattling on about needing special toasting flutes for the champagne and a quill pen for the guest book because it would be so much classier than a ballpoint one, and it was too late.

Chapter Twenty-two

The call from Donna Marin came at ten o'clock on a Friday morning. Snowflakes were falling outside of Alyssa's bedroom window, adding to the drifts leaning against the sides of the B-and-B. The forecasters had been right; it was going to be the snowiest winter in Vermont in years. Alyssa was cocooned in bed, staring at the view and feeling as if she were inside a snow globe.

"Your red letter arrived!" Donna's voice popped with excitement.

This must be her favorite part of her job, Alyssa thought. The red letter was travel approval, the final hurdle in the endless adoption process. All that was left was a sprint to the trophy, the grand prize, the miracle: Grace.

"You'll—I mean, Rand will—spend a week in her province, Jiangxi, and then the second week in Guangzhou, where you'll wait for the consulate appointment," Donna said, infusing the Chinese names with a flawless accent. "When would he like to go?"

"As soon as possible," Alyssa said. She was crying now, but she didn't try to muffle the sounds. Donna must be used to that reaction. "I'll talk to Rand and we'll call you later. Is that all right?"

"Of course it is," Donna said. She didn't sound like a prim young woman in severe glasses any longer. Donna had transformed in Alyssa's mind into a grandmother who smelled of talcum powder, one with pillow-soft arms and a ready smile. She'd been so kind when Alyssa had phoned to tell her about the pregnancy, immediately congratulating her and saying that Grace would be lucky to have a little sister or brother.

"It usually takes a few weeks to organize things, so don't book the tickets for tonight!" Donna was laughing. "But another two or three weeks should be safe."

"Thank you," Alyssa whispered before she hung up.

She lay back, feeling her emotions swirl like the snowflakes caught up in a gust of wind just outside her window. She'd fantasized so often about the moment she'd first see her daughter. She'd walk toward Grace slowly and then stop a few feet away, letting Grace get a good look at her. *Remember me?* Alyssa would think as the little girl's eyes traveled over her face. *We've always belonged to each other.*

She wouldn't try to grab Grace, or hold her, not right away. She'd move gently, reaching out a single finger to see if her daughter wanted to wrap a hand around it. She'd drink in every inch of her little girl, from her cap of shiny hair to her delicious nubs of toes.

She wouldn't bring her camera to that first meeting. She wouldn't need one. Every detail would be engraved upon her memory for the rest of her life.

And then, when Grace was ready—this was the part that made a hard lump form in Alyssa's throat—she would take her daughter into her arms, and inhale her smell. She would close her eyes and rest her cheek next to Grace's. Grace would be coming home, but in that moment, so would Alyssa.

Somehow along the way, Rand had slowly gone from having a costarring role in her fantasy to being relegated to the background. She'd subconsciously known all along that he was teetering on the edge of ambivalence about fatherhood, that this was all too much for him, too fast—two children, one with a very real risk of being born dangerously prematurely, one who'd come from an orphanage and might have adjustment issues or other emotional concerns.

She thought back to how easily he'd accepted the news that her appendicitis had probably caused infertility. What had he said, there in the parking lot, while she'd twisted her wedding ring around and around on her finger? She heard his voice as clearly now as if his words were a boomerang, swinging back at her: *Who needs kids anyway?*

She'd believed he'd let go of the idea of having

children so easily because he worried she'd blame herself for her infertility. She'd imagined his words were steeped in generosity and kindness and love. But she'd once heard that every joke contained a grain of truth. And now she recognized—or finally *let* herself recognize—that there was a hard nugget of it buried deep inside his lighthearted tone, like an unpopped kernel in a handful of fluffy popcorn.

She'd been the one to come up with the idea of adoption. She'd filled out all the paperwork, telling herself Rand's dyslexia would make it difficult for him to do so. She'd written their essay pledging to love Grace without his help for the same reason. She'd selected the photographs for their dossier, because she was the photography expert, after all. He'd gone along with everything, like a water-skier being pulled by a powerful motorboat.

She was still holding on to the phone when he brought in her lunch—a glass of lemonade, a dish of mixed berries, and a toasted cheese sandwich.

"Thanks," she said as he set the tray on the bed next to her.

Rand had come back quickly after his fight with Peter, which surprised her. She'd figured he'd disappear for a while, trying to outrun his emotions. But she'd still been on the couch when the front door opened and he walked inside, his lips tinged blue from the cold.

He hadn't said a single word. He'd just approached her and knelt down and rested his head on her lap.

She'd known he needed comfort, so she'd pulled the blanket off the back of the couch and tucked it over his shoulders and patted his back, like he was a little boy. He'd stayed like that for a long time, his cheek resting against her belly so that his head rose slightly with every breath she took. She'd been grateful when she'd seen Dawn start to enter the room with a dust mop in hand, then quickly wheel around to return to the kitchen.

"Do you need anything else?" Rand asked. He'd been subdued ever since his fight with Peter—his voice muted, his movements softer and slower. Rand had always seemed larger than life, but now he looked diminished.

"No, this looks wonderful. Kira always knows what I'm craving," Alyssa said.

"Actually, I made it," Rand said. "I know I'm not much of a cook, but . . ."

"Oh," she said, surprised. She took a bite of the sandwich. It was overbuttered and on the verge of burned, but she smiled appreciatively. "It's good."

She needed to tell him about the travel approval, but first she had to ask the questions that had been building in her mind.

"Why did you go ahead with the adoption if you had doubts? Why didn't you say, 'Hey, let's talk about this,' before I sent in the paperwork?" she asked.

He sat down next to her on the bed. "They told us it would take years and years," he finally said.

Rand never focused on the future, Alyssa thought. It was a quality they'd shared, until recently.

"So you figured your feelings would change?" she asked. She wasn't challenging him; she was truly trying to understand, and she made sure her tone conveyed that. "Or that it might not happen?"

"I don't know," he said. "I guess I just didn't think about it much. It just— It didn't seem real." He ran a hand over his forehead. "And now I can't stop thinking about it. We wouldn't even get to ease into it, to see if one was enough . . . And you can't get out of bed, and the damn snow never stops, and Kira's jabbering on like she's throwing the royal wedding, and I'm just—I guess I was feeling stuck."

She nodded.

"But I don't want to be that guy any longer," Rand said.

"What guy?" she asked.

"The guy who cops out when things get tough," he said.

"Oh, Rand," she said. Peter had needed to speak those words—he'd deserved to, even—but they'd cut Rand deeply. She reached out for her husband's hand, running her fingers over the rough calluses on his palm and tracing the wormlike scar in the crease between his thumb and index finger. He always had dirt or car oil under his nails, and one of the tips of his fingers was slightly misshapen from a long-ago carpentry accident. She loved his hands; they told stories about his life.

"I never stayed with a woman for longer than a few months, a year tops, until I met you. People can change, right?" he asked.

"I think so," she said. *I don't know,* she thought.

"Is it easy for you?" he asked. "All this? I'd go crazy staying in bed, but you make it look so simple . . . you don't have any doubts."

They'd always been in sync. He must've felt so alone with his fears.

"With Grace, yes," she answered honestly. "I fell in love with her the second I saw her picture. The baby took a little longer because I wasn't prepared for him or her . . . but I'm so happy about them both now, Rand. I really am."

"I messed up," he said. "I know that."

He reached out a hand and rested it on her abdomen, and she realized something: When he'd laid his head there after his fight with Peter, she'd thought it was because he needed comfort. But suddenly she knew he'd been trying to give something instead of taking it.

He'd been trying to form a connection with the baby.

．．．

"Have you seen my bread knife?" Kira asked as she crossed the kitchen and pulled open a drawer.

Dawn busied herself stirring a pot on the stove. "Which one is that?"

"The one with the blue plastic sheath," Kira said. "Remember you used it that time you hollowed out the mini–bread bowls for chili? I always keep it in this drawer, but I can't find it."

"I might've put it in the wrong place when I unloaded the dishwasher," Dawn said. Only Kira was organized enough to have a mental inventory of every single utensil and device in her kitchen, as well as dedicated places to keep them.

"Hmm. I just can't imagine where it went," Kira said, opening another drawer and rummaging through it. Kira had seemed especially agitated ever since the incident or argument or whatever it was that had transpired in the living room. Maybe it was just the fact that the wedding was approaching so quickly, but something bigger seemed to be going on, Dawn thought.

Kira turned to look at Dawn. "Hey!"

Dawn startled and nearly dropped the wooden spoon she was holding.

"Your glasses! You're not wearing them," Kira said.

"I don't really need them," Dawn said. "I just wore them because I thought they'd help me stay hidden."

"Well, you don't need to hide when you're here," Kira said. "You're perfectly safe."

Dawn thought of the knife tucked in an inside pocket of her purse and the way she'd begun to hear creaks as she lay in her sleeping bag at night. Sometimes the wind moaning outside sounded almost human. Her little room was comfortable enough, with the heaters and futon, and she'd added an old cardboard box draped with a bright cloth as a nightstand. Kira had given her a little lamp, too, but Dawn couldn't help noticing the light cast long, eerie shadows against the walls.

"I need to run into town and hit the grocery store later today," Kira was saying. "Want to come?"

Dawn took a deep breath. She hadn't had a chance to touch up her hair, and the light roots might make her stand out. People would probably remember a girl with a skunk-like stripe down her part. But she was through being intimidated by Tucker, she reminded herself. "Sure," she said.

The money would have arrived at the firm by now. Kay would have had to sign for the package, and Dawn knew her well enough to know curiosity would've gotten the better of her. She imagined Kay opening the box, reading the note, and peeling back the layers of newspaper to see those stacks of hundred-dollar bills. Kay would've marched into John Parks's office, her back straight and her expression serious, but inside she would've been bursting with excitement at being part of this intrigue.

The question was what John Parks would do next. He'd tell the police about the package, but would they be satisfied now that the money was back in its rightful place? Or would they intensify their efforts to find her?

"Let me review this one more time," Kira said, reaching for her wedding binder. "Then we can go."

"Is Peter coming?" Dawn asked.

She enjoyed having him around and felt the most comfortable with him of the foursome. But if Tucker was in town, it would also be good to have a guy there for Kira's protection.

She noticed Kira, the woman who never stopped moving, suddenly grow still.

"I doubt it," Kira finally said. "Why?"

Dawn shrugged. "No reason."

She tried to keep her voice light as she wiped down the counter, but she could feel Kira's eyes lingering on her.

Kira flipped through the pages, musing that Jessica's day was going to be a very long one. The flowers would arrive by noon, the cake would be rolled in at 2:00 P.M., and the ceremony would begin at 4:00—which meant guests might start coming as early as 3:00 P.M. So the B-and-B would have to be fully ready by then. No—

actually, everything needed to be finished an hour earlier, Kira realized. Jessica was spending the morning having her hair and makeup done in town, and she'd arrive with the rest of the wedding party by 2:00 P.M. to get dressed. If things weren't in place, Kira would hear about it. At length. Better to wake up even earlier, and scramble harder, than have to answer to Jessica.

Kira made a mental note to get a tray full of Jessica-tinis to the bride's room the moment she arrived. Better yet, she'd have Rand deliver them. That would either ward off potential problems or create a slew of new ones.

Rand had been making himself scarce since the brawl with Peter, but Kira noticed he was spending a lot of time in the bedroom with Alyssa, their door firmly shut. She couldn't stop thinking about Peter's prediction that Rand would desert his wife and kids. Surely Peter had a skewed perception because of his troubled history with his brother, Kira thought. Rand and Alyssa had been hit with so much overwhelming news in the past few weeks, and Rand's silence, his absences from the house—maybe it just meant he was trying to absorb everything.

Alyssa was facing the exact same news, though. You could argue that it was even more intense for her, since she was the one on bed rest, with a baby inside of her threatening to emerge dangerously soon. And Alyssa wasn't withdrawing; she was fighting for her kids. She'd never seemed more focused or intent.

The wedding, Kira thought, jerking her attention around again. She had to focus on the wedding. It was what was going to pull them all through this year, and even though Rand and Alyssa seemed carefree about money, when their children arrived they'd realize how important it was. In a way, handling the wedding would be a gift from Kira to them—a financial bonus when they needed it most. She just hoped they had good health-care coverage.

Kira walked into the living room and tapped her index finger against her chin as she surveyed the space. They were going to move out all the furniture the morning of the ceremony, except for a few chairs in case elderly relatives needed to sit down. Two local guys were bringing by a U-Haul, and they'd carry out the sectional couch, dining room tables, and benches—then carry them right back once the reception was under way. That way the guests would have room to cluster around while Jessica and Scott stood in front of the fireplace, exchanging vows.

As soon as the I dos were uttered, everyone would be ushered outside. The big white tent was scheduled to be delivered and set up on the front lawn a day before the wedding. Kira knew they'd need a window of time so Peter and Rand could get the chairs and tables into place for the dinner, the tables could be set, the sound system tested, the dance floor and the heaters arranged. But maybe she should ask the local guys to do all that, too, so that Peter and Rand could avoid each other, given their history at weddings.

Everything was under control.

A prosecutor, though? Why couldn't Jessica's father be a plumber, or a pediatrician, or . . . a zookeeper, for God's sakes? Out of all the hundreds of possible professions, he had to have the most dangerous one.

Kira realized she was biting her fingernails, and she yanked her hand away from her mouth.

She wondered why she was the only one of the four of them who was worried about the surcharge. She knew they deserved it; her thickening notebook was proof. But the idea that she was *taking* it chafed her.

Kira felt the beginning of a headache throbbing between her temples.

"You're going to be in the kitchen with me," she said to Dawn, "but we'll need to hire extra waiters and a bartender. Or two bartenders? I have no idea how many we'll need. I've never done this before!"

"I bet a local restaurant will let us hire a few waiters," Dawn said.

"Good idea," Kira responded. "Can you ask around when we get to town?"

She should've added on ten percent to Jessica's

proposal, not twenty! Ten percent would've been easier to justify.

"Okay," Dawn said. "How many do we need?"

"Hmm? Oh, let's see . . . A hundred guests," Kira said. "We'll have four different passed hors d'ouevres—I'm going to make a hundred pieces of each item—and there will be ten round tables under the tent."

"So four waiters?" Dawn suggested.

"Better make it five," Kira finally decided. "And two bartenders. I only budgeted for three and one, but we'll eat the extra cost. I thought we could have waiters circling the crowds with glasses of wine right after the ceremony, since most people drink wine at weddings. Then the guests can carry the drinks with them when they walk to the tent and they won't have to wait in line at the bar unless they want something else."

"Five waiters and two bartenders," Dawn repeated.

"Just . . . can you make sure they don't try to give us some seventeen-year-old?" Kira said. "Ask how long the waiters have been working there, how much experience they have . . . And make sure to tell the restaurant that we'll keep a copy of their menu here in the future to steer guests to them, as a way of thanking them."

"Okay," Dawn said. "No problem."

Why did Dawn want to know if Peter was coming with them? It rankled Kira that the two of them had spent so much time together lately, especially since she and Peter were barely speaking. She'd caught the way Dawn gazed at him with hero worship in her eyes, and how quickly she laughed at his jokes. And Peter seemed to be a little different around Dawn, too —more confident and verbal. It wasn't that she was jealous; she just wished things were better between her and Peter. How had they gotten so bad, so quickly?

"Should we go to town now?" Dawn was asking.

"Sure," Kira said. "I'll grab my coat and meet you at the car."

Kira hesitated, then went into the bedroom, where Peter was working on his laptop.

"Do you want to come into town?" she asked. "Dawn and I are going."

He closed his laptop. "Sure," he said, his voice brusque. "I feel like getting out of here anyway."

Kira felt a little sting of rejection. He wasn't coming because he wanted to be with her; he'd made that clear.

He followed her to the car, but instead of taking the seat next to her as she'd anticipated, he held open the door for Dawn, then climbed into the back.

"Oh, I can sit in the back," Dawn said.

"Nope, ladies get the front," Peter said.

Kira started the engine and shivered, rubbing

her hands up and down her arms. She wondered if Peter wanted to keep his distance from her. She'd invited him because she wanted to shake up the dynamic that had formed with Peter and Dawn's constant pairing off, but now she wondered if she'd made a mistake.

She pulled out of the driveway and realized the streets still had spots of snow and ice. She steered the car to the side of the road and turned to look at Peter. "Actually," she said, "would you mind driving? I get a little nervous in the snow."

"Sure," he said.

She switched places with him, climbing into the backseat. She tried to think of something to say, some joke to lighten the mood, but she came up empty. Then Peter reached for the radio to turn on music and her opportunity vanished. Her husband, the guy who never got upset, was still angry with her, and for once in her life, the girl who always had a plan didn't know what to do.

"So, do you want to know the gender?" Dr. Natterson asked.

Alyssa's eyes skipped from the ultrasound screen to the doctor's face. "You can tell?" she asked.

Rand had driven her to the hospital that morning for a routine checkup while she'd reclined in the front seat, dipping it as low as possible and propping her feet up on a stack of pillows so she could be close to a horizontal position. An orderly had met her at the entrance with a wheelchair and had pushed her to the exam room while Rand went to park the Jeep.

First Dr. Natterson had revealed the fantastic news that her cervix was hanging in there. Then he'd checked out the baby with an ultrasound. The little one was growing so quickly! Alyssa could make out the shape of its nose and its impossibly delicate, graceful fingers. They were the fingers of a pianist, or a sculptor, she thought.

"I can tell," Dr. Natterson confirmed.

"Wow," Alyssa said. "We haven't even talked about it . . . Rand? What do you think?"

"It's up to you," he said.

Wrong answer, she thought. She wanted Rand to show some excitement, to take a stand one way or the other. He could've said he was looking forward to the surprise, or that he was eager to know so they could start thinking about names. His nonanswer was a tremendous disappointment.

"Alyssa?" Dr. Natterson was saying.

"Let's wait for now," she said. She knew Rand was trying, but feelings were slippery entities with their own agendas. They couldn't be forced to fall into line, no matter how hard you wished for them to. The heaviness in her chest returned, and she turned her head to hide the expression she knew must be flooding her face.

"Sure," the doctor said. "You can always call me if you change your mind."

He removed the wand from her stomach and gently rubbed away the gel with a tissue. "Just keep on doing what you're doing," he said. "I'll see you next month."

Rand stood up from his chair, his knees making a little cracking sound. "I'll go warm up the Jeep and bring it around front," he said. "I'll call your cell when I'm there, okay?"

She nodded, and he left the room. She expected Dr. Natterson to follow him out, but he stayed seated.

"Is everything okay?" he asked, his voice gentle.

"Is it that obvious?" she asked, trying for a joke but knowing her tone was falling flat.

"Being on bed rest is incredibly difficult," he said. "A lot of women get depressed being stuck there month after month. If you need to talk to someone, I can give you a referral."

She shook her head. "It isn't that," she said. "My husband and I are having some . . . difficulties. Is that normal, too? Maybe it's one of the stages I haven't read about yet in *What to Expect When You're Expecting*."

Dr. Natterson smiled. "Sure, it can be tough on a marriage."

"I'm just not sure . . . I don't know . . ."

She gave up the pretense and succumbed to tears. "I'm worried Rand's only staying with me out of guilt," she sobbed. "I don't think he really wants to be here, even though he's trying to pretend he does. And I'm so scared it's not going to work out between us."

Dr. Natterson just nodded, as if he didn't find her words shocking or horrible.

"He's going to go to China to pick up Grace alone," Alyssa continued. "We just bought the tickets, and he's supposed to leave in a couple weeks. And I don't want her introduction to her new life to be a father who isn't sure he wants her. Kids are really bright. She'll probably pick it up."

She wiped her eyes with the sleeve of her hospital gown.

"What you said before, about bed rest being hard on me . . . It isn't, not really. Other than not being able to pick up Grace—that's the only bad part. But Rand's the one who feels like he's stuck."

"Maybe he should talk to someone," Dr. Natterson suggested. "Or couples counseling . . . you could find a counselor to do it over the phone."

"I guess," Alyssa said.

"I don't mean this to minimize what you're going through," Dr. Natterson said. "But I have seen it before."

Alyssa's head snapped up. "You have?"

"Sometimes parents completely freak out, for lack of a better term, around the birth of a child.

The advertising industry doesn't help—they make it look like all you have to do is give your kid a lavender-scented bubble bath and your problems will be solved. But the truth is, this is the biggest life change you'll probably ever endure. Some people are exhilarated by it, some are scared—there isn't any perfect reaction. But it's often a bumpy road."

Alyssa nodded.

"Give it a little time," Dr. Natterson said.

"Okay," she said. "Thanks."

She got dressed after the doctor left, and a moment later, a nurse came back with her wheelchair.

"Ready?" the nurse asked.

"I don't think my husband's here yet," Alyssa said. She looked at her cell phone. "He went to get the car."

What if Rand just kept going? she suddenly wondered. What if he eased the key into the ignition and pulled out of the parking lot and flicked on the car's right blinker instead of its left one? He could be in Canada in hours, or Mexico in a couple of weeks. He could continue with the kind of life he'd always wanted.

"I'll check in a few minutes, then," the nurse said. She had a hint of a southern accent. Alabama, maybe. Or South Carolina.

The bachelorette party.

Alyssa's thoughts flitted back to that event, as

they had so often lately. When she'd awoken the next morning after her heavy, dreamless sleep, Rand had been beside her, snoring loudly, the way he always did when he'd had too much to drink. She'd run her eyes over his strong features, the stubble on his chin, the hollow at the base of his throat that she loved. She'd leaned down to give it a kiss.

He'd smiled without opening his eyes and pulled her closer.

"You smell like beer and cigarette smoke," she'd said, nuzzling his chest.

"Mmmm . . ."

"Was it a late night?" she'd asked.

"Not really." He'd opened his eyes and stretched. "We got in around midnight. Maybe one."

Alyssa had immediately felt better. She'd never held tightly to Rand before, and she didn't intend to start doing so. She'd wanted to stay in, Rand had felt like going out—they were married, not conjoined twins, so what was the harm in that?

A few minutes later, she'd peeled herself out of his arms—he'd fallen back asleep—and gone into the kitchen to discover Kira layering yogurt, blueberries, and granola into parfait cups. Kira's granola was homemade, and had dried cherries and almonds and golden raisins in it. It was out of this world.

"Should I set the table?" Alyssa had asked.

"Dawn's doing that," Kira had said. "But

maybe you could squeeze some juice? I bet those girls need rehydrating."

"Rand said they didn't get in too late last night, so hopefully they're not feeling bad this morning," Alyssa had said.

"Well, yeah, but they were in the hot tub after that. Didn't you hear them shrieking and splashing?"

"I must've slept through it," Alyssa had said.

She'd finished gathering silverware and coffee mugs, then walked into the dining room. Rand wouldn't have gone in the hot tub with the girls, would he? That taste of tequila on his lips, Miss South Carolina's hand on the curve of her hip, a smile playing across her full lips as she asked Rand to fix Nutty Irishmen . . .

Knock it off, Alyssa had ordered herself. When she and Rand had begun dating, they'd both had to untangle themselves from other liaisons. Alyssa had met a guy from New Zealand during a round of her travels, and they'd spent a few weeks together in hostels and on beaches. He was working his way across the United States, and was planning to come visit her. And Rand had had a half dozen women chasing him; they called his cell phone incessantly, and showed up at his house late at night. Once, when Alyssa was lying in Rand's bed, still naked and flushed and sweaty after an incredible lovemaking session, a girl had pounded on the door. Rand had wrapped the sheet around his waist and gone out to talk to her. Alyssa could hear the girl growing belligerent and arguing, and she'd walked into the hallway to listen.

"I'm not going!" the girl had been yelling at Rand, her voice a mixture of anger and pain. "So why don't you get rid of *her?*"

"I'm sorry," Rand had said after he'd finally managed to ease the girl out the doorway, but Alyssa didn't think he had anything to apologize for. If he'd wanted to be with that other girl, Alyssa would have felt gutted—she was already in love with Rand by then—but she never would've begged. What was the point in trying to cling to someone who'd obviously moved on?

She'd reached into the refrigerator for oranges to juice, and by the time the girls had come downstairs in matching Juicy Couture sweat suits—apparently they'd purchased them specifically for the trip—the coffee was brewing and a platter of Kira's banana-pecan pancakes was warming in the oven. In the light of day, the girls had seemed so very young, and Alyssa had felt silly for her momentary worry.

Later, though, she'd helped clean up one of the guest rooms. When she'd gone to empty the trash can, Alyssa had noticed a crumpled piece of paper in it and something had made her reach for it.

It was a to-do list for the bachelorettes: *Drink*

a fuzzy navel! Get as many guys as possible to sign your shirts! Dance on top of a table!

Some of the items were checked off. Alyssa had continued reading: *Find a guy who can wiggle his ears! Do three different kinds of shots!*

And at the very end of the list was written: *Walk up to the hottest guy in the bar . . . and kiss him!*

That final item had a big check mark next to it.

Alyssa had crumpled up the paper and thrown it back into the trash can. So what if Rand had kissed one of the bridesmaids? A quick peck on the lips while the other girls cheered and giggled would mean absolutely nothing. She, Alyssa, sometimes kissed her male friends full on the lips when she greeted them.

She wasn't going to ask Rand about the hot tub. She wasn't going to ask him how much he'd had to drink. And she was going to forget she'd ever seen the list, she'd vowed.

She was still trying.

Chapter Twenty-three

By the time Kira and Peter returned from town, the color was leaching out of the sky, leaving behind a dull, oatmeal-gray swath, and the wind was like a whip. Dawn had told them she had something important to do and would take a cab back to the B-and-B.

"Are you sure?" Peter had asked. "We're not in a rush."

"You waited long enough for me the last time we ran errands," Dawn had said, and she and Peter had laughed together again while Kira had stood there, understanding the joke but not quite feeling in on it.

Dawn still wasn't back a few hours later, when the B-and-B's newest guests—a mother, a father, and their twin college-age daughters—arrived from the ski slopes, looking half-frozen and exhausted.

"I'm starving," one of the daughters whined, even though she was clutching a mug of the cocoa that Kira had handed out practically the moment the family came through the door. "Is it always this cold here?"

Terrific, Kira thought. Most visitors were pleasant enough, and some were truly likable— such as the young woman named Becca who'd come with her boyfriend for a ski getaway a few weeks back. Kira had loved chatting with them about their life in Los Angeles, a city that had always fascinated her.

She'd gotten good at sizing up guests quickly, and she already knew this family fell into the impossible-to-please category. Peter had carried their bags up to the guest rooms while Kira hurried to the kitchen to put the finishing touches on her tray of après-ski goodies. Everything was hot, as a rebuttal to the weather: a pot of cheese fondue, kept bubbling by a lit can of Sterno underneath, and surrounded by things for dipping. There were chunks of crusty farmer's bread, roasted Granny Smith apple slices, sweet potato wedges, and blanched asparagus spears with the ends artfully trimmed away.

She looked down at the platter that was worthy of a spread in *Gourmet* magazine, added a few more asparagus spears, and pronounced it perfect. She lifted the heavy platter and brought it into the living room.

"Just put it right here," the father said, gesturing to the coffee table.

"Finally!" a daughter said. Kira couldn't tell if it was the same one who had complained before; they looked exactly alike—long, blond hair; long, thin bodies; and long, unhappy faces. "I'm about to pass out!"

You're welcome, Kira wanted to say in a prim voice, but she merely set down the platter and returned to the kitchen. She pulled a pan of angel food cake out of the oven, saw that the edges had turned golden brown, and cut thick, fragrant slices. She fanned them out on a plate and started to bring the dessert into the living room, then circled back to the refrigerator and scattered a few ripe raspberries in the middle.

"Ouch!" one of the daughters cried as Kira came through the swinging doors with the cake. The girl dropped her fondue fork, and it clattered against the edge of the pot, sending a splatter of cheese onto the coffee table. She touched her lower lip and winced. "It burned me!"

"The cheese?" Kira blurted.

"No, the fork!" The girl looked at Kira accusingly.

"You should warn people about resting their forks near the flame!" the father said, frowning.

"But—I—" Kira began, then she took a deep breath. How was it her fault that the guests hadn't realized metal would heat up when it was placed next to a fire? God forbid this family ever went camping; they'd probably try to use their fingertips to toast marshmallows. Still, the customer was always right—wasn't that the hospitality industry's motto?

"I'm sorry," Kira finally said.

"Some ice," the mother commanded, her tone indicating Kira was an idiot for not having brought it already.

Kira put down the cake and hurried into the kitchen, her cheeks flushing. She grabbed the ice pack out of the freezer and wrapped it in a clean cloth, then steeled herself to go back into the living room.

She handed the ice pack to the girl, who accepted it without a word. "Just let me know if you need anything else," Kira said and escaped to the kitchen. Tears pricked her eyes. The jerks in the living room were treating her like a servant. They hadn't even commented on the meal she'd so carefully prepared!

She swept apple cores and bread crumbs into the trash, then gathered up the block of cheese and wrapped it up tightly in plastic before returning it to the refrigerator.

"Miss?"

She ducked her head so the father wouldn't see her tears. Not like he would care.

"We'd like some water."

"Be right there," she said, keeping her face averted as he let the kitchen door swing closed behind him. She wiped her face with a paper towel and blew her nose and washed her hands. She filled a pitcher from the tap instead of using the filter on the refrigerator, and stacked up four of the cheap plastic glasses they didn't usually give to guests, and she brought everything into the living room. She left it on the coffee table and exited without a word.

The family hadn't bothered to clean up the cheese splatter, even though they had plenty of napkins on the tray, she noticed. Well, she wasn't going to do it either. Let Dawn or Rand or Peter deal with the guests for the rest of their stay. Where were they, anyway?

She hurried down the hallway toward her bedroom.

"Peter!" The word shot out of her—half shout, half accusation—as she opened the door.

He was bent over his laptop, his expression intent.

"What are you doing?" she asked.

He set his laptop aside. "Hey," he said. "I was just checking something for Dawn. What's wrong?"

"The obnoxious guests are ordering me around. Why wasn't anyone helping me?"

"What do you need?"

"It's all done now," she said. She tried to peek at his computer screen, but he shut it.

"I was just trying to look up some legal stuff for Dawn," he said. "To keep her ex away."

Kira bit back the words: *Well, I'm glad you had time to help* her. She felt horrible for being so catty, but Peter had all but ignored her on the trip to town, and she'd been humiliated. Obviously Peter wasn't just feeling angry, as she'd tried to tell herself after their argument on the anniversary of his mother's death. He was angry with her, specifically.

"I've been meaning to talk to you about the background check for Dawn," Kira said. "Before we give Alyssa the info to pass on to the agency, maybe we should check her out first."

"Okay," Peter said. "I'll do it."

"You need to get Dawn's birth date and social security number," Kira said. She sat down on the bed. "It was a little odd . . . Did you notice how she flinched when I mentioned the background check?"

"No," Peter said. "I didn't."

"Well, she definitely flinched. She looked a little . . . not scared, exactly. But wary. Something seemed off."

"Hey, the woman's been through a pretty traumatic experience," Peter said. "It's understandable."

"No, it was more than that," Kira insisted. "And there's something else: A knife is missing from the kitchen."

"Kira, come on. Are you accusing Dawn of taking it?" Peter asked. "What, do you think she's going to slice us all up in our sleep?"

"We have no idea who she really is," Kira said. "Some con artists are really convincing. We need to be careful."

"She's a victim, Kira," Peter said, his voice almost as cold as the air outside. "And she didn't ask to stay here—we invited her. I practically had to beg her to stay after that first night."

Kira exhaled. How did their conversation get so off track? "All I'm saying is, we need to uphold the promise to Alyssa and Rand's adoption agency. It wouldn't be right otherwise."

"Well, I did a preliminary check and everything's fine," Peter said.

Kira turned to look at him. "You did? When?"

"A few days ago," Peter said.

"Why didn't you tell me?"

"Because nothing turned up!" Peter said. "Dawn's exactly who she says she is: a young woman who got abused by a really bad guy."

Kira was about to respond when she heard a sharp rap on the bedroom door: "Miss!"

She leapt at the sound. Had the guests overheard her conversation with Peter? She jumped up and opened the door. It was the mother of the group this time.

"We'd like some more water," she said.

What was she, a waitress? "I'll be right there," she said, forcing a smile.

"I'll do it," Peter said. He got up from the bed and left the room.

Exhaustion suddenly crashed down on Kira. She wanted to lie in her soft bed and sleep for a year, but she'd gotten two texts from Jessica within the last hour. They contained her song choices for her first dance with Scott as well as the one with her father.

Did you listen to them yet? Jessica had texted just a moment ago. *What do you think?*

Kira downloaded the songs to her iPod, wishing Peter would come back. Then she straightened the comforter on the bed and checked the laundry basket to see if she should run a load. The basket was empty, so she swept the spare change Peter always left scattered on the dresser into the little jar she kept just for that purpose.

A disturbing thought flashed into her mind: Her mother had always turned on the vacuum cleaner instead of engaging in difficult conversations. Was she, Kira, so determined to avoid becoming like her father that she'd overlooked the fact that she'd taken on some of her mother's traits?

She sat down on the bed and began to listen to Jessica's music. The first dance for the newlyweds would be lovely: Ray Charles's "Come Rain or Come Shine." It was an unexpected choice; she would've thought Jessica would select something contemporary and over-the-top rather than soulful. Kira was sorry when it ended.

Kira had never heard the song for the father-daughter dance before. In her text, Jessica had explained that her father had chosen it. Apparently he was content to let his daughter dictate every other detail of the wedding, but this song was important to him.

The music was by Paul Simon. His voice was gentle, but it soared into the room, filling the space:

I'm gonna watch you shine, gonna watch you grow, gonna paint a sign, so you'll always know . . . As long as one and one is two, there could never be a father who loved his daughter more than I love you.

The DJ for her wedding had asked which song Kira wanted for the father-daughter dance, and she'd told him there wouldn't be one.

She'd kept her composure when talking to the DJ, and she'd smiled when she walked down the aisle alone. So why, Kira wondered, was she crying now?

Chapter Twenty-four

Tucker was here.

The knowledge crashed into Dawn suddenly and absolutely. Had she spotted a glimpse of him in the distance—the cadence of his walk tripping something in her memory and sending an electric charge through her body? Or maybe there was a current traveling through the air, linking the two of them together. She reached into her purse to grip the knife, which suddenly seemed too small for defense.

She wheeled around and hurried back to the grocery store, telling Kira and Peter she was going to run errands after checking into hiring the waiters, and that she'd take a cab home. Then she went back out to look for Tucker.

She wasn't surprised, she realized, as she prepared to turn a corner, wondering if she'd come face-to-face with him. Vermont was a relatively short distance from New York, and she was hiding in a small town. Tucker was probably a gambler—Dawn had the feeling that could be why he'd needed so much money so quickly. Now, he was betting everything on finding her.

She looked into shops and cafés and peered down side streets, trying to formulate a plan, her father's wisdom about thinking more than one step ahead echoing in her mind. If Tucker approached her on the street, she'd scream for help. There were a ton of guys around, strong-looking men who'd spent the day engaged in physical activity. Surely one or two of them would come to her aid. What was Tucker going to do? Drag her off somewhere and threaten her?

Probably, she thought, and she tightened her grip on the knife. He wouldn't want the police involved any more than she did. He still thought she had the money, and he'd figure it would be relatively easy to get it back. He'd remember her as the mousy, quiet Dawn, pathetically eager for attention, still under his thumb.

She walked for hours, searching for a glimpse of his blond hair, her fingers and cheeks growing numb from the cold, an icy dampness seeping in through her cheap sneakers. The wind was picking up by now, but crowds still filled the sidewalks as people headed to the warmth of restaurants and bars.

Finally, as the sky darkened, Dawn called off her search. She needed to fulfill her promise to Kira and find waiters for the wedding. She stepped into an elegant seafood place, the sudden warmth as shocking as a slap, and asked to speak to the manager.

He approached her, smiling but looking harried, then stopped short, his eyes locked on her. After a beat, he closed the distance between them.

"Can I help you?" he asked.

Dawn explained about needing waiters and bartenders for the wedding, and the manager nodded.

"Why don't you come by tomorrow afternoon after I check schedules and I can give you a few names?" he said.

"We'd be really grateful," Dawn said. "And we'll keep a copy of the restaurant's menu at the B-and-B and steer our guests here."

The restaurant was busy, with waiters in white shirts rushing by with trays full of drinks and plates of food, and a cluster of people waited for tables by the hostess stand, but the manager didn't make any move to get back to work.

"What did you say your name was again?" he asked suddenly. She noticed his eyes shift to the scars on her cheek.

"Oh. It's D-Diane," she said, then she quickly turned and left.

Why had the manager hesitated when he'd first seen her? Dawn wondered, trying to analyze the look on his face.

Something told her to get away quickly. She managed to find a cab outside a hotel, and as the driver started toward the B-and-B, she scanned every person they drove past. She'd tell Peter about her suspicion, and she'd ask him to call the restaurant to get the names of the waiters. She wasn't going to return in person.

But as they got farther away from town, she began to doubt herself. She'd been on edge for so long. Paranoia could be warping her instincts. Still, if Tucker was showing people a photo of her, maybe telling a story about her being his long-lost sister, that could account for the manager's hesitation, and the strange look that had come into his eyes. Or Tucker could be pretending to be a private detective. Maybe he was saying there was a reward for information about Dawn. He was a terrific liar, after all.

She'd made a huge mistake. She'd told the restaurant manager the wedding would be held at a B-and-B. Luckily she hadn't said which one, but if Tucker really *was* searching for her, she'd just narrowed his search considerably.

Alyssa awoke before dawn, a burning sensation erupting in her chest. For a brief, terrified instant, she wondered if it was a heart attack. Then she remembered the lasagna she'd had for dinner. Heartburn, she thought, and she propped another pillow under her head. She suddenly felt wide awake, so she turned on her tiny reading lamp and picked up the journal she was keeping for the baby. She had one for Grace, too—a pretty fabric-bound book with unlined pages.

She wrote down all sorts of things that she thought her children might be curious about one day: her memories of the first time she'd seen Grace's photograph, the first time she'd felt the baby move, how the snow glittered when the early-morning light shone down on it . . .

She wrote for a long time, then set aside her children's journals. Rand was sleeping soundly beside her, but she wasn't tired.

When she'd first arrived home from the hospital, she'd wondered if she'd feel confined by bed rest, if it would chafe at her. Curiously, all her traveling was what had prepared her for it. She'd once spent three days on a rickety bus moving through India, squashed into a too-small seat next to a woman in a blue-and-gold sari. The woman had pulled fresh samosas out of a sack and handed one to Alyssa without a word, as Alyssa had admired the intricate henna patterns painted onto her seatmate's hands. When Alyssa had broken apart the golden, crispy crust, steam had wafted out, and the filling was studded with peas and chunks of potatoes. It was the best thing Alyssa had ever tasted. They'd ridden in silence for the rest of the trip, with nothing to occupy Alyssa's mind but the view out the window and the rhythmic snores of the old man across the aisle. She was practiced in the art of patience.

Alyssa picked up a novel from her nightstand and read a few pages, then dozed for what felt like a moment, but when she opened her eyes again, Rand was gone and a bowl of homemade granola with yogurt had appeared on her nightstand. Alyssa could smell the toasted oats even before she peeled back the Saran Wrap. Kira knew it was her favorite breakfast.

Poor Kira, Alyssa thought. The burden of the wedding was falling on her shoulders. Although Peter and Rand and Dawn were assisting, Kira was the one running the show, and Jessica had to be making her life difficult. Yet she'd never once complained to Alyssa. Instead she brought in trays of food, and left new books and magazines on her nightstand every time she went into town. She and Peter had even bought a DVD player for Alyssa's room—a pre-baby shower gift, Kira had said.

Alyssa was just scraping the last mouthful out of the bowl when the bedroom door slowly opened.

"Hey," Rand said as he stepped inside. Bits of snow clung to his eyebrows and hair. Just looking at him made her feel cold.

"Hey," Alyssa repeated. She put down her spoon, and it made a bell-like sound as it met the empty bowl.

"So . . . ," Rand said. He cleared his throat. He was still standing by the door, still wearing his boots and gloves. "I wanted to show you something."

He walked out of the room and came in a moment later carrying something. He set it by the window and then looked at her, apprehension on his face. "If you don't like it you don't have to use it . . . I just thought, it would be nice for both of them maybe . . . for Grace and the baby . . ."

It was a rocking chair, made of wood that seemed to glow. Soft amber mingled with lighter shades of butterscotch and honey. The arms were wide and generous, and there wasn't a sharp edge anywhere. The chair was a collection of graceful curves, one flowing into the next.

"The back braces are flexible, so it'll be comfortable even without cushions," he said. He shifted from one foot to the other.

This was why he hadn't been around much lately. He must have been in the garage, selecting wood and cutting it into the right sizes before fitting the pieces together. He'd been smoothing and shaping, easing away the splinters and rough edges, then polishing his creation until it gleamed.

"It's a little wider than most chairs, just in case

. . . I thought maybe if one of us were rocking the baby, and Grace wanted to sit there, too . . . see, there's plenty of room."

In just over a week, two days after the wedding to be precise, he'd go to China to pick up Grace Elizabeth Lopez-Danner. His ticket was on top of the bureau, along with his passport. Every time Alyssa looked at it, she felt a little stab of worry. Would Rand feel differently, once he'd seen Grace? Would he carry her in his arms as he wound his way through the final bureaucratic hurdles in China, making silly faces to get her to laugh, feeding her tastes of different foods, stroking her hair and staring down at her while she slept at night?

She'd gone online and lurked on some adoption chat groups, notably one with the headline *Help—my husband is freaking out!* A few women had rushed to give counsel, writing that their husbands—or they themselves!—had also panicked once the adoption was imminent, but that their fears had evaporated when the child came home.

It was so hard to know if this was a temporary state or if it would be a permanent one for Rand.

"Do you like it?" he finally asked. He touched the back of the chair to set it gently rocking.

At least this one question was easy to answer. "It's perfect," she answered truthfully, and she reached out her hand toward her husband.

Chapter Twenty-five

The wedding was one day away. Twenty-four hours! And everything was going wrong.

The huge tent that was supposed to arrive by noon and give them plenty of time to arrange the tables, chairs, bar, dance floor, and heaters had been "delayed" by the weather. *Delayed*—a slippery, disturbingly ambiguous word.

"So does that mean it'll be here this afternoon?" Kira had asked the nervous-sounding guy who'd phoned to deliver the news.

Silence.

"Tonight? Please don't tell me it'll be later than tonight."

Already they'd had to tweak their original plan of setting up the tent on the lawn. With the heaters and the weight of a hundred guests, it would sink into the snow, potentially suffocating their guests while simultaneously electrocuting them. Jessica wouldn't approve (unless she wanted to punish them for talking during the toasts). So now the tent would be placed atop their big paved parking area, which wasn't the classiest option, but what else could they do?

"We have no control over the weather," the tent rental guy was saying, which, ironically, was exactly what Kira had said when she'd told Jessica about the tent placement. "We're doing our best. We'll get it there as soon as we can."

Her phone had rung again seconds after she'd hung up on that call.

"Kira!" Jessica's voice was a shrill squeak of a teakettle emitting steam. "My grandfather and grandmother were supposed to drive in from Connecticut today but they can't because it isn't safe for them to drive with the snow and I don't know what to do. We can't have the wedding without them!"

Kira was concocting her third giant bowl of marinade for the salmon. She'd gotten up at 5:00 A.M. to make the stuffing for the figs, and she had a dozen butternut squashes rolling around on the countertop, waiting to be peeled and cubed and roasted and turned into spoonfuls of soup.

"Your grandparents," Kira repeated dully. She was squeezing limes into the marinade, and the acidic juice was stinging a tiny cut near her knuckle. Jessica's grandparents were two of the more complicated pasta primavera entrées, so Kira wasn't inclined to like them much at this point. *Stay home!* she wanted to shout at them.

"So . . . what would you like me to do?" Kira asked, struggling to keep an edge out of her tone. She half-expected Jessica to ask her to go pick them up.

"I don't know!" Jessica squealed. "My dad's trying to book them a flight instead, and then they'll drive to the wedding with him."

"So it sounds like it's all under control," Kira said slowly, trying to remember to breathe. She was Jessica's therapist now, too, which surely justified adding twenty percent to the bill.

"I guess so," Jessica said. "Ooh, Scottie's calling on the other line. Gotta run! I'll call you back!"

"Can't wait," Kira said into the dead receiver.

Private snowplows. She still needed to find someone with a private plow to make sure their road and driveway were constantly cleared. How could the sky contain so much snow? She finished squeezing the limes and rinsed her red, raw hands under warm tap water.

She looked over at Peter, who was on his computer, trying to book a shuttle bus to ferry guests from the bottom of the hill up to the B-and-B, since all the parking spots would be taken up by the tent and guests would have to leave their cars parallel-parked on the road.

"Any luck yet?" she whispered, and he shook his head.

She finished adding crushed ginger and lime to the three giant bowls and covered them with Saran Wrap. She stole a glance out the window: Thick, wet flurries were coming down as steadily as ever. It wasn't a record-setting storm, but to a warm-weather girl like herself, the sight of that relentless white was intimidating.

"I finished slicing the veggies for the pasta primavera," Dawn said, coming in from the dining room. "But some of the asparagus was turning brown . . . I don't think it'll be good tomorrow even if we keep it in the crisper."

"Let me see." Kira hurried out to the dining room. Dawn had used two big wooden cutting boards to protect the table as she sliced yellow and orange bell peppers and cherry tomatoes. Dawn was right—the undersides of about half of the spears of asparagus were turning soft and brown.

"Should we leave it out?" Dawn suggested.

Kira shook her head. It was the only green vegetable in the mix, and the topping would seem sparse without it. "I can run into town and get some more."

One more thing on her list.

Rand came inside from clearing off the parking area for the second time that day. He took off his gloves, stomped his snowy boots on the mat just inside the front door, and blew on his hands.

"It's a bitch out there," he said. "How many heaters do we have again?"

"A dozen," Kira responded. "The tent people assured me it would be enough. They better be right."

The phone rang again, and Kira stared at it

384

warily. The phone didn't have a record of carrying good news today. Perhaps Jessica had chipped a nail and needed Kira to FedEx over a file.

Peter looked at her expression, then said, "I'll get it." He answered the phone while Kira walked back into the kitchen. What next? The soup. She reached for a squash and sliced it in half, fighting to work her knife through the hard shell of the vegetable.

"Peter?" she asked as he came back into the room. "Who was it?"

He walked over to the charger and set the cordless phone back down.

"The salmon supplier," he said. "They're not going to make it."

Kira gasped. "No," she said. "That's impossible! They were going to deliver a hundred fillets today! Did you tell them they had to do it?"

"Yes," Peter said. "But it's not just us. They had to cancel all the deliveries to our area. There was an accident with the truck. Everything spoiled."

"Call them back!" Kira said. "That isn't acceptable!"

Her mind whirled. A wedding without a main course at dinner? Maybe they could scrap the appetizers and change the service to a buffet, or just give everyone heavy hors d'oeuvres, but either way Jessica would be fully justified in refusing to pay. The sit-down dinner was the centerpiece of the event!

"Should we phone around to restaurants in town?" Dawn suggested. "I bet some of them have frozen fillets. If we can gather enough, we can still do it."

"Okay," Kira said. "Try."

Dawn grabbed the phone book and began flipping through the yellow pages.

"Shit!" Kira snatched up a paper towel and wrapped it around her index finger.

"Are you okay?" Peter asked.

"I cut myself," she said. Her finger throbbed, and spots of red appeared through the wad of paper toweling. She'd been sloppy, thinking about too many things at once, and the knife had slipped. "Shit, shit, shit!"

"Look, you gotta calm down," Rand said. "So there's no salmon. Everyone can eat pasta, right?"

"That wasn't in the agreement!" Kira said. "Jessica wants salmon!"

"It's a dinner," Rand said. "One meal."

"A dinner that's going to save us all financially," Kira pointed out.

"Whatever," Rand said, lifting his hands up in surrender.

"Lay off," Peter said, looking at his brother. "Can't you tell she's stressed?"

Kira felt dizzy. Maybe she needed something to eat. Who had time to eat? Peter had been ignoring her for days, but at least he'd defended her to his brother. *Don't let them start fighting again,* she thought.

"I'm going to check on Lyss." Rand started to walk out of the room just as a loud crack sounded from somewhere outside. The lights flickered once, then twice.

Everyone froze.

"What was that?" Kira asked. She noticed Dawn clutching the countertop and gasping.

"Are you okay?" Peter asked.

Dawn nodded. "It just startled me," she said. She peered through the window.

"It was a branch," Rand said, coming back into the kitchen. "The snow's heavy and it cracked under the weight. I'll go see if I can clear it away."

"Ouch," Kira said. She peeled away the paper towel and found a Band-Aid and some Neosporin in a cupboard above the dishwasher. The cut didn't seem deep enough to need stitches, but it throbbed.

The soup. She needed to prepare the soup. She'd slept poorly last night, waking at 1:00 A.M. and then again at 4:00 imagining a crate of champagne glasses crashing to the floor, the minister failing to show up, Jessica's ring getting lost . . . So many things could go wrong at weddings. And something always did.

Her head felt fuzzy, and her throat was a little sore. She hoped she wasn't coming down with a bug.

The lights flickered again, then went out.

Come back on, Kira prayed. *Please.* But nothing happened. Outside, clouds were snuffing out the sun, so even though it was early afternoon, the room was dim and gray.

The little digital clock on the stove was blank. Kira walked over to the toaster and depressed the switch, but it popped back up. So it wasn't just a blown fuse. The power was out.

The front door slammed, and Rand's voice rang out: "The branch that fell got tangled up with the power line. I can't move it."

Could this actually be happening? Their refrigerator contained hundreds of dollars' worth of cheeses, and fillings for the tarts, and raspberries, and fig spread, and heavy cream for the soup . . . her entire meal would be destroyed if the power stayed off.

Kira fell onto a stool and put her head in her hands, trying not to hyperventilate. Jessica's father would be furious. He might even sue them.

You know how daddies are about their little girls, Jessica had said.

Why hadn't her father come to her wedding? Kira felt a pain pierce the center of her chest and spread outward, growing until it seemed to consume her.

Maybe it wasn't because he wanted to avoid her mother, as Kira had told herself. Maybe the truth was that he'd long ago replaced Kira with his stepdaughter. She tried to rub away the tears that threatened to spill down her cheeks, but there must've been some lime juice left on her hands, because her eyes began to burn.

Her cell phone buzzed on the counter. She started, realizing she was falling behind schedule. She needed to preheat the oven, and cube the squash, and find some asparagus . . . But she couldn't preheat the oven, not without electricity. Her tears were coming harder now, but no one noticed.

"Why aren't there any shuttle buses available for rent in the state of Vermont?" Peter was saying in an exasperated tone.

Her husband was barely speaking to her. She'd have to refund the deposit for the wedding if she didn't uphold the terms of the contract. Even if Jessica's father didn't sue, they'd end up losing money if they had to eat the cost of the alcohol and food. All these months in Vermont would be a complete waste, just like her time at the law firm. She'd embarked upon two careers, and failed spectacularly at both. And to think she'd once expected to do great things.

Dawn's voice broke into her thoughts. "Should I call the electric company on a cell phone? They're probably used to outages here all the time because of the weather . . . Kira? Do you want me to call?"

Dawn. She'd escaped from her own life when

things got rough, with no plan or agenda or support, Kira thought.

"Was it hard?" Kira asked, keeping her head low.

"Sorry?" Dawn said. "I'm not sure what you mean."

Her phone buzzed again. It must be Jessica. Jessica's father wanted a special dance with his daughter. He was paying for Cristal champagne to toast her. Only the best for his little girl. *There could never be a father who loved his daughter more than I love you,* Paul Simon would sing. Kira wondered what song would play while her father danced with his stepdaughter.

She'd lost her father long ago, and now she knew she was losing the only other man she'd truly loved. Peter was across the room, frowning at his computer. Ignoring her again.

"Do you want me to get it?" Dawn asked, motioning to the phone.

"No," Kira said, avoiding Dawn's gaze. If Peter would only look up at her, acknowledge her in some way . . .

"I need to . . . go . . . ," Kira whispered.

She walked to the hall closet and put on her coat and hat, then reached for her purse, her movements slow and precise. Her keys and wallet were inside her purse, and her boots were by the front door. She slid them on and reached for the doorknob.

Peter was still with the others in the kitchen. He hadn't noticed she was leaving. No one was coming after her.

She slipped outside quietly, easing the storm door shut behind her so it wouldn't bang. Snow lashed against her cheeks, and the wind whipped her hair as she walked to her Honda and started the engine. Oddly enough, she didn't feel the slightest bit cold.

It wasn't hard to walk out of your own life, she thought as she carefully drove down the hill and turned left, the B-and-B receding in her rearview mirror and then disappearing completely. Not hard at all.

Chapter Twenty-six

"Kira?" Peter looked up from his computer. "I found a shuttle bus."

Dawn stopped flipping through the yellow pages. "She's not here. She said she had to go out."

Peter frowned. "Where?"

"Maybe to get more asparagus?" Dawn guessed. "She left about an hour ago."

"She hates driving in the snow," Peter said. "I'm surprised she went alone."

The front door slammed and Dawn flinched, but it was just Rand.

"Did anyone call the power company?" he asked.

"I did," Dawn said. "I told them a live power line was down, and a lot of people were going to be walking around the area because of the wedding, so we're on a priority list. They said they'd come within four hours."

Rand gave her a high-five. "Should we put all the food outside, just in case? I mean, who needs a refrigerator when we've got the world's biggest one in our backyard?"

"Let's give it a couple hours," Peter said. "Did Kira say anything to you guys before she left?"

Dawn shook her head.

"Kira left?" Rand asked. "Not the greatest weather for her to be out driving."

Peter picked up her cell phone off the counter and looked at it. "Five missed calls," he said. "All from Jessica. Can I borrow your Jeep?" he finally asked Rand. "I want to go into town and look for her."

Rand scooped up his keys off the counter and tossed them to his brother.

"Need help?" he offered, but Peter just shook his head and walked out.

Alyssa made the slow journey to the couch. It was a shower day, so she'd taken advantage of the authorized movement to travel to the living room. She couldn't do much to help with the wedding, but maybe there were some small tasks she could handle while lying down.

The house seemed so quiet. She'd expected it to be awhirl with activity, with Kira holding court in the kitchen, and Rand and Peter carrying things out to the tent . . . but she couldn't hear a thing. She looked out the window. Where was the tent?

"Hello?" she called out, and Dawn swung through the door from the kitchen.

"Where is everyone?" Alyssa asked.

"Rand's outside, and Peter went to look for Kira," Dawn said. "She ran an errand in town. At least, we think that's what she did. We were all worried about the power being out, so things were a little confused . . ."

"How long has she been gone?" Alyssa asked.

"Maybe an hour and a half?" Dawn guessed.

"She'll probably be back any second now," Alyssa said. "So what can I do to help? We've got a wedding to throw, right?"

Dawn nodded. "Kira was going to do the soup next, so I took it over. I cubed the butternut squash, but maybe you could chop up the scallions and stuff? I could bring you a cutting board."

"Perfect," Alyssa said. "It'll be good to feel useful."

As Dawn turned to go back into the kitchen, Alyssa spoke up again. "Did anyone try to call Kira?"

Dawn hesitated. "That's the odd thing. She left her phone behind."

Alyssa glanced out the window. "The snow's really coming down," she said. "I'm glad Peter's going to look for her. The roads must be getting slippery."

As Dawn went back into the kitchen, Kira's cell phone rang. Dawn snatched it up, thinking it might be Kira, but the call was from Peter.

"Hi," Dawn said. "Did you find her?"

She could hear the disappointment in his voice. "No. I was hoping she'd be home by now . . . I've driven all around town and haven't spotted our car. Call me when she comes back, okay? I'm going to keep looking."

"Sure," Dawn said. She glanced at the long to-do list Kira had taped to the front of one of the kitchen cabinets. Kira had allotted certain amounts of time for each task she needed to complete today, and according to the schedule, they were almost two hours behind. It shouldn't have taken more than forty minutes for her to pick up asparagus, even if she'd had to drive slowly because of the weather. Dawn felt the hairs on her arms stand up. What could have happened to Kira?

When she spoke to Peter, though, she made sure to keep her voice light and reassuring: "You probably just missed each other. I bet she's on her way home right now."

Chapter Twenty-seven

Two police officers showed up at the B-and-B around 8:00 P.M., responding to Peter's call. One was a bleached-blond woman who looked to be in her fifties, and she had a younger male partner who kept touching his gun holster—a nervous habit, perhaps, but a disconcerting one, too. Everyone sat together in the living room except for Peter, who couldn't stop pacing. The power had been restored hours earlier, and now every lamp and overhead fixture in the room blazed. Peter had turned them all on and lit a fire in the hearth; it was as if he wanted the B-and-B to be a beacon in case Kira needed a light to guide her home, Dawn thought.

"Can you go over exactly what happened before she left?" said the female officer, whose name badge read *Wilson*.

"The power went out," Peter said. "She disappeared right after that."

"Did she get any phone calls?" Officer Wilson asked. "Text messages, maybe?"

Peter shook his head. "Just a few from this bride of a wedding we're holding tomorrow. She calls all the time, though. I don't think Kira even talked to her before she left. It certainly wasn't anything unusual, in any case."

"Has she ever done anything like this before?" the officer asked. She was taking notes in a small spiral pad while her partner surveyed everyone with an impassive expression. "Has she ever run off and not told anyone?"

Peter gave a little laugh. "Never. Kira is the most responsible person I've ever known. She wouldn't just do this, especially not with the wedding coming up. It makes no sense."

"No . . . fights?" Officer Wilson looked directly at Peter. "No marital upsets?"

Peter folded his arms. "I mean, sure, we bicker sometimes," he finally said. "But it isn't that."

"Is there anything else you can think of? Even a small thing. Something she said before she walked out, maybe."

"She asked me if it was hard."

Everyone turned to look at Dawn, who was sitting on an ottoman, not quite within the circle.

"If what was hard?" the officer asked, shifting in her seat to face Dawn.

"I don't know," Dawn said, twisting her hands. "We were talking about the power going out and then she just said, 'Was it hard?' But it was almost like she was talking to herself. That was the last thing she said before she left, other than that she had to go."

Officer Wilson wrote something in her pad. It seemed to take her forever.

"Do you have any idea what she was talking about?" the officer asked when she finally raised her head again.

Dawn swallowed against the lump forming in her throat. This was it. She'd almost fled when Peter mentioned calling the police, so great had been her worry. But then she'd remembered the soup Kira had made for her on her first night, and the extra bread Kira had slipped onto her plate when Dawn had been so hungry. There had been a hundred such small kindnesses: the lamp Kira had found for her room, the soft futon she'd ordered online, the delicacies Kira had slipped to Dawn while they cooked together.

"She was asking me if it was hard to disappear," Dawn said, her voice a scratchy whisper. Everyone leaned closer, straining to hear. "She asked because I disappeared once before."

Both officers visibly tensed.

"There's one more thing you need to check," Dawn said. She was shaking, but she forced herself to sit up straight and to meet Officer Wilson's steady gaze. Kira's safety was at stake, which meant Dawn needed to offer up her own, just as her mother had on that long-ago day when she'd rushed to help the little boy who'd been choking.

"There's a guy named Tucker Newman," Dawn

began. "He may be in town, and if so, he's after me. I don't think he has anything to do with this, but you should know about him."

The officer picked up her pencil again. "What should I know?"

Dawn took a deep breath, feeling the eyes of Peter and Rand and Alyssa on her. Then, starting at the very beginning, she told the officers everything.

Chapter Twenty-eight

The heat was shocking. Kira had forgotten what it felt like to sweat, for her upper lip to grow damp and her armpits sticky and to have to gather her hair into a ponytail to get it off her neck.

She'd begun shedding layers the moment she stepped off the plane. First her hat, then her coat, then her heavy wool sweater. She was down to a long-sleeved shirt and her jeans and boots, and still she felt too warm. It was eight o'clock at night, and she was in a completely different world. Amazing how easy it had been to slip inside it: a swipe of her credit card, a flash of her driver's license, a quick walk through security . . . Disappearing was so exquisitely simple.

She hadn't known where she was going, until

the ticket agent at the airport asked for her destination.

"Florida," she'd said instantly, the word sounding confident and comfortable on her lips. She'd paid more than eight hundred dollars for a ticket—she, who clipped coupons to save fifty cents on a carton of yogurt!—then she'd waited for two hours, until it was time to climb aboard the plane. She'd stared out the window for the entire flight.

When you were feeling lost and desperate, where else would you go but home?

Kira walked through the terminal, heading toward the exit. Everyone had kept telling her to stop stressing, and now she was doing precisely that. She'd left her cell phone buzzing on the counter. Peter or Rand could explain to Jessica about the lost power and missing salmon and everything else. She was handing off her worries, like a bundle of dirty laundry passed over the counter at the dry cleaner's. She passed a pay phone and paused, then used her credit card to make a quick call, dialing the number from memory.

She pushed through the glass doors and walked to the end of the line of people waiting outside for taxicabs. There was a glowing young couple who looked like newlyweds, a few exuberant families probably heading to Disney World, solo business travelers wearing suits and weary expressions, and a tanned older couple who looked like they were returning from a cruise. Funny, but they were probably all living different phases of essentially the same life, Kira thought. In another ten years, the newlyweds would be back, this time more haggard-looking and with a few kids in tow, heading toward Space Mountain and mouse ears again, and a decade after that, the business travelers would be returning from a sail to the Bahamas, their strained expressions replaced with serene ones, their pallor giving way to tans.

"Where to?" the cabdriver asked when Kira climbed into the backseat.

Again, the destination slipped easily off her tongue. She named a certain restaurant, a place with a clubby atmosphere, where the martinis were bone-dry and the walls were paneled in a dark, knotty wood, and entrées couldn't be had for less than thirty dollars.

It was a Friday night. He'd be there, of course. He was a man who enjoyed elegant routines, and this was his end-of-the-workweek ritual.

She walked into the restaurant a half hour later and spotted him holding court in a corner booth. It felt as if decades had passed since she'd stood in his office while he'd turned his back on her to take a phone call, but he looked exactly the same: expensive gray suit, crisp white shirt, cuffs shot through with gold monogrammed cuff links, florid red cheeks, and a crescent of silver hair sweeping around the back of his mostly bald head.

Thomas Bigalow was dining with three other men who exuded the same kind of look: power that was sourced in great wealth. She recognized one of them as the district's congressman.

She'd felt as if she'd been in the throes of a dream ever since she left the B-and-B, gliding along, her emotions pleasantly numb, following a script that her subconscious was writing but that she couldn't predict. Now she realized what had brought her home: It was finally time to stand up to her old boss. Their last encounter had trailed her all the way to Vermont, tainting her new life there. Jinxing her ability to succeed.

She walked over to stand in front of their booth, marveling in a detached sort of way at her complete lack of fear. He didn't notice her, not at first. He was talking to the guy on his left, the congressman, while the other two men leaned in to hear. On the table in front of her old boss was a plate holding the last bit of his steak dinner. The meat was leaking blood-red juice onto the white china. She watched as he picked up a gleaming, serrated knife and sawed off another bite, then gestured for the waiter to bring the bill.

"Mr. Bigalow," she said, moving to stand directly in front of him.

He regarded her for a long moment, and as she felt his eyes run over her, she suddenly became aware of what she looked like: no makeup, hair that needed a trim swept up into a messy pony-tail, heavy winter boots in the eighty-degree heat.

"Yes?" he said, amusement lacing his voice. "Are you here to tell us about the desserts?"

The other three men burst into laughter.

"No," Kira said. Her voice stayed steady, her palms dry. They were nothing more than school-yard bullies. They probably *had* been school-yard bullies. "I'm not here to offer you something sweet."

She raised her chin and stared at him. *Shame on you,* she thought. Maybe that would be a good opening line. But slowly, chillingly, she became aware of something: His eyes held only wariness and defiance. They didn't contain a trace of recognition.

All the breath left her lungs in a whoosh, as if she'd been punched. Sure, she looked different from how she had during her law firm days, when her hair was always sleek and she wore nice suits, but how could he not remember her? She'd devoted six years of her life to his firm, more than two thousand awful, soul-crushing days in which she'd done her best every single minute. She was prepared for anything—for him to yell, or demand to have her tossed out, or mock her winter boots —*anything* but this. Being forgotten gutted her.

He was turning back to his friends now, finishing his cocktail and cracking another joke. Maybe he thought she was the daughter of a client whose case he'd lost, or a job applicant he'd turned down. Or more likely he wasn't the slightest bit concerned about why she'd appeared. Confrontation didn't faze him; he was steeped in it every day in the courtroom, plus he'd been married three times. He *thrived* on it. She was a gnat buzzing in his ear, something inconsequential to be swatted away.

The waiter approached, cleared away the dirty plates, and set down the black leather holder containing the check as Thomas looked at her again. "Was there anything else?" he asked, his voice pointed.

He'd forget this encounter by the time she stepped onto the sidewalk outside, but Kira knew it would haunt her. She couldn't leave like this, defeated and meek. Not again.

Kira reached for the leather holder and waved it in the air. "Be careful when it comes to Tommy and bills, because you'll probably end up paying more than your fair share," she said, her voice ringing out in the hushed, elegant room. "That's what some of his clients were beginning to complain about when I worked at his firm. Over-billing. Just ask Skyrim Holdings. You should watch yourself, Congressman, because I'd hate for your constituents to think you're as corrupt as your dinner host. Guilt by association and all."

She tossed the bill at Thomas and spun around to leave, but not before noticing two things: The congressman was leaning back, away from Thomas. And recognition had finally snapped into her old boss's eyes.

Dawn tried to prepare herself for the feel of heavy metal handcuffs clicking onto her wrists. She thought she'd be read her rights, then led outside to the police car, a hand pushing down her head as she was guided into the backseat. Blue and red lights would reflect against the snow as they sped through the streets, and then she'd be locked in a grimy cage somewhere in the underbelly of this charming town, a place happy vacationers never even knew existed.

But the police officers didn't move once she finished her story.

"So you sent back the money?" Officer Wilson finally asked. "When?"

"A little while ago," Dawn said. "It would have arrived by now."

They made her repeat her entire story, this time peppering her with questions, making her loop back again and again, probably to see if she'd change her tale, or trip herself up. By the time she finished talking, Dawn's voice was growing hoarse.

"This Tucker Newman," the female officer

finally said, flipping back a page in her notebook to find his name. "What makes you think he's here?"

"Mostly just a sense," Dawn said. "But he did tell me in an e-mail he wouldn't stop looking for me, and I think a friend from work figured out I was in Killington. I think she told him."

She stole a glance at the others. Peter had known the whole story, of course, but it must have come as a shock to Rand and Alyssa. Alyssa gave her a gentle smile, and Dawn felt tears of relief prick her eyes. She looked at Rand, who appeared a little taken aback. But then he winked at her. Maybe they'd suspected there was more to her story all along, or maybe life had thrown so much at them recently that their threshold for shock had been raised to a whole new level.

The officer finally returned her notepad to her pocket, and she and her partner stood up.

This was it, Dawn thought. She'd been so worried about Tucker appearing, but it turned out to be the police who'd discovered her first, after all.

"Do not leave town without first informing us," said the male officer. "We may want to question you more tomorrow."

"Of course," Dawn said. Her heart beat against her chest like a small, frantic bird. The officers were putting on their coats. Were they actually leaving?

"As for your wife," Officer Wilson said to Peter, "we can't consider her a missing person until forty-eight hours have passed. She left of her own volition. There's no evidence of foul play."

"Can't you do anything?" Peter asked.

"We've got her description and the plate number of her car," she said. "We'll keep a lookout."

The police left, and Dawn almost collapsed to the floor. Her confession had drained all the energy out of her, like water spiraling from a sink. Peter came back into the room and slumped on the couch, looking as exhausted as Dawn felt.

"Can I make anyone coffee?" she offered. She hesitated. "And if you guys want me to stay somewhere else in town tonight, it's no problem."

Rand stood up. "Coffee sounds great," he said.

Peter was reaching for his jacket. "I'm going back out to look for Kira," he said. "And don't be ridiculous. You're staying here."

"I'll call around," Alyssa offered. "Maybe some of the local hotels? She might've just needed to get away from the wedding and everything."

Peter nodded. His eyes were red-rimmed, and he was pale. He probably shouldn't be driving, Dawn thought. It was dark, and the roads were slippery . . . she thought of her parents' accident, and her throat constricted.

But now Rand was putting on his coat, too,

and walking over to stand next to his brother, and holding out his hand for the keys.

"Can I come with you?" he asked. "I want to help."

Peter hesitated, then gave him the keys.

"Why didn't you tell me?" Alyssa's voice was kind, but Dawn still flinched.

They were together in the living room, the lights still blazing, but by now Dawn had brought out cups of tea and the fire had been reduced to glowing embers. She thought about all the things she could say—that she was scared, or lonely, or desperate—but finally settled on the most honest, raw answer, the words that hurt the most to release: "I was ashamed."

"Ashamed of being tricked by a con artist?" Alyssa asked.

Dawn shook her head. "Of falling in love with him." She remembered Tucker brushing the hair from her face, and saying, *Let's be each other's families from now on.*

"Oh," Alyssa said slowly. "I see."

"I'm so sorry. I should have told you. And I don't think Tucker had anything to do with Kira's disappearance," Dawn said. "But if he does, I won't ever forgive myself."

"I don't think that's it either," Alyssa said. "In fact, I'm sure of it. I bet she just needed to escape for a bit. We can all relate to that, can't we? It was one of the reasons why I used to travel so much. And Rand . . ." Her voice trailed off, and she reached for her tea again. "Kira left before she knew the power would come back on. I bet she just had a mini-breakdown because she was worried the lack of electricity would ruin the wedding."

"And the salmon," Dawn added. At Alyssa's questioning look, Dawn explained about the supplier not delivering the fish. "But I've called a bunch of restaurants, and I've come up with eighty-four fillets. They're charging the same price they would for the entrée on the menu, and it may not be as good quality, but it's still salmon."

Alyssa smiled. "Good for you." She paused, then added, "I feel a little guilty, too, you know. We all agreed to do the wedding, but Kira's the one doing the bulk of the work. I didn't expect to be on bed rest—I never expected to get pregnant, truthfully—and I've been so wrapped up in worrying about the baby and Grace and . . . and some other things, that I haven't fully appreciated how much Kira has had to shoulder. I know you've been helping a lot, but I think she feels responsible. And she's worried about money, and the wedding was going to be a big help with that."

"Where do you think she went?" Dawn asked.

Alyssa shrugged. "My bet's a quiet hotel, where

she can have a glass or two of wine and a dinner she didn't have to cook. I bet she sleeps for twelve hours straight and comes back tomorrow. I just wish she'd taken her phone. Peter is so scared."

She frowned. "I just thought of something. Can you check the cell phone in my room?"

"Sure." Dawn got to her feet. "Where is it, exactly?"

"Probably on the bureau."

Dawn came back a moment later, holding the cell phone, and Alyssa reached for it and switched it on. "Two messages," she said.

"The first one's from an old photography client," Alyssa said. "Hang on . . . She's rambling . . ."

She listened for another minute, then withdrew the phone.

"Kira called," she said. "She's okay."

Dawn squeezed her eyes shut. "Thank God. Where is she?"

"She didn't say," Alyssa said. "But she asked me to tell Peter that she's safe." Alyssa was already dialing his number on her phone.

"Did she say when she was coming back?" Dawn asked, but Alyssa shook her head. "Oh, I wish there was something we could do!"

"We can," Alyssa said, smiling at Dawn. She was holding the phone to her ear, waiting for Peter to answer. "We can try to pull off the wedding."

Chapter Twenty-nine

It was growing dark now, the temperature cooling by a few degrees. The air was softened by humidity, and palm trees rustled in the gentle breeze, sounding like pages turning in a book.

Kira hadn't eaten in hours, but she wasn't the slightest bit hungry or tired. After leaving the restaurant, she walked down the street, watching people devour ice cream cones and sip white wine in outdoor cafés. She felt neither aimless nor intent; she was just waiting to see what would unfold next, as if she were a bystander in her own life story.

She hailed a cab and asked to be taken to a certain intersection, then she got out and stood there for a moment, orienting herself before she began to walk. She passed under the yellow glow of streetlights and stopped to pet a gentle old dog resting in his front yard. She wandered by a house where a half dozen newspapers had piled up in front of the door, and was doused by a sprinkler someone had set to water their flower borders. The air grew thicker, and she heard a rumble of thunder as she walked on. Her feet felt heavy and sore, but the rest of her was still numb.

She turned up a front walk and climbed the steps to the house, feeling as if she were in a trance. There was a new mat, one that didn't say "welcome," and the front door was shut. A big pot of lavender sat on the top step. She could see a light on somewhere in the house, but no noise came from within. She lifted her hand to knock, then dropped her head against the door instead.

She didn't know why she'd come, or what she'd say if she saw her father again. The last time they'd gotten together was a few weeks before she left. She'd picked him up here, but she'd waited at the curb until he came out. They'd gone to a crowded diner and had both ordered coffee and sandwiches. Kira had swirled a spoon around in her mug while they made conversation that was so stilted Kira had been grateful for the noise and bustle around them. It helped camouflage the fact that she couldn't think of anything to say to her dad.

The door opened.

Kira nearly fell inside the house, but she managed to jerk back and regain her balance.

"Kira," he said. "I thought I heard someone— Why are you . . ."

He held open the door wider. "Come in."

She shook her head. "It's okay. I was just in the neighborhood and figured I'd stop by. I need to get going, actually."

"Are you sure?" Her dad stepped outside. "It's so late." He wore a navy-blue bathrobe, belted over his thickening waist, and glasses that caught the reflection of the light over the front door. Those were new, she thought.

"I heard about the wedding," she blurted.

"Oh," he said. His forehead wrinkled, then smoothed out. "Well, I hope you can come."

"Probably not," she said. "I live in Vermont now, you know."

"I know," he said. "The B-and-B, right?"

"Yep," she said.

He looked at her closely. "You seem tired," he said. "Everything okay?"

She nodded. "Sure. But I do need to go, so . . ." She turned and started to walk away, but her father put a hand on her shoulder.

"Hang on one second, okay?" he asked. "Let me just get you . . ." His sentence trailed off as he went back inside, and she wondered what he could possibly bring her. Maybe an invitation to the wedding. She'd stick it in her purse without looking at it, then tear it up and toss it in the trash.

But when her dad came back, he was holding a tall, clear glass filled with water. "Here," he said, handing it to her. "It's so warm out."

She stared at it as if unsure what to do with it. Then she raised it to her lips and took a sip. The moment the cool fluid trickled into her mouth, she realized she was parched. Her lips felt cracked, and her tongue was thick from dehydration. The plane ride, the heat, the long walk, her heavy clothes . . . she gulped greedily until the glass was empty.

"You need more," her father said. "Come on." He opened the door, and this time she followed him inside, through a small living room that was cluttered but clean and into the kitchen, where a light over the stove illuminated the middle of the room but not its corners. Her father refilled the glass from the tap, and she drank it all down again, more slowly this time.

"That's better," he said.

There was a red teakettle on the stove, and a small wooden table with two matching chairs alongside the wall, and a Far Side calendar hanging by the sink. The refrigerator was covered with magnets and photos. Kira moved closer to look. There was a picture of his stepdaughter, Margie—she must've been ten or eleven—building a sand castle on the beach. Kira had met her briefly a few times; she was a pretty girl, with dark hair and a sprinkling of freckles. There was another photo of her dad's wife caught dozing on the couch, her mouth slightly open and a calico cat resting on her chest. There was a whole row of his stepdaughter's school pictures, capturing her progression from year to year, including a college graduation photo. And one of Kira exiting the church on her wedding day.

She reached out and pulled away the magnet, freeing the photograph. She'd never seen it before; it wasn't one of the shots taken by the professional photographer she'd hired.

"Where did you get this?" she demanded, shaking it at her father. "Who gave it to you?" Had her mother sent it—perhaps as a way of shaming her dad for not coming?

"I took it," her father said.

"You weren't there," she protested.

"I sat in the last row," he said. He cleared his throat. "I, ah, came in late and I left early. Same for your high school graduation. I've got a picture of that somewhere, too. I think it's in an album in the living room."

She stared at him, the contours of the room suddenly becoming sharp and crisp, the languid sense of her day evaporating.

"You said your leg was hurt and you couldn't come!" she cried. Her voice was too loud—she'd probably wake his wife—but she didn't care.

"Ah, Kira," he said. "Do you want to sit down?" He gestured toward the table, but she shook her head. She was clutching the photograph so tightly her fingertips were turning white, and her heart was pounding.

"Things with your mother and me . . . Well, I don't have to explain to you, do I?" He managed a smile. "No love lost there. I figured it would make things awkward if I showed up. Unpleasant, on a day that's supposed to be a happy one. Easier all around if I stayed away."

Easier for who? Kira wanted to cry. For her mother, yes, and for her father, too. But not for her. Why hadn't anyone asked what she wanted?

But her father was a man who'd always taken the easy way out, so it shouldn't have surprised her that he'd selected that path again. Maybe he wasn't solely responsible for their fractured relationship; she'd turned away from her father, too. But she'd been a child. She was trying to be loyal to her mother; she was angry and confused. He should have tried harder. But for the first time she acknowledged that she should have, too. It wasn't solely his fault they'd lost each other.

She put back the photograph, carefully, centering it just so and pinning it with the magnet. She gave it one final look. In it she was smiling, her veil fanning out behind her, her face shining. And there was something else in the photograph, something vitally important, that she hadn't noticed until just now.

"I'm glad you were there," she finally said. Her father didn't say a word, but she felt his hand on her shoulder again. She stayed perfectly still for a moment, then leaned her cheek against it. She wasn't sure, but she thought she heard him whisper her name.

"It's late, like you said." She finally spoke up. "I need to get going."

"Where are you staying?" he asked. "Do you need a ride somewhere? Or you could sleep on the couch here, if you want. It's supposed to rain, so . . ."

She nodded. "If you could take me to the Holiday Inn, I'd really appreciate it."

He didn't hesitate. "I'll go change."

She heard his footsteps on the stairs, then the creak of a door opening overhead. She stepped back outside to wait. She breathed in the scent of lavender and felt the first few warm raindrops splash onto her hair. She didn't yet know that when her father came downstairs, he'd bring a fresh Band-Aid to wrap around the finger she'd cut that morning, or that when she woke up tomorrow, she'd call and ask him for a ride to the airport. She didn't yet know that he'd kiss her on the cheek when they pulled up in front of the terminal, or that she'd get out of the car, then lean back in through the open passenger's-side window and invite her father and his wife to visit the B-and-B for a weekend. She couldn't foresee the rebirth of their relationship, which would slowly unfold in the future.

She was only feeling a sense of wonderment about the fact that she'd thought she needed to confront Thomas Bigalow, but she'd been wrong.

This was the ending she'd been yearning to rewrite all along.

Chapter Thirty

The day of the wedding dawned bright and clear, with a chance of flurries in the late afternoon—exactly as Jessica had wanted it. Apparently even the weather didn't dare defy her wishes. She'd look like a snow princess in her full-skirted dress and floor-length veil, surrounded by towering pine trees and sloping white drifts, Alyssa thought.

Miraculously, the streets were clear and all of the food had been delivered as promised, with the exception of the salmon. But Dawn had headed into town with a huge cooler in the back of Rand's Jeep, going from restaurant to restaurant until she'd picked up eighty-four fillets. They were short by four, but Alyssa figured they'd manage somehow.

The tent was set up in the parking area. It had arrived six hours late, but Dawn had had the idea of asking the waiters to come for a few extra hours last night, and they'd not only arranged the round tables and chairs and bar but set all the tables with the rented china and glassware and tied gauzy bows onto the backs of the chairs.

Alyssa reclined on the couch, a pillow under her knees and another one propped under her head, her growing belly up in the air, helping as best she could by trying to fill in the last-minute organizational gaps. She flipped through Kira's three-ring binder, thankful that her sister-in-law had left such detailed instructions.

"We should move the beer and wine into the tent now," she told Rand. "But keep the heaters on low, so the ice doesn't melt and the beverages stay cold."

Inside the tent, the tables were draped in blush-colored cloths, the dance floor was in place, and the DJ was coming to arrange his speakers and microphone. Rand had snapped pictures with her camera and shown her the images. They were *ahead* of schedule, unbelievably.

"The flowers!" Dawn looked at Alyssa. "Wasn't the florist supposed to have been here twenty minutes ago?" Alyssa reached for her cell phone, but before she could dial, she spotted a white van climbing the driveway. "They're here!" she cried out.

A few minutes later, the driver was carrying the first of ten centerpieces into the B-and-B. Alyssa checked over the flowers: She wasn't sure what Princess Diana roses or ranunculus looked like, so she couldn't say if the bouquets were what Jessica had ordered, but they were gorgeous.

"Please put them on the tables in the tent and leave the bouquets and bouttonnieres in the master bedroom upstairs," Alyssa said. "Dawn, can you show them the way?"

Peter came into the room and immediately looked at Alyssa. His expression went from hopeful to disappointed, just as it did every time he searched her face and realized there was no news. Kira hadn't been in touch since she walked out the previous day, save for that one brief message.

"Okay," Peter said. He inhaled and rubbed his hands down the sides of his jeans. "What's next?"

"Cheese," Alyssa said.

She peered at Kira's handwriting. "There should be a few rounds of Brie, wedges of smoked Gouda, and blocks of sharp cheddar in the fridge. And there's some goat cheese that needs to be topped with fresh raspberries. It should all be arranged on two big platters, and she wrote that the empty spots should be filled up with clusters of red grapes and rows of crackers."

"Got it," Peter said.

"Don't forget the fig spread."

Alyssa was lying on the couch with her back to the door, so she couldn't see Kira, but she could hear Peter's exclamation of surprise, then a quick rustling sound, and a long murmuring. She wasn't sure, but she thought she caught the whispered word "Sorry."

After a few moments Kira walked into Alyssa's line of view. "Hey," she said. "I'm back."

All the questions that had been on the tip of Alyssa's tongue—*Where'd you go? What have you been doing? Why didn't you call again?*—disappeared when she saw Kira. Her sister-in-law was smiling. The pinched look was gone from her face.

"I'm glad" was all Alyssa said instead.

"So!" Kira said. She rubbed her hands together. "Put me to work. Apparently we've got a wedding to run."

"How about helping Peter with the cheeses?" Alyssa suggested.

"I can do that," Kira said.

She turned and followed her husband into the kitchen, the swinging door fluttering behind them.

Kira's foot skidded on a patch of ice, and she nearly fell before managing to restore her balance and lose only a single cracker off the cheese platter she was holding. She delivered it to the tent and took a long look around. It was spectacular. Little white lights snaked through the ceiling supports, and lush green topiaries softened the corners. The dance floor was already set up in front of the bar, and crystal and silver gleamed on the rich linens draping the tables. In the corner, the florist's assistant was using a helium machine to blow up white balloons.

Kira returned through the back door into the kitchen, which was a disaster—wine was still stockpiled in crates everywhere, though Rand

420

was moving it case by case into the tent, and a big metal contraption containing racks of warming trays filled a corner. Cutting boards and bunches of romaine lettuce and dribbles of sauces cluttered nearly every inch of the counter-tops, but everything smelled and tasted wonder-ful. The aromas of roasted garlic and lime and the buttery crusts of baking sun-dried tomato tarts filled the room.

"Should I start boiling the water for the next batch of rice?" Peter was asking.

"Sure," Kira said. She wrapped her arms around his waist and leaned her head against his back. "I'm sorry," she whispered again. She wanted to say it hundreds of times, to try to erase the hurt of not just her recent absence but of the last few months, too.

She thought again of the wedding photo on her father's refrigerator. The picture had been of her alone, but she was holding on to Peter's hand as she walked down the steps of the church. You could just see his fingers clasping hers, and part of his thin, pale wrist, at the very edge of the photo. That was why her face was shining. Peter was the reason she hadn't minded coming down the church aisle alone. She knew she would look straight ahead, into his eyes, and that he would be all she'd be thinking of in that moment.

He was the finest man she'd ever met.

Tonight she'd throw away her birth control

pills and let him see the half-full packet in the trash can. She'd tell him about the visit to her father, and try to explain why she'd been so scared. Her parents may not have done the best job raising her, but she wouldn't repeat their mistakes. She could almost hear Peter's joke: *We'll make new mistakes of our own!* She squeezed him tighter, breathing in his scent.

"Excuse me?" Kira reluctantly let go of Peter and turned around. A man was standing in the doorway to the kitchen, a camera slung around his neck. It was the backup photographer they'd hired when Alyssa learned she couldn't do the job.

"Hi," Kira said. She introduced herself and steered the photographer toward the tent to set up his equipment and snap some photos, telling him she'd give a shout when Jessica appeared.

Then she returned to the kitchen and rolled up her sleeves. It was time to get to work.

Dawn filled the glasses on one table with ice water and added a slim round of lemon to each, then walked back to the kitchen to refill the pitcher for the next table. Rand had asked the tent guys to help him erect a temporary structure to shield everyone from the wind and snow as they ferried things back and forth. It wasn't much more than a few plastic tarps attached to stakes and shaped into a tunnel with rubber mats placed atop the shoveled footpath, but the makeshift shelter would provide some protection and might prevent people from slipping while carrying trays of food.

When she started to enter the kitchen, Dawn saw Kira walk up to Peter and give him a lingering kiss as his arms wound around her waist. Dawn quickly turned and walked the other way, toward the front of the house.

She wasn't in love with Peter. She'd known that all along. She'd just been craving what he and Kira had with an intensity that left her aching. Even when Kira got tense and snapped, or when Peter withdrew—and Dawn had seen both things happen more than once—their love was apparent, shimmering just below the surface.

She was lost in thought, her head ducked low, which was why she almost walked straight into Tucker.

She saw his boots first; then she slowly raised her eyes up over his jeans and black coat before looking at his face. As they stared at each other, she realized that he'd changed his appearance, too. But she doubted Tucker's transformation was deliberate, even if it was also born of desperation. He was painfully thin, his cheekbones jutting out in sharp triangular planes, and his hair had grown past the point of flopping charmingly into his eyes. His left arm seemed to be at an awkward angle, and she realized it must still be in a cast. She blinked, wondering if he was an apparition, then she saw him exhale a little puff of white.

Of course he'd found her. Kay had overheard the comment about the Pickle Barrel, and Killington was only a half day's drive from New York. Dawn had left clues like bread crumbs around town when she'd canvassed all the restaurants in search of salmon fillets and waiters. Tucker had only needed to follow her trail.

"I don't have the money," she blurted.

He took a step closer, and she flinched. "Where is it? Where'd you hide it?"

She forced herself to stand her ground, even though everything in her was begging to retreat. She tested the weight of the water pitcher in her hand, in case she needed to use it as a weapon.

"I gave it back," she said. She hoped he couldn't tell that she was shaking.

Anger swept across his features. "You bitch," he said. He lurched forward and grabbed her arm. Tears flooded her eyes, more from shock than from hurt. She thought she'd steeled herself against Tucker, but seeing him again conjured a complicated swirl of emotions in her. She'd laughed with this man, memorized his features while he slept, and made love with him. She couldn't completely disconnect the part of herself that had once cared so deeply for him.

He lifted his hand, and she braced herself for the feel of his fist cracking into her face, but it never came. Instead, he did something that shocked her into momentary silence.

"What am I supposed to do now?" he yelled.

His tone was furious, but there was something else mixed in, too. Despair.

Somehow, she realized, they'd reversed positions. Now Tucker was the one who was trapped. New York was probably no longer safe for him. She didn't know why he'd needed the money, but he must be so desperate. Maybe he'd have to be on the run from now on. She wondered how long he'd be able to hide.

"I really loved you," she said. She let the pitcher slip down onto the thick layer of snow because she knew she'd never be able to strike him with it.

He blinked, taken aback, but recovered quickly. "Then you're even stupider than I thought."

His words stung, but not as much as they would've a few weeks ago. "I guess I was," she said. "But I was smart enough to FedEx the money back to the firm. You can check with your friend Kay; I had the box delivered to her."

What was holding him back from hitting her, or trying to drag her off somewhere? That was what she'd always imagined he'd do if he found her. She hadn't foreseen this encounter ending any other way than in violence. But he was just standing there, staring at her, his expression inscrutable. The note of despair in his voice still seemed to echo between them.

Toward the end of their relationship, there had been one night when Tucker had awoken, sweaty and frantic, from a nightmare. He'd told her he'd dreamed about his father hurting him when he'd been a boy. She knew now that was probably a lie, like most of the other things Tucker had said. But they'd curled up together in the darkness, her head resting on his shoulder, his rapid heartbeat growing slower and steadier beneath her cheek, and Tucker had talked for hours. He'd confessed that he'd been a screwup for most of his life, but he felt powerless to change. He'd lost most of his friends, and his family barely acknowledged him. She'd listened to his words as they poured out, sensing he'd never talked about all this with anyone else.

That was what she'd responded to, because it had been real. There was still a bit of goodness in Tucker, and she'd brought it out in him. At least a small part of their relationship wasn't manufactured. She had to believe by the end, not everything had been a game for Tucker. Maybe that was why he couldn't hit her now, because he remembered, too.

"I loved you," she repeated. She felt warm tears roll down her cold cheeks, but she didn't wipe them away, because she had nothing to be ashamed of. "I felt so alone after my parents died. I was lost. And I think that's why I didn't recognize you were using me. I was just so happy you wanted to be with me . . . But I'm not the same person anymore, Tucker. I've changed."

She slid her arm out of his grasp. "I won't tell anyone I saw you," she said. "You can go somewhere new, too. Maybe you can start over like I did." She couldn't believe it; she actually felt sorry for him.

Unlike Tucker, she knew exactly what she was going to do next. Once the wedding was over, she was going to climb aboard another bus— hoping it would be the last one she'd ride for a while—and return to New York and walk into the investment bank. She'd repay John Parks the final bit of cash, with interest, using money from her father's life insurance policy. She'd accept whatever punishment came her way.

And then she'd begin again. Maybe she'd stay in New York, or maybe she'd move somewhere new. She'd been hesitant to leave because the city held so many precious memories of her parents, but now she knew she'd feel their presence no matter where she went. Eventually she'd find a good man, someone kind and warm and gentle. Someone like Peter. He'd shown her that they existed.

I forgive you, Dawn thought as she stepped backward, away from Tucker. She didn't say the words aloud, though, because they weren't meant for him. She'd finally forgiven herself.

Tucker wavered, and Dawn could see the turmoil raging in him. His eyes looked tortured. She waited for him to say cutting, terrible things, to lash out and make her suffer the way he was.

But then someone yelled, and they both turned toward the sound.

"Get away from her!" Kira shouted. She came running up beside Dawn and stood there holding, of all things, a metal spatula. Rand and Peter were following close behind.

"Everything good here, buddy?" Rand asked, stepping in front of Dawn and Kira as Peter approached from the other side.

"It's okay," Dawn said. She didn't want Tucker to get hurt. She just wanted him to leave.

Tucker held Dawn's eyes a beat or two longer, then he shook his head. She heard him mutter something, but she couldn't make out the words. He turned around and walked away, and she noticed the sole of his boot was coming loose and flapping with every step. His foot must be frozen, she thought, and she felt a surge of pity that made her realize she was finally, truly free. Tucker climbed into an old brown car in the driveway, started the engine, and sped down the hill, skidding on a patch of ice before regaining control of the vehicle. Dawn watched until the car was out of view, the tears drying on her cheeks.

"If he didn't leave, were you going to sauté him?" Rand asked Kira, gesturing to the spatula. "I'm not sure our bride approved that entrée."

Dawn took a deep breath and turned to Kira. She'd been anxious when Rand and Alyssa had learned her story, but facing Kira was the hardest of all.

"I'm sorry," Dawn said. "I should've told you."

"Yeah," Kira said. She looked at Dawn steadily. "You should have. Peter filled me in on everything a little while ago."

Peter put a hand on his wife's arm. "I didn't want to put you in a position of having knowledge of a crime," he said.

"I get it," Kira said. "You were trying to protect me."

"If you want me to leave—" Dawn began, but Kira cut her off.

"Are you kidding? We've got a hundred guests coming, and you're the only other one here who knows her way around a kitchen."

Dawn felt her body sag with relief when Kira smiled and put an arm around her shoulders. "I'll go with you to talk to the police again tomorrow and let them know if they have any more questions, they'll need to come through me."

Kira looked at Peter. "Did I tell you I got licensed to practice in Vermont before we moved here? I figured it would be good to have a backup plan, just in case."

Peter laughed. "Why am I not surprised?"

"And we can work on how to approach your old boss, but I doubt he'll be pressing charges," Kira told Dawn.

"You don't think so?" Dawn asked.

"For a hundred thousand bucks that you've mostly returned?" Kira shook her head. "That's like pocket change to those guys. They're not going to want any publicity either, trust me. I can call him for you, if you want."

"You've done too much for me," Dawn said. "I know I keep saying that, but it's true . . ."

"Hey," Kira said. "I don't mind. I'd like to close out my law career this way. End it on a high note."

Rand looked at Peter. "Ever notice how nothing gets in the way of women gabbing? It's twenty degrees out, there's a heated house fifty feet away, yet here we are, freezing our asses off."

Kira wasn't sure if Peter would acknowledge his brother—he'd been avoiding Rand ever since their fight—but he finally smiled, and they all began to walk toward the B-and-B together.

Chapter Thirty-one

"Can I get you anything?" Kira asked her sister-in-law. Alyssa was in bed by now, safely out of the way of the wedding chaos, a magazine spread out on her lap. Kira caught the title of the magazine and hid a smile: *Organic Mothering.*

"Are you kidding? Like you don't have enough to do?" Alyssa was laughing.

"I'll bring by your dinner as soon as the guests are served," Kira said. "We've got a little Do Not Enter sign on the hallway door, so no one should come down this way and bother you. I have to get back now, but just call if you need anything, okay?"

"Kira?" Alyssa called out as Kira began to leave. "Could you leave my door open?"

"Of course," Kira said.

"I'd like to listen," Alyssa said. "It makes me feel like I'm a part of things."

Alyssa could hear Rand playing an acoustic version of "Isn't She Lovely" and she knew that Jessica was about to walk down the white silk runner that was serving as an aisle. Rand was warming up the crowd, putting everyone in a good mood with his songs. He looked so handsome in his white dress shirt and black pants. She could hear the murmur of voices, an occasional laugh.

Kira and Dawn must be busy in the kitchen, Alyssa thought. They'd be stirring the huge pot of savory soup and stuffing the last few figs and making sure the tarts were being kept toasty on the rented warming trays while the waiters poured wine, poised to head into the living room moments after the minister pronounced Scott and Jessica man and wife.

The living room would be filled with creamy flowers and candlelight, the high, exposed ceiling beams glowing amber, the big arched windows showcasing mounds of snow.

Jessica's friend had been right when she'd said, on that long-ago night, that the B-and-B was a spectacular place for a wedding.

What was a wedding, after all, but a new beginning, a pathway into a different sort of life, the linking together of a brand-new family? She hadn't gotten married here, but the B-and-B had supplied all of that for Alyssa, too. Its magic had wound around her like an embrace.

Tears ran down her cheeks as she listened to Rand's rendition of "Here Comes the Bride." She heard a big rustling and knew everyone was turning around to see Jessica; then came a wolf whistle—Scott's stoner cousin was the most likely suspect—and the minister began to speak. He had a deep, strong voice, and Alyssa made out snatches of what he was saying: *gathered today . . . share in the joy . . . joining together of two souls.*

She closed her eyes, wondering if people could ever truly change. She thought about a friend she'd met years ago when she lived in Chicago, a fit and healthy size ten who ran marathons several times a year. Over cocktails one evening, the woman had revealed she'd once weighed 350 pounds. Then one day she decided to run. She'd made it a block before she bent over, heaving and gasping. But the next day she ran a tiny bit farther. Within a month she was logging a mile a day, and a year later, she completed her first 10K. It wasn't so much that first decision to jog around the block that had changed her life, Alyssa's friend had said. It was the decision she still confronted every single day, just before she laced up her shoes and renewed her commitment. She hadn't changed her habits; her habits had changed her.

Grace would be here in a few weeks, and the baby in a few months. Alyssa had been thinking about moving to live near her mother once her children arrived. She wouldn't be of much help in the B-and-B with two small children, and their presence would be off-putting to guests. Kira and Peter could decide whether they wanted to stay on and run the B-and-B themselves, or whether to hand it off to a professional innkeeper.

She'd miss them, Alyssa thought. But she'd invite them to come visit often. She closed her eyes and visualized being in the kitchen with Kira again, cooking a holiday dinner, the scents of roasted potatoes and melted butter and apple pie swirling around while they listened to squeals and laughter coming from the living room as Rand and Peter played with the children. They'd pour wine for themselves and grape juice for the kids, and they'd all gather at the table and raise a toast to their time at the B-and-B, reminiscing about Hugh the inspector's visit, and Kira's attempt to learn how to ski, and the wedding they'd somehow managed to pull off. *It was fun,* Alyssa would say. *I'm so glad we did it.* And she'd reach for Rand's hand under the table.

Sickness and health, the minister was saying. *Love and cherish.*

Alyssa opened her eyes and looked at the rocking chair, placed precisely where she'd imagined one would go the first time she saw this room. She thought about how Rand had volunteered to help Peter look for Kira, driving late into the night even though he'd been exhausted. He hadn't been there for his brother in the past, but Alyssa could see him trying to change that, too.

She knew now, without a doubt, that she wanted Rand to move with her when she left the B-and-B. To be her coparent and partner. She'd tried to imagine going forward without him, but the thought made her heart ache. It would be like leaving a part of herself behind. They belonged together, along with Grace and the baby. Maybe the road wouldn't be a perfect or easy one, but when did life ever promise anyone a smooth course?

In two days, her husband would go to the airport, carrying the bag she'd packed for Grace. Rand would be the one to give their daughter a bath, and tie on her ducky robe, and tuck a blanket around her while she slept. Alyssa also wanted him to be the one to teach Grace to play the guitar, and to change the oil in a car. She needed Rand by her side when she panted and groaned, pushing their baby into the world. She wanted him to place both of their children in her arms for the very first time. She yearned to see the look on his face when it happened.

Sometimes love exploded in your heart, and sometimes it grew slowly. But the end result was the same. Did it really matter so much, after all, which path you took?

She had faith in her husband, and right now, that was enough.

I pronounce you man and wife, the minister said.

The living room erupted in applause and cheers.

To love, Alyssa thought, and she didn't try to stop the tears that flowed down her cheeks.

• • •

The appetizers were a hit!

The waiters kept returning to the kitchen and refilling their trays and dashing back out.

"How's the cheese display?" Kira asked Peter, who ducked into the tent to take a look.

"It's hanging in there," he reported when he came back. "There's some left, but people are tearing through it."

Kira checked the schedule taped to the wall, even though she had it memorized.

"We need to start toasts in a few minutes," she told Peter. "Can you pull out the bread and put it on a warming rack as soon as the oven buzzer sounds?"

She headed into the tent. It was stunning, with votive lights circling the table centerpieces and dozens of helium balloons drifting overhead, looking almost like clouds against the tent's ceiling. She searched the crowd for Jessica and spotted her leading Scott around by the hand.

"Kira!" Jessica squealed, letting go of Scott and reaching out her arms for a hug. "Everything's so pretty!"

"I'm really glad you're happy," Kira said, meaning it. "Is it okay if we ask people to sit down now to dinner?"

After a lot of thought, Kira had decided Rand would be the best person to manage the toasts. He could wrangle a long-winded brother-in-law away from the microphone and make it seem funny. Where was Rand, though? She looked around. He wasn't behind the bar mixing drinks alongside the bartenders they'd hired. His guitar was sitting on a chair up by the stage, with a beer on the floor next to it, but Rand wasn't there either . . .

"It's Jessica-tini time!"

She turned around to see Rand holding a pink beverage aloft. "I've got a Scott scorpion here, too," Rand was saying to Jessica. "Why don't you guys go sit down and I'll carry them to your table?"

Relief flooded through Kira's body. "I've got to get back to the kitchen," she said to Rand. "Remember, three minutes for the toasts. Her dad gets five."

Kira had met Jessica's father briefly before the wedding and had suppressed a shudder. He was exactly as she'd feared—a crushing handshake and sharp, narrow eyes. He was a barracuda in an Armani suit. He probably tore up witnesses in court, made drug dealers and murderers beg for mercy. But he hadn't said a word about the bill. He'd already sent a check over for half of the total amount, and he was supposed to give Kira a second check tonight.

"On second thought, let her father talk as long as he wants," she told Rand before she hurried off.

All that was left to do was ladle Caesar salad onto eighty-five small plates—fifteen of the guests hadn't shown up—then they'd serve the salmon and pasta primavera. And dinner would be done.

Just as she took a step out of the tent, she heard a crashing noise. A collective gasp rose.

"Oh, no!" she heard Jessica wail.

Kira made herself turn around. The wedding cake, which had been perched atop a small table, was lying ruined on the floor, and one of the waiters was sprawled out next to it, his tray of figs overturned beside him, his face turning red.

"I tripped," he said to no one in particular, his voice loud and disbelieving. "The floor was slippery! I grabbed for the table and the cake just fell!"

Kira froze. She could make more appetizers. She could get a liquor store to rush in a delivery of more wine. The one thing she couldn't do was create a three-tiered wedding cake! Her mind spun and came up empty. She felt as if everyone was looking at her, waiting for her to take charge. Why couldn't she think of what to do?

"Ladies and gentlemen, that kicks off the entertainment portion of tonight's events." Rand's voice boomed over the microphone, his warm tone inviting everyone into the joke while drawing attention away from the debacle on the floor. "If you'll please find your seats now, we're going to begin toasting the gorgeous bride and her dashing groom . . . Jessica and Scott, can you come up here so your family and friends can all talk about how wonderful you are? Don't worry; we paid them extra to do so."

People laughed and took their seats, and the waiter rushed out of the tent and came back with a broom and oversize dustpan. Kira exhaled and went back into the kitchen to plate salads.

The wedding was going by so quickly. Dinner had been served—raves had poured back for the entrées—and dishes had been cleared away. The waiters were scraping the plates and stacking them in crates to return them to the rental company, which would wash and sanitize them.

Kira had thrown together a vanilla dump cake— you dumped all the ingredients into one bowl, mixed, and stuck it in the oven—with vanilla icing. She'd found four round pans and had stacked up the layers. Luckily she had plenty of butter, eggs, and confectioners' sugar on hand. She'd decorated the top of the cake with fresh flowers, and had wound a pink ribbon around its base. It hadn't looked half-bad, and Scott and Jessica took their first taste while the photographer snapped a flurry of shots.

Kira did a final check: The DJ was spinning Beyoncé's latest hit, and writhing bodies filled the dance floor. The furniture was back in the living room now, and some guests were gathered in front of the fire, finishing their slices of cake and sipping coffee.

Kira sank onto a kitchen stool and took a sip of coffee herself. Her feet ached, her throat was sore, and it would take her days to get the smell of onions out from under her nails.

"Here," Peter said, handing her a champagne flute.

She smiled and clinked it against his. "Never again," she said, rolling her head around on her neck and hearing it crack.

"Think about how much money we made, though," Peter said.

"Maybe in another six months," she joked.

"I offered to pay the waiters an extra hundred bucks each to stay around for another hour and clean everything up," Peter said.

"I love you," Kira said, and this time her voice was serious.

"Has Jessica's father given you the check yet?" Peter asked.

Kira shook her head.

"We need to pay out the waiters and DJ," Peter said. "Don't you think we should collect it?"

Kira sighed and pushed herself to her feet. She opened a kitchen drawer and pulled out a plain white envelope, then headed for the tent. This was the moment she'd been dreading for weeks.

She found Jessica's father sitting at his table,

chatting with another guest. She waited until the conversation broke up, then forced herself to smile.

"Jessica looks radiant," she said. "I hope she's having a wonderful night."

"She seems to be," he said. Bruce was his first name, but Kira knew she'd never be able to bring herself to call him that.

"I have the final bill for you here," Kira said, handing him the envelope.

"Ah," Bruce said. He reached into his breast pocket for his reading glasses and withdrew the sheet of paper. He read through it silently. Kira felt her armpits grow sweaty.

"Of course, you can't possibly bill us for the wedding cake one of your waiters ruined," Bruce finally said. "There should be a little compensation for that, in fact. And we had eighty-five guests, not a hundred."

"Yes, but . . ." Kira's voice trailed off. It was true that not all of the guests had shown up, but she'd been asked to prepare dinner for a hundred!

"We drank a lot less alcohol than you budgeted for, given that we had fifteen percent fewer guests," Bruce said. He folded the paper back up.

"I think we should go over this in the morning, given all the changes," he said.

Kira's cheeks flushed. That wasn't the agreement! He was supposed to write a check tonight, and Rand was going to rush to the bank tomorrow to deposit it, so that the checks *they'd* written to the florist and grocery stores and waiters wouldn't bounce.

Were people staring? Kira was wearing a white apron while Bruce was clad in a tuxedo, leaning back in his chair and sipping espresso. The balance of power clearly tilted in his direction. Jessica's fake tears and veiled threats suddenly made a lot more sense to Kira; it was clear where she'd learned her tactics. Kira began to tremble, feeling a sense of déjà vu. Bruce could be Thomas Bigalow's twin brother.

"We're not going to go over this in the morning," Peter said. Kira looked up at her husband in astonishment.

"We'll take off a thousand bucks for the cake," Peter said, his voice soft but steady. "We paid in advance for the alcohol based on *your* requirements and guest list, so you can take whatever's left over when you leave tomorrow. The same with the food. We can wrap it up and pack it in a cooler."

"What am I going to do with a crate of salad?" Bruce asked.

"What are we going to do with it?" Peter shot back. "Breed rabbits?"

This couldn't be her husband, Kira thought wildly. Her sweet, nonconfrontational Peter taking on a prosecutor?

"We have a written agreement that the check will be provided tonight," Peter said. A few guests were turning to look, but Peter didn't back down or lower his voice. "We'd like that check now."

"Minus twelve hundred?" Bruce was raising an eyebrow, but he didn't look mad. He must be used to blustering on both sides before an agreement was reached, given his job, Kira thought. Maybe he even respected it, in an odd way.

"Fine," Peter agreed. "Even though it was an accident, and my wife whipped up a damn good cake on the spot."

Bruce pulled out his checkbook and began to write.

"Thank you," Peter said, putting the check in his own pocket.

"It's a nice wedding," Bruce said.

And now it was done, Kira thought. Really, truly over. She was going to take the world's longest bubble bath and then climb into bed and wrap herself around Peter. They'd order pizza for the next week.

She and Peter began to walk out of the tent and snow flurries fell down upon them like confetti, blown sideways under the tarp by the strong wind.

"Wait," Kira said. She reached for her husband's hand, remembering the photograph on her father's refrigerator.

It was dark and freezing, and neither of them had on a coat, but she didn't want to go into the kitchen yet, where the waiters were washing platters and wrapping up leftovers and sweeping the floor, where everything was loud and bright and busy.

The DJ was playing "At Last" by Etta James, and the slow, sweet opening notes of the music carried outside to them. It was a song Kira had always loved. It was the one she and Peter had first danced to at their own wedding.

She reached up and wrapped her arms around Peter's neck, and they swayed back and forth.

There was no place she'd rather be.

Acknowledgments

Though it seems impossible, my adoration and appreciation of my editor, Greer Hendricks, continues to grow. Her expert guidance, ability to inspire, and natural knack for storytelling strengthen all of my novels—and none more so than this one. If you enjoyed *Catching Air*, please know that Greer's fingerprints are on everything from the structure to the language to the cover. It would be a privilege to work with her under any circumstance. The fact that she's someone I can (and do!) laugh with, identify with, and talk with for hours leaves me awed by my spectacular good fortune.

My smart, funny, ridiculously hard-working agent, Victoria Sanders, is as fierce and loyal as they come (she's soft-hearted, too, but don't mention that at the negotiating table or she might haul off and kick you). V has created opportunities for me that seem like a dream— actually, they *were* my dreams, just a few short years ago. As with Greer, somewhere along the way, Victoria has transformed into a cherished friend.

Marcy Engelman somehow agreed to take me on as a client (I'm still trying to figure out how I deserve this), and has worked magic on the publicity front while writing the funniest, sassiest e-mails in e-mail history. Marcy, you are one in a million—and I adore you.

You would think I'd used up my allotment of good luck, and I'd agree, but somehow I hit the publishing jackpot with publisher Judith Curr, Carolyn Reidy of Simon & Schuster, and the rest of the creative, cutting-edge, and just darn *likeable* folks at Atria who have published every book I've ever written. From dashing publicist Paul Olsewski and his imaginative colleague Elaine Broeder, to the fabulous sales force who work so hard to bring my books into stores, to Ben Lee, Lisa Sciambra, Lisa Keim, Carly Sommerstein, Hillary Tisman, and Jackie Jou . . . it is a pleasure to work with each and every one of you. Then there's the incredible Sarah Cantin, an all-around star who brings grace, intelligence, and unerring good instincts to every single thing she does.

Chandler Crawford does an outstanding job of selling foreign rights to my books, and I'm proud to be associated with someone so well-respected in the industry. Bernadette Baker-Baughman (B3!) is smart, funny, and an excellent partner in squealing when good news arrives. My deep thanks also to Chris Kepner, for everything he does, and does so well.

To Angela Cheng Caplan, my film agent! Talk

about dreams coming true. I look forward to many, many years of working with you and Kim Yau.

Erin Wittenmyer kindly answered dozens of questions I had about the adoption process, and she forwarded pages and pages of materials that provided essential information as I crafted Alyssa's storyline. I'm very grateful to Erin.

Kudos to copy editor Susan Brown, proofreader Wendy Keebler, and book jacket designer Anna Dorfman for another stellar job.

To all the amazing book bloggers, booksellers, and librarians—I would never get to do this without your support, and I am deeply thankful to you for being so welcoming to me, and for championing books in general. And speaking of championing books, there is no one who is more supportive and generous to her fellow writers (not to mention more funny and charming) than the author Jennifer Weiner. Jen, you stand up for us all when it would be easier to look away, and I'm proud to call you a friend.

Chatting with readers who have found me on Facebook and Twitter is always a highlight of my day. Thank you all for sharing the publication process with me, and for making it so much more fun! If you haven't already found me on social media, please do, because I'm probably hanging out there, procrastinating (note to my publisher: Please don't read that last line).

My parents are endless sources of help, fun, and laughter, and I'm so grateful they live close by and are an important part of our lives. "Alvie"—Olivia Cortez—is an angel, and I don't know what I would do without the good cheer she brings into my home.

And as always, to my family (in this case, last place isn't a bad thing, kids!), for filling my life with chaos and carpools, messes and baseball games—and moments of joy that my heart can barely contain.

Catching Air

SARAH PEKKANEN

A Readers Club Guide

Questions and Topics for Discussion

1. In what ways do Alyssa and Kira discover that they are more alike than they originally believed?

2. How are Rand and Peter contrasted throughout the novel? What are their different approaches to running the bed-and-breakfast?

3. For Dawn, following her heart rather than her head leads her into a disastrous outcome. Have you ever found yourself in a difficult situation because you were blinded by love?

4. Alyssa recalls a friend who went from weighing 350 pounds to running several marathons a year: "She hadn't changed her habits; her habits had changed her." What's the meaning behind this distinction? What are some of the new habits that these characters develop because they are running the B-and-B?

5. Even though Kira, Dawn, and Alyssa are all grown women, how are their childhood

experiences—particularly, the degree to which they felt safe and cared for—impacting them throughout the novel? Particularly for Kira and Alyssa, how are these experiences shaping how they think about becoming mothers themselves?

6. In thinking about her marriage to Rand, Alyssa notes, "Their relationship had never been truly tested." Given that they regularly moved and traveled—and likely faced financial uncertainty as a result—did this analysis surprise you? What kinds of life events do you think really test a romantic relationship?

7. How do each woman's memories of her mother drive her forward, or inspire her?

8. Kira becomes frustrated when she feels she's bearing the weight of planning the wedding and the daily management of the inn without Peter equally contributing; Alyssa starts to panic when she realizes that perhaps she never really ensured that Rand also wanted a child as much as she did. To what degree is each woman responsible for the situations she finds herself in, and to what extent should they expect their husbands to behave differently?

9. Alyssa says that she was worried she'd "feel confined by bed rest" but that surprisingly, "all her traveling was what had prepared her for it." What are some other seemingly polar opposite experiences that end up being mutually beneficial?

10. Consider where we leave Rand at the novel's conclusion. What do you think will happen to his and Alyssa's marriage? Do you think men are less likely than women to change their patterns of behavior?

11. Kira disappears from the B-and-B and confronts two men when she arrives in Florida. What kind of power has each man held over her sense of self since she and Peter moved to Vermont, and why is it essential for her to find closure with each of them?

12. Consider the different types of relation- ships that are depicted in the novel— romantic bonds, blood relations, in-laws, and friends—and discuss the expectations and "norms" associated with each.

Enhance Your Reading Group

1. Would you ever want to move to a vacation destination and open your own business? If yes, where in the world would you pick? What would the business be? Who would you want to run it with?

2. Sarah Pekkanen is the author of four other delicious novels! If you haven't yet read *The Best of Us*, do so as a group, and think about the marriages depicted in that novel. Using the couples of these two books as examples, what would you say are the keys to a successful relationship? And where do the breakdowns that each couple face seem to originate from?

3. Throughout the novel, Kira perfects certain recipes that work well for feeding larger groups—like her butternut squash soup, or her fondue, or her pancakes. Do you have any tried-and-true recipes that you break out for guests spending the night, or for hosting a larger holiday meal? Did any of those dishes ever go disastrously wrong when you were hosting? Bring a recipe or two—and stories!—to share with the group.

Center Point Large Print
600 Brooks Road / PO Box 1
Thorndike ME 04986-0001 USA

(207) 568-3717

US & Canada:
1 800 929-9108
www.centerpointlargeprint.com